Two hours later the snow stopped, leaving the battlefield covered by an additional foot.

I was on watch with Ox. The white made it difficult to concentrate and I had to close my eyes every few seconds to keep from getting dizzy; even though I had spat out the zip a long time ago, its effect still bounced in my head, keeping the edge off but blurring my sense of time and vision. Something moved out there. It looked like a piece of rubble melted into the snow and then rose from a new position, closer, so when it happened again, I told Ox.

"Button up," he said. The mood shattered in an instant. Ox's and the others' fingers blurred as the Marines yanked on vision hoods and snapped the cables into place, and it got dead quiet when Snyder killed the music. All I had to do was put on my helmet, but I was the last one finished.

"Cycle the air."

Snyder hit a button and I heard a hiss, watching the temperature gauge on my heads-up drop rapidly. It stopped at five below zero. Burger popped open a firing port under the window and the floor light flickered from green to red at the same time he shoved his grenade launcher through. Ox and Snyder popped their ports, too, and ⬚⬚⬚⬚⬚⬚⬚⬚⬚⬚⬚⬚⬚⬚⬚e, so I poked my car⬚⬚⬚⬚⬚⬚⬚⬚⬚⬚⬚⬚⬚⬚and it clicked against ⬚⬚⬚⬚⬚

"Contact."

BY T. C. McCARTHY

The Subterrene War

Germline

Exogene

GERMLINE

The Subterrene War: Book 1

T. C. McCARTHY

orbit

www.orbitbooks.net

Copyright © 2011 by T. C. McCarthy
Excerpt from *Exogene* copyright © 2011 by T. C. McCarthy
All rights reserved. Except as permitted under the U.S. Copyright Act of 1976, no part of this publication may be reproduced, distributed, or transmitted in any form or by any means, or stored in a database or retrieval system, without the prior written permission of the publisher.

Book design by Giorgetta Bell McRee

Orbit
Hachette Book Group
237 Park Avenue
New York, NY 10017
www.orbitbooks.net

Orbit is an imprint of Hachette Book Group, Inc. The Orbit name and logo are trademarks of Little, Brown Book Group Limited.

Printed in the United States of America

First edition: August 2011

10 9 8 7 6 5 4 3 2 1

GERMLINE

ONE

Crank Fire

I'll never forget the smell: human waste, the dead, and rubbing alcohol—the smell of a Pulitzer.

The sergeant looked jumpy as he glanced at my ticket. "*Stars and Stripes*?" I couldn't place the accent. New York, maybe. "You'll be the first."

"First what?"

He laughed as if I had made a joke. "The first civilian reporter wiped on the front line. Nobody from the press has ever been allowed up here, not even you guys. We got plenty of armor, rube. Draw some on your way out and button up." He gestured to a pile of used suits, next to which lay a mountain of undersuits, and on my way over, the sergeant shouted to a corporal who had been relaxing against the wall. "Wake up, Chappy. We got a *reporter* needin' some."

Tired. Empty. I'd seen it before in Shymkent, in frontline troops rotating back for a week or two, barely able to walk, with dark circles under their eyes so they looked like nervous raccoons. Chappy had that look too.

He opened one eye. "Reporter?"

"Yep. *Stripes.*"

"Where's your camera?"

I shrugged. "Not allowed one. Security. It's gonna be an audio-only piece."

Chappy frowned, as if I couldn't be a *real* reporter, since I didn't have a holo unit, thought for a moment, and then stood. "If you're going to be the first reporter on the line, I guess we oughta give you something special. What size?"

I knew my size and told him. I'd been through Rube-Hack back in the States; all of us had. The Pentagon called it Basic Battlefield Training, but every grunt I'd met had just laughed at me, and not behind my back. Rube. Babe. Another civilian too stupid to realize that anything was better than Kaz because Kazakhstan was another world, purgatory for those who least deserved it, a vacation for the suicidal, and a novelty for those whose brain chemistry was messed up enough to make them think it would be a cool place to visit. To see firsthand. Only graduates of Rube-Hack thought that last way, actually *wanted* Kaz.

Only reporters.

"*Real* special," he said. Chappy lifted a suit from the pile and dropped it at my feet, then handed me a helmet. Across the back someone had scrawled *forget me not or I'll blow your punk-ass away.* "That guy doesn't need it anymore, got killed before he could suit up, so it's in decent shape."

I tried not to think about it and grabbed an undersuit. "Where's the APC hangar?"

He didn't answer. The man had already slumped against the wall again and didn't bother to open his eyes this time, not even the one.

It took me a few minutes to remember. Sardines. Lips

and guts stuffed into a sausage casing. Getting into a suit was hard, like over-packing a suitcase and then trying to close it from the inside. First came the undersuit, a network of hoses and cables. There was one tube that ended in a stretchy latex hood, to be snapped over the end of your you-know-what, and one that ended in a hollow plug (they issued antibacterial lube for *that*), and the plug had a funny belt to keep it from coming out. The alternative was sloshing around in a suit filled with your own waste, and we had been told that on the line you lived in a suit for weeks at a time.

I laughed when it occurred to me that somewhere, you could almost bet on it, there was a certain class of people who didn't mind the plug at all.

Underground meant the jitters. A klick of rock hung overhead so that even though I couldn't see it, I felt its weight crushing down, making the hair on my neck stand straight. These guys *partied* subterrene, prayed for it. You'd recognize it in Shymkent, when you met up with other reporters at the hotel bar and saw Marines—fresh off the line—looking for booze and chicks. Grunts would come in and the waiter would move to seat them on the ground floor and they'd look at him like he was trying to get them killed. They didn't have armor on—it wasn't allowed in Shymkent—so the guys had no defense against heat sensors or motion tracking, and instinct kicked in, reminding them that nothing lived long aboveground. Suddenly they had eyes in the backs of their heads. Line Marines, who until that moment had thought R & R meant safety, began shaking and one or two of them would back against the wall to make sure they couldn't get it from that direction. *How about downstairs? Got anything underground? A basement?* The waiter would realize his mistake then and usher them into the back room to a spiral staircase, into the deep.

The Marines would smile and breathe easy as they pushed to be the first one underground. Not me, though. The underworld was where you buried corpses, and where tunnel collapses guaranteed you'd be dead, sometimes slowly, so I didn't think I could hack it, claustrophobia and all, but didn't have much choice. I wanted the line. Begged for a last chance to prove I could write despite my habit. I even threw a party at the hotel when I found out that I was the only reporter selected for the front, but there was one problem: at the line, everything was down—down and über-tight.

The APC bounced over something on the tunnel floor, and the vehicle's other passenger, a corpsman, grinned. "No shit?" he asked. "A reporter for real?"

I nodded.

"Hell yeah. Check it." I couldn't remember his name but for some reason the corpsman decided to unlock his suit and slip his arm out—what remained of it. Much of the flesh had been replaced by scar tissue so that it looked as though he had been partially eaten by a shark. "Fléchettes. You should do a story on *that*. Got a holo unit?"

"Nah. Not allowed." He gave me the same look as Chappy—*what kind of a reporter are you?*—and it annoyed me because I hadn't been lit lately and was starting to feel a kind of withdrawal, *rough*. I pointed to his arm. "Fléchettes did *that*? I thought they were like needles, porcupine stickers."

"Nah. Pops doesn't use regular fléchettes. Coats 'em with dog shit sometimes, and it's nasty. Hell, a guy can take a couple of fléchette hits and walk away. But not when they've got 'em coated in Baba-Yaga's magic grease. Pops almost cost me the whole thing."

"Pops?"

"Popov. Victor Popovich. The Russians."

He looked about nineteen, but he spoke like he was eighty. You couldn't get used to that, seeing kids half your age, speaking to them, and realizing that in one year, God and war had somehow crammed in decades. Always giving advice as if they knew. They *did* know. Anyone who survived at the line learned more about death than I had ever wanted to know, and as I sat there, the corpsman got that look on his face. *Let me give you some advice...*

"Don't get shot, rube," he said, "and if you do, there's only one option."

The whine of the APC's turbines swelled as it angled downward, and I had to shout. "Yeah? What?"

"Treat *yourself.*" He pointed his fingers like a pistol and placed them against his temple. The corpsman grinned, as if it was the funniest thing he had ever heard.

Marines in green armor rested against the curved walls of the tunnel and everything seemed slippery. Slick. Their ceramic armor was slick, and the tunnel walls had been melted by a fusion borer so that they shone like the inside of an empty soda can, slick, slick, and double slick. My helmet hung from a strap against my hip and banged with every step, so I felt as though it were a cowbell, calling everyone's attention.

First thing I noticed on the line? Everyone had a beard except me. The Marines stared as though I were a movie star, something out of place, and even though I wore the armor of a subterrener—one of Vulcan's apostles—mine didn't fit quite right, hadn't been scuffed in the right places or buckled just *so* because they all knew the best way, the way a veteran would have suited up. I asked once, in Shymkent, "Hey, Marine, how come you guys all wear beards?" He smiled and reached for his, his smile fading when he realized it had been shaved. The guy even looked around for it, like it fell off or something. " 'Cause it keeps the chafing down," he said. "Ever try sleeping and eating with a bucket strapped around your face twenty-four seven?" I hadn't. Early in the war, the Third required their Marines to shave their heads and faces before going on leave—to keep lice from getting it on behind the lines—but here in the underworld the Marines' hair was theirs, a cushion between them and the vision hood that clung tightly but never fit quite right, leaving blisters on anyone bald.

Not having a beard made me unique.

A captain grabbed my arm. "Who the hell are you?"

"Wendell. *Stars and Stripes*, civilian DOD."

"No shit?" The captain looked surprised at first but then smiled. "Who are you hooking up with?"

"Second Battalion, Baker."

"That's us." He slapped me on the back and turned to his men. "Listen up. This here is Wendell, a reporter from the Western world. He'll be joining us on the line, so if you're nice, he might put you in the news vids."

I didn't have the heart to say it again, to tell them that I didn't have a camera and, oh, by the way, I spent most of my time so high that I could barely piece a story together.

"Captain," I said. "Where are we headed?"

"Straight into boredom. You came at the right time. Rumor is that Popov is too tired to push, and we're not going to push him. We'll be taking a siesta just west of Pavlodar, about three klicks north of here, Z minus four klicks. Plenty of rock between us and the plasma."

I had seen a collection of civilian mining equipment in the APC hangar, looking out of place, and wondered. Fusion borers, piping, and conveyors, all of it painted orange with black stripes. Someone had tried to hide it under layers of camouflage netting, like a teenager would hide his stash, just in case Mom didn't buy the *I-don't*-do-*drugs, you-don't*-need-*to-search-my-room* argument.

"What about the gear in the hangar—the mining rigs?" I asked.

A few of the closest Marines had been bantering and fell silent while the captain glared at me. "What rigs?"

"The stuff back in the hangar. Looked like civilian mining stuff."

He turned and headed toward the front of his column. "Keep up, rube. We're not coming back if you get lost."

Land mines. Words were land mines. I wasn't part of the family, wasn't even close to being one of them, and my exposure to the war had so far been limited to jerking off Marines when they stepped off the transport pad in Shymkent, hoping to get a money shot interview, the real deal. *Hey, Lieutenant, what's it like? Got anyone back home you wanna say hi to?* Their looks said it all. Total confusion, like, *Where am I?* We came from two different worlds, and in Shymkent they stepped into mine, where plasma artillery and autonomous ground attack drones were things to be talked about openly—irreverently and without fear so you could prove to the hot AP betty, just arrived in Kaz, that you knew more than she did, and if she let you in those cotton panties, you'd share *everything*. You would, too. But now I was in *their* world, land of the learn-or-get-out-of-the-way-or-die tribe, and didn't know the language.

A Marine corporal explained it to me, or I never would have figured it out.

"Hey, reporter-guy." He fell in beside me as we walked. "Don't ever mention that shit again."

"What'd I say?"

"Mining gear. They don't bring that crap in unless we're making another push, to try and retake the mines. If we recapture them, the engineers come in and dig as much ore as they can before the Russians hit us to grab it back. Back and forth, it's how the world churns."

There were mines of all kinds in Kaz, trace-metal mines *and* land mines. The trace mines were the worst, because they never blew up; they just spun in place like a buzz saw, chewing, and too tempting to let go. Metal. We'd get it from space someday, but bringing it in was still so expensive that whenever someone stumbled across an earth source, usually deep underground, everyone scrambled. Metal was worth fighting over, bartered for with blood and fléchettes. Kaz proved it. Metals, especially rhenium and all the traces, were all the rage, which was the whole reason for our being there in the first place.

I saw an old movie once, in one of those art houses. It was animated, a cartoon, but I can't remember what it was called. There was a song in it that I'll never forget and one line said it all. "Put your trust in Heavy Metal." Whoever wrote that song must have *seen* Kaz, must have looked far into the beyond.

I needed to get high. The line assignment had come from an old friend, someone corporate who'd taken pity and thought he'd give me one last chance to get out the *old* Oscar, not the one who used to show promise but couldn't even write a sentence now unless he'd just mainlined a cool bing. Somehow, I knew I'd screw this one up too, but I didn't want to *die* doing it.

My first barrage lasted three days. I was so scared that I forgot about my job, never even turning on my voice recorder, the word "Pulitzer" a mirage. Three days of sitting around and trying to watch them, to learn something that might keep me from getting wiped—or at least explain why it was I had wanted this assignment in the first place—and always wondering what would drive me crazy first: the rocks pelting my helmet, not having any drugs, or claustrophobia. Living in a can. The suits had speakers and audio pickups so you could talk without using radio, but I'd never realized before how important it was to *see* someone else. Read his face. You couldn't even nod; it got lost in a suit, same as a shrug. Meaningless.

Ox, the corporal who had educated me about mining gear, was a huge guy from Georgia. Tank big.

"I friggin' hate curried chicken," he said. Ox pulled the feeding tube from a tiny membrane in his helmet and threw a pouch to the ground. "Anyone wanna trade?"

I had some ration packs that I'd gotten off a couple of French guys in Shymkent, and threw one to him.

"What the hell is this? I can't read it."

"It's French. That one is wine-poached salmon."

Ox broke the heat pack at the pouch's bottom. When it was warm, he stuck the tube through and squeezed. I swore I could almost see his eyes go wide, the *no-friggin'-way* expression on his face.

"Where'd you get *this*?"

"Foreign Legion."

He squeezed the pouch again and didn't stop until it was a wad, all wringed out. "Un-fucking-real. The French get to eat this every day?"

I nodded and then remembered he couldn't see it. "Yeah. And they get booze in their rations. Wine."

"That's it," Ox said. "I'm going AWOL, join up with the Legion. *You,* rube, are welcome in my tunnel."

And just like that, I was in the fold.

Occasionally the Russians lobbed in deep penetrators, and near the end of the second day, one of them detonated, breaking free a massive slab that crushed two Marines instantly. One of their buddies, a private who sat next to them, got splattered with bits of flesh and bone that popped from their armor, like someone had just popped a huge zit. The man screamed and wouldn't stop until a corpsman sedated him, but he kept rocking back and forth, repeating, "I can't find my face." Finally the captain ordered the corpsman to sedate him further, tie him up, and drag the Marine into the rear-area tunnel, where they could pick him up later.

"Good thing they did that," said Ox.

I pulled my knees up to my chest. "Why?"

"I was about to wipe him."

Things returned to normal for a while. Muffled thumps of plasma still shook the ceiling, and suit waste pouches opened automatically to dump human filth on the floor—because someone had been too scared or too lazy to jack into a wall port. *That* was normal for subterrene.

The only flaw in the captain's plan was that eventually the guy who had been sedated came to and picked up where he had left off. Over the coms net, his voice screamed in our ears that he still couldn't find his face, every once in a while adding "the shitheads left me."

Ox picked up his carbine and muttered, "He's dead," but fortunately for both Ox and the crazy guy, a corpsman was close to the tunnel exit and sped off to deactivate the man's communications.

I knew what the crazy guy meant. Ox did too, and that was the problem: nobody wanted to hear it; nobody needed to be reminded that none of us could find our faces. Without being able to touch it, I had begun to wonder if maybe I didn't have one anymore, like it got left behind in my Shymkent hotel so that some half-Mongolian puke could steal it for himself because I had forgotten to leave a big enough tip on the pillow to make stealing not worth it. I *needed* to find my face, knew that it had to be around there somewhere, if I could just take off my helmet for a second.

By the end of the third day, the barrage lifted, and I sat quietly, watching the Marines and feeling like I was the uninvited guest who didn't know what fork to use at dinner, too scared to say anything because my stupidity would show. I'd left my rig in the hotel too, hadn't thought I'd have to go this long without juice, and now I felt the shakes, got that chill, a warning that if I didn't get lit soon, it'd be bad. Even so, nobody moved. Everyone soaked in that stillness, and only an occasional click as the armorer went down the line, checking weapons and suits, broke it. Then the captain slapped the four men closest to him. They stood and moved slowly to a ladder before disappearing through a hole in the ceiling.

"Where they going?" I asked.

Ox checked his carbine for about the hundredth time. "Topside watch."

"Why?"

"'Cause Pops is shifty. Sometimes, when neither of us has a barrage on, he'll try and move in topside."

I shivered, a mental wind that preceded whacked-out thoughts. No way I could deal with all this shit; I wasn't ready. It wasn't what I signed up for; someone else could cover the line, get the first story. My next question proved to me, to everybody, that I was terrified, a rube.

"What about the sentry fields? The bots. Won't they deal with anything topside?"

Ox laughed. "Pops can make magic in his land, and Kaz *is* his land. Sentry bots don't always work."

"Come on, reporter-guy," Ox said. "You want a story, this'll give you a story."

It was Ox's turn on watch, so he and two of his buddies, Burger and Snyder, moved toward the ladder, motioning for me to follow. I had no saliva. I don't even remember willing my legs to work, yet there I was, heading to the ladder, and in that instant I knew exactly how the Marines had felt— the ones who had wanted to eat dinner in the basement of my hotel. You didn't go up; it was all wrong. Anything could happen up there, and the rest of your unit would be far below, unable to help and just glad that it wasn't them. My legs seemed to have grown a mind of their own, refusing to work the way they should have, almost detached from the rest of my body as they resisted efforts to move them toward danger. This was tangled. *I* knew it was tangled, Ox knew it, the captain knew it, and even the guy who had lost his face knew it, but everyone except *that* guy managed to pretend it was all cool, all smooth. Normal.

"Come on," said Ox.

When I got to the base of the ladder, the captain stopped me.

"Hold a sec." He grabbed a Maxwell carbine from the closest Marine, snapped the hopper from the kid's armor, and then rigged me with it. The carbine felt heavy and I slung it over my shoulder.

"Anyone who goes topside is a cranker," the captain explained.

"Sir, I'm a reporter. I didn't think I'd even be allowed to carry a Maxwell on the line."

He had taken off his helmet during the lull in shelling, and smiled. "You're DOD—a civilian who wanted this crap, right?"

I nodded.

"Well, you got it. Here…" He lifted my helmet and placed it over my head, sliding the locking ring into place. "You're going topside, you button up. Period."

When I caught up to the others, they had stepped off the ladder into a tiny mining elevator, about a hundred feet up from the main tunnel. Ox laughed and pointed toward my carbine.

"You know how to shoot one of those?"

I could barely talk, realizing for the first time how important spit was. "Yeah. I fired one in Rube-Hack."

"Going up," said Snyder, and our elevator jerked.

The car rattled. I wondered how often the thing had been used, recognizing what it was from some of my earliest stories on deep-mining operations in Nevada, where collapses and explosions had made mine rescues something boring, not even newsworthy anymore. It was ironic. The elevator was a modified rescue rig, two cages welded together to fit four men, but it wasn't doing its job anymore; it wasn't taking men out of danger but throwing them in. You can hate an inanimate object on the line. Every bump and shake made me want to throw up, rip the yellow wire cage apart and scream, because it wasn't supposed to move people to their deaths, and I just knew that the thing was laughing at our expense, that the elevator had clearly lost its way, been corrupted. It was an orphan. A street kid that had learned to make the best of it and survive any way it knew how—at our expense.

It took us a little under an hour to make the trip topside and we had to switch into three different shafts to do it. When we got to the top, the other watch was waiting and didn't say anything as they fought to get on the elevator, to get back inside Mother Earth, while we tried to dismount as slowly as possible. We still had one more ladder to climb, another hundred feet up to the observation post, and when we got there, I had to blink from the sudden light, a bright bluish glow that made me remember everything, including that there was a world aboveground and that it rested under a thing called the sun. There was snow. Fall had made its escape while I had been tunnel-bound, and winter claimed the land with its pale blanket.

I had never seen a battlefield and hadn't expected it to be so...clean. You sensed the rubble but couldn't see it under what looked like about two feet of fresh snow, and the land was flat, vacant except for wind. The war had vanished. But at the same time there was a thrill, an undercurrent of danger, because you knew that no matter how peaceful it looked, here, exposed, you had reason to be scared. The position allowed us to see in three-sixty, from a concrete bunker that just barely protruded from the rubble fields and had four narrow windows, their glass three feet thick.

My face pressed against the nearest window, looking north, and I stared, hypnotized. Somewhere out there was Pops, looking back at us, and I just wanted to see him. I knew there was a word for my type, but my brain hadn't been working since getting on the line. Choked up. It had clogged with ass puckering, with the sound of my own breathing inside the helmet, and with dreams of getting wired again, plugged in. Words started coming to me as I stared out across the rubble field, words that described me to a T. "Voyeur." "Spectator." "Pulitzer-fanboy." "Coward."

Ox yanked his helmet off and I nearly choked in surprise. "What are you doing?"

He laughed and the others took their helmets off too. Vision hoods came next, and Ox and Snyder carefully disconnected the series of cables that connected coms and goggle units to the suit. Burger kept his hood on. The goggles made him look funny, like a bug with big green bottled eyes, and he grinned at me.

"Rube, you're about to get initiated into the brotherhood. First reporter on the line, first reporter to get *zipped*!" He took a seat near the north window and stared out.

"Get down here," Ox said. When I sat next to him, he popped my helmet and helped me out of the hood.

"What about Russian sensors?" I asked.

"We're tight." Ox pointed to two lights on the floor next to us, one green, the other red, and I saw the green one glowing dimly. "Green means go. A good seal, so they can't see our therms, even if we unbutton, and we don't need the chameleon skin in *this* domicile."

Snyder pulled a small tin from a belt pouch and began flicking it, his finger snapping against the lid. His teeth were unbelievably yellow. "The good life," he said.

Ox laughed, slid a small player out of his pouch and hit a button. I couldn't believe it. Old music from the ancient world, rock. Nobody listened to that shit anymore except me, and as I sat there, it seemed...right. I didn't know these men and hadn't really seen much of them down in the tunnels, since we had been buttoned up for most of the time, and the only one I really spoke with was Ox. But I had listened and watched. They all had a look, and it wasn't the one you saw on any of the troops that made it to the rear for R & R; out here the look was more raw, a tightness in their faces and eyes that manifested in a kind of cornered-animal thing even when they grinned. Always looking for signs of danger, always moving.

Snyder was a kid, from Jamaica, I think, and like the rest of them, he'd grown out his beard, but it grew only in patches, so it looked as though someone had ripped out tufts of hair.

"What's zipped?" I asked.

"Zipped?" Snyder thought for a minute. "It's a long trip."

Ox grabbed the tin and opened it. He pinched the dark

material inside—it looked like finely ground dirt—and pressed a tiny wad inside his lower lip.

"It's tobacco. But we add a special ingredient, tranq tabs."

"Tranq tabs?"

"Illegal shit," Snyder explained. "They give them to the crazies, the Gs, to make 'em not so crazy, keep 'em fighting and energized."

"The Gs," I said. "Genetics."

Ox tossed the tin to Burger, who repeated the ritual and then threw it to Snyder. "Around their second year of service, Gs start to lose it, unstable. At first they didn't give 'em anything and some Gs went nuts, wiped an entire battalion of Army on the push northward from Bandar. Then came tranq."

"What is it?" I asked.

"It's a mixture of haloperidol, fentanyl, and some kind of speed—in elephant-sized doses. We got some from a very friendly supply sergeant last time on leave. You crush up the tabs, mix it with dip, and there you go. Zip. We can't smoke anything on the line—screws up the air handling when everyone lights up—and there's no way a human could take a G-dose of these things. Can't inject anything through suits unless you're a corpsman. So mixing tranq with dip gives us just the right cut and a new way to see the war."

Snyder finished and handed it to me. I looked at the stuff suspiciously, not because I didn't want it—I wanted it more than anything—but because I didn't know if I could keep my fingers steady long enough to take some. When the shakes eased for a moment, I dug in.

"Whatever you do," said Snyder, "*don't* swallow." He held up a finger and spat onto the floor. "You spit."

Cool and easy, all grins. Everything seemed smooth
and I swore I smelled the snow, even over the stink of our
own bodies. The music got louder. It took me a second but
I realized that there was no fear—no war, even—just us
and music that I could see coming out of the speakers,
and I started giggling, unable to stop even if I had wanted
to. I was about to swallow when Ox warned me. His voice
sounded faraway and slow, so damn slow.

"Spit."

"What's your name?" Snyder asked.

I don't remember telling him, but I must have.

"Oscar Wendell?" Ox asked. He and the others started
laughing then. "No, no, no, *hell* no. We're gonna give you
a new name, your war name, 'cause you been born again,
son of Kaz. Oscar Wendell will now be known as Scout."

"Scout?"

"Well, Scout," said Snyder. "Welcome to the jolly
green brotherhood, no turning back now, nothing to do
but crank on. Crank fire."

Crank fire. We cranked fire, and looking back, I realize I was glad for the drugs, for the cushion they gave me,
a cocoon that filtered reality and kept out the really bad
stuff or made it seem as though nothing was *actually* happening and everything was a dream. Two hours later the
snow stopped, leaving the battlefield covered by an additional foot. I was on watch with Ox. The white made it
difficult to concentrate and I had to close my eyes every
few seconds to keep from getting dizzy; even though I
had spat out the zip a long time ago, its effect still bounced
in my head, keeping the edge off but blurring my sense of
time and vision. Something moved out there. It looked
like a piece of rubble melted into the snow and then rose

from a new position, closer, so when it happened again, I told Ox.

"Button up," he said. The mood shattered in an instant. Ox's and the others' fingers blurred as the Marines yanked on vision hoods and snapped the cables into place, and it got dead quiet when Snyder killed the music. All I had to do was put on my helmet, but I was the last one finished.

"Cycle the air."

Snyder hit a button and I heard a hiss, watching the temperature gauge on my heads-up drop rapidly. It stopped at five below zero. Burger popped open a firing port under the window and the floor light flickered from green to red at the same time he shoved his grenade launcher through. Ox and Snyder popped their ports, too, and gestured for me to do the same, so I poked my carbine into the narrow opening, and it clicked against the sides as my hands shook.

"Contact." Ox's voice crackled in my ear, over the radio. "Grid Foxtrot-Uniform-one-six-five-three-five-zero."

The captain answered, his voice surreal, a caricature of what it should have been, as though someone pinched his nose while he spoke. If things hadn't been so tense, I might have laughed. "Roger. Artillery off-line, weapons free, sentry bots show green lights. Green light."

The shapes crept forward. It was almost impossible to detect, and had I not been paying attention, they would have crawled all the way, hundreds of white blobs that moved forward in a continuous line, so slowly they seemed barely to shift. Chameleon skins. Our suits, and theirs, had been coated with a reactive polymer, wired to the suits' computers and power systems so that it sensed one's surroundings and changed to the same color as the closest objects. That was why they had been so hard to see, and it reminded me of what Ox had said, how he'd described them. Spooky. Popov was a ghost.

"Why are they moving so slowly?" I asked.

Ox grunted. "'Cause of our sentry bots. The bots can detect heat, but armored suits mask heat. That leaves motion and shape detection, but if you've got your second skin activated, move slow enough, and stay low..."

"Crafty little bastards," said Snyder.

I shook my head, trying to concentrate. "How slow?"

"Once they reach our security zone," said Burger, "about two feet a minute."

Two feet a minute. Outside. If a plasma barrage came and you were out there when it hit, instant crisp. I'd seen the bodies and wreckage on flatcars in Tashkent, smelled it when the wind was right. Ceramic melted at plasma temperatures, and the dead bodies looked like lumps of rock. These guys had come from their own lines, almost three klicks away. Slowly. That meant they had been out in the weather for almost a day, come plasma, snow, or anything, and that kind of dedication indicated that whoever these men were, they *really* wanted to kill us. What had we ever done to them?

"I think I'm going to puke," I said.

"Well," said Ox, "then let's get this over with. *Burger.*"

Loud pops sounded from my right as Burger worked his grenade launcher up and down, left and right, arcing deadly eggs toward the oncoming shapes. Posts on our flanks must have opened up at the same time, because brilliant flashes blossomed over the snow several hundred meters away, toward the Irtysh River, and then from the opposite direction. *Big push,* I thought. There were thousands of them. Burger's grenades—alternating between thermal gel and fléchettes—melted or punctured anything they hit, and the Russians reacted immediately; advance troops rose from their crawl and sprinted forward, firing at our bunker so that all we saw were lines of tracers leaping out of thin air.

"Right about..." Ox said, "now."

Sentry robots beeped to life at the appearance of moving targets. Metallic columns popped up from buried tubes across the entire front and sprayed explosive fléchettes, strafing and mowing like avenging angels as they sucked ammunition from bunker magazines far below.

"Crank up, Scout!" said Snyder. *"What are you waiting for, man?"*

I didn't have time to think, not even like, *Wait a second, I'm about to wipe someone I don't even know.* Didn't happen. Those thoughts came only later, in nightmares. Daymares. As soon as my finger touched the trigger, a green sighting reticle appeared on my goggles, and I heard the tinkling of fléchettes as they fell through the flexi-belt and into the carbine. I didn't feel a thing. No kick. The barrel magnets launched the fléchettes down and out so that all I saw was a line of red streaks—each one the tiny fleck of phosphorus that lit up when a fléchette hit air. I had time to think then. Time to think that it was beautiful, like fireworks, but just a few seconds later, there were no more targets and the sentries lowered slowly into their holes to leave me gasping for air and searching the horizon for something, anything, that might be trying to kill me.

"Grid clear," said Ox.

Burger pulled his launcher in and slapped a new clip into its base. He probably thought it was over; we all did.

"Man," I said. My finger ached. I didn't realize I had been squeezing so hard, and smelled the sweat, the awful smell of terror and salt, inside my suit.

Suddenly a salvo of enemy grenades arced toward us. They came unexpectedly, and from the popping of their launchers, I guessed that some Russian troops had remained in the rear, motionless. The grenades hit directly on our position, most of them concentrated on Burger's section, and thermal gel smoked as it tried to burn through the glass. I heard them then; the Russians screamed and it seemed like an entire army charged at us.

"Oooo-rah! Pobieda!"

"What the fuck does that mean?" I asked.

"Oooo-rah means 'kill,'" said Ox. *"Pobieda* means 'victory.'"

A second wave rose from the rubble, and the sentries again sprang from their holes, picking them off easily. Windblown snow fell in gentle swirls as once more the front became quiet.

We didn't say anything.

Our relief showed up later, and it took us about two hours to get down. Burger had bought it. One direct hit on his port burned through the tiny alloy door, and then a fléchette grenade followed to send a bunch of needles through his chest and out the back, opening a quarter-sized hole on either side, and I wondered if from the right angle you could look clear through. It took us longer than normal to descend, because it was hard to fit into the elevators with a corpse.

When we got back to the tunnels, I yanked off my helmet and threw up, my body trying to rid itself of the tobacco and drugs, but it was the *memory* I wanted to vomit out. We hadn't even known that Burger had bought it—not until someone tapped him on the shoulder and he slumped over. On the way down in the elevator, his guts had started coming out of the hole, and for a moment I remembered my real job.

Burger would make some story.

The genetics came a few days after we lost Burger, and that word popped into my head again. "Pulitzer." Nobody in the press had been this close. A hundred of them showed up in the tunnel, silent and eerie, all identical, all girls. *Engineered.*

I wished I had my holo unit as they passed in front of me. Beautifully deadly, and all grace. The girls had mustered out of the factories, ateliers, manufactured at a trickle for now, but it was a trickle that made a difference—one that even the Press Corps noticed. Since the Russians had shown up a year earlier, every action where we were able to retake the mine had involved the use of genetically engineered troops. Line units had entire legends built up around the Gs. *"You should have seen them, man, just one squad of Gs wiped an entire battalion of Pops, moved like lightning on speed."*

They were probably about sixteen or seventeen years old, and their bald heads were nearly flawless, would have been if not for thick calluses formed by the friction of their hoods. These didn't wear helmets for some reason. Maybe it was because they were too cool, like Amazons in formation, and they knew it. Instead the girls carried their lids like I had, on straps hanging from their belts, and they marched into the tunnel without a sound, silent phantoms in black armor.

"What's all over their faces?" I asked. Their heads had been coated with something like grease, a dark green that hid most of their features.

"Thermal block," Ox said. "Gs hate helmets worse than we do. Especially the ones near the end of their term. Thermal block cuts down on emissions. Not perfect, but they're crazy anyway."

"End of their term?"

He laughed and leaned his carbine against the wall. "The young Gs wipe the old ones when they turn eighteen. Honorable discharge. By then they're too crazy to keep on the line, too far gone. At that point they're sucking down tranq tabs like candy, and it doesn't even faze 'em."

"Yeah," said Snyder. "But they're here. Only one thing to do now."

"What's that?" I asked.

"Pucker," Ox said. "And ask the captain if you can have another weapon. We'll be pushing into the mines again, or else these chicks wouldn't be here."

One of the girls approached the captain and handed him a stack of tickets. Orders. He nodded, and everyone watched then, looking for some sign of our fate in the captain's face, not willing to give up hope that maybe it was all a big mistake, maybe this time there'd be no push.

The girl returned to her group and on the way she passed me, close. Whatever they were, they *smelled* like girls, and for a second I felt like screaming, because if you closed your eyes and couldn't see her, it *smelled* like she should have been sitting in school, driving guys crazy with a miniskirt. But she *looked* like a killer. *That* was subterrene; that was Kaz—where opposites existed simultaneously and just laughed at you, like, *Yeah? So?*

She sat against the wall and bowed her head with the rest of them.

"Now what are they doing?" I asked.

"Praying," said Ox. "They've been fed some messed-up religion; it keeps them going."

I grabbed my recorder and turned it on, just in time.

"Death and faith," they said. The words were soft, sounded like a children's choir, and filled the quiet tunnel with an echoing murmur. "I believe in God, the Father Almighty, creator of heaven, earth, and death. I believe in warfare and destruction, his only children, conceived by the power of the Holy Spirit and taught through honorable suffering. I believe that death on the field is my proof, a sacrifice, to show that I remain among the faithful. The loyal. I believe in the atelier, the forgiveness of enemies brave enough to die, and the communion of sisterhood."

I shut the recorder off. Somehow I felt dirty, because as part of the human race, I had helped create these things, monsters who prayed to death, wanted it. Animals.

"That's *beyond* fucked up," said Snyder. "Just when I think I wouldn't mind getting it on with one or two of them, they have to spout that kind of crap."

From the main exit tunnel we heard a high-pitched screeching. As the volume increased, I saw the Marines getting nervous. I hadn't been there long, but long enough to know when something was up, and when Ox handed me a tin of zip, I took some without thinking, because who knew how much longer we'd get to keep our helmets off? The screeching made me wince, sounded like someone running hundred-foot metallic fingernails over a mammoth chalkboard, until the drugs kicked in and made everything OK.

Twenty minutes later, a fusion borer rolled into view. A team of engineers in orange jumpsuits manned the vehicle and jockeyed it against the north wall, its front end pointed at the Russian lines.

"*Screw* this," said Ox.

The captain waved us over.

"Push is on." He waited until the grumbling subsided. "Sappers are going to start digging in about twenty minutes. It's roughly three klicks to Pop's lines, so I figure you've got just under three days to write letters or grab some rack. But stay alert. Pops might try a topside infiltration, and if it works this time, we'll be busy. Questions?"

Ox raised his hand. "Standard assault?"

The captain nodded. "Except for one thing. The Gs won't be with us this time, not underground, anyway."

"What the hell?" someone asked.

"Take it easy. Division has a bright idea about trying to screw Popov at his own game. We'll start a barrage twenty-four hours before jump-off, to keep their heads down, and the Gs are going to use it as cover. They'll move out topside and infiltrate the Russian positions from above at the same time we crash their lines underground. Wendell?"

I raised my hand.

"You coming with us?" he asked.

"Yeah, if that's all right."

"Whatever. Ox and Snyder, stay with Wendell in the rear, keep him safe. Dismissed."

I looked at Ox and caught him staring at me like, *What the hell, are you crazy?* I didn't know—maybe I was—but something told me that I had to see this. *Stripes* wanted a story, and I had to have one to write about. For at least that moment I wanted the Pulitzer so bad I could taste it, could almost see it floating in midair, and it made me forgot how much shit I was in. *They* could party sub-terrene all year if they wanted, but this was my last chance and *I* was going to get laid. *I* partied Pulitzer.

A few minutes later, the fusion borer ground to life. I still had my hood on, and the vision kit switched to infra-red, showing the secondary coolant lines in glowing white. The thing looked like a cross between a lamprey and a freight train, a perfect cylinder with coolant and muck lines trailing behind it. Superheated water flowed through them. I was glad I had zipped, because in infra-red, it looked really cool. Space-age. I wished I could be there when it punched through, to see the thing vent plasma into Russian tunnels so they couldn't shoot at it. You can't shoot at something when you've been charred beyond recognition.

The borer slammed into the wall. A rock face immedi-ately melted and chunks broke off to land in a screaming grinder, which pulverized the blocks and sent them along with spent coolant water in a muddy mixture to the rear. It didn't just scream; it laughed, banshee-style. I grinned widely, because the zip told me things—that the screech-ing was for me, announcing to the world that Scout was coming, while magma oozed over the ceramic sides of the machine, chilling instantly to glass against water-cooled skin.

Ox had zipped too. It was full-on; I could see it in the

way he slouched. "God bless the engineers, for it is they who make subterrene slick."

"That's some of the coolest shit I've ever seen," said Snyder.

"Wow." We all said it at the same time and then collapsed, laughing.

Once the borer had pushed into the northern wall, we waited. I thought that by now the Marines would be used to it—thought that even *I'd* be used to it. But nobody was—you couldn't *get* used to it—and I began to suspect that the more you experienced the line, the *less* capable you were of waiting. Eskimos had a thousand words for snow. Marines had about two thousand to describe time; I heard them over and over, like mantras. Crap time, rack time, grab-ass-and-jerk time. But *this* was the worst kind, the one that Marines hated the most, because it moved slowest, gave you a chance to think about what waited for you, to write emails and death letters. This was push time. Anyone who had booze drank it. Ox, Snyder, and I stayed zipped while we were awake, which was most of the time. Only the genetics seemed unaffected, just sitting there. Statues. Once in a while, one or two would jack into the waste ports or slap in a fresh fuel cell, but other than that, they stared at the wall.

"I need a beer," I said. The borer was long gone, and we could barely hear it screeching now.

"Why didn't you say so? I have one more." Snyder rummaged through his pack and produced a can, tossing it to me.

"I don't want to take your last one."

"Nah," he said. "Take it, man. I'll get plenty when I rotate to Shymkent. You're with us now. Crank fire."

*   *   *

"Stay on *me*," Ox said. I wasn't going to argue. I had a carbine again and it felt strange, like I was eight and playing make-believe soldier.

We had marched two and a half klicks of the attack tunnel, heading north through no-man's-land. I imagined Marines across the front doing the same. When we headed in, the genetics had gone topside and we felt the Marine barrage, heard it get louder as we approached Pop's territory. But we didn't care. That was Pop's problem. In less than twenty minutes, if our Gs weren't detected, they would drop in from above at the same time our fusion borer punched through, and then Mr. Popovich would have two more problems.

The order came over the headset. "Hold."

"Christ," said Ox. "You all right, Snyder?"

Snyder didn't say anything but reached up and tapped the side of his helmet, where he had written something new: *Angel of Death.*

"What happens now?" I asked.

"Well, there's always a chance that Pops will stealth bore and try to wipe us from the rear."

"What?"

Ox sounded like he was laughing but I couldn't tell. "Take it easy. There's another group behind us about a klick, ready to deal if they try it. For now, we wait. You anxious to get shot?"

"I want to go home," I said.

"Don't we all."

We didn't have long to wait. I didn't even know it had happened until ahead of me I heard what sounded like firecrackers, something far-off and dreamlike, as if Chinese New Year had arrived early. Then someone's voice came over the headset—not the captain's; a voice I didn't recognize.

"Move in."

The Marines in front of me surged forward. One second I was in the tunnel, so scared I couldn't move; the next second I was in hell and everything drifted, so slowly that I had time to wonder how I got there. It must have taken ages for me to move in. I mean, it *had* to have; there were a thousand men in front of me. But then, before I knew it, Ox and Snyder were on either side and we broke into the Russian positions, where the two of them threw me to the ground. It knocked the wind out of me. At first Ox thought I had been hit, because I couldn't talk and just lay there, but after a few seconds, I breathed again and gave him the thumbs-up.

"Wind knocked out of me."

"Christ," he said. *"Stay down."*

Another world. The Russians had extinguished their lamps, so I saw everything in shades of green and white, except when thermal flashes overloaded my vision kit with every grenade burst. I couldn't figure out where I was. It looked like a sandbag pit, but once I got used to seeing through the goggles, it became clear that we'd landed on top of dead Marines, who were so close that I read the names stenciled on their armor and saw flecks of tissue and blood pasted to the inside of their faceplates. The dead protected me. The dead liked me, whispered that they'd take care of everything.

We had punched into the mine itself, and in front of us a huge hangar stretched beyond my vision range. It looked like the Marines had spread themselves out in a rough semicircle and were pushing forward, one group leap-frogging over another, and eventually the reporter got the worst of me, too stupid to be scared. I prairie-dogged it—poked my head up to get a better view—when a swarm of fléchettes nearly took it off, whining past my temple.

"Stay down!" said Ox.

Snyder looked at me and—I shit you not—popped his lid. Took it off in the middle of the firefight.

"What the hell are you doing?" Ox asked.

"I can *see,*" he said. "I see now, man, for the first time." Snyder pulled out his tin and zipped. "It's unreal, Ox, you should try it. Invincible. I don't care what the captain said. Scout can take care of himself. Let's go *crank.*"

"Put your helmet on. Come on. I mean, what the ... ?"

Snyder spat on the back of a dead Marine and then grinned. I didn't know what to do. It seemed crazy, but at the same time it seemed normal, because the whole place was insane, something I had never experienced, so who was I to say what *wasn't* normal?

"Nah," he said, "I can't see with it on. But now I do."

A grenade landed behind him and I saw a fléchette punch through Snyder's shoulder, sending a few drops of blood my way. It didn't affect him. He just smiled at the hole, looked up, and started singing. There was no tune, but it must have sounded right to him, because he started singing more loudly, a series of random notes that formed some screwed-up song. Kaz had claimed Snyder as its own. Ox must have suspected there was no way to pull him back into our world, and he couldn't have tried any-way, because as soon as Snyder paused to breathe, the Russians counterattacked.

"Pobieda!" They were so close that the scream sounded like a roar.

"Oooo-rah!" Snyder said. *"Pobieda!* Man, that's the shit, why don't *we* have words like that?"

I howled like a little girl. Something had hit me, my ass felt like it was on fire, and suddenly in my suit I smelled burning flesh.

Ox started laughing. *"You're hit."*

"Aw, man," I said, tasting the fear and getting cold with it. "Shit, shit. Where? How bad?"

"Relax. You got splashed with a little thermal gel is all. On your ass."

Let down. Relief. We both laughed then and couldn't stop. I felt the Russians coming, heard the change in tone of the commands being barked over the coms net, but somehow being splashed in the rear with thermal gel made it bearable.

I was still laughing when Ox went quiet. He pulled himself over to Snyder and shook him, kept shaking him for a minute, but he was gone. Snyder had absorbed most of the thermal gel that had hit me, and one entire side of his armor was missing, along with a wide swath of skin, so we saw muscles twitching. Electrical impulses were the only things left.

"At least he's not singing," said Ox, trying to be cool. But I could tell it had hit him. He just lay there, curled up as close to Snyder's remains as possible, and then sobbed while he held the guy's head against his shoulder.

Normally, I would have been concerned only with *my* injury and screw the dead. Worry about the living, about me. But all I could think of now was that Snyder had given me his last beer. I felt it then, can pinpoint the instant when Kaz took me and refused to let go, drawing me down into the depths of subterrene so that I could never really leave.

I popped my helmet. The smell was like nothing I had experienced before. Imagine taking everything in a house—the family, the furniture, the carpets, even the dog and cat—and shoving it all into a bonfire along with a thousand liters of fuel alcohol. That's the smell of war in subterrene, and with every breath I inhaled some of Snyder.

I grabbed his tin and zipped.

"Check it," said Ox. He popped his lid and joined me—children of Kaz. We both lay there on our backs, our heads resting on Snyder's armor, and looked up at the ceiling as red tracers zinged overhead and flashes of brilliant grenade light went off like strobes.

I got splashed a couple more times, and so did Ox. We both caught a few fléchettes, and a ricochet took half my right ear off, but I didn't even feel it; I was too zipped up. Ox even pulled out his player and cranked music. He thought that Snyder had been trying to sing an old, old song, "Kids in America," but I didn't know the song, or any kids, and besides, it had all been so whacked that I hadn't bothered to really try to figure out *what* he was singing. We lay there for what felt like hours, not even noticing when the firing died off.

"Holy shit." A corpsman looked down at us. He seemed far away and his eyes went wide, so we must have been hit worse than we thought, but there was no way to tell; we didn't feel a thing. "Stretchers!"

"What's wrong?" I asked. "Is the war over?"

Ox started giggling and the corpsman just looked at us

like we were crazy. "For you guys it is. Besides, Russians pulled out. Gs pushed them back ten klicks."

Once they loaded us onto stretchers, Ox turned his head to look at me. "Man. You're all bloody. I think your ear is missing."

"What's that?" I said. "I can't hear you, I lost an ear."

Man, did we laugh at that. So hard it hurt my stomach. Then the corpsman injected me with something and the world turned off, went black so that I couldn't see a thing, but just before I went totally under, I had the strangest thought.

Screw the Pulitzer.

TWO

Winter Offensive

Headaches. Hallucinations. Snyder and Burger came to see me every day and stood there all bloody and messed as they grinned because they knew there was nothing I could do, nothing to be done about phantoms in my mind, the products of withdrawal. Ox had been sent to a field hospital closer to the lines, while they'd sent me with the bad cases to Shymkent for a month in bed and recuperation. Two weeks of that was because I kept screaming, wouldn't shut up. The doctors didn't know about a la canona, the lack of drugs that makes your skin turn inside out, and they thought I was a psych case, so when the day for my release arrived, one of them said I was supposed to get in touch with Bandar 'Abbas because they had called my editor's desk *concerning my mental state*. "Great," I'd said. "I'll get right on that."

"Haloo!" the doorman to my hotel greeted me on my return. "Welcome bag, mister!"

"Yeah, you too."

My suite seemed smaller. I breathed through my nose, trying to catch a whiff of Marines, alcohol, something, but all I got was Shymkent and sulfur from the coal-burning power plant. Civilization.

I reached once more out of reflex for my tin—Snyder's tin—and then remembered. It was at the mine. My suite melted around me and I was right back there, wallowing in the dead and shaking from the explosions. I just went with it, prayed for it to end—*God, bring me back to the real world and save me from Kaz. Or send me back to subterrene.*

When the hallucination was over, the sun had set and only the telephone message indicator lit the room.

"I gotta get away from straight." There wasn't anyone there, but talking made me feel better, like the sounds of my own voice would keep me company. I'd do the phone call. Make the desk think that it was my injuries that messed me up, that the doc didn't know what he was talking about. I'd lost an ear, for Christ's sake, and the desk wouldn't understand that I needed to be *wired up,* to re-submerge and escape from the sun and snow. To get loose. The Marine supply base was on the north side of the city, and that friendly supply sergeant was in there somewhere. Straight was all wrong, I thought, and I needed Pavlodar, dreamed in subterrene green—the only way. I didn't know why, but I had this crazy thought going through my head and couldn't get rid of it: if I didn't get back to the line with Ox, the ghosts of Snyder and Burger would haunt me forever.

A tired voice answered the phone after I punched in. "Erikson."

"Hey, Phil, it's Sc...Wendell."

"Jesus!" He sounded awake now. "My head case at the front, you going to assemble a story that makes sense for once? I hear you finally went psychotic."

"Look, I don't know what the docs told you but I'm

fine. I got shot, and they must have given me something that was past its shelf life. I'll have the story for you—"

He cut me off in midsentence. "Just shut up. People around here are already talking about it, and we have a pool to guess how long it'll be before you crash. I didn't want to send you there; Jackson or Martha should have gotten that posting. I don't know who's pulling strings for you up top, but I swear to shit, your ass is mine from now on. Get me the story before tomorrow morning, or you're done."

"I'll have a draft emailed to you in two hours. Look, it won't even be rough. I'll give it to you polished." The lie came to me then, easily, like all of them did. "You won't be able to reach me once I send it, though. I have a chance to get back on the line."

"Screw that," he said. "Screw another promise from the wonder kid. I'll believe it when I see it, so get it to me."

Phil didn't say goodbye; he just hung up. The laptop's glare blinded me for a second, until my eyes adjusted, and I stared. Blank. I couldn't remember a damn thing about what I had done, where I had been. There was a vague feeling of terror and of horrible things, but also a sense that if I sat there long enough and relaxed, it would all come back in a wave of shit. It did. I wrote the story while crying, in an hour, and, after sending it, thought about what it would take to make it all go away. I was going back to Pavlodar.

As I walked out the door, my phone started ringing. It was probably Phil, I figured, pissed off about a period I had forgotten, so I shut the door and left.

Son of two parents: reporting and subterrene. I needed the story, needed to see the war, like some psycho Peeping

Tom with an addiction to scoping out unsuspecting housewives—only *my* addiction was watching death in its million forms. Kaz gave me clarity, focus, because it made everything simple. No ass grabbing at the water-cooler, no having to worry about shitbags breaking into your computer and stealing your contacts, your research, your story. The irony of subterrene was that it provided the intangible and priceless: decency. Gestures that weren't only gestures, like Ox's holding Snyder's head because it had totally mangled his state, or Snyder's tossing me a beer because somehow I'd become one of them—worth his last can. Then, just as quickly, Kaz took it away, leaving you with its aftertaste, enough to get you hooked on guys like Snyder and Burger before ripping them from your grasp, as if to say, *Ah-ah-ah, not too much, I want you coming back for more.* And you would. I knew *I* would. Decency was like a drug to someone like me, someone who almost never got to see it and who rarely showed it except in trade to screw you over.

I remember running into a Special Forces guy sitting on the side of the road when I first got to Kaz. He didn't even look at me. So I walked up to him and laid on my slickest rap, the one I used to hit some source, pry out the information with finesse. He looked at me then and smiled, said really quietly, "You'll find out, Kaz will suck you in, won't let go. And you'll go down smiling like we all do, because there is no world anymore. Except Kaz." I didn't get it back then, and didn't really take it now, but thought I did, only it never became clear until much later what the guy had really been saying. This was only the beginning of a mind trip. Call it false clarity on the way down, a misguided belief that crept in on my way out of the hotel to fool me into thinking I had it all figured out: you *smiled* at the war because it *took* war to show you good shit, to show you human beings. Back then, I thought *that* was the answer.

The walk to the north side of Shymkent went quickly and it took only an hour to find someone at the Marine supply depot willing to deal. Zip. I bought a month's worth. The train station wasn't too far, so I hit it, trying to move fast enough to keep from freezing, and on the way thought about how I would get north.

As soon as I stepped onto the station platform, a colonel slapped me on the back.

"*Stripes,* right?"

"Yeah, Colonel. Wendell. How'd you know?"

He lit a cigar and blew the smoke over his shoulder. "I thought I recognized you, saw you in Pavlodar. Can't wait to see your piece on my Marines, son."

"Yes, sir," I said, "I just gave it to my bureau. Headed back to Pavlodar now."

"That might be a problem," he said.

"Why?"

"Only genetics are being allowed transit passes to the northern sector." The colonel thought for a second. "But I could get you in *with* them."

The idea made me shiver. I remembered what I had seen of them, innocent murderers. "Sir, I don't have a combat suit and it's freezing."

"I'll be back in a second, to bring you a suit." He pulled me toward a passenger car and helped me get inside. "Get in, hang tight."

I had my pack and sat on it, waiting for my eyes to adjust to the darkness, and when they did, I nearly freaked.

Wall-to-wall betties, all around me—genetics—who stared at me with a vacant, *I-could-kill-you-or-screw-you-and-not-care-about-either* look.

The suit didn't fit right. Getting into the undersuit in front of those chicks was another hassle, a tale of embarrassment that I'm sure would have been hilarious to Ox if he had been there. Forty of them, watching me deal with the hoses, my face red.

Horses—they were like horses or mules. It occurred to me after sealing the suit and hanging my helmet that these girls were low, way down in the order of things, lower than grunts. Draft animals. The military had taken a passenger car and ripped everything out except the steam heat and a samovar so they could cram as many bodies in as possible, stack Gs like vertical cordwood one layer thick.

I cracked my first tin, then smelled it. Like a summer vacation, the first bit went in easy, hit all the right mental spots, and I melted from the inside, grinned for the first time since leaving Shymkent—until the girl across from me grinned back. That killed it. I just wanted to zip, to ignore the fact that I had been shoved into a train full of Gs, and never thought the things would actually talk to me. Who knew they smiled?

"You wish for the line," she said. The others glanced up then, curious.

I nodded. "Yeah. I left a friend there."

"I left many friends there, sisters. I miss the line too. It is where we find our best selves."

"Baby, you have no idea how much I understand that."

It took me a second to figure out why they looked so different this time. "Don't you guys usually wear thermal block?"

She touched her face, like she wasn't sure whether she had any on. "Some do, but we all wear helmets in combat. Time enough for thermal block, time for everything. I remember you."

"Excuse me?"

She reached out and placed her hand on mine. It screwed me up. These things weren't acting like I thought they would, and it became hard to reconcile that this was a killing machine with her touching my hand, making small talk.

"Do not fear. You are the first man who has ever advanced with us into glory. I remember you from our last action in Pavlodar. You stared at me and I thought you were ugly." I had to spit, so I did, on the floor in front of me.

"Why did you do that?" she asked.

"It's zip." But I could tell she didn't get it, because her face scrunched, so I tried something different. "Like tranq tabs."

She got *that* and brushed her hand across my beard, the one I had grown on the line. "We think you are so interesting."

That was all it took. I changed my mind on the spot, had to grin at how easy a sell I was, because it didn't take much to get me to change my mind. Sexy, they really were. In a train and without the crap on their faces, it was different from the last time. I thought, *Man, if you guys had any clue how freaky this is for me, you wouldn't come any closer and would give me a second to normalize.* Beautiful. Check it, you'd think that without hair and in a combat suit they couldn't be beautiful, but they were. Like perfectly wired athletes, a high school track team gone bad, and all with the same chiseled face. I didn't care that they were totally bald. It didn't matter in Kaz.

"Thanks," I said. "Interesting is better than ugly."

Man, I was tired. I hadn't rested since getting out of the hospital, and it began to catch up. They weren't *really* human. So I didn't care when they saw me spit the zip out, and cared even less when I realized that as I'd fallen asleep, I had said something to the girl, the one who had done the talking.

"You are *beautiful*. Just unreal, and thanks for being so normal this time. Like a girl."

I dreamed. A psychotherapist sat across from me on the train and laughed while he spat out words, which landed on the wooden floor and shattered into droplets of mercury, disappearing through cracks. *Only the weak-minded crumble after just one time on the line, the cowards and shit-for-brains. There is a word for people like you, but I hesitate to use it, because it implies that you are human when in fact you've never been anything of the sort, have you, Oscar? You're a parasite. A mosquito that buzzes around and annoys people, sucking them dry and then moving on to the next victim, the next meal. Anyway, the word is old and perhaps overused, and there are actually several different terms for this kind of person, but I like this word: "narcissistic."*

She woke me by whispering in my ear. "My name is Bridgette."

The train had stopped. "Are we there?"

"Pavlodar? Yes. Come. It is for death and faith."

She had begun to stand when I noticed that we were the only ones left in the car, and I grabbed her hand. "Wait. I've heard that phrase before. Why do you guys say that, death and faith?"

"Because it is time. It is the end of my term. Tomorrow I turn eighteen and today I die. These are *good* things. Without death or faith, I am nothing; with both, everything."

She helped me up and I was about to grab my bag when she kissed me, quick and awkward, an eighth-grade kiss from the shy girl in the front row who didn't have clue one about holding hands. Swear to *God,* it was *cool.*

"I..." she began. She shouldered her Maxwell and slid a grenade into her combat harness. "I needed to do that, before my discharge. We wonder what it is like to kiss and I can tell them now. It will help when their time comes. Follow me, because one of my sisters, Kim, acquired a Russian Maxwell for you. Without your Maxwell, you can't be perfect."

Those kinked-up stories we all told about the Gs and how they were crazy and all messed to hell, they were part right, but now I could see where they missed. The Gs *weren't* crazy, not exactly. I hooked up for dinner once with a lieutenant colonel from the Army, a real manicure-and-polish guy, who wore a pair of old-style automatic pistols—chemically propelled rounds, which were about as useless against armor as thrown flowers. I wouldn't have wasted time with him except for one thing. He'd been there since day one, on the trip from Bandar, the landing, and D-day. There was a story there, I figured, one for which I'd whore myself.

The guy laughed as if Bandar had been spring break in college when he was younger. "Wendell, you really should have been there, strapped it all on and gotten into the shit a little earlier. It felt like Caesar and the Rubicon, and you can quote me on that."

"Why should I have been there, Colonel?"

He laced both hands behind his head and leaned back. "Well, all of a sudden, these APCs come out of nowhere—I mean balls out and screaming up the beach—headed straight for about a thousand enemy prisoners. Fucking things ran right over them. Those Iranian boys—what was left of them—looked like ketchup mixed with sand, spaghetti, and purple eggplant. I would have been pissed, but the APCs missed *my* guys entirely, so I figured…who cares?"

"Jesus."

"Nah," he said, raising his beer in toast. "Genetics. The APCs were filled with, and driven by, our Gs. To the wonders of science, and to hell with the Russians—along with all who stand in our way. Although without Popov, you and I would have no war. The genetics may be lunatics, but at least they're *our* lunatics and God bless them."

Kim and Bridgette stood outside the railcar waiting for me, and as soon as I dropped to the ground, Kim handed me a Maxwell and then kissed me. They all lined up after that, one after another, and did the same. Twisted. You'd think it would have been sweet, like having a huge harem, but no way; it wasn't the same as when Bridgette did it. By the time they finished, I must have kissed a whole battalion, too many to see as they filled the rail yard, and I had to fight to keep from crying. *Not* cool, not after I realized what was happening.

The colonel had got it all wrong. They weren't crazy,

not from their perspective. Gs just *were*. The factories designed and raised them that way, but nobody had bothered to get rid of other instincts, and now they had to deal with being part human. *Hey, Kim, I got me a hundred confirmed. How many did you kill today? I don't know, Bridgette. I forgot because I was thinking about what it would be like to have kids.* How did they deal with that?

As soon as they broke into a trot, Bridgette waved for me to catch up. "Come, it is a nice day for combat. What is your name?"

"Scout."

She laughed before slipping her helmet on. "Scout. We like you, Scout, and I like you especially. Hurry. We lost communications with Third Marine less than a week ago, and Division suspects something went wrong. Today, before dying, we will see about Russians."

Pavlodar brought it back. They were funny things, memories.

General Margaret Jensen, commanding officer, First Armored Division, had set up her HQ in Aktau in a hotel that had a brothel on the ground floor and overlooked the Caspian Sea. On my first visit there, I thought I had the wrong place. I walked around the block again, just to check, because Aktau had some messed-up system—a leftover from the old Soviet Union days—where there were no street names, just block and building numbers. Turned out I'd had the right location in the first place.

The hotel was filled with hookers. Wall-to-wall, unbelievably hot betties, with skinny bodies and an Eastern sensibility when it came to makeup—that more was

always better. But despite their smiles, you could tell they
were off, just as dirty as the rest of Kaz. Most were sad,
their grins concealing pitted, rotten souls, and *they* didn't
want to be there, but as long as they were, they sure as shit
didn't want *us* there, and every time I turned around, I
suspected that those chicks gave me the finger.

On that particular day, the general was in her suite,
which had been converted into a radio room and tracking
station, stuffed with computers and holo-displays. She sat
behind a huge desk with two hookers on her lap.

"*Wendell!* Siddown."

"Yes, ma'am," I said.

"So, what do your readers want to know?" she asked.
The general had a plate of Vienna sausages, which she fed
to the girls, one at a time.

"Ma'am, we got a report that for the first time since
this started, you're seeing action at Group West, that
Popov launched a major armored offensive."

"Probes," she said. "That's it. Pops knows we'll kick
his ass back to the Urals if he tries anything in force."

The general didn't know about my visit to her hospital. I
had already interviewed her tankers, who had just been
flown in from south of Saykhin near the Russian border.
One of them was charred from head to toe, and assured me
that the fight was on, two divisions of Russian armor
headed south, and I gathered from his sobbing and attempts
to chew off his own tongue that *he* wasn't confident about
kicking *anyone* back to the Urals. *That* wasn't a probe.

"My sources say different. First Armored is collapsing, and you have plans to move your HQ eastward, before
the Caspian sector is isolated, cut off."

Her face went dead white and she ordered the hookers

out. I had a cousin who was a cop. He always told me
never to be afraid of someone who was angry and red in
the face—*that* was normal. Only the truly whacked got
pale when pissed, and you were supposed to run if you
ever saw that.

She waited until the two girls left. "Shithead, whose
side are you on?"

"Ma'am?"

The general pulled out a sidearm, a fléchette pistol,
and pointed it at my head. "You put any of the shit in your
rag and I'll find you. Wipe your shit from here to Almaty.
Get out."

I ran. Kaz was that messed sometimes, each sector
like a fiefdom where a general called the shots, got to
decide what to believe, often making decisions completely disconnected from conditions at the front. With
video feeds and instant coms, it was hard to imagine how
that could be, but it was. Some called it the human factor.
An inability to see real-time information for what it was,
as if commanders' minds had a filter that changed the
data into Picasso-like pictures except with *no* tether to
reality. Later I found out that General Jensen had been
arrested for trying to send girls back to her home in the
States so her girlfriend there could sell them to pimps.
White slaves. That betty had way more than a screwed-up
filter; Kaz had nothing to do with it. She was fucked
before subterrene.

This time around, the Pavlodar line reminded me of
that, of Aktau and the hotel, a forgotten land, disconnected from the world and isolated, left on its own to
mutate into whatever it chose. The tunnel Bridgette and I
moved into was part of the Marines' sector, and men sat

on crates or lounged on the tunnel floor amid meter-high piles of ration packs, spent hoppers, and broken equipment. They had given up on pumping suit waste into wall ports. Human filth caked their legs where it had fallen from their dump valves, and piles of it collected on the floor. This wasn't the Pavlodar I had left.

A captain greeted us, his accent foreign, but at the time it didn't seem strange; plenty of foreigners fought with us, hoping for American citizenship. "Welcome to Pavlodar!" he said.

I let the Gs do their thing and went to talk to a sergeant.

"Top, what outfit is this?"

He looked up, barely moving. "First Battalion, Third Marine."

"Where's First Marine?"

"Other side of the city, about three or four klicks west. Who are you?"

"He's not a friggin' G," another one said. "*That's* good."

I slumped against the wall and popped my lid. Needed it bad. I grabbed my tin, packed it, and scooped a massive pinch before noticing that my teeth had begun to hurt. Who cared? Soon I wouldn't feel anything.

"Scout, civilian reporter with *Stripes*."

"Oh man," the sergeant said. Suddenly he was awake, animated. "You should have been here yesterday, we pushed and got our asses kicked, didn't even have time to blow our tunnels, just plugged 'em. I lost half my guys, woulda made some story."

I looked where he pointed. A huge circular alloy plug had been sealed into the north wall, blocking what had once been an attack tunnel, and was the only thing between us and an empty passage—one that ran straight to the Russians.

"When did you guys lose coms?" I asked.

The sergeant and his men looked at each other like I was crazy. "What are you talking about?"

"That's why the Gs are here, said they lost communication with Third Marine a few days ago. There's an entire division of genetics spreading out across the lines right now."

"Man, that's off," said the sergeant. "I don't know who told you that but we've been in communication the whole time. I was just back at Battalion yesterday, all normal. Either someone got it backwards, or that's just a story they told the Gs. What're they like?"

"What?" I asked.

"The Gs. You came in with 'em?"

I nodded. The zip had kicked in by then and I grinned like a madman. "Wild."

If I hadn't been wired to the gills, I might have been able to figure out that everything was wrong. Didn't fit. But I didn't care anymore; I was back in subterrene, rock walls on every side so that nothing could hurt me.

Dan Wodzinski. Greatest reporter who ever lived. He blew a head vein when he found out that I'd got the nod for subterrene, for the line, and he didn't try to hide it. We got piss drunk in the hotel, the bartender shaking his head until he left the bottle so he wouldn't have to keep pouring. Dan had covered the Syrian Campaign back in '45. He went in with the Special Forces when they first inserted behind the lines, and was practically a movie star, the Supreme Chancellor of the Press Corps, the one we all wanted to be. We hated and loved him at the same time, because he knew he was good but was so damn generous with his experiences—handed them out like candy to anyone who wanted a taste. That made it worse. It would have been easier to handle him if he had been good *and* a total prick, but because he was gracious about it, everyone assumed that he was a world-class jerk-off, not your garden variety.

"You goddamn *rube!*" he said. "Man, I can't believe you got the nod, serves me right for going freelance, no machine to bribe the right people anymore."

"Are you insinuating that I had to buy my way to the line?"

"Yep. You couldn't write your way out of a bad romance novel. *No* way. You could eat my 'puter, and you *still* wouldn't be able to shit a sentence as good as my worst."

He got all serious then. Stared off in the distance, same look I saw on that Special Forces guy on the road—somewhere else, in a different world, channeling demons and ghosts.

"It'll end badly," he said.

"Don't give me that crap. I don't want to hear it."

He shook his head. "Nah, not you. You'll be fine, go get some. I'm talking about the war. Even if we win, it'll end badly."

"I don't follow."

"The genetics. We played with nature and soon we'll get it shoved in our faces, rammed into our bungholes whether we like it or not."

He must have seen the confusion on my face, read it.

"How long do you think it'll be before Popov makes his own genetics?" Dan asked.

I didn't know how even to *start* answering that one.

That was a long time ago, but when I woke up in the tunnel, I remembered it. Bridgette had found me slumped over, and I had forgotten to take out my zip before passing out. Luckily, I *had* taken off my helmet. A puddle of puke had dried around my head, and as soon as I sat up, I dry heaved, and the tunnel wouldn't stop spinning. It didn't matter. What mattered was that the edge was still off, everything smooth, and I did my best to wipe my face with an empty ration pack.

"You are ill," she said.

"Nah, I'm OK."

"We attack soon." She pointed to the tunnel plug and I saw a team of sappers working plasma torches, cutting through while a forklift waited to catch it. "I thought you might want to come, to share."

I kissed her. She was real close to me, and her breath was incredible, feminine. It had been a long time, and I was so gone that I just did it without thinking, not considering that maybe she didn't want to kiss someone who had just puked. But she kissed me back. And when it was over, she smiled.

"I will miss you, Scout."

Bridgette stood and hesitated before leaving. "Remember me. It will be nice to leave this place and know that we will be remembered."

"Yeah. I won't forget, kid."

When the plug fell out with a clang, Bridgette moved into the tunnel with the others and it screwed with me. I didn't want her to go.

The fact was that although I didn't see it, the downward slide had begun long before, a transformation in which the human part of me had begun to dissolve to be replaced by a hybrid thing, part earth and part war, a shift that was clear only in retrospect, maybe looking back when you hit sixty years old. Bridgette reminded me of the old Oscar—before Kaz. She had a light in her face that said nothing about what she had been designed to do, because it was the glow of someone young who still had things to experience, the same things I had taken for granted or forgotten, and her presence reminded me of them. Bridgette made you forget where you were.

"Get some," the sergeant said.

"Huh?"

"I can't believe you'd even touch one of those things. Gs and reporters screwing. Now I've seen it all."

It finally started to break through then, that something wasn't right. These weren't the Marines I remembered; they were nothing like Ox, and I wished he was there, actually missed Burger and Snyder too, wanted their corpses to show up and keep me from having to look at the sergeant.

I stood and moved toward the attack tunnel, slipping on my hood to see in the darkness. Screw the Maxwell, I thought. It was too heavy.

The captain stood near the tunnel entrance and nodded at me.

"Welcome to Pavlodar!" he said again. "No weapon?"

"Nah—I'm a reporter, with *Stripes*."

"I haven't heard of this," he said.

"You haven't heard of *Stars and Stripes*?" I asked. It was *all* wrong, and even through the zip, it started to tingle, the pucker starting early. "Where are you from?"

"Poland. I joined up last year so I could get my citizenship."

I had to get out of there. It was too amped up, even for me, and there wasn't anything in particular that got me on edge; it was more a feeling that somewhere in my subconscious an internal computer had crunched the numbers while I wasn't looking and now sent me a message that it couldn't divide by zero. The girls had vanished into the tunnel, but I thought if I walked after them, I might get to the Russian lines in time to see it. To get some, or at least get away from the captain.

That's when the shit started.

"You can't go there," he said. The guy was grinning and it occurred to me that he was too young. Like a teenager. The vision hood had concealed it from a distance, but now that he was close, it was obvious and crazy. He grabbed my arm with one hand and nearly broke my wrist in a grip so strong it was like nothing I had felt before; then he lifted a carbine with his free hand.

The others never had a chance. Fléchettes ripped through the Marines, cutting some of them in half, and none of them even got to return fire; they weren't ready. A couple started running toward the exit tunnel, and the captain let go of me so he could steady his aim and cut them down.

It was slow. A plasma torch lay on the floor and I grabbed it, no clue how to turn it on, but guessing it involved the red button on its side, and while I fumbled, he aimed at the running Marines carefully. I heard the shots, like a spray bottle.

The plasma torch hissed, nearly cutting my fingers off, and I saw the captain smile again as he swung the carbine toward the noise. He didn't even scream. The torch cut through his midsection. It cauterized everything, so there was no blood, but his two halves glared white on my infrared and then slowly faded as they cooled. He coughed once before the tunnel went quiet.

Dan's words ran through my head again. *How long do you think it'll be before Popov makes his own genetics?*

I was so dead and knew it, but for some reason I ran after her, into the tunnel, when every part of me screamed, *Run the other way.*

They were way ahead. I sprinted for as long as I could, then stopped to button on my lid before hitting it again. Pops must have been jamming us. Static filled my coms, and with relays I should have been reading the Gs clear, even from the far end of the tunnel, but the girls didn't click in until I'd moved almost a kilometer. The static cleared, replaced by her voice, but then again, *all* of them had her voice.

"There will be a moment of reckoning," one of them said, "and He will look down and judge, not our thoughts or words but our actions. Eternal life for the warrior, certain death for our enemies."

They all chanted then, low and reverent. "We were made in their image and we will die for their salvation."

The girls were somewhere up ahead. I heard one's voice echo through the tunnel when she yelled, *"Fire, fire, fire,"* and then I saw them, crouching, stiff and tight with weapons pointed downrange. Not the ones I had kissed back at the train; these were different organisms, made of bone and ceramic that had been stitched tight so that when they blew the next tunnel plug, the group filed through a narrow gap, into Popov's burrow, not even hesitating.

"Bridgette!"

One at the rear turned and straightened.

"It's a trap!"

The gas bloom flashed, so brightly that even though I didn't hear or feel it, its glare forced liquid crystals in my goggles to align—to frost over and keep me from getting flash burns. Plasma illuminated everything, like a tiny sun. The realization hit me at the same time the pressure wave did: the Russians had used artillery underground, probably manned by Popov's Gs, and I wouldn't feel a thing.

By the time the overpressure hit, my goggles still hadn't cleared, so I felt only the sensation of being lifted off my feet. Then something collided with me. Finally my goggles went transparent again, and I saw the tunnel walls whiz by, another body floating next to mine until we both hit the floor, sliding for a hundred feet.

Her helmet had shattered and blood came from both nostrils, but she blinked. Alive.

"Bridgette?"

She nodded. "What happened?"

"Popov has genetics. One of them infiltrated back in the tunnels, the captain. This whole thing was a trap. Pops cut off coms and arranged it so Third Marine *thought* they were communicating with the rear. They *wanted* you guys to come."

Bridgette blinked, then sat up. "I have to go back. My sisters."

"Are you nuts? You're the only one left."

"It is not a choice," she said. "I am at the end; it is *time*."

"Screw that." I grabbed her wrist and pulled, putting her arm around my shoulders until she got steady. When I started leading her toward the rear, I had a guess why I did it—why I wanted to save her. The zip was out, gone for now, so everything was clear and made me realize that I didn't have many friends. Not among the living. This wasn't about my attraction to her. I didn't care if she was a G or a dog; I couldn't take any more, at least not now, didn't want to inherit another ghost.

The Russians shouted from behind us. *"Pobieda!"*

"I'll die anyway," said Bridgette, matter-of-factly. "As soon as we return to Shymkent, it will be over for me. Discharged. There's no difference."

"There is to me," I said. "We can get you out. Down to Bandar. From there you can go to Sri Lanka, Argentina, anywhere."

We heard footsteps from the Russian lines and I saw her think, some cold calculus of war ticking through a machinelike brain.

"You," said Bridgette, "are too slow."

She slung her carbine and grabbed my arm, and at the same time Bridgette started dragging me like a sack, I thought, *Man, she is mad hot. Exotic.* Even with Pops on our ass, she was *still* beautiful enough to take my mind off everything else.

Or *maybe* my mind was gone.

You couldn't get a sense of how empty the steppes were until you saw them from the ground, alone and in the open. We had cruised through Pavlodar's ruins and stopped at the south side on a small hill, and when I looked out over the emptiness, it nearly made me cry. Snow covered the grasslands in a dirty gray layer, stretching toward a horizon that was a slightly darker gray. It was the first I had *seen* infinite. Somewhere out there lived Burger and Snyder, prowling and searching for me with all the time in the world, not wanting me to rest or forget that I was almost ready to hang out with them, if only I'd die and get it over with.

There was no thought of stories or Pultizers anymore; everything had been distilled down to three needs: to move south, to stay low, and to get wired up. Aboveground, you spent most of your time trying to ignore the facts that you had a bull's-eye painted on your back and that attack could come from any direction, anytime; aboveground, you spent all your time wishing for the underground, for fungus and waste that signaled a kind of safety only moles and Marines really understood. It was the second time I'd felt it—the sensation that I was horribly exposed and that somewhere overhead were Russian eyes that bored into my soul because I had become so obvious, outlined against a backdrop of snow.

We heard the sound of engines and dropped facedown into a shallow depression. Marine APCs roared from underground hangars and sped southward, their turbines whining as they bounced over the broken terrain like eight-wheeled beetles. Behind the APCs, swarms of Marines ran from the exits and filled the steppes as they sprinted after them, trying to keep up.

"It is still winter," said Bridgette.

"Yeah, so?"

"In 1942 the Germans invaded Russia and were forced to retreat. It was winter then, and many Germans died from the cold, and so will those men, the Marines. Let's move. The clouds are low and for now we won't have to worry about aircraft."

From behind us I heard the thumping of big guns, followed by the blasts of plasma over the lines we had just vacated. I didn't need more convincing, and we pushed through the snow.

"You're full of good thoughts, huh?" I asked.

"I do not understand."

"That story about 1942. It's depressing."

She cocked her head, but I saw her face now through her broken helmet. It had that scrunched-up look of *I-don't-get-it.* "It just…is. It is fact. We will have a hard time moving through this snow, over twelve hundred kilometers to Shymkent. One can assume that Popov will follow, and I would imagine that by now our rear forces are dismantling artillery for retrograde. There is no depression. Just fact and necessity." Bridgette looked up at the clouds and then at me. "What is the temperature?"

I checked my heads-up display. "Zero F."

"It will snow soon. We need to find shelter."

The static had returned on my headset and I tried switching channels but couldn't get anything. "We're still being jammed."

Bridgette just nodded and smiled. *Way* cool.

I'd had a breakdown back in D.C. Kept it quiet and just sort of disappeared for a while after calling in sick. Ten days. I curled up in my apartment and cried, positive that if I moved, something bad would happen, that they'd come and get me—*who* wasn't exactly clear, but *they* would, I was sure—as payback for all the mistakes I had made, people I had screwed. It went away on its own. Thirty pounds lighter and somewhat dirtier than before, I got up and barely made it to the shower, where I passed out. So I've always had crazy in me, mostly dormant.

After that episode, I started seeing a shrink out in Bethesda—didn't want to, *had* to. What did you do when you didn't trust your own mind? I expected it to ambush me—grab me in the middle of an interview, turn me into a blabbering schizo, and make me rip my clothes off to run down the street naked. The shrink said Kaz was a bad idea.

"Why?" I asked.

"Look at your past. Rock climbing. High-risk sexual liaisons. Drugs, and not just pills; I'm talking intravenous. Drinking to the point of self-destruction. Oscar, Kazakhstan is just another way to put yourself in harm's way so that you won't *have* to kill yourself; someone else can do it for you. I think you should reconsider and think about treatment at a facility."

"To hell with you," I said, paid her, and left. But looking back, I realize she was right. Death scared me but at the same time I wanted it, because *life* was too painful and the only thing that had taken that pain away was subterrene, Kaz, because I was too much of a coward to hang myself or put a gun in my mouth. I thought about ending it, though, all the time. But now? In the open, on the run, I felt like the only thing between me and total collapse was zip, but part of me *wanted* to collapse, to give Pops his chance at catching us so it could be over. It was the easy way out.

Bridgette had run out of tranq tabs. She started crying, and as we sat under the burned-out hulk of an APC, she shook.

"I can see them," she said. "Kim and my sisters. They want me to go with them."

I snapped my tin to pack it and held it out to her.

"You said it was like tranq tabs. What is it?"

I explained and she snatched the tin from my hand, making me smile. I thought of that day with Ox and the others and repeated their advice. "Spit. Whatever you do, don't swallow. And these doses are lower than what you're used to, but hopefully the nicotine will do you some good too."

After a moment she sighed and rested her head against the APC. "Why do you smile at me?"

"That suit," I said. "It's totally melted and obviously not a Marine suit. They'll see you coming a mile away. If we're going to try and get you south, hide who you are so you can get out of the war, we'll have to get a replacement."

"You want me to stay with you. Alive."

I couldn't bring myself to kiss her, not with that crap in her mouth, but I wanted to. "Yes. I'll get you a suit."

We had found the corpse of a Marine corporal outside the APC, a guy who'd killed himself with a Maxwell shot to the head, and I didn't spend more than a millisecond wondering *why* he had done it—kind of made sense to me, a last demonstration that he still had control over destiny. His armor was intact. I ducked into the snowfall and enjoyed the soft quiet as I dragged him out of the carapace, getting it ready for her, hoping that it would fit, because she was smaller than most Marines. Getting him out was tough. The guy had stiffened and cold only made it worse, forcing me to snap both his arms to bend them into the right angles. I dragged the armor under the wreckage and dropped it in front of her.

"Get in," I said.

She grinned. When Bridgette slid from her suit, I marveled, thanked God for what she was. Perfect. Precise. Everything curvy about a girl that you could imagine, but all of it dangerously fluid. I grinned back at her. I think I drooled when I forgot about my zip, and we cracked up.

"How does it fit?" I asked when she had finished.

"Loose. But it will function. How do I seem?"

"Perfect."

We'd have to start moving again in a few hours, so we spat out the zip and lay down together, huddled in a corner of the APC, where she rested her head on my shoulder. I don't think I slept; I didn't want to. I just wanted to breathe girl for a while.

A few days later a thick layer of ice and snow collapsed underfoot as we marched, and both of us fell through, hitting a rock floor about twenty feet below. There hadn't been enough time even to yell. Once my vision kit adjusted, I saw that we had fallen down a narrow access shaft and into an abandoned tunnel, making me think it was probably an old artillery position. In front of us the chamber stretched into darkness but headed in the right direction, south. It felt good to be underground again, superslick and in control.

She nearly wiped them. Bridgette flicked off her safety and swung her Maxwell in a blur when a group of four Marines rose from behind a pile of rubble.

"O'Brian?" one of them asked.

I froze. O'BRIAN had been stenciled in white on the right side of Bridgette's suit so you could see it for miles.

"Holy Christ!" the man said. "It *is* you, what the hell?"

"You know this guy?" another one asked.

"Yeah, Lieutenant, guy from my platoon."

The Marine slapped her on the shoulder and I saw his name: Bauer. "Man, it's good to see you. I thought all of Dog Company got wiped. What happened?"

Bridgette stood still for a moment. "I got out," she said finally.

One good thing about being in a suit, about being buttoned tight: the speakers were for shit. You couldn't recognize voices. I wouldn't have known it was a girl if it weren't for the fact that I *did* know it was a girl, and as soon as I heard what she sounded like, I went loose, trying my best to breathe out slowly so my relief wouldn't be obvious.

" 'I got out,' " said Bauer. "Shit. So did I, but I had to get away from a battalion of Russian Gs to do it. Who's this?" he asked, pointing his Maxwell at me.

"Oscar Wendell, with *Stars and Stripes,*" I said.

"A reporter?" the lieutenant asked. "Out here?"

"Yeah," I said, "what are you gonna do?"

They all laughed and I relaxed a little when Bauer shouldered his carbine.

"You got one hell of a story now," said the lieutenant. "Pops is heading south, probably just ten klicks north of us, and he's pissed. Gonna take it all back. Command net just broadcast a sector-wide recall, telling us to stuff grass, leaves, anything between our undersuits and carapace. Fuel cells dragging everywhere and the weather's too shitty for resupply, so I hope you brought your long johns."

I had no clue what in the hell a long john was, but got the rest of it and shivered, already cold at the thought. My current fuel cell had about a day or two left of power, and I didn't want to think about it, tried to find anything to say, and felt embarrassed and out of place as soon as the words came out. "At least the weather's keeping their drones grounded," I said, and they all just stared at me.

We marched. Nobody felt like talking, least of all me, but there was something in the air. Not just the anticipation of Popov's coming. *That* was a given, and the thought constantly ran through my mind in an undercurrent of gut-wrenching fear. This was something else: the idea that she was a G, walking in a Marine suit—the suit of a Marine who had been a friend to these guys. Sooner or later she might have to take off her helmet and they'd see what she was, which would lead to the next question: "What did you do with our friend?" And because she was a G, they'd assume that she'd killed him. It was going to be bad. I knew it, and I tasted it.

The tunnel broke into a large underground hangar, empty except for a small scout car that had two doors near the front and an open ramp at the rear. The Marines popped their helmets with a hiss.

"Phew," one said. "Some luck for a change. Let's see if this rattrap works."

I noticed Bauer staring at Bridgette, waiting for something. "Come on, get that helmet off," he said. "The scout car will shield our therms if it works. You need to conserve, man, unless you got a pack full of spare fuel cells."

My palms got slippery. Sweat on the palms and no spit almost made me laugh, because by now they were familiar, my long-lost cousins: Fear and Kaz.

"No," she said.

" 'No'? What, are you nuts? Your fuel cells are already

draining, they won't last as long as it'll take to reach Shymkent. We may have to go as far as Tashkent if Pops breaks the southern line."

Bridgette didn't move. I was too strung out on terror to say anything, but with what might happen next, I thought I'd better keep my own lid on.

"What's wrong?" Bauer asked.

"Nothing." With one hand on her carbine, she popped her helmet, and they all went slack-jawed.

"That ain't O'Brian," the lieutenant said.

Bridgette raised her weapon and dropped into a crouch. "Please. Do not move."

"Motherfucker," said one of the others. *"Motherfucker."*

"Don't do it," said Bridgette.

The guy started lifting the barrel of his grenade launcher and I dove to the ground, waiting for what I knew would come next: a shit storm of a firefight with nowhere to hide, so you could only pray for some way to get small. The man didn't listen. If only he'd listened, thought for a second before acting like an asshole, he might have lived a bit longer; maybe Bridgette wouldn't have done anything to them. For a second I wondered: if she *could* do it to them, to friendlies, would she do it to me? First came the sound of a spray, then the firecrackers of fléchettes breaking the sound barrier, snapping through ceramic and slamming into the rock walls beyond. But the man *hadn't listened.* I opened my eyes and found that all of them had bought it, although one was trying to crawl away, barely alive.

"Whiskey seven, this is Talon one-five," the lieutenant said.

I was about to go to him when she rested a boot on his neck and fired into his head.

"I am sorry," she said to me. "I had to. It would have been the end for both of us—for you because you helped me—and these men were too stupid to make it south if I had let them live. It was a tactical decision."

But she didn't have to say sorry, not to me. I didn't give a shit, not about the stupid. It was over for them; they were lucky. Popov wouldn't get to catch them in the open and drop thermal gel, toy with them a little before sending Gs to finish the job. Truth be told, I felt nothing. Empty. I even got it when Bridgette started popping their fuel cells, pushing them into a pack that she ripped from the lieutenant's dead hand, because what else was there to do? The dead didn't need fuel cells; the dead were at home in the cold. She waved me over after throwing her helmet into the back of the scout car.

I didn't like feeling nothing. Wanted something. So I kissed her there, among the silent Marines, and heard our ceramic chests click. The thought of two insects getting it on kind of killed the moment for me, but not for her; there was something new in Bridgette that I hadn't seen. She was hungry, wouldn't let me go until *she* had finished, and when she had, Bridgette leaned over to press her mouth against my ear.

"I need you."

It took us a while to get out of our armor, and we shivered, but she had started the scout car and it was warm by the time we were ready to screw. And after we finished in the car, we just lay there. Did it again later, with Popov bearing down and not even a second thought except for *fuck it*. She didn't know anything; I had to teach her. But she was perfect—dug it and made me feel so *cool* about everything.

That was when *my* calculus clicked, when I figured out why it felt like a gut wound once she gunned the car to head south again. I loved that betty. It was easy to fall in love, because neither of us was likely to live long anyway. I thought that the realization would make me feel better, like, *Don't worry, just feel it now because it might be over tomorrow,* but it didn't. I had to zip before I started bawling. Kaz had antibodies for anyone who started to feel good, and sent battles to scream in at a moment's notice and chew on anyone who began to feel happy.

All *we* had for now, to keep the feeling, was zip.

From the top of a low hill, I saw them, a slow-moving mass of retreating soldiers, stretched like a wide green snake across the steppes. There was no point in avoiding them. We had used up most of the spare fuel cells, and the car had run out of juice a few hours earlier, so our only chance was to hook up—join them in a last push to friendly lines and a supply depot. I hadn't thought much about what I was going to do to get her out of Kaz, make it safely, but we were close now and I'd have to think of something before they took her from me. Bridgette shouldered the carbine and wiped her faceplate clear of ice, and ten minutes later we joined the column.

Sometimes, Kaz was *really* banged up, in a trippy, what-are-the-odds kind of way. Seriously. As soon as we entered the column, I heard a voice asking if someone wanted to trade for a chicken curry.

"All I've got is this French shit," I said. "Wine-poached salmon."

It was him. Only Ox hated chicken curry; it was the

one pack worth eating as far as most Marines were concerned, but not him. He tackled me. At first Bridgette thought he was attacking, and dropped into some fighting stance as she leveled that damn carbine, but I waved her off.

Ox didn't even know how close it had been. "You little shit, *you stupid rube!*"

"What the hell are you doing here?" I asked. "Thought you'd still be in the hospital or on light duty, rear-style for a while."

He looked away. It was hard to tell, since he was buttoned, but I'd been at it long enough and realized it was the wrong question. A killer question. "You know how it is, Scout. I had to get back." That was all he had to say, and I knew what he meant.

Ox didn't realize that Bridgette was with me, and I didn't push it, didn't want to risk another scene. But as we walked, trudging through snowdrifts, I noticed her acting funny. First the snowfall started to lighten and she got all twitchy, unslinging her carbine and smacking the ice from its barrel while looking rearward. A few minutes later, she stopped and stared at the ground.

"What's wrong with that guy?" Ox asked. "He with you?"

I stopped too and was about to whisper to her that she needed to start acting normal, when she grabbed my harness. *"Move."*

I moved, followed her out into the nowhere, pushing through chest-high snow that hadn't been packed down by a column of men, so it was incredibly hard going. Like torture. I was in one of those nightmares you'd see on shitty holos, where a character ran but didn't get anywhere.

"Come on, Ox," I said. He knew me well enough to listen, and followed.

When we had gotten about a hundred meters away from the column, she dove into the snow and motioned for us to get down. I hit it and then slapped her ankle.

"What's up?"

"Look." Bridgette held out her hand and for a moment I didn't see anything, but then, all of a sudden, it was there. Her shadow. The weather had begun to clear and that would mean only one thing.

"Aw, mother of..." said Ox. "Scout, make sure that chill can is on. And chameleon skins."

The chill can sat below the suit exhaust, cooled it to the same temperature as ambient so we'd be invisible on thermal sensors. Mine was fine, and there was power enough for a short time with chameleon skins. Then I saw it. A group of Russian drones flew overhead, supersonic, so that we didn't hear anything until the boom cracked and shook the ground, covering us in a minor avalanche that only got worse when the bombs fell, over and over. I tried digging. Wanted to get underground so badly that nothing else mattered. Eventually my gauntlets hit dirt, frozen solid into concrete with no way to get through, but I couldn't stop and found out it was over only when Bridgette and Ox pulled me up, the tips of my gauntlets sanded flat.

A few minutes later it started snowing again. I don't know how many guys bought it in that attack, but we walked over them for a couple of hours, on a road paved by corpses.

Ox went down one day out from Shymkent. At first he just looked tired, like everyone else, and I almost didn't notice when he dropped his carbine. It seemed normal. I was so tired that I felt asleep on my feet, my muscles beyond screaming and at the verge of quitting, so *I* would have dropped the Maxwell ages earlier. But then I heard him laugh. Ox started hitting the buckles on his carapace, one at a time, opening them so that he could get out—until I grabbed his wrist.

"What the shit are you doing?"

"I'm so hot," he said. "Gotta get out of this suit." His words slurred and I didn't notice that Bridgette was right next to me.

She put her hand on my shoulder. "Hypothermia. Symptoms include lethargy, disorientation, euphoria, hallucination. Then death."

It had gotten dark and the column came to a halt, which was good because I had to stay there, to keep Ox from unbuttoning while she watched. But it was bad because with the night, temperatures would drop even further.

"I'm so tired," he said. "Just let me sleep for a while."

After that, he fell over, and I couldn't wake him up.

"What are *they* doing?" asked Bridgette, pointing.

Several of the Marines had collected webbing, ration packs, and other flammable material and threw them into a pile. Atop this they placed several frozen corpses. Then one of the men pulled the caps off three flares and tossed them on top so that the flash overloaded my infrared.

"Bonfire," I said.

Men gathered around it, jockeying for position as they loosened their armor—to enable the heat to penetrate more quickly. I was about to drag Ox closer when I heard someone shout.

"Goddamn it!" An Army colonel pushed into the circle. "Put that shit out now, you'll draw fire."

"Screw you," someone said, a Marine. "They can't send aircraft through this shit, and even if they could, let 'em. The weather's killing my men."

"Captain, you listen to my orders or so help me God—"

The Marine drew his fléchette pistol and fired. He pointed at two of his men, who then liberated the dead colonel of his suit, tossing the already freezing corpse onto the flames.

Bridgette cocked her head, and I smiled. The last few days had been so bad and I was so tired that I had forgotten what she looked like, hadn't seen her face since the scout car. That one gesture brought it back. I pulled her into the snow next to me.

"I think that the captain was right to do that," she said.

"I do too."

"Do you want to know what else I think, Scout?"

"Sure," I said. "Love to know."

"I think that you and these men are not so different from me and my sisters. Come. We need to get your friend near the fire."

The closest thing I'd ever had to a real friend in Shymkent was Pete German, a freelance photographer. We went everywhere together, arrived in country at the same time. It was good, because I needed a photographer; the guy from *Stripes* had gotten appendicitis and had to leave, and they didn't know when a replacement would arrive. So I picked up Pete.

He was one of those shits that caused trouble. Anywhere, every time. One night we got completely wasted and decided to hit the USO show in Shymkent's downtown rubble, a real blowout with some comedian from the States. Pete was gay, and I think he had a crush on me, because he kept trying to get me loaded, always had the best drugs and wouldn't share with anyone except me. I'd have to fight him off at the end of the night, though, remind him that I hadn't yet joined the team.

On the night of the USO thing, we popped about ten pills each—ecstasy, meth, and I can't remember what else—for what he called an on-the-town appetizer, arranged on a plate with a bottle of vodka to wash. We got *beyond* wasted that night. After getting there, Pete couldn't keep his shit straight and started screaming at the performers, accusing them of stealing his cameras just before he stumbled onto the stage. That was when he puked. We had just eaten spaghetti for dinner and it came out undigested, like guts and blood, all over the comedian's shirt and the whole place got quiet. Then Pete said, in a serious voice, "I think you've been shot." Pete got more laughs than the comedian, because all the troops in the audience gave him a standing ovation as the MPs dragged him out.

He bought it the next day. I got him out of jail, and we walked past an abandoned phosphorus plant, the structures rusted and sad remnants of a time gone by. I could almost sense it a millisecond before it happened, as if my ears felt the pressure change just before picking up the sound. *Boom.* Kazakh insurgents touched off a bomb, probably thought we were military. The blast took off half of Pete's head and sent me across the street, where I landed in the dirt before shaking it off to discover that my friend had been scattered across the road in about ten pieces. At the time I thought it was especially bad because I hadn't gotten a chance to say goodbye. But it wasn't. Getting to say goodbye made things worse; I just hadn't learned that yet, *wouldn't* learn it until Bridgette and I got Ox back to Shymkent.

We saw ground fighting for the first time in weeks. She carried Ox by the shoulders and I had his legs, both of us stumbling and trying to stay awake. A few klicks away from us, on either side, plasma thundered, and I saw the brilliant globes of light burst upward from the steppes, Popov trying to cut off our escape, pinching inward from the east and west so that we were moving through a narrow gap about a mile across. I was about to suggest to Bridgette that we drop Ox for a rest when a loud cheer made me look up. We had made it. A few minutes later we passed the outer observation posts, and then the ruins of Shymkent's suburbs, home free.

A loudspeaker broadcast a continuous automated message, which got louder as we made our way into the city. "Arriving troops, report to the assignment center at Hotel Dostyk. Follow the signs marked in blue. There you will be reattached to your units and given orders. Wounded, report to the hospital at town center. Follow the markers in red. Arriving troops, report to the assignment center at Hotel Dostyk..."

There were a Marine APC and a group of corpsmen on one side of the street, and we veered toward them to drop Ox at their feet.

"Take him," said Bridgette.

"What's wrong with him?" one asked.

"Frostbite and hypothermia," I said. Like it mattered;

the guy was hurting and it was their job. I nearly lost my shit waiting for them to move, but two of the Marines grabbed Ox and carried him to the APC.

"Move up to the relocation center, and fast," one of them said. "Popov is only a few klicks out."

Bridgette saw a pair of MPs approaching and dragged me into an alley, where she popped her lid and then mine. We kissed, and I couldn't imagine that she liked it, because after spending all this time in my suit, I was rancid. But *I* liked it and wouldn't let go, so she finally had to push me away to breathe. Then we did it again. It was weird, gentle; I barely felt her tongue brush against mine.

"I'm so happy to have met you," she said.

"Me too."

Bridgette was crying. I had an awful feeling then, like I didn't get it but something major was about to happen. "What's wrong?"

"It's time for me to go. I love you."

I remember what I said next; it will be etched in my gray matter forever. "I love you too. Let's get married and have kids. A hundred Bridgettes, all with killer instincts and dead-on aim."

She cracked up at that—half laughing and half crying while she wiped the tears from her eyes, unable to look at me. Then Bridgette shook her head. "I can't have children, Scout, don't be stupid. They didn't design us that way."

And that was the last thing she said. That was how she said goodbye, just before she walked over to the MPs. I stood there, in shock, unable even to move. Maybe I was too tired, but I don't think I ever anticipated what she would do that day, not after spending all that time retreating through Kaz, keeping me together, making it in the scout car like mad teenagers. She walked over and said something, and the MPs drew down on her, put a few fléchettes right through her forehead. When she collapsed, I lost it. Screamed. I ran across the street and threw myself at them, just before one of them slammed the butt of his carbine into my head to keep his buddy from being strangled.

Once I recovered from the MP's butt-shot to my head, I found out that Phil Erikson at the Bandar desk had gotten my Kaz tickets yanked. The MPs actually drove me to the airfield to put me on the next transport flight out of Tashkent to the States. Apparently, the story I had sent Phil wasn't a story at all. I swear I don't remember doing this, but I typed "fuck you" about ten thousand times and slapped on a title: "What I Like About Doing Phil Erikson up the Ass," by Scout. That last phone call—the one I had ignored on my way out the door—was *him,* calling to tell me I had been fired.

Still, having a friend in Brussels High Command helped a lot. It was even better because this guy was a Marine general, a hard charger who spent half his time in Kaz scoring dope, and the other half sniping Popovs from the front line. A military genius. General Nathan Urqhart was a small man, stout, like a midget, only bigger and with a barrel chest, and his kids, every Marine in the theater, loved him. I loved him too, because for all his shortcomings, the guy had his war bonnet on straight, knew the drill, and had subterrene in his veins.

Before I met him, one of his aides pulled me aside and gave me some advice.

"Don't call him this at first," he said, "but after you've developed rapport with the general, you should suggest that he needs a nickname."

"A nickname?" I asked. I mean, *come on.* What the shit was this guy angling at?

"Yeah—the general digs them. Keeps waiting for someone to compare him to Chesty Puller." I think the aide must have seen my blank face. Like, *Uh…what?* "You know, Chesty? Famous Marine from the twentieth century?"

"Nope," I said. "Drawing a blank over here."

The guy looked like he was about to take a dump on me, right there in the staff room. "Never mind. Who cares if you know who Chesty is? What's important is that the *general* thinks you do. Just say something like he reminds you of that hard-ass in the twentieth century, blah, blah."

Blah, blah was something I understood. Perfectly. *Blah, blah* I could do; I was a reporter, for Christ's sake. "Not a problem," I said. "And thanks."

I should have bought him a drink, because with God as my witness, the second I actually *did* it, the instant I suggested to General Urqhart that he was like old Chesty, I owned the guy. When I put the comparison in one of my stories, I could have screwed his daughter and he would have asked how it was, could he get me a beer? The old son of a bitch made it a point to put me up in his Bandar HQ every time he was in the area—five star and any chick I wanted—as long as I promised to go everywhere with him, like I was writing his biography or something. Did I do it? Hell yes, I did it. Of all the self-serving prick officers I encountered in Kaz, General Urqhart was the only prick who at least reserved part of his mental energy for caring about Marines. So when he found out what that pair of Army MPs had done, he took a big verbal crap, right on their CO's face, and came to see me himself.

I cried on the plane as it sat on the tarmac, and not even zip made it better. I just missed her, couldn't get Bridgette out of my head.

Suddenly the whine of the transport engines died, and I saw a ramp being wheeled out to the main hatch. When it popped open, old Chesty himself burst into the plane, and the MPs who had arrested me followed him in, unable to look me in the eye.

"Goddamn it to hell!" he said. He liked to bellow, and just hearing it made me feel a little better, like being on the good side of a war god. "Jesus, son, what happened to you?"

"Pavlodar. I was on the retreat, and these shit sacks"—I pointed at the MPs—"wouldn't even let me shower."

General Urqhart looked at the men and said quietly, "Get out of my sight."

They did. Once we were the only two people on the entire transport, the general sat beside me, putting his arm around my shoulder. "What's this about a genetic?"

I told him. I couldn't *not* tell him; I had to get it out to keep it from eating through my gut, and by the end of it, my shirt was soaked from tears.

He just sat there quietly for a second and then grinned. "That there is some fucked-up shit, Wendell. I haven't tried genetics, and sure as shit haven't tried zip—is it good?"

I nodded.

"Well then, son." He stood and lifted me to my feet. "It's been a while since I've been a line Marine, but I know one when I see one. You've changed. No more normal civilian life. A guy like you has a hard time reinserting into the world, and if I'm guessing right, the last thing you want is a ride back to the States. Am I right?"

Like I said, the guy was a real genius. Omniscient. I nodded again.

"Well, I may have an idea. You want another assignment, to stay in Kaz?"

"Please, General." I wiped my nose, felt like a little kid.

"Done."

He pushed me toward the hatch and then outside. At the bottom of the ramp, the general spoke to me quietly, his shit-eating grin getting wider by the second. "We're counterattacking. Pops overextended and we were ready for it. Ten more factories came online a few years ago, so we've been building up two divisions of genetics in reserve. They were ready to jump from Uzbekistan the moment Popov hit us."

"What does that mean?" I asked.

He lit what looked like a cigar, but I could smell the weed, sweet and heavy. "It means we'll be back at the mines in a couple of weeks. And beyond. Boy, do I have a posting for someone in as fucked-up a state as you." The general handed me a ticket. "Report to the reassignment center at oh-eight-hundred tomorrow for DOD duty as our civilian historian. I'll make sure to get orders for your buddy Ox to join you there. You'll be going somewhere quiet, with no women in sight, so you'll have time to wind down and get some of that shit out of your brain."

I didn't know what to say. I just stood there and did some weird sobbing thing.

"It's OK, son. Kaz is a nasty mistress and no thanks are necessary. I'm doing it for one reason: you can't avoid the world forever but you're not ready to return to it. Not yet. This'll be over someday, and if you don't find a way to deal, nothing will work. Ever. Use the time to ease out, son, let it all go if you can."

When he left, I collapsed on the side of the airstrip and thought about her. I could still smell Bridgette and knew that I had meant it when I had said we should have kids—wanted her that badly.

But Kaz had wanted her too.

THREE

Ad Hoc

They brought in heating units that baked everything and made the smell worse; the same smell that used to make me think *Pulitzer* now brought only dysentery and sickness. Eventually I stopped noticing it. That winter was one of the most awful on record, which, ironically, *helped* us as much as it hurt, because it blunted the Russian push, forcing them to grind down and crumble in the face of our genetic counterattack. Once my assignment came in, they gave me a rack in an underground barracks, and occasionally I'd hear people talk about the topside action and how our forces hit from Uzbekistan, like Urqhart had said they would, pushing the Russians back to Pavlodar. None of these stories mattered. The concrete and rock seemed more interesting than anything else, safer than conversation. Bridgette sat next to me on the bed sometimes and smiled, nearly real enough that I felt her hand on my shoulder, and at those moments I couldn't handle it, had to go outside and almost never bothered to suit up. The cold made me tremble. Winds blew from the north, and with nothing to block their path, they tore through our rubble fields and flung dry snow against my face and bare chest in waves of needles. Sometimes I'd stand outside for less than a minute. Other times, if I was high, I'd last for half an hour, praying that the cold would numb all of it, even the parts that drugs couldn't touch, until eventually I'd pass out and collapse in a pocket of snow, forgotten. Inevitably someone would find me and pull me underground. My body had gotten so used to the cold that when the summer arrived, it made me feel sick, the heat forcing me to toss in my bunk. There was no spring that year—or, at least, none worth remembering.

And there were no more thoughts about writing; Phil had been right to fire me. I'd fail at being a unit historian too—you could bet on it—but this mattered less, because I hadn't been given the job to succeed; I'd been given the job as a life preserver, Urquhart's last try at keeping me alive. And there were times I hated him for it. Who was he? He hadn't known Bridgette, and I still smelled her if I pulled out my old undersuit, the one they had tried to confiscate but for which I'd sworn to kill if anyone took it. Eventually, that too disappeared. Lost. Time became a fog bank, and I moved through it recklessly, hoping that I'd fall off a cliff and wishing when I went to sleep that the morning wouldn't come, but then the fog would break to give a glimpse of the barracks, of the war, of the facts that I still lived and that she was still gone.

A week before our unit officially went active, Ox lifted me from the rack, got me to my feet, and hugged me. *You* tell *me* what he said. I don't remember. The zip had done its job, so everything looked soft and fuzzy, and one could guess that he said something about being grateful for my having saved him, about having lost only bits of toes and fingers as a result of frostbite, but he'd make it, had just barely avoided being discharged on medical, and wasn't that the worst luck? He grabbed my gear, shoved it into a duffel, and left with it. Then he came back a few minutes later and took me to new quarters, where we'd be bunkmates. That's when it turned. Ox brought reality back, a little at a time, so that I started eating normally again, got dressed every once in a while, and even made it outside to see what remained of Shymkent after the snow had vanished. I remember the first day that I inserted back into reality, at least partially, and recall that it was like sticking my toe into a pool to test it because I suspected the water was way too cold. It was the day they announced our deployment.

We assembled in a makeshift training area, where a Marine captain stood at the head of the parade ground and coughed. "At ease," he said. The field went quiet a moment later, so he continued, and I did my best to concentrate, but the words seemed strange, foreign.

"As of eighteen-thirty hours last night, allied forces have retaken the Pavlodar mines and our lines crystallized north of the city, inside Russia itself." He paused to allow some of the men to cheer. "That's the good news. The bad news is that it's mop-up time, which is where we come in. Our scouts report that some Russian genetics survived our push north and may have linked up with guerillas to harass the supply lines, somehow managing to stay out of sight. Rest time is over. At oh-eight-hundred tomorrow, Task Force Karazhyngyl will be activated and deployed northward, so that we can go after the remaining genetic units. Get to your racks early and, NCOs, have your men at the train station for embarkation at oh-seven-thirty. Dismissed."

Even I, only half sane, operating under a mixture of drugged confusion and self-loathing, knew that calling that unit a task force was a joke. I looked at Ox, who looked back at me, and we didn't have to say it. Something had changed since the war had started, since the Marines had engaged with Pops more than a year earlier, and over the past week we'd talked about it, because Ox had seen it too. Draftees weren't the right age anymore. Some were old, sometimes into their forties, while others couldn't have been more than fourteen. And "task forces" were ad hoc things, the phrase a euphemism for turd units thrown together using whatever was on hand, anything that could be spared. This one was no different. We'd be deployed with a unit that consisted of sub-rubes, old men and boys who'd had less training than I'd had in Rube-Hack, with no clue what it meant to face real Russian forces, let alone their genetics.

Everyone knew what was *really* up; all you had to do was spend time in town or at the bars and it was the only thing people talked about. Both sides were hurting. Press reports from home raged about a congressional committee that had been formed to investigate lowering the draft age to sixteen and raising it to fifty-five; women chafed at government campaigns encouraging them to have children, to breed; and bonds, the administration's only hope for financing more ateliers, more Gs, were issued. Command needed warm bodies, *any* bodies. And Pops had it just as bad. The last battles, which had raged aboveground across the entirety of Kaz, had resulted in unbelievable losses, and neither side would have new stocks of genetics for at least six months, so the number of young men and engineered girls able to die on the line had dwindled, evaporated to the point where the word "reserves" had become the punch line to a joke.

Hence, the birth of ad hocs. A new term for "holy-shit-we-need-somebody-who-can-we-use-to-stop-the-leaking." At least there was an upside. Nobody wanted a fight right now, and both sides, for the moment, happily stayed put behind their lines.

Ox had been made a gunnery sergeant, the unit's senior NCO, and after the assembly, he showed me his roster; I hadn't guessed wrong. His new men consisted of Navy cooks, Army supply troops, Marine clerks, and anyone who could be spared from rear duties, pressed into combat service and issued weapons that most had probably never fired in anger.

It was funny, I thought as we headed back to Ox's quarters. I wasn't a combatant. Not even a reporter anymore. But I had "the look," same as Ox, because we'd been there and knew what to expect, while everyone else just looked terrified.

A single overhead fan spun slowly and barely made a breeze as I collapsed into my rack.

"We're doomed," Ox said.

I smiled and pushed in a wad of zip. "Speak for yourself, gunny. I'm just a unit historian, a civilian. I could quit anytime."

"Yeah. You were screaming again, last night. Keep waking me up like that and I'll wipe you."

I knew he was kidding but felt bad anyway. "Was it about her?"

"Yeah. It's nasty. You need to insert a morphine drip at

night or something, anything to keep that shit out of your head while you're asleep."

He was right. I missed her just as much now as I had five months earlier, still saw her everywhere I looked.

"I can't get out of this."

Ox just nodded. "To hell with it then. Maybe you should just stay high."

Before reporters had been allowed on the line, some of them got only as close as the supply depots well south of the front. Dan Wodzinski was one of them. One day, when he got back from his third trip, he came into my hotel room. The air-conditioning had gone out, making the place steamy, and there was no breeze, so I had been lying on my bed in a wet towel, trying anything to stay cool. Dan leaned against the wall and slid to the floor, the color gone from his face.

"What's wrong?" I asked.

"Karaganda."

I shook my head. "What?"

"I was in Karaganda," he said, "the Third Marine supply depot, south of Pavlodar. We should go home now, Oscar. This place is gone."

I cracked the small fridge next to my bed and tossed him a beer. He finished it in about three gulps and asked for another.

"That bad?"

He nodded. "When I got there, military investigators had discovered a camp, one set up by the Kazakhs back when we were pushing north from Iran." Dan stopped talking and just looked at me, but I didn't want to say anything—

it might shut him up—so I waited. When he had taken a few gulps from the second beer, he continued. "There used to be a huge Indian population there, immigrated I don't know when, and the grunts told me that it was an Indian-staffed corporation that discovered the rhenium mine outside Pav. The company had its headquarters in Karaganda.

"Apparently the Kazakhs decided to nationalize the mines after their discovery, and when the Indians made a stink, they rounded up every single Indian in the country—from all over—and shoved them into this camp. Marines found over ten thousand of them, slaughtered, in shallow graves. Most of them had been beheaded. Kids too."

The locals had almost disappeared during the war. You used to see the women in the streets and slums, trying to sell anything they could to make a buck, but eventually they too vanished. Dan hadn't seen many locals either, not in Karaganda. But he had seen their work.

"We should wipe them all and do the world a favor," he finished. "Karaganda is a no-man's-land, frontier, but at least our troops are there. I'd hate to be posted in one of the really small towns. No support for miles. Who knows the kind of shit that goes on there? We'd never even hear about it, I bet."

I remembered that conversation as if it was playing out in front of me again, on video, when we moved out. Karazhyngyl *was* one of those really small towns, south-east of Karaganda, and according to Ox, the only other units might be too far to help if anything went down.

And she refused to leave my head. The memory of Bridgette rotted inside me, so that most of the time I couldn't eat, instead cramming in drugs. In more lucid moments it really messed me—didn't make any sense. *I hadn't known her long.* But the more I thought about it, the more it took, until one day, on the back of a truck, it hit me between the eyes so hard that I started crying. Not sobbing. Just a steady stream of tears that left tracks in the dust that had caked to my face.

Innocents. Bridgette and the others. She had been everything I dug about Kaz, the selflessness and the lack of bullshit, no strings. *Death and faith. That* was what they were all about, and she never would have cheated on me, thought I hung the moon, because by being her first, I had shown her something besides war, so even though I hadn't intended to give *that* to her, I had. And she had given it back. Take all the betties in the real world, human, and line them up in front of me and I wouldn't even look. Didn't want them. Somehow, I'd have to get back with the Gs, and even with Ox I began to feel like I didn't belong. He didn't get it. But I did, and in my worst moments I wished I didn't, because it was like a sucking chest wound, messy and offering little chance of recovery. Only drugs made it OK. Maybe an overdose would kill me, I thought, *and that would be all right too.* Death and faith, drugs and painlessness, bullshit and Kaz. The Gs were better than any human I had ever met.

It took Ox's task force, almost two hundred men and a pack of rusted-out trucks, several weeks to make the journey by rail and another two days to off-load vehicles and supplies. Most of Karazhyngyl—a tiny railway village— had escaped the devastation of plasma but had been deserted. It was creepy, like a ghost town. Ox ordered the men to construct a defensive perimeter around a hotel close to the station, but it was well into the summer before they erected a network of motion sensors and sentry bots.

Despite the defenses, I felt uneasy. There was no sub-terrene here—subterrene didn't exist in the outposts—and all we got were holes, dug into a sickly tan soil. Ox said it best.

"We're out here now. Alone. And I hate this place."

We had been there a couple of months when one day, in the distance, a long low whistle sounded and the nearby tracks rattled with the approach of a train.

Ox sat up. "That ain't right."

"What's wrong?" I asked. He had already punched a button to put the men on alert, and a stream of them came running out of the hotel to man the perimeter. I did a mental calculation, counted one hundred and forty, with sixty out on patrol.

"There's no train scheduled for now," said Ox. He clicked on to the net. "Heads up. Keep your eyes and ears open. First patrol, status."

Thick static made the response hard to understand. "One hundred klicks north of base, turning back now."

"Second patrol?" asked Ox.

"OK, gunny, on our way back now."

Slowly the train lumbered into town, moving at less than thirty kilometers per hour, and shook the hotel's few remaining windows as it clacked over a road crossing. I threw up when I saw it.

The train consisted of an engine and an attached string of flatcars that stretched as far as we could see. At first I thought the cars had been loaded with recycling material: vehicle wreckage, parts, and anything else that had been taken from the battlefield to be reused and reshaped when time allowed. But I was wrong. It became obvious once the train got closer. Dead bodies had been stacked on each flatcar like logs, the men still encased in shattered combat suits that barely kept their occupants in one piece, and neither I nor any of the others had our helmets on, so we struggled to snap them in place. Several of us were too late. Like me, some of the others puked into their fighting holes as the odor drifted through town, and I caught a glimpse of one body that had bloated to the point where it split the combat suit at its seams. It took twenty minutes for the last car to disappear.

"Jesus." Ox ducked into the hotel and ran down into the cellar, where we had established the task force's headquarters. There they kept a tac-net radio, which had a much longer range than suit radios, wired to a mobile fusion reactor. Ten minutes later, he returned.

"Russian push. They hit our front lines hard, and the flanks are being probed. So far our guys are holding but we can expect activity all along the rail line for the next couple of days. Task Force Agadyr captured an insurgent and got him to talk—a local, not a G-boy. Pops has partisans in all the towns around us, ready to go as soon as they get it wired."

"How long until patrols report in?" I asked. I was only a division historian, a civilian, but somehow I'd wound up as the unit's administrative assistant. I didn't mind, kind of liked it. Finally felt useful in the war.

"About ten hours for each of them," said Ox.

Out here it was a different Kaz, one I hadn't met. Out here, ten hours was a lifetime.

A few hours later, night settled on Karazhyngyl. My external thermocouples indicated thirty degrees centigrade, and I thanked God for climate control. Ox had asked me to make the rounds of the perimeter while he and his command group—two corpsmen, an armorer, and a vehicle mechanic—huddled in the hotel cellar.

I was about to jump into the nearest hole when a flash of light overloaded my vision kit, followed a few seconds later by a rumbling boom. I ran to the hotel and down into the basement, where Ox bent over the tac-net.

"First patrol is getting it," the armorer said. "Gunny's talking them through."

"Someone just blew the rail line, about five klicks north."

Ox heard me and turned. "Any movement on the perimeter?"

I shook my head.

"Fine. We'll deal with it later." He turned back to the radio. "Calm down. How many are there and what are you getting hit with?"

There was a second of static before the guy clicked in, the popping of grenades in the background. "Hard to tell, gunny. *They're everywhere.* Grenades and fléchettes, no plasma. I didn't see any vehicles; they must be on foot."

"You have a shitload of firepower on your scout car. *Use* it."

I almost laughed. "Scout car" was one way to put it. The Marines had taken a bunch of abandoned cargo trucks, slapped in salvaged engines, and then welded Maxwell auto-cannons to the beds. Voilà. Supercharged coffins, also known as scout cars.

"Scout car is out, I've lost half my guys. We need support."

"Negative, you can do this, kid. Get one of your guys

into the scout car now. Even if it's on fire, your suits can take it for a while. *Get on that goddamn auto-cannon.*"

We listened to static for a moment before Ox clicked in again. "Matthews?" He was gone, though, and we all knew it.

The next morning, second patrol arrived safely, and Ox sent them out to bring back what was left of first. They returned a few hours later, empty-handed. All they'd found were drag marks and bloodstains, along with a battered scout car.

That was the new Kaz, way spookier than the one I remembered from Pavlodar. You could get hit from any direction and never even know what wiped you. And somewhere north of us, at the front, Bridgette's sisters got it on, so anytime I wasn't wasted, I prayed—that some of them would make their way back to our position, just so that I could see them and get another look at her.

Sometimes Karazhyngyl made us laugh. The train became our main source of entertainment, the thing that broke up the boredom and could be counted on, a reminder that to our north we had friends and to our south we had a place to escape to, to hope for if things went badly. The engineers would toss dirty magazines and video chits from the engine car, and we'd throw them our old ones, a commerce of sorts that kept all of us sane, up and down the rail lines. And at times my thinking turned for the better. Bridgette still dominated it, but every once in a while the train would roll through and I'd think about something else, something besides joining her. Still, "think" was a strong way of putting what I did; my mind had eroded.

Before coming to Karazhyngyl, I had arranged with supply at Shymkent to have regular deliveries made, not just of zip but of anything they could get their hands on, so on any given day, you'd find me lit on straight fentanyl or one of a hundred pharmaceuticals intended for field hospitals. Mai tais all the way. But check it: I functioned OK because I had everything rigged so that if I needed to get it straight after going down on zip, there was another cocktail ready to go, able to counteract whatever I took in the first place. Still, sometimes the plan didn't work out. I was totally gone when the white coats arrived, and Ox didn't give me enough time to find a good antidote. Instead of taking something to counteract the zip, I took something that made it worse.

The train actually stopped in Karazhyngyl, which was way odd, and then Ox called me to the hotel, which filled me with dread. At first I thought I'd been busted. Two guys in suits sat in the hotel lobby, their black shoes covered with Kazakh dust, and over it all they wore white lab coats, which had turned a sickly yellow from the long train ride northward. Both of them were old and wore glasses, and you could tell if you'd spent any time in D.C. at all that they were Feds, civilians, here for some reason that was bound to make you sick.

Ox looked grim. When he saw the expression on my face, and my need to prop myself against the doorframe, he shook his head.

"These guys want to talk, Scout. You *can* talk, right?"

One of them stood and shook my hand when I approached. "I'm Dr. Stephens and this is my colleague Dr. Franks. Thanks for joining us, Mr. Wendell. We won't take too much of your time."

"You guys look like shrinks. Did you come to take me away? Because I like it here. I don't want to go back, not yet."

They looked at each other, and one pulled out a clipboard while the first kept talking. "No, Oscar, we didn't come to take you away. We just came to talk."

"Man." I sat near them on a soft chair, its cushion half burned. "I'm freakin' tired. They don't get many holovids out here and the restaurants are awful."

"I'll be downstairs in ops," Ox said. "If you need me, just yell." When he was gone, the room went quiet except for the sounds of a basketball game outside.

"Mr. Wendell, we were wondering if you wouldn't mind talking to us about Bridgette."

"What about her?" I didn't let it show, but the question turned me cold despite the heat, and I could see a hunger in them that made everything outside go dark and the room get a little dimmer. Something about them said *killers. Murderers.*

"According to our records, you had a relationship with her. You two were close, is that correct?"

"That's correct."

"And she helped you on the retreat from Pavlodar, last year?"

"Yeah." The quiet one's hands looked jumpy as he took notes, and I couldn't tell if it was a hallucination or reality, but the hands appeared to vibrate—so fast that he looked about to break a finger while writing. When they disappeared in a blur, I knew that I was more messed up than anyone realized. "She helped me."

"Did you love her?"

I glared at him and then his friend. "Who are you guys?"

"Relax, Mr. Wendell. We're with the Defense Policy Board—actually, a special subcommittee under the DPB, established to represent the interests of contractors engaged in war production. We're here to ask questions, to learn from you."

"Learn what?"

The other one spoke then, and his voice was high, like a girl's, but quiet. "About Bridgette. So we can optimize."

"What he's trying to say," the first one explained, "is that you got closer to one of our products than we ever could, near the end of its service term. You're not the only one to, uh…have feelings for one of our units. We've been tasked to interview you and others like you so we can figure out what the units are thinking, in general, when they're close to discharge; why they would want to be with a real human."

"But what good would that do? And I have a few questions of my own, like why did you make them all the same? Why did you make them girls?"

He looked at the floor. The room went quiet again and I could hear the other one gulp loudly as he took a sip of water, the plastic bottle sweating with condensation. The first one tapped a finger against his thigh before answering.

"To answer your first question, we use the information to extend their shelf life. If we can get a more accurate picture of the things they focus on after two years on the line, what issues they have, psychologically, it's entirely possible we can establish a protocol—either with drug therapy or mental preconditioning—to prevent them from collapsing so quickly. To make it so they don't get attached to men like you. If we can do that, we have a product that's useful over a greater period of time and, consequently, worth more to the Defense Department. It's all about lowering production and maintenance costs and making a larger profit. Commerce.

"To answer your second question, we make them all identical for the same reason each soldier is issued the same armor, the same weapons, why we have one kind of main battle tank and one kind of APC: it too makes production and maintenance more simple. To answer your third question, we tried producing men a long time ago. It didn't work. But the details are classified."

"That's about it," the other one said, pausing to lick the end of his pencil. "Now will you help us?"

The train engine hissed in the distance, hydraulic brakes locking and unlocking as someone shunted it off the main line just in case another rolled through. I hated these men. The train had brought them here, so they had corrupted even that, the one thing we all looked forward to, and from now on its arrival would make me wonder if it carried something awful, something that feasted on the minds of people like me and then vomited on the potential of someone like Bridgette. Even with my brain melting each second, enough of me was there to realize that this was all insane; why did they need to wear lab coats in Karazhyngyl? They thought that she had been only a recreation for me, that I was perverted, and it occurred to me that all I wanted to do was get back in my hole, outside, just sink back into the dust and fossilize.

"She was wild," I said.

They leaned forward, the quiet one taking notes again. "How so? What do you mean 'wild'?"

"I mean that she ate rats and mice, bugs, anything she

could get her hands on. She tried eating dirt too, had lost her taste for standard rations."

"That's . . . unusual."

I clicked into Ox's personal channel so he could listen in. "And that's not all. I think that she wanted to become a lawyer."

"A what?"

"Swear to whatever, man, she wanted to make a break for it and become an entertainment lawyer for some reason, said that she could make tons of money and live in Beverly Hills, that some guy had given her and her sisters a bunch of vids of what it's like to be rich in California. She and a few of the others had a plan to escape and become hookers to put themselves through law school in San Diego. Either that or start an all-girl rock band to keep their days free for school."

The room went quiet again. Ox laughed in my ear and I did my best to keep from cracking a smile, but there's not much you can do when you're that high. It took all I had just to string the sentences together, so when the egghead one asked his next question, I lost it.

"Was she satisfying? Sexually, I mean?"

Boom. I don't even remember hitting the floor but there it was, right in my face, as I grinned and shrieked, unable to hold back the laughter anymore and hearing Ox crack up in my ears, louder. Both men stared. Then the quiet guy dropped his pencil so that it rolled toward me, and I grabbed it, not even noticing a transition to rage before I slammed it into his foot, through the dusty synthetic leather and down through flesh. His screams didn't faze me. It was all so funny that when they carried him from the hotel, his partner shouting something at Ox, I passed out from lack of oxygen.

Ox poured water on my face to bring me back and I glanced at my suit clock. An hour had passed.

"They wanted me to court-martial you."

"You can't," I said. "I'm not military, and they freakin' deserved worse."

"I know. But, Oscar, you've got to get a grip, man. My guys are all starting to think you're bad luck and that I can't control you, that you're going to screw up and get someone killed. And they're right. You're fading, going way, way out there."

"Let's zip, Ox. Like we used to."

He shook his head and what happened next freaked me: he started crying. Just a few tears, but it wasn't right.

"You're dying, Scout. I don't want it anymore. You're nothing but a screwup and I've asked for a space for you on the soonest train out to Shymkent. As soon as we get a billet, you're gone."

It was cold that night. My suit said otherwise, but when I tried to sleep in my hole, it felt like an ice bath. I shivered and hoped that morning—and any empty trains—wouldn't come. As bad as Karazhyngyl was, it was all I had, and the thought of leaving Ox made me pucker.

There were no empty trains. All of them carried wounded back from the front lines, or wrecked vehicles, or mountainous piles of dead, so each time Ox tried to signal one, he got the same reply over the radio, one we all heard on our headsets. Without direct orders from headquarters, no members of ad hocs would be permitted to abandon their posts, except in the case of seriously wounded. The dead would be buried in place. After a couple of days, he gave up. But I did my best to stay out of his way, and in my more lucid moments I really felt bad about the way I had acted and the fact that we headed in opposite directions. Ox had gone clean. He didn't do *anything* anymore and I never even saw him drink as much as a beer, which made me feel even worse for being so weak, because deep down I knew: there was no way I would quit. I was weaker than him and it let him down.

About three weeks after the incident with the two Feds, we got a call from an ad hoc north of us, Task Force Kiik. Ox nearly blew a fuse. I was in the basement, picking tobacco out of my teeth, when he threw his helmet against the wall, startling all of us, including the doc who had been stitching up a kid who'd shot a hole in his foot by accident. It was the third "accident" that week; Ox had gotten wise to it some time before and made it a policy not to send anyone rearward unless the man had been wounded under enemy fire. This kid must have been extra stupid— or didn't get the memo until it was too late.

"What's up?" I asked.

He stared at me for a second and then grinned. "You're going to Kiik."

"Kiik? Why?"

"They're under attack. We have two patrols out, so I can only spare thirty guys and two trucks right now, and I need you out there. Every weapon counts. Get your shit together, Martin will lead from truck one."

I had been feeling good until then—like maybe it wouldn't be such a bad day—but Kiik killed it. Somehow I knew it would be extra crappy. The day was especially hot—so hot that I had made it a point to wriggle my way into the basement command post and stay there, even though I wasn't supposed to. But that wasn't what bothered me. Somewhere out there was Pops. I hadn't seen him in forever, and during his absence, I'd gotten soft, terrified, and I just knew that he'd been preparing, gathering his strength all this time we'd been sitting around. The stairs felt magnetized. As I crept up them, Ox's orders went out over the net, and by the time I stepped into the Kazakh sunlight, squinting, Karazhyngyl had come alive. Guys ran back and forth loading the two trucks with ammo, water, and food, and I pulled my vision hood on and cinched it. Tight. The goggles dimmed the sunlight, made everything a bearable bluish green, soothing in a way, despite the fact that nobody was happy about the orders. Martin saw me on the hotel steps and tossed me a Maxwell.

"Truck two."

I just nodded; there wasn't anything to say. You'd have been hard-pressed to hold a conversation as we all readied. By the time I climbed aboard, everyone had found a seat, leaving me a spot on the bed, just below the auto-Maxwell, where I sat, cross-legged. We set out, and still nobody said a word.

The road northward took us over low rises, but for the most part, this section of Kazakhstan was as flat as the rest of it. I'd never been to Texas. But a friend of mine had once shown me pictures of the state's west side, near El Paso, with dry plains that stretched forever, here and there covered with a pathetic kind of scrub grass; Kaz was just like that. In the distance we saw an auto-drone every once in a while, and someone would get jumpy, calling both trucks to a halt so that we had to spill out and find cover behind the railroad tracks, but inevitably it turned out to be ours. The monotony nearly killed me. Every once in a while Ox would check in with Martin and relay Kiik's status reports, but that didn't do anything to improve our mood; it made things worse. The insurgents were hammering those guys, and it sounded like we'd be too late to change anything, even though Kiik was only two hours from Karazhyngyl.

Then they hit us.

Our trucks were old Tedoms that someone had confiscated off locals in Shymkent. They should have been tossed into a junkyard. The rebuilt engines were good enough. But the frames had all but rusted out, and rudimentary ceramic armor had been fixed to all the surfaces so that they looked like hybrid nightmares, some sort of Frankenstein truck, part vehicle, part scout car, but all of it crap. Martin's truck exploded in front of us. Our driver panicked, and instead of stopping so we could all get out and find cover, he hit the gas, slamming into the back of Martin's flaming wreck and then bouncing over what I assumed were the bodies of our own men, but I never found out if they were alive or dead before we ran over them. Then three more rockets came out of nowhere. Two roared over our heads and disappeared in the plains beyond, but the third hit our rear wheel, and the next thing I knew, I was airborne, moving forward at roughly the same speed the truck had been. When I slammed into the dirt, everything went black.

I woke to the sound of grenades. To my right a group of men in Russian armor fired at the men from my unit, who had taken cover on the other side of the railroad tracks. I was behind the Russians. The four of them moved quickly, throwing each other hoppers or grenade clips to make sure nobody ran out of ammunition, and at least two of them fired at all times. I felt myself about to scream, recognizing their swiftness and efficiency immediately. These were genetics. Cables dangled from their helmets and connected to the power packs on their backs, and I tried to stay as still as possible, thinking that I could wait it out and crawl from the dust once it was over. Then one of our guys' grenades overshot, pelting me with fléchettes.

My carbine was a few feet away and I reached for it slowly, inching my hand across the dirt so a sudden movement wouldn't attract any attention, praying that none of my guys would fire at me by accident, mistake me for Russian. The reticle popped into sight. After I emptied my hopper, it was over, only a few seconds later, and I lay there, shaking, barely getting my helmet off in time to dry heave, trying not to think of the fact that it had been close. The last genetic had noticed me just before I squeezed the trigger, and had begun swinging his grenade launcher around. The barrel looked wide and empty, pointed at my face. Most of my fléchettes missed him, but a few passed through one of his vision ports and out the back of his helmet.

Martin nudged me with his foot. "You OK?"

"I thought you bought it."

"Me too. We lost more than half our guys; there's only ten of us left. You should have seen how much air you caught. And thanks for taking them out."

Now that the fighting was over, the shakes got worse, and my neck began to feel as though it had been twisted. "I'm messed up. What do we do now?"

"One of the guys thinks he can scavenge the burned-out Tedom, use it to get the other truck back on the road. Ox wants us to come back; Kiik's holding its own now, don't need us, and even if they did...we're *all* messed."

I turned to look at the vehicles. One truck had burned out almost completely, and the other one had lost its rear wheel, but a group had already begun jacking up the burned one and ratcheting off a replacement. The sun had passed its zenith. In the quiet, as I sat on the rails, the breeze on my face felt peaceful—like maybe this wouldn't have been such a bad place to visit before the war—and some of the guys even started joking as they struggled with the trucks. We'd leave our dead, pick them up the next day with a reinforced unit. But for now, Martin did the rounds and downloaded their data into his computer, to make sure that their names got recorded and sent home even if their bodies didn't.

Twenty minutes later we had piled into the back of the Tedom and were bouncing over the dirt road and heading south toward Karazhyngyl, but this time I rode on the bench. We were less crowded. At my feet one of our corpsmen worked on someone, but I didn't know his name and wasn't sure if I wanted to, because the guy kept staring and reaching for me, like he recognized something on my face. Flecks of blood covered his cheeks and the corpsman cracked his armor, so we all got a look. A grenade had gone off near his side, leaving only a fist-sized hole in his carapace, but the fléchettes had ricocheted around inside the armor, which, as it turned out, had been the only thing holding him in one piece. Blood and a good portion of his intestines washed over my feet, and a Marine next to me threw up into his helmet after the guy died.

The corpsman dropped his bandage, the one he had

been planning to use before his patient spilled out. "I couldn't fix this."

"It's OK," said Martin.

"I can't do anything for this, all they gave me was a first aid kit, how am I supposed to do anything with that?"

"I said it's OK. Just snap him shut. He's gone now anyway."

The corpsman's expression changed then, to the same one I'd seen so long ago on that guy Ox had nearly wiped in the tunnels, the one who'd lost his face. "No, Martin, you don't get it, man. I can't do *anything*. What the fuck is wrong with you, are you even hearing me?"

"I said *fuck it*!"

All of us were getting on edge, catching whatever it was that the corpsman had, and Martin felt it. You could see in his eyes that if the guy said one more word, he'd be tossed from the truck. So I knelt. I moved the corpsman gently into my seat and began scooping up everything that had fallen out of the wounded guy, doing my best to get it all back in before snapping the armor shut, and then rubbed my hands on the truck bed, on my legs, anywhere that might let me get rid of some of the blood, exchange it for oil or dirt—anything.

The corpsman whispered when I sat back down. "They didn't give me anything for this, swear to God they didn't."

"I know, they're a bunch of nut jobs."

"Damn right they're nuts. I mean, did you see him? Did you get a good look at that?"

"And all they gave you was a first aid kit; doesn't seem right."

"You're damn right it doesn't. You're damn right.

What am I supposed to do with a first aid kit? You're damn right it doesn't..."

And then I knew he'd be OK. He shook his head back and forth for the whole ride back, repeating the same thing over and over, but we didn't care; this wasn't the tunnels. The sun had begun to set, turning everything an orange pink, and with the noise of the truck and the wind, we couldn't hear him except if we *tried* to hear him, and I knew from my own experience that he'd repeat himself as long as he needed to—maybe forever—but that it didn't matter, and it beat the option I had chosen, the option of pharmaceutical oblivion. Getting high wasn't on the menu that night. All my gear was where I'd left it, plenty of dope and zip, but when I crawled back into my hole and looked at it, it didn't look back, didn't beckon to me with its promise that everything would be better once I got lit, because I knew it was bullshit. It wouldn't make anything better. I went to sleep that night praying for Bridgette to come back, and in the distance I heard the guy, all night.

"You're damn right it doesn't. What do they expect me to do with a first aid kit? I can't do *anything*."

My prayers were answered a month later. I had walked outside the perimeter to take a leak when on the horizon a dust cloud appeared, growing. We had taken to powering down everything except climate controls—to conserve fuel cells—and it took me a moment to remember how to activate my vision hood. I was so *high*. A group of Marines had laughed when I'd shuffled past; I was barely able to stand, so finding the forearm controls and the right sequence of buttons seemed impossible. Finally I got it. The cloud zoomed in, nearly making me puke, and eventually the goggles focused so that I saw a single APC, dust-colored, cruising northward along the rail line in our direction.

Ox came out to see it. "Friendlies," he said. "Let's find out what gives."

It took the APC about ten minutes to reach us, and the bottom hatches opened, disgorging a group of them, genetics, who took up positions around the vehicle while one of them approached.

"Task Force Karazhyngyl?" she asked. The voice made me flinch, brought back all sorts of memories. I had to helmet up—in case I freaked.

Ox nodded. "Yeah. What's going on?"

"You sent a distress call. We're here to help with the town's defense."

"What?" Ox looked around before clicking onto the net. "Everyone into their holes. Any patrols out right now?"

A voice responded immediately. "Negative."

"You did not send a distress call?" she asked.

"No. We didn't."

I shit you not. The chick popped her lid then, so that I could see that grin, and I wanted to run up and grab her, swore that it was *Bridgette*.

"This is good. Maybe it's a trap. Russian genetics are operating in this area and we will meet them. With your permission, my sisters will evaluate the town's defenses and determine what changes should be made, where to put our APC as a pillbox. We're out of fuel alcohol and have been running the secondary plasma engine, but now we'll need the reactor for firing and can't spare any plasma."

Ox nodded. "OK. Cool."

"Yes." She grinned again and then resealed her helmet. "Death and faith."

One of the guys nearest to me cursed. "Screw death and faith. Come on, man, let's bolt. This is for shit. I'm an *IT guy,* for shit's sake. I worked on computers." He scrambled out of his hole, almost making it before one of his buddies pulled him back in.

"You're not going anywhere."

"I gotta get outta here. *Come on.*" The guy pulled his helmet off then and began popping his seals to unsuit. "I can't breathe."

But before he could finish getting out of his suit, the man just slid to the bottom of the hole and curled into a ball. He cried. We all heard the sobs, punctuated by some kind of moaning, and it made the skin on my neck crawl, but nobody did anything to him—just let him keep going. We all knew how he felt, and it was OK, because everyone realized that the next day *you* could be the one cracked up and balling because there was nothing you could do with a computer or a first aid kit; they were the same damn thing in Kaz.

I watched as the girls formed up to walk the perimeter, Ox's voice clicking in again. "Anything these betties say, you do. *That's an order.*"

An hour later it was ready. The girls had our guys dig deeper holes, laid out additional sentry bots, and rigged a hundred meters of remote-detonated fléchette and gel mines, directional like the old claymores but specifically designed for Kaz—to look like grubby rocks. The girls concealed their APC near the hotel, checked its field of fire, and smiled.

Standing next to a hole and staring southward, I hadn't

moved since they'd come, and didn't hear her when one of the girls approached.

"You should take cover."

I smiled. "I'm glad you're here."

"Why are you out of your hole? You're exposed."

"I'm insane."

"You need to take cover. We don't know what they plan, but you must get into a hole, stay still."

"I missed you. A lot. But I can't get back in my hole, it's full of scorpions."

She checked it, saw that it was empty, and then cocked her head. "Your hole is empty."

"I'm insane. I'm spoiling."

She caught on. I heard her take a breath and it reminded me of Bridgette, who had breathed just like that when she got excited or upset, and it took me a second to gather the courage even to look at this one, and when I did, it nearly killed me. Green thermal paste coated her face, but it was her. All beauty. It was Bridgette on the train, in the old days, when things were good and we ran across the steppes, too scared to stop running but too into each other *not* to stop, for a second, just to screw.

"Do you know me?" she asked.

I shook my head. "I knew Bridgette. She was one of you."

"And she was yours." It wasn't a question, so I just stood there. A second later she took my hand and led me to a hole, gently pulled me into it, with her, and made me lie on my back. She lay next to me. I wouldn't let go of her hand.

"Bridgette is with Him now. It is natural, you should be happy for her."

I shook my head. "No. It's not natural. That's what

you've been taught but it's not." I tried to kiss her then, grabbed her face and pulled it toward me, but she backed away.

"We are not the same," she said. "I am not her, and I don't want you."

For a moment we said nothing, waiting as the sun set and the sky darkened, bringing out stars for as far as we could see. I smelled her breath and pushed another wad of zip into my lip, waiting for the relief to come. My eyes started to flicker shut.

"Don't sleep," she said.

"If I don't sleep, the scorpions will come back and I don't want them to. If I close my eyes, nothing can see my face and I won't exist and it will be as though I'm dead so that nothing more can hurt me. It's cool, though, don't worry about it. I'm insane."

The chick rolled onto her side and looked at me, brushed the dirt from my cheeks and grinned. "I am glad that Bridgette got to know you before she died."

"Where are they?" I asked. "The girls who want to live? Don't any of you want to live?"

Her smile faded then, and she raised her head, listening. It took her less than a second to snap on her helmet. *"They come."*

A party had gone wrong. The embassy set up shop in Almaty, moved south from Astana, but the funny thing was that they moved into an ancient compound, the *former* site of our embassy, back in the twenty-first century. All things moved in circles; this proved it. As a kind of celebration, a bunch of Marine guards threw a party, one of those don't-ask-don't-tell sex fests that became a thing of legends, more hookers than guys, more drugs than sense. It didn't take long for me to become paralyzed, on Thai stick, probably dipped in *something*.

He was like a shimmering vision, unreal. A Special Forces guy. His Class A had been pressed, with so much fruit salad that it looked about to rip the fabric, but there was one imperfection. He had just thrown up. A large stain covered the front of his uniform and I saw the bits of hot dog that had gone undigested, like *real* war decorations from Kaz, proof that he had been there.

"I hate this war," he said.

"Why?" My voice sounded like a machine, a robot's, and I swore I wouldn't smoke any more of that shit if only everything would go back to normal.

He frowned. "I'm out. No more line for me, no more long-range patrols."

"That's OK," I said. "It looks like you've done enough; your bros will take care of it."

"Bullshit." He wouldn't look at me and it began to freak me out; his head was turning half shark's, half man's. "They're pulling us off the line, all of us."

"That's nuts. Why?"

"Refit. Retrain. We're going to be cops and assassins." He *did* look at me then and must have seen the cluelessness on my face. "*Genetics,* man. We're going after them. Hard."

"Their genetics? How is that any different from what you've *been* doing?"

He lit a cigarette, and I swear, every time he exhaled, dolphins swam through the smoke, jumping straight upward and diving back in. "Not theirs. Ours. We're losing track of them, ones who don't think that eighteen is a good time to die. So they're sending us to hunt them, in rear areas and in other countries, and when we find them, we're to slaughter 'em. I loved this place, man, speak the language, you know? I don't *want* to leave."

I nodded, but it was a lie. I didn't know, hadn't been on the line yet. Even wasted, I understood what the guy was saying, but it didn't connect with anything I had yet experienced and the guy seemed crazy for it. A lunatic. How could anyone love Kaz, love the dust-and-sulfur smell, tinged with the odor of shit?

I handed him my pipe. "You need this more than I do." And left.

I thought about it in Karazhyngyl after the betty said they were coming—knew what the Special Forces guy had meant, and knew that she had heard *something*. Precognitive, both of them. Bridgette and the others were just like that guy, a different kind of organism that breathed plasma and had thermal gel for blood, perfectly suited for life in battle. They could *smell* war on the wind.

Almost immediately after she said they would come, they did. Stealth bored, all the way into our pos, and before we knew what had happened, Russian genetics popped from the ground inside our lines and their rockets slammed into the front of the APC, which shot a ball of fire skyward while tracers flew in every direction, in every color. She rose to the edge of the hole and started firing, her carbine shifting methodically as though it was attached to a machine, ticking from side to side.

At one point she ripped a grenade from her harness and tossed it, looking for another. I grabbed one of mine and flipped it to her. Then another.

"I'm out," I said.

"Do not fight." She pulled a new hopper from her harness and slapped it onto her shoulder with a click. "Stay down, and do not fight. When this is over, head east first—put as much distance as you can between you and the rail line—and then south. Make for Almaty. Then on to Bandar 'Abbas, because those of us who want to live all head there. To Bandar."

And then it ended. A flash illuminated her face for a second, and I watched as a cloud of fléchettes buzzed overhead, through her faceplate and out the back, spraying everything with her blood. She collapsed on me, and I froze. I wanted to scream but Karazhyngyl went quiet then, and a breeze had picked up, blowing smoke over the hole like fog.

Their voices made me want to shrink, disappear. *Mentally evaporate.* They sounded like boys, teenagers who giggled and laughed as they ran through Karazhyngyl, looking for something. I didn't speak Russian, didn't understand the words, and couldn't imagine what they meant. One of them peeked over the lip of my hole. He saw her and pumped a few more fléchettes into her head before popping his helmet off to survey the job—to grin. The boy couldn't have been more than sixteen, but several teeth were gone, knocked out so that his face resembled a round jack-o'-lantern, with glassy black eyes. He spat once and then disappeared.

I hadn't been breathing, and let the air out slowly, scared that they'd hear the slightest noise. She saved me. The girl's body covered mine completely, and I prayed that they wouldn't come back to bury her. I didn't have to look to know that everyone else was dead, that Ox wouldn't be there when I crawled from the hole, would be shredded like the rest, an empty shell, and by the time I got the courage to move, the sky had brightened with morning light.

Karazhyngyl was gone. Everything. The hotel had burned to its foundations, and every fighting hole had been hit, sprawled bodies lying everywhere. I found Ox. His helmet was off, and he seemed to smile, staring at the sky without seeing it. He didn't show any wounds and looked as though his body had sunk into the dirt, so I tried to lift him, surprised by how light he had gotten. I dropped him when I saw it. His entire back side was gone—he was filleted straight down the middle, leaving only the front half.

I didn't remember the next few minutes until after I found myself in a truck, east of town. One of the task force's Tedoms had gone untouched. It was partially covered with rubble, so it took a moment to free the vehicle, after which I loaded it with alcohol, fuel cells, and ammunition. Ox's carbine rested on the seat next to me.

Eastward. Her words echoed in my thoughts and I tasted fear, a salt-tinged terror that made me see Russians behind every bush. Whenever the truck bounced over a rock, I flinched, thinking that I had come under attack, expecting a rocket to scream through my ear. With Karazhyngyl so far behind me that I couldn't see it, I stopped, and the truck idled quietly, a cloud of exhaust rising to merge with airborne dust.

Drugs, I realized. There weren't any. It wasn't clear how long it'd take to reach Almaty, and I had left everything back in Karazhyngyl, in the hotel's rubble and in my hole, my stash probably soaked with her blood so that even if I went back, I wouldn't be able to touch it. But part of me wanted to turn around, see if anything could be salvaged for one more fix, one for the road. I gunned the engine before giving in to the temptation—promised myself that I could make it to Almaty with no problem, didn't need the drugs for now and would just do it.

I was wrong.

FOUR

Cold Turkey

Bridgette had hair now, still short, but just above her ears in some kind of bob, and she wore jeans and a white tank top. She cocked her head to the side. I reached out to touch her and she disappeared with a wink, leaving me on the cab seat with nothing but a carbine.

Outside, a storm rocked the truck. Sand and dust surrounded it in a tan blizzard so that I saw only about four feet ahead, the truck stopped in the middle of it to sway back and forth, making me wonder how strong the winds had to be to move a Tedom that way. Grit pelted the windows and I closed my eyes to imagine rain, a storm that had blown in from the ocean over Annapolis. But this wasn't Annapolis. And my hands felt as though they had inflated to twice their normal size.

It had been less than a day since I'd left Karazhyngyl, and already I was gone. Withdrawal. Sweat poured down my forehead, stinging my eyes so that I had to blink, and in the dim light I saw a puddle of vomit on the seat next to me, dried. It was so cold there. I checked my suit temperature and saw it at eighty Fahrenheit, so I should have been comfortable, but I wasn't, and even though external temperatures read ninety, it felt like I would freeze.

Then Ox showed up. One second nothing, and the next he sat on the seat beside me, the back half of him bleeding everywhere. "A la canona," he said. "Welcome to the evening, no more daytime, Oscar. Scout. Not for you."

"Screw you."

"You got a case of it, man, and it's cold because you're going through withdrawals."

I wanted to slap or strangle him, but I was afraid. If I tried to touch him, he might leave and I didn't want to be alone. "Help me."

"Can't, Scout," he said. "You have to find your own way now. All alone."

"I'm heading south. To Almaty."

He shook his head. "Then where? A dealer? Drop it. Let it all go and come with us. Off yourself."

The shakes got bad and I felt like puking, wanted to crawl out of my own skin and couldn't stop shivering. Ox said something and it sounded like he was talking through a pipe, a mile away. Man, I was spiraling down. I was dying and knew it, and now that it was happening, I almost felt glad.

"What's wrong?" he asked. But when I looked up, it wasn't him anymore; it was her, and I started crying, couldn't sit still when a new wave of chills hit, made me slide down the seat and under the steering wheel.

"Stay with me; don't go."

"I'm not going anywhere, Scout." She brushed a hand through that hair and closed her eyes. "Come down with me, where it's warm. Let's have kids."

And I passed out. The next time I woke she was gone,

and the dust storm had ended to leave an empty panorama in shades of brown, the air wavy in the distance. My suit temperature said one hundred. Its fuel cell had died, and I felt as though someone had trapped me in one of those old steam cabinets from the cartoons, my face getting redder by the second. After I swapped fuel cells, it took half an hour for the temperature to drop, by which time the cold sweats had returned.

I sensed it long before it came, and rolled out of the cab to land on the steppes with a thud. *Come on in,* I thought, *right here.* My carbine was dull in the sunlight and I lifted it, the reticle shaking wildly on my goggle lens as I aimed in the general direction. It came silently. A single Russian drone sped toward me, passing directly overhead until the air cracked with its boom a few seconds later, at the same moment I fired. Tracers rocketed from the barrel and chased the thing, disappearing into the blue sky as the craft banked for a second run. I dropped the carbine, stood, and then shut my eyes, hoping it would be quick.

The thing boomed again, passing only a few hundred feet overhead before speeding away.

"Kill me!"

Sobbing, I dragged the carbine and crawled back into the cab to sleep.

My suit chronometer showed two weeks had passed. I had lain in the truck the whole time, eating and drinking barely enough to keep alive while the main valve emptied my waste all over the cab and—after the valve failed— inside my suit. Standing outside the truck, I felt as though my legs would give. Their muscles had gotten so weak that I had to rest several times while doing my best to clean up the mess, and I fell asleep again, so it was noon before most of the crap lay on the ground outside. A quick turn of the key, and my truck coughed to life.

The map display said it was over three hundred klicks to Almaty, most of it cross-country. *Less than a day away, maybe.* I shifted into gear and began the slow drive overland, hoping that I wouldn't pass out or drive into a gully, because walking to Almaty wouldn't work at all, I thought, but it turned out that I wouldn't have to drive the whole way either. At times I drifted off with the gentle bouncing, only to snap awake when I ran over a rut or a log. It would take a moment for me to reorient myself and make sure that the truck still pointed in the right direction. Whatever I had once loved about Kaz was gone. You can take only so much openness, and the one thing that prevented me from going off the deep end were the screams I let out in frustration, making it clear to the landscape that it was a piece of shit and that soon I would leave it, so that Kaz wouldn't be able to mock me with never-ending horizons and total emptiness that gave nothing but took everything.

Near the northern shore of Lake Balkhash, I ran into an outpost. The Army unit manning it fired on me, and a torrent of red tracer fire came straight at my forehead, peppering the engine block so that the cab filled with an odd pinging sound. I dove to the floor. Once the truck rolled to a stop, I kicked open the passenger door and threw out my carbine.

"Friendly!"

A face appeared at the driver-side window. "Who the hell are *you*?"

"Wendell. Civilian DOD, attached to Task Force Karazhyngyl. We got overrun."

Another guy joined his buddy and opened the door, helping me sit up. "You all right?" When I nodded, he grinned. "Shit. You shoulda *told* us you was coming, we nearly fired a rocket up your ass. Ever hear of radio?"

"Guy says he was in Karazhyngyl when it got overrun."

"Overrun, *hell*." The second one lifted me out and handed me my carbine, helping to reattach the flexi. "Karazhyngyl was wiped."

"Genetics," I said.

Both of them nodded. "That's what we heard. You're luckier than hell to have made it out." The first one waved for me to follow when they started walking back to their position. "Come on. We'll see if we can get you back to civilization. Welcome to Task Force Tombstone."

I followed them, struggling to keep up, and the first one stopped to help, draping my free arm over his shoulder. "You sure you're OK? Not hit anywhere, are you?"

"Nah. I've just been sick, sleeping in the truck for two weeks and—" I dove to the ground at the sound of an explosion and saw flames rise from my Tedom.

"Easy," he said. "We just whacked it with a rocket, don't want Pops to get his hands on anything when they make it this far south."

"This far south?" I asked. "What do you mean?"

Both of them looked at each other and the second one slung his carbine, the metal clicking against armor. "You must have been off-line for a good while. Pavlodar is gone, Russians hit us hard and are pushing this way. Their Gs have some new kind of suits, powered, and they're tearing it up. Division thinks they'll be here in a few days, maybe less, so we came up here to blow the ferry docks, make it so's Pops has to take the long way around or risk his APCs in the water."

"What about *our* genetics?"

He got quiet then and spat before answering. "Don't know about them. From what I hear, we sent the whole bunch northward to stop the bleeding. They bought our guys a few days extra to bail southward, but most of them haven't come back. Not this way, anyhow. A few days ago the entire Fifth Marine cruised through here, hammered all to hell, but they had their gear and I'll be damned if they weren't hard."

"But it's bad," the other one added. "Everyone's headed back to Shymkent, to try and hold there. Division at Almaty is bugging out, you're lucky you came when you did. One more day and you'd been all alone out here. The second-to-last ferry is leaving in an hour, you oughta get to Almaty in time, maybe hop a ride to Shymkent from there."

Those two didn't show anything, seemed calm, but when we reached the rest of their unit, you could tell something was up. There was a quiet hum. Nobody said anything and lines of men handed boxes to each other, one after another, passing equipment and supplies from a depot to the docks for loading onto boats. Officers muttered their orders to hurry it up. *Whisper* quiet. We passed the perimeter, and most of the ones manning it didn't have their helmets on; they just stared over the horizon to look for any sign of Popov. *Everyone* was watching. You'd see the guys passing ammo, and once in a while, during a pause, they'd turn to look northward, checking the sky.

A clerk sat near a field terminal at the dock and took my information after the two soldiers wished me well. His fingers moved so quickly that I couldn't hear the individual keystrokes; they just hissed while he entered my data.

"You're dead," he said. "Oscar Wendell, civilian historian attached to Task Force Karazhyngyl?"

"Yep." I showed him my ticket.

The clerk shook his head. "Dead. Welcome back to the living. Get out of the way and stay clear of the docks so we can on-load. I'll call your name when it's time."

A group of engineers were the only ones building something while everything else got torn down. Point defenses. Four towers were already in place and linked to portable reactors, the fifth one almost complete.

"Come on," one of them said. *"Speed it up."*

The worst of my physical withdrawal was over, but I agreed with the engineer that everyone needed to hurry, and thought that I could really use something right then. *To take the edge off.* You couldn't see Pops yet, but he'd be there. I just hoped that the Russians didn't decide to hit us on the water, and willed the engineers once more to hurry it up, to give us some *cover,* because didn't they know how scared I was?

Popov came before the clerk called my name. I heard the whine from the tower servos and a roar when plasma transferred from the reactors into the gun coils, telegraphing what would happen next. I hit the dirt. Guys ran around me, shouting at each other, and to their credit, the ones manning the lines for transferring equipment didn't budge. They moved faster. As soon as the guns started pounding, though, sending vibrations through the dirt, the men broke for cover and left the crates where they lay.

I never even saw the aircraft. Missiles shrieked in from the north and slammed into any target they could find, the overpressure from detonations hitting me like a hurricane. A deep kind of groaning noise caught my attention, and I looked up, just in time to see one of the five towers collapse slowly, and when the plasma coil ruptured, it sent a jet of hot gas into one of the fighting positions, turning a group of soldiers into instant charcoal. They didn't even scream.

Someone dove to the ground next to me, one of the engineers.

"Where the hell is our air cover?" I asked.

"Got none." We both ducked when a missile impacted behind us, near the water. "It's all reserved for the pullback from Almaty."

He stood then and sprinted to join the team, who had already shut down one of the reactors to stop the gas flow, and who were now trying to fix the plasma line—so they could erect the tower more quickly after the attack ended. A final missile homed on their movement and slammed into the group, sending body parts in every direction, just before a cluster bomb detonated far to my left. It cracked and scattered its bomblets to the wind so that they sounded like a string of firecrackers, after which the area went quiet again.

Someone blew a whistle over the dock loudspeaker.

"*Everyone out.* Blow the remaining stockpile and board the ferry now, we're pushing off. Pass the word."

I didn't need any encouragement. Each step felt heavy,

like my legs weren't sure of what my brain told them, and wet soil tugged at my boots. Before I knew it, the dock was underfoot, solid and easy to negotiate, and I sprinted across the gangplank as fast as I could. The clerk was already on the boat and pushed me into a corner.

"Stay there. *Stay down*."

Time seemed to slow down, forcing me to fight the urge to scream, to tell them to hurry up and get us the hell out of there. There is no way to describe having to wait like that. My carbine was gone, left on the shore, and a line of men had formed on the dock, pushing and shoving each other to be the next ones on board. I got the shakes then, bad. I didn't know who was in charge. Maybe nobody was, and maybe once everyone got aboard, we'd just sit there and wait, a big fat target for one missile to take out. Easy. Maybe it was an illusion, a trick of my mind, but in the distance I heard something like the squeak of APC wheels and the rumbling of armor, only it couldn't be that, because there was so much noise from everyone panicking that it would be impossible to hear the Russian advance.

The boat had overloaded. Water lapped at its sides, three feet below the gunwale, and I had just begun praying that the craft wouldn't shift too far to one side or the other when a horn sounded, signaling us to pull away. That's when it got horrible. Someone had decided they couldn't warn the others, the ones who were about to get aboard, and the gangplank collapsed, sending men into the water, their suits—unhelmeted—rapidly filling and pulling them under. Others, still on the dock, leapt across the gap and grabbed the side, hoping to hold on or scramble over the edge, but they carried too much weight and guys on the deck didn't even try to help. After the first one splashed in, I stopped watching.

Halfway across Lake Balkhash, I looked back. A line of men stood on the shore, trying to shrug out of their armor and undersuits, to get ready for the swim, oblivious to what had appeared on the horizon. Dust clouds. The point defense cannons scanned back and forth but couldn't fire at ground targets, wouldn't provide any cover to our forces when Russian APCs got within plasma range. We were only a hundred meters from the far shore when the first rounds hit. Some of the men had already started swimming and dove under, trying to avoid the blasts, but those still on the shore had nowhere to go. The globes of plasma burst among them, and if the round hit in the right place, you could see their dark figures silhouetted against the glow, poses burned into my memory before the men collapsed into piles of black matter. As soon as I got off the boat, I ran, not caring where I'd wind up.

A Marine corporal waited near the dock, his scout car idling beside him, and it took a second for me to hear what he was shouting.

"Wendell. *Oscar Wendell!*"

I raised my arm. "That's me."

"Jesus." A look of relief crossed his face. He was unarmored, in fatigues, and when I saw the staff emblem on the front bumper, I knew what he would say next. "General Urqhart sends his regards. He was in Almaty when the net reported you were here, alive, and sent his car. He's waiting on the airstrip, so I suggest we get it on. Sir."

I never even looked back. The mass of soldiers I had come with milled on every side, looking for a way out, and some of them had already begun moving across country, not wanting to take the chance of waiting for a formal retreat order that might never come. Any organization that once existed had broken down into total chaos, so I got in quickly and shut the door. "Get us the hell out of here."

"Aye, aye. You're lucky, sir."

"Oh yeah?" I asked. "I keep hearing that."

He nodded, struggling to keep the scout car in a straight line when he gunned it. "Yep. Russian Gs have just been spotted, a whole division on the way. Ten more minutes and I woulda left you there with the stupid Army homos."

As we drove southward, I had time to reflect on Ox and Bridgette. I looked out the window and watched the salt flats pass, wondering where the two of them were now, and feeling empty. There would be no more drugs, nothing to sandbag the wave of grief that I knew had been building, and that would slam into me without warning. For now, there was nothing at all. But Kaz had taught me many things, and one of those was that the longer you stayed, the more friends you lost, and the more ghosts you collected. You could run from them for a while, but they never got tired; they knew it was a marathon and not a sprint, and they would be more than happy to wait for you to collapse so they could catch up.

At one point or another, everyone faced the dead.

Almaty was worse than the docks—almost—and we barely made it through the city. Military traffic choked the roads, or what was left of them, and everyone headed in the same direction: toward the airfield. Drones boomed constantly. I didn't know if our air cover had engaged any incoming targets yet, but the fact that we hadn't seen missiles made me feel a little better, like maybe Pops was still working on getting across the lake, like maybe there was time to breathe.

An MP stopped us at one point, about a mile from the airfield. "No go," he said.

"I'm on direct orders from General Urqhart." The corporal handed him his ticket, but the guy didn't even bother to insert it into his computer, and handed it back.

"Nope. We got it straight from Division. Only combat vehicles—no soft skins—beyond this point."

"Hey, guy." The corporal turned to me and pointed at my vision hood. "You got coms on that thing?"

It occurred to me that I had turned them off, probably during my withdrawal episode in the Tedom, and had never turned them back on. I flicked the button on my forearm and nodded. He ripped the hood from my head, leaned over so the wires would stay connected to my suit, and pushed it against his ear.

"Hit channel two-seven." I did. The corporal gave his call sign multiple times before getting frustrated. "Screw this. Cal, answer *the fucking line!*" He must have gotten through, because he calmed down. "Yeah, listen up, we're almost two klicks out and they've stopped our car. We'll have to finish on foot. Tell the general we're on our way, and if you leave us, I swear to God I'll have your ass."

The MP hammered on our hood. *"Get this thing off the road!"*

"You ready?" the corporal asked me, and I nodded. "Then let's go."

We ditched the car where it was, still idling, and the last thing I saw was the MP having a conniption. No shit. The guy actually unslung his carbine and fired in the air, was about to aim at us when we disappeared around a corner and hightailed it through an alley.

I had never run so fast. I knew that I'd pay for it later, that I hadn't even begun to recover from two weeks on almost no rations, but it's a funny thing when you're that scared. You don't *feel* anything. Mother adrenaline kicked in and took over, giving me everything I needed, telling me it was only a mile, a cakewalk.

By the time we reached the airfield, my fuel cell had expired. I stopped at the gate to unsuit, and thought the corporal would have a heart attack while waiting, begging me to hurry up. The smell offended even *me*. It had been over a month since I'd last showered, and sweat had made an amazing pattern of dried salt on my undersuit, the legs caked with excrement. I considered ditching the undersuit too, just showing up at the plane naked, but I doubted they would let me through the checkpoint.

By the time I finished, he had almost lost it. "Can we go now? *Please?*"

"Sure."

But it was too late. We both heard it at the same time and then looked to see a huge transport roar down the airstrip. We caught a glimpse of it between two buildings before it drifted off the ground, barely clearing the trees at the end of the runway and banking right for its trip westward. I sunk to my knees. The ground felt unsteady and it took me a second to figure out that an awful wailing sound wasn't coming from me; it was coming from an alarm siren that now screamed over loudspeakers. Just as I was about to lose it completely, I heard him.

"Damn, son, you smell awful. What'd you do, pass out in a pile of pig shit?"

The corporal stepped forward and took the general's briefcase. "General, what's going on?"

"Popov pushed south to prevent our escape to the west. To our east, they're moving down into Uzbekistan with mountain units so that, our scouts say, by tonight we'll be cut off. Get my car." He slapped me on the back. "Glad to see you made it, Oscar."

I found my voice and got up. "General, why'd you stay? You could've gone."

"Simple. My boys are here. Once I saw they couldn't make it out, there wasn't any other option but to get off the plane. You really *do* smell horrible, son; let's get you a new undersuit and armor, and you can tell me all about Karazhyngyl." He lit a cigar as we turned and headed away from the airport, toward the city, where the corporal disappeared into the crowds to try to recover the vehicle we'd abandoned earlier, and I stopped to examine my new surroundings.

A blue haze hovered over the city. I'd never seen Almaty, but liked it more than the rest of Kaz, felt comfortable with the hills and low mountains flanking it to the south so that you couldn't look out and keep looking forever to the end of the earth. Other than that, it was identical to Shymkent, or any other city. Air strikes and artillery had reduced its buildings to blocks of concrete or piles of brick, and almost all the locals had vanished except for the entrepreneurs who stayed behind to make money off the troops—whoever's troops happened to be there. An armored column appeared out of nowhere, scattering people and bearing northward where you could barely see flashes on the horizon, and although you couldn't yet hear it, you could almost feel it: the vibration of artillery.

The general grinned. "Well, Oscar, we're in the shit now. So I need to get drunk."

I'd never had the shakes so bad. This wasn't the result of withdrawal, not the product of something with which anyone should have been familiar—least of all me. This was something entirely different, a kind of awakening, a realization that everything was real and that it all surrounded us in a panorama, the ugliness of which couldn't be ignored. Like having my eyes taped open. A clarity descended on the world so that even through the city's pollution I saw the outlines of our troops with a kind of crispness, the globs of mud that had caked to their boots transforming as my gaze shifted upward to see that it went from a sticky mess near their soles, faded to a medium brown at their shins, and then ended below their knees, where the mud completely dried and broke off with every step. Some of the soldiers had a purpose. As we drove carefully through the packed Almaty streets, I stared at them as if it was all a kind of freak show, and noticed the ones who still had hope because they stopped to salute as we passed, and, more importantly, marched northward or westward, toward the trouble. But this wasn't Kaz in the war's first year. This was Kaz aged, a Kaz within which mold had taken hold and the faces of our men showed signs of rot, caving in as the underpinnings decayed and disintegrated. Most of the men looked lost. They stood or slouched, lounged against blocks of rubble, having to move their legs at the last minute, barely avoiding being run over by the general's vehicle. The worst ones didn't look at us. Those didn't see anything.

I wanted to be like them—not the ones with purpose; I connected with the ones who had already given up. The thought of crawling into a corner seemed logical, because fighting our situation was pointless given the distance to our main battle groups in Shymkent, hundreds of kilometers to the west. You could imagine the higher-ups debating it all in Bandar, and only one answer would float to the surface: abandon Almaty. That was the logical conclusion. How could retreating forces—broken themselves—rescue us from as far away as Shymkent? But a part of my mind dusted itself off in that moment, a part that hoped. I listened as the general shouted into his headset, rattling off options to his staff, and I latched on to one of his ideas, made it my life preserver. He wanted to concentrate forces and push south now, into Kyrgyzstan, where there was a chance that we could overpower the encircling forces and break through, head southwest to link up with the main retreat and on to Bandar 'Abbas. To home. The other options chewed at my thoughts, kept tugging at them with their threat of submersing me into a pool of despair, one that whispered that no matter what happened, the outcome would be brutal. But as long as I focused on the *possibility* of breakout, gripped it tightly without letting go, I'd get by and wouldn't hear the whispers.

In the end, it all became clear. I wanted to get high again; this was no time for reality.

"Stop the car," the general said, and it lurched to a halt, throwing me against the front seat. He pointed at me. "Get out."

"What? What for?"

"Change."

A pile of discarded combat suits and undersuits lay on

the sidewalk. Many of them hadn't been cleaned, were filled with whatever remained of the men they'd once held, and I did my best to find a set that was at least partly non-bloody and my size. There was no embarrassment this time. I changed in the open, discarding my old under-suit in favor of the new one, and did my best to shrug into armor, finishing the hose and cable connections once I was back in the car.

The general waved the corporal on. "Turn this box around, head south."

"South?" the corporal asked.

"South. General Stinson is assembling the main force to move out at three a.m.; we're going to attempt a break-out and I want to see the front before our boys head toward trouble." He grinned at me then and lit a new cigar. "We have wonderful boys, Oscar. The best."

"Sir, they're spent. Most of them are too old or too young."

"Hell. Look at me. You think *I'm* too old?"

I thought for a moment, the urge to zip up and check out beginning to fade with a new sense of *maybe-this-will-be-all-right*. "OK. Screw it."

"You really have changed, son. I remember when we first met, you looked like a kid, a real rube, and now look at you. Ox would be proud. You're a new-worlder whether you want it or not, and hell, all these boys are. I know what's in your head, their heads, and don't let that bother you, the doubts, the fear, the inevitability. Ignore it. That stuff, it comes and goes in war, and all you have to remember is this: Popov is no different. When they see our tanks and APCs charging down their throats, they'll shit their pants, and I guarantee you, they'll flinch. They'll break and run."

The general nodded and looked away, spitting a fleck of tobacco on the floor. "We're going home. I'm getting our boys out of here, whether they're Marines or not. All of them."

The mountains rose on either side as our scout car wound its way up the road south, out of the city, and we wove through massive APCs and tanks that made the scout vehicle look like a toy, a rabbit in the middle of wild rhinos. The sun had gone down. Still, Kaz's sky glowed orange and cast an even light over everything, making it spooky, because there were neither shadows nor the appearance of depth, which, when combined with the quiet tankers who leaned against their vehicles and smoked, watching us pass without a word, made the breeze seem a little colder. Gone were the smiles from the early war, the confidence that had infused everyone. This was a battle group already spent. And I sensed it in myself too, the terror kneading my gut no less than it had before, all the worse because I had no more options—no more drugs. The general lit a joint and blew smoke over his shoulder so that I smelled it, my thoughts a mix of *Should I ask for some?* and *Should I jump out and head into the mountains, make for Uzbekistan on my own, where one man might be overlooked, missed by Russian forces?*

We stopped at the entrance to a national park, maybe the only one Kazakhstan had, and I recognized the place. Much of it had already been leveled, its alpine meadows stripped of trees and brush, the ground blackened from plasma barrages and littered with armor fragments.

The general must have seen me staring after we dismounted. "Many things happened here, son."

"When?"

"Long time ago, back when we first lost Pavlodar and had to fall back; airborne held out in the park, made their last stand until we were able to mount a full counterattack, just after I found you on the plane."

"I've seen pictures of this place, I think. Maybe when the war started, and it used to be beautiful."

The general grunted. "Not anymore. And they disbanded the one hundred first airborne after the action. Only two hundred men survived out of a full division, and they just couldn't replace it. Come on. Battalion HQ is this way."

The general led me into the meadow, and in the open we felt exposed, all of us crouching and buttoning helmets as we jogged forward. Eventually the corporal disappeared into the ground, next the general, and then I saw a ramp heading down into the earth. The hole swallowed me. A few seconds later I had popped my helmet, and waited for my eyes to adjust to the dimness of combat lamps in a wide concrete vault, its space filled with computers and men. The general and corporal had already found the line commander, and Urqhart was deep in conversation, so I found a quiet corner and sat, sliding to the floor to wait.

A few hours later, the general shook me awake and whispered, "Let's go, son. *Move it*."

"What's going on?"

"Popov. He's not waiting for us to attack."

That woke me up. We sprinted from the command bunker and headed for the road, and I had to dive to the side to avoid being run over by a tank. At least a hundred of them lumbered past to head in the direction of Russian forces, and their treads kicked up dirt and chewed wide divots into the ground, which almost tripped me once I got to my feet. Without warning, bright light turned the meadows white. It was as if a million camera flashes had gone off. I instinctively dove, landing next to the general just as the booms arrived. An intense heat cooked the back of my scalp, through the vision hood. Someone dragged me to my feet, and before I knew it, I was in the scout car again, the corporal speeding back down the mountain road until a plasma round detonated nearby, sending the car into the air. It was strange. Your mind went into overtime when something like that occurred, and deep down you knew that it was bad, but there was a detachment, as if it was happening to someone else, and when the car impacted, I felt nothing, flying forward at first and then bouncing around inside as it tumbled over and over. We had left the road. When the car stopped, I crawled from the wreckage and looked up the slope we had just rolled down, a steep ravine at the top of which was the park entrance, backlit by plasma rounds and explosions that even from this distance ripped the air from my lungs and forced wind up the mountainside, blowing so hard that I had to lean against it.

The general grabbed my arm. "We have to get back to Almaty, Oscar. Now."

"Does it matter anymore? If they're coming, they're coming."

"Half our armor is buying us time. The rest is falling back to cut off the southern approach to the city, and we need to get inside the new perimeter. There won't be any breakout now."

The hopelessness of it hit me in a wave. I stumbled

after him as we clawed our way back to the road, but there was no more energy, no goal, and although my legs moved, there was no will motivating them, so my flight was more a function of autopilot than any instinct for survival. None of it mattered. A glance over my shoulder showed men firing from holes in the ground only to be swallowed by plasma, and our tanks, their cannons bucking with each round, launched a continuous barrage against an enemy that remained invisible, somewhere beyond a bend in the valley. That made it worse. With no sight of them, my mind created a scenario in which an endless mass of Russians advanced, oblivious to our fire. They were supermen. Inhuman. And as I stumbled down the road after the general, I laughed at *my* inhumanity, realizing that not only had I given up the title of Oscar Wendell, but nobody would classify me even as an animal, because didn't animals want to survive? The general turned at one point and spoke. But the words disintegrated in my ears and may as well have been a foreign tongue, only able to convey a sense of a question, something like *What the hell is wrong with you?* but they didn't fully register, and I laughed all the harder. Whatever was wrong with me, did it matter? What did the general think he could do if I answered? Help me? All my experience of warfare had accumulated into a critical mass of horror so that "the present" transpired outside time, in some universe that made a second an hour and an hour a week, made the road stretch and elongate so that my legs moved in slow motion and would never get me to the safety of Almaty.

And once Almaty, what then? Ox and Bridgette had taken the easy way out, the path of least resistance, and didn't have to face the war anymore, and I whooped with a new energy, the realization that it wouldn't be long now making me happy. I'd join them. My legs carried me past the general, faster now that my feet recognized what I had just begun to suspect—that we were all dead already, and that when it happened, the moment would be one of painlessness, of emptiness. I hadn't felt anything when our scout car crashed; it was an epiphany. The scout car had taught me that when my moment came, I'd be ready, and I knew that it would be a happy event, a festival in which all trouble would be shed, all sadness and terror. It would be a moment—if that—of pain, maybe a millisecond of incredulity, and then freedom via death.

The sight of men surprised me. Endless lines of them guided fusion borers into steep dives or dug massive holes into which tanks had begun to inch, to bury themselves in a protective mantle of earth and rock, leaving only turrets exposed. It took a moment for me to realize that someone was in my face, screaming, pointing a pistol at my forehead.

"Your suit computer won't sync, give me the fucking call sign," he said.

"I don't get it. You don't get it."

He slammed the butt of his handgun against my chin and knocked me to the ground. "Who are you?"

"I'm all of it, man. Do it. Take me out, and then it'll be cool because you don't get it but I do, you don't matter but I do. Take it down. You didn't know her and now I'm nothing and let's look into the abyss because once you do that you'll see it's all OK, that it's just the way it is."

"What?" The soldier looked up and then drew to attention so that I knew before hearing the voice, knew without turning around, that he'd saved me again.

"It's OK, he's with me, son. Where's General Stinson's HQ?"

The man pointed his pistol in the opposite direction, behind him, and I felt the general lift me by the shoulders, push me down the road and back into the Almaty rubble. The bubble burst then. I started crying and hung my head, wishing that it had ended back on the mountain, in the meadows that had once looked so beautiful and calm.

The general shook his head. "I didn't know you were so far gone, Oscar."

"I'm not gone. I'm here."

"Don't. Just don't."

I heard the blasts again, in the distance now, but when I looked toward the mountains, it was clear that the fighting had intensified, and even more plasma lit the sky. "They're coming. They want us all, General, even you, even our dead. You said you'd get us out."

"Not anymore. Now I just want to kill as many as I can before they kill us."

"Not me; I just want to die, to go. It'll be OK then. I know it. Let the Russians come in, General. Dying won't be so bad."

"Son, you don't get it at all. They might not kill you, they might capture you. And that's a hell of a lot worse."

Just before we arrived at the command post, I looked around. "Where's the corporal?"

"Dead. Decapitated in the wreck."

We jogged down a ramp and back into the earth again, but the feeling of security that subterrene had once lent me was long gone, so that now the earth felt like a prison.

*   *   *

We felt them closing in. There wasn't any moment that a historian would be able to point to, declaring with certainty that *this* was the instant Popov closed the circle around us, but we all sensed it happening, a feeling that made your hair stand up, and it took everything to keep from turning to jelly. Men sat at terminals in the command post and smoked nonstop and nobody chewed them out, because air handling didn't matter anymore. The floor rumbled with far-off detonations. A digital map unit rested on the main wall and showed Almaty with friendly forces marked in green and blue and Popov in red, but nobody needed it; you felt the perimeter and the false sense of security it lent, because all those men had a nervous energy that pulsated and expanded, keeping you warm. The command post had been dug into rock, under the city center, and our forces assembled themselves into two concentric rings with us in the middle. I breathed a sigh of relief the one time I did look at the map, recognizing that some of the forces had survived the mountains—had dug in just at the edge of the park to keep Pops out of south Almaty.

My problem wasn't just being trapped: I was a lunatic. I wanted drugs, anything to take the edge off and let me roll into a deep hole, escape the reality of our situation and get out—even though I wouldn't *really* be out. But juicing up wouldn't work and I knew it, because deep down the recollection of time in the mountain meadows, the wilderness after Karazhyngyl, all of it played in a continuous loop to remind me that getting lit would be just as useless as it always had been. I'd get high and then what? The comedown would be worse, darker with the added benefit of knowing that nothing had changed except that I'd failed again. I swear to God that at that instant, with Pops encircling us and getting ready to attack, I didn't worry about the Russians as much as I wondered how I would get through life without drugs, which *really* was a wacky thought. Like there would *be* a life beyond Almaty. The thought of spending my days with nothing to help me get by, like a normal person, made me cringe, because it didn't seem possible.

A voice asked for volunteers to check different sections of the perimeter and I raised my hand. Not because I wanted the job. It was clear that someone else would have been better suited; I just wanted to do something, to get out of my head for once, because the thoughts never got brighter and the only way to escape was to escape them, to do *something* that would make me stop thinking.

The general handed me a new helmet and a carbine. "Take them."

"I didn't know I'd lost my helmet."

"You left it in my car on the mountain. If this were another war, I would have made you climb back up and get it, but it doesn't matter now. Take the northern section, from areas ten through fifteen. Just make for the Premier Hotel and then north on what's left of Dostyk Avenue from there."

He punched keys on his suit and a map popped onto my faceplate, showing the section of the line, one where Popov still hadn't arrived in force.

"What do you want me to do?"

"Tell the boys we're doing fine; for now our guys are giving air cover to keep the skies clear, and that's something. Ask if they need anything. Give them a hand job if they want one."

The general walked me to the ramp and my night vision clicked in, the stars twinkling in greenish yellow.

"Come back and tell me what you learn," he said, and headed back into the ground.

I crept over the rubble. Our engineers would have an underground defense network established eventually, and we prayed that it would be soon, but this time it was almost guaranteed that Pops would also hit us topside. Remnants of an Army battalion had emplaced all their sentry bots around the perimeter and had some artillery, but it wasn't nearly the amount we'd need, not even close to what would make topside attacks too risky for the Russians. Overhead, drones whined and fought each other. But the real battle hadn't started yet—this was the quiet before the attack—and I felt my nerves begin to slip again, so I had to play games of counting blocks of rubble as I traversed the city streets, and of watching the map display to make sure I headed in the right direction, reminding myself that thinking was just as real an enemy as the Russians.

In the darkness, a square shape emerged from the rubble, a building. It had sustained some damage but was largely intact, a huge thing that had once been Almaty's biggest hotel, the Premier, and it stopped me in my tracks so that I stood, dumfounded, just staring. How had we gotten this far? Almaty had once been a city like any other, with people who had dreams of doing something other than being invaded and killed, and I doubted that many of them even knew the current market price for rhenium or selenium or lanthanum; they probably didn't even know what the metals were used for. But we did. The Russians did. At the moment word got out that Kaz had something everyone wanted, someone at the Pentagon dusted off the abacus and did the math, a simple equation that estimated cost of deployment, engagement, and retreat, to be balanced against the estimated reserves of rhenium and someone's wild-ass guess at how much we could get out—a kind of lottery that the locals hadn't even known they'd played until they were notified of winning the grand prize: us. I recalled the discussions when I first arrived in Bandar, when reporters in the bar would still haggle over the amounts we'd be able to pull out before the Russians countered, and how I'd engaged in them too, because it had all been so important back then. Now? Now it was like seeing a trillion one-dollar bills in person versus hearing it described; if you saw the cost of getting our share, it was indescribable, and you'd realize that there had been no words for all this until now. The cost was a hotel in the middle of an empty rubble field, surrounded by the dead. Useless. I pushed past and did my best to shake the feeling that the Premier watched me as I left, staring at my back with a look of *you-did-this-to-me-and-I'll-never-forget-it*. Its empty windows made strange noises in the breeze, and if Ox or Bridgette lived there now, I wasn't ready to see them.

When I reached the inner perimeter, I dropped into a trench manned by three Army guys, and one of them nearly shot me.

"Jesus." He lowered his Maxwell and turned to face north. "Jesus Christ."

I asked, "How are you guys doing?"

"What do you mean how are we doing? Who the fuck are you?"

The other two didn't even look at me, hadn't thought I was worth shooting, much less speaking with.

"Command sent me to check on things, to let you know that we still have air cover. Where's your CO?"

"Yeah, right. *CO*. I'm the CO. My name's Private Jerkoff. I don't know, smart guy. *You* tell me where he is, because I haven't seen an officer since they put us here."

"What did they tell you to do?"

The question made all of them laugh, and the one who had almost fired at me leaned his Maxwell against the trench and slid into a crouch. He popped his helmet.

"They told us to watch north, toward the outer perimeter, and if we see any of our guys booking this way, to give them cover, because it means Pops is coming." He lit a cigarette and then looked at me, his night vision goggles glinting. "Hey, you got any drugs?"

"No. I'm heading to check the outer perimeter, but I'll be coming back this way, so if you see someone headed toward you, don't shoot."

And I booked it. Pops waited, gathering strength so he could roll in and roll over, and when he did arrive, I didn't want to be trapped in a trench with those guys. They were lepers. My stomach turned at the realization that all those green and blue dots, which were supposed to represent able-bodied soldiers on the map, hadn't really meant anything. These *were* soldiers in a way. But none of them were in one piece.

Sentry bots hissed, popping out to scan as I approached the outer markers, and then returned to their holes, allowing me to pass and slide into a second set of trenches. This one was filled with men, shoulder to shoulder, who faced north and ignored my joining them. I tapped one on the shoulder and waited for him to turn.

"Command sent me to check on the lines, to let you

know that we still have air cover and the engineers are working out a tunnel network. You guys see anything?"

"Yeah." He faced north again. "I see it all now, like in daytime. Jesus is on a white horse at the head of Popov's army, and he's pissed. He'll be coming soon. Jesus wants revenge."

This time *I* was the one who slid to the trench floor, trying to figure out how I'd do it, how I'd make it across the entire sector, because that close to the front, you knew like these guys did, sensed it: the Russians had finished prepping and were just waiting for the right time to come in. It was obvious.

I picked myself up and wormed through the trench, heading east, unable to shake the feeling that sooner or later I'd get high again.

FIVE

Cut Off

The Russians *didn't* attack. It was lucky for us, because the respite gave engineers the time they needed to dig their underground fortifications, ringing Almaty's subterranean territories with tunnels and bunkers so that the men topside could take cover in rock. By the time the tunnels were complete, massive piles of soil and mud dotted the city's rubble fields, monuments to the amount of material removed. There already were tunnels in place from the first defense of Almaty, which saved the sappers time and effort, so on the third day I found myself back where it had all started, underground, albeit under different circumstances this time and without any friends. Some men stayed topside. Most rotated down to be replaced at eight-hour intervals, but the tank and APC crews didn't get that luxury and had glared at us when we'd first descended to leave them behind in the dirt, exposed. I didn't blame them for hating us; they had been assigned to die first, to take out as much Russian armor as they could before plasma fried them in ceramic coffins, and *that* was if they were lucky. If they weren't, and we lost our air cover before Pops attacked, the auto-drones would come before our tanks had a chance to get off a single shot.

I had been assigned to General Urqhart's staff, in the new command post three kilometers underground, and it was empty—it was all empty. Not the tunnel—*that* was packed with people. Thoughts were empty, like something seen out of the corner of my eye but never caught; they came and went, and although a part of my mind heeded them, processed whatever they were, the thoughts left as soon as they arrived, because by then I was outside myself looking down, there but *not* there at the same time. And mail came, just before Pops jammed all outside coms. Letters from home, from a time I barely remembered, arrived in a bolus of emails that automatically uploaded to my suit as soon as I came within range of the main server, but it's not like it was a good thing. Family hadn't mattered before the war—drugs had; writing had—and now family was unwanted because of the reminder they carried that outside Kaz was a different world, one that nobody could process and that seemed illusory because it was so ancient. The world at peace was a black-and-white 2-D film, an old documentary. So correspondence threatened to incite madness, because letters grabbed us by the short hairs and shoved our faces into the reality that while we died, the rest of the world went on. You wanted to know about the National Mall in springtime, but you *didn't* want to know, because that memory was a threat, a corruption. Still, you read them and did your best to pretend that it wasn't you who your mother wrote to complain about D.C. traffic and the fact that your dad was still disappointed you hadn't gone to Georgetown Law. And the neighbor's son had finished medical school and was now practicing in McLean, happy, a success. Sure, you read them. There was nothing else to do except read them, one at a time, and then delete the things from your suit computer at the same time you wished for a mental delete.

Before I had finished my second email, the general nudged me with a boot. "I need a favor."

"Sure," I said, closing my display with relief.

"We're going to try something, an attack from the northern sector to probe Popov's lines. Get out there and report back what you see."

"Won't you get news over local coms?"

"The jamming might screw it up, and I want a pair of eyes that I trust. Get it on."

And I got it on. The path northward snaked through the underground positions, and through men who tried to sleep or forget. Now that we had submerged again, they had taken off their helmets and pushed vision hoods back, exposing the bushy beards of the old or the barely-there ones of the kids, and all of them looked wide-eyed and vacant. Panic was contagious. We'd all caught it. Dirt had become our makeup and all of them had slathered it on so that the faces looked gray with dark patches that would never wash off in just one shower. It *had* to smell. I recalled my first exposure to the front, the smells that had once made me dream of some journalistic blow-job fest, but now there was nothing, because once you were immersed in all of it, the odor became an extension of Kaz itself, something that *couldn't* be sensed. It was like trying to feel my own liver. If it had smelled good, that would have been different; I would have noticed it in less than a second. There was nothing left to do but button up, and a blinking light on my helmet display led me to a bank of elevators, where I stepped in, grabbing hold of the cage as it rattled upward.

Fall temperatures made my gauge drop as soon as I climbed into the morning darkness, and I hurried through the trench toward a forward observation post. Two men waited there. They stared into the distance and I looked in the same direction, vaguely making out a row of shapes in long narrow green boxes with eight wheels on each side and two turrets on top. They looked like armored cars, but a kind I had never seen before, with an impossibly thin profile.

Once I reached the post, one of the men crouched and began working at a computer, its red light barely visible.

"You come from General Urqhart?" the other one asked.

"Yeah."

"Good. Then we can get going." He gestured to the other one, and the vehicles roared to life, beginning their movement north toward the Russian positions.

"What are those?" I asked.

"Bots. Engineers had a thousand in storage; we thought we'd give them a try. They're armed with Maxwell auto-cannons and grenade launchers."

And for the first time in a long while, I felt good. We were doing something other than wait. It didn't matter that there were only a thousand bots against God knew how many Pops, because maybe some would get close enough to take them out, disrupt Russian operations, or at least let them know that we could sting.

"Fully automated," the crouching one said, and he slapped the computer shut.

I watched. Before the things disappeared from view,

they increased speed, bouncing over the rubble and jogging side to side, some moving out ahead while others lingered in the rear at a slower speed so the group spaced out before I lost sight.

"Now what?" I asked.

"Now we wait. Don't worry, those things are smart, like drones. Some might make it through."

We didn't have to wait long. A few minutes later the fields in front of us lit up with tracer fire, and then plasma rounds fell, bursting amid the robots to send them flying before they disintegrated into clouds of wheels and pieces. It ended less than a minute later. As the robots fell, one of the men counted down out loud, the numbers steadily decreasing to zero.

"And that," the other one said, "is why we don't bother with ground bots anymore. Useless."

Just as quickly as my mood had brightened, it went dark. I don't recall my trip back to the tunnels. The Russians lobbed a few plasma shells in our direction, but they only guessed at our positions, and the rounds never came close, so I didn't bother to crouch while making my way through the trench. When I returned to the command post, General Urqhart waved me away, having already heard the news, and I slumped back to the floor, opening my email again even though it was the last thing I wanted to do. The only other option was to sleep, but nobody wanted to sleep at that moment, and I knew that aboveground, the sun had begun to rise.

I volunteered for regular topside duty. A week after the bot experiment, Popov still hadn't attacked, and none of us figured out why they waited, but the general guessed they were concentrating on our main forces, pushing them back to Tashkent, and would get to us eventually. Occasionally drones transmitted information, so we learned that the rear-guard task force in Tashkent had blunted the main Russian advance to our west, allowing the rest of our forces to withdraw into Iran. After hearing that, I wanted topside duty more than anything. The general didn't understand; he hadn't expected me to join the duty roster. But I couldn't explain that waiting and thinking had begun to take a greater toll than I had anticipated, that I had stopped trying to read emails because I couldn't concentrate, or that hearing news made me want to put a fléchette through my own forehead; it felt like the walls would collapse at any second, and I couldn't stand the other faces anymore. All of them looked the same: scared. And thick blue smoke began accumulating near the tunnel roof once restrictions were lifted. Everyone smoked so much that it had become a concern, because when the cigarettes started running out, people were really going to lose it, and what then? I didn't want to be around to find out, and decided to spend as much time as I could aboveground if for no other reason than to breathe cleaner air.

When I got to the elevators, someone was already there and held the cage open for me. A kid, a Marine. His grenade launcher hung from its strap and he struggled to untangle it from the bars as the elevator shuddered on its way to the surface.

"Where are *you* going?" I asked.

"Topside. Skipper said to wait for some guy named Wendell." The kid tried to look tough—glared at me, even—but I saw his eyes, which darted around and couldn't stay focused on any one thing for more than a fraction of a second.

"You got any drugs?" I asked.

"No."

"Get some. Soon. You'll need them, trust me. And put your helmet on."

The pair already on watch duty didn't wait for us to relieve them. They pushed me against the wall in their haste to get below, and when we arrived at the post, we found it empty. It was barely a pillbox, and not linked to the underground defenses. The engineers had done their best to resurrect the old topside positions, so this one showed the blackened surfaces of multiple plasma attacks, the glass of its vision slits long ago melted away or shattered, letting the evening breeze course through. The sun had already set. Just before ducking inside, I paused and took off my helmet, pushing the hood back so I could look at the sky with my own eyes, careful to make sure that my head was below the trench lip. There must have been a million stars. You couldn't see all of them yet, because the sun still cast a weak glow to our west, but you saw enough to know that under different circumstances, Kaz wouldn't have been so bad.

I don't remember much of what the kid said during those first hours of darkness, and did my best to ignore him as I arranged myself on an old wooden box, but maybe I *should* have listened. In the distance, something moved. Within a second I had yanked my vision hood in place before snapping my lid shut, and then I slid my carbine through the empty view slit, ratcheting up the magnification.

"What is it?" the kid asked.

About three kilometers away, the Russian lines had erupted into a glow, with flames that twinkled in green sparks.

"Fires. Bonfires."

"Jesus. It's like they don't care."

"They care." We both went silent. A faint sound reached us then and I tuned up, struggling to figure out what it was before I laughed. "They care, because they're singing; they care about having some fun while they can."

"I remember before I left, a few months ago, we had a cookout..."

The kid popped his helmet and pulled his vision hood back, still peering into the night at the Russian lines. I didn't notice his head was bare until it was too late.

"...and I got so wasted that I had to—"

The fléchette didn't even crack. Whoever fired must have amped down the muzzle velocity to keep it below the speed of sound, and I was staring at the kid when it hit— just about to tell him to button up, that he was an idiot for looking out without a helmet. The kid's head snapped back. There was nothing to be done; he died before his body hit the floor, and the one that hit him hadn't been a tracer, so I couldn't pinpoint the shooter's position.

It's funny what you think about at moments like that. Most people would have felt terror at the thought of Pops out there, somewhere, wriggling his way through the rubble and scoping for targets, and maybe also some sadness because the kid had just bought it, and a natural reaction would have been to wonder how old he was or whether he would be missed, and whether he at least got *laid* at that cookout. Had he *ever* gotten laid? I felt nothing. It just clicked. I activated my chameleon skin, radioed down to the tunnels what had happened, and then scanned the horizon for any sign of movement, my view reduced to whatever fed into the eye of the Maxwell, a circle of green that spat ranges and temperature and any other data it could think to throw, anything that might affect range or accuracy. That was what life had become. A reduction had occurred so that whatever madness had afflicted me on the mountain was gone, along with any kind of caring about life or death or drugs or Ox, replaced by a kind of mathematics—the calculus of *wanting* to kill. Needing it. The search for a target became so consuming that I barely noticed when someone else arrived at the outpost, pulling the kid's body into the trench before taking a position next to me, joining me in a silent hunt. It clicked because that kind of concentration made everything go away. Maybe it was the same way people enjoyed carpentry, or surfing, or building model airplanes, things that took so much concentration that whatever else was going on in your life didn't matter; bad stuff just melted away during the time it took to complete the task.

Movement. Something shimmered about a hundred yards from our position and I zeroed, waiting for whatever it was to move again so I could make sure I hadn't imagined it. We squeezed our triggers at the same time and twin lines of tracers reached into the darkness, some of the fléchettes bouncing off concrete to go spinning wildly into the night. Whoever that Russian had been, he was dead now, and it felt good.

I spent the rest of my watch like that, staring at the Russian positions, knowing that one of them had died and praying for another one to show up to give me something to do. I never met the guy who replaced my kid, but it didn't matter. Killing, for the moment, was the only thing on my mind.

When the attack finally started, it came on one of the most beautiful days of the war, an especially crisp fall afternoon that carried the hint of burning charcoal from the Russian lines, which drove us crazy, because we had just been put on half rations to conserve our food supply. The charcoal reminded everyone of cookouts. Not only that, but Pops must have been roasting something, because on top of the charcoal was the smell of burning meat, which wafted through the observation post and tortured us to the point where some people buttoned up whether they were exposed or not—just to keep the smell away.

On that day I shared the post with two others, a Marine corporal and an Army private. The corporal sighed and slumped down from the viewing slit so he could face me.

"When will they hit us?"

"How old are you?" I asked. I didn't need to; I heard it in his voice, but I mentally flinched anyway, wondering why it was that all the kids found their way into my post.

"Fifteen."

"Did you have to get your parents' permission or something?"

"Nah, not for the draft, but I wanted this and would have volunteered if I needed to."

"A fifteen-year-old corporal? You're an idiot."

The other one sat beside him. A helmet hid the private's face but he sounded about the same age, and I imagined cheeks covered with pimples, maybe a little peach fuzz. "Screw that. We need the metals. Where I come from, they shut down a bunch of electronics factories, and people can't find jobs. They needed *us*. To stop the Russian aggression."

"They don't need you. They need about a million genetics, an army of betties, and maybe then we'd be OK."

"You're an asshole," the corporal said.

My mind warned me to shut up—some part of it that could still compute and realized that these two weren't worth it. But that wasn't going to happen, because my chest needed to vent before I puked in frustration.

"Maybe. Maybe I'm all asshole, I don't know, but I *do* know that you won't live to see sixteen and that I don't even remember sixteen. And I know that there wasn't any Russian aggression; there was just us, and we pushed over into Popov's territory, and now your propaganda is totally for shit. Does your ass itch yet—from the tube? Mine does. The last time I saw a medic, he said that everyone's ass is infected, and just to rub my suit against a wall as hard as I can, but that won't get it, man, because my ass itches on the inside."

The private began to sound angry. "Screw you. If old men like you hadn't messed up in the first place, we wouldn't be here. How old are *you*?"

"Twenty-eight."

"Wow," said the corporal. "That's old."

The pressure in the bunker shifted slightly and I felt the skin on my neck go cold, just before I shouted at them to get down. It shook the ground when the shells hit. Plasma rounds impacted all around the bunker, filling it with an otherworldly glow that shifted from one color to the next, and when I risked a glance, I saw streamers of hot gas snake in through the viewing slits, playing against the ceiling to leave blackened patterns. I don't know which one started it, but within a moment both the kids were screaming and one yelled that he couldn't breathe. It was probably true. My suit temperature indicator leapt into the yellow zone and a blinking light popped on to let me know that it had switched to the emergency oxygen supply because the plasma had sucked up all the air.

"Cry on, idiots!" I yelled, and then started laughing. "This is what you wanted, boys. Isn't it fantastic! Popov aggression! See what you two can do to stop it, *because I'm still waiting for the day when guys like you teach him a lesson, for the day when I can finally itch my own ass.*"

You lost track of time during moments like that. Part of it was fear. Whatever had changed in me wasn't enough to negate a primal instinct that returned unexpectedly and lodged in my throat, an almost overwhelming urge to book from the pillbox and make for the rear—anywhere but there—regardless of the fact that it would mean certain death to get caught in the open. Instead I curled, not even noticing that I had done it until long afterward, because my attention had shifted to the constant *whump-whump* of containment shells as they impacted in the fields around us. During momentary lulls, I heard the hissing of water boiling off, water that had soaked into the dirt or concrete blocks during some rainstorm that I had either missed or failed to notice.

Every once in a while the general would click in to check on me, to let me know that I should announce when the barrage was over and report in so they'd know if there was any sign of a topside infantry attack. Somehow I found a voice. It wasn't obvious if he heard my responses, but it was likely he did, because the general always clicked off with an acknowledgment.

It ended about eight hours later. The fields went quiet except for the cracking and popping of partially molten bricks, and I flicked on my chameleon skin before rising to peer through the slit. There was no sign of them.

A group of three Marines popped in, shutting the door behind them, and I wasted no time, slapping one of the kids on my way out.

"Let's go."

The corporal started to get up and then stopped, glancing at his friend. "What's wrong with him?"

A plasma tendril must have arced through a slit and played over the private, because his ceramic had melted, along with most of the function-control unit on his back.

"He's dead, kid. Suffocated." I grabbed the corporal by the shoulders and kicked him in the rear, forcing him toward the door, which he barely remembered to open.

It was slow going. Some of the trench works had collapsed during the barrage, so we had to slide out and into the rubble, doing our best to keep as much space between us and the Russian lines as possible. When we made it to the elevators, we popped our helmets and I saw that the corporal really was fifteen and that he was crying.

"Nothing you or I could have done," I said.

"I want to go home. This doesn't end."

The elevator dropped underneath us and I nodded. "Nope. It doesn't. But always check your emergency air bottles and make sure they're full before going on watch. Always, kid."

The kid stayed with me after that. I tried a couple of times to get rid of him, but nothing worked—not reporting him to his unit or begging his sergeant, who informed me that he had a bunch of babies and old men to look after and he'd be damned glad for me to take a few more, show them a thing or two. He had a crazy look and started calling them over, so I booked it as fast as I could, headed back to the command tunnel before the guy succeeded in saddling me with more teenagers. It was madness. At the same time, though, it made sense, because it was Kaz, after all, and the same thoughts that had once plagued me had infected these kids with some vague notion of glory and sacrifice—that maybe you could learn something through hardship and become a better person for it. Right. When I got back to the tunnel, the kid was asleep, using my carbine for a pillow, and I had to chuckle, because he looked like such a baby. The tunnel wall, wet with runoff, felt slick and cold against my head, and I slid down to start reading the emails never gotten to, wishing a moment later that I hadn't bothered.

My father was dead. Mother spelled it out like she always did, plainly and without emotion, explaining how he'd been playing golf and just keeled over from a heart attack in the middle of the afternoon a few months earlier. At first it didn't hit me. But by the third time I'd read the note, a feeling had begun to build that no matter what happened, I couldn't die in Almaty, that I had to make it out because I didn't want to wind up like my old man. Funny. Every fight we'd ever had raced through my mind, and it occurred to me that the last time he'd seen me was when I'd flicked him off because I was too high to realize that he'd been crying upon finding out about my Kaz assignment, that he wanted me to stay home. He'd been smarter than me. Always. Looking back, I realized the guy had been smarter than all of us, never missing a chance to tell me how stupid it was for someone to join the military or to have anything to do with it, always finding ways to get me jobs or get me into different schools to follow in his path. That was the bottom—the worst moment of my life—sitting in a cold tunnel while plasma shells rained topside, with a sudden realization that I wanted more than anything to get a second chance, to live, and that odds were it'd be over within the next couple of weeks. It was too late to let him know he'd been right. But this sensation of having to get home wasn't about making something up to him or my mother; this was something inexplicable, like the news had opened the throttle on an internal engine so that it revved out of control, making me feel as if something would crack if I didn't get out soon. He was dead; that was all that registered. And living was better, so being in Almaty just wasn't going to work for me anymore.

There they were again: thoughts. As if I hadn't learned my lesson, they crept in unnoticed, then ambushed me because I'd let my guard down.

The kid woke up and glanced over. "What time is it?"

"Does it matter?"

"What's wrong with you?"

I thought about it for a moment and then shook my head. "Nothing. You got any food?"

"Nah. But I'm starving. Wanna go on a run?"

"Sure."

We geared up and left. I felt better already. Food runs were the least risky of activities, because you didn't have to go topside—not at first, anyway. Not until you'd exhausted all possibilities. Over the past week I'd lost weight. It wasn't like there was a scale to tell you it had happened, but one day you woke up and realized that the undersuit wasn't tight and that the hoses and wires hung a little more loosely, rattling against the inside of the carapace whenever you moved. Hunger was a constant companion—a demanding one. The only way to forget it was to pull topside duty in the middle of one of Pop's barrages so that you'd be too scared to think about how long it had been since your last pouch, and it had gotten so bad for some that guys had started risking topside during lulls to hunt rats. And there weren't any supply drops. The Russians had taken the skies some time earlier, so no help would be given to us from the outside, and Urqhart wasn't able to work any magic on that one, his insights useless in Almaty. I hadn't seen the general that much lately, but when I did, he never smiled and almost seemed not to recognize me, so I took to avoiding him as much as possible. It was one thing to see panic on some kid's face, or on a sergeant's. It was another to see it on his.

We were on our way to one of the ration distribution points, to see if we could trade or scrounge, when the pounding overhead ended, as if someone had flicked a switch and turned off the barrage. The kid looked at me. We didn't have to say anything and both of us buttoned up as we sprinted for the elevators, meeting ten or twenty guys who had the same idea. When we got to the cars, we had to fight for room, eventually cramming ourselves into the last one.

Once we got to the surface, everyone fanned out, not bothering to check through the rubble closest to the exit, because the ground had already been covered, scrounged. The kid and I developed a system. He'd watch the skies while I crouched, occasionally stopping to lift a small block that might hide a basement or a crawl space, something unnoticed that might contain food. We worked our way through the city like that for an hour before he tapped me on the shoulder and pointed.

"What?" I asked.

"Look. That's just whacked."

The hotel was still there. It was late in the evening, so the building's shadow fell long over the rubble, and I marveled at the fact that even through all the recent barrages, the structure *still* remained much the way it had been the last time I'd seen it—albeit a little more charred. The Premier Hotel.

"I don't like this place," he said.

"Me neither."

"We should go back down into the tunnels. Pops never stops for more than an hour."

"You hungry?"

"Yeah."

I grunted. "Me too, and there's nothing in the tunnels. I say let's risk it."

"Don't you think guys have already scrounged here?"

"I think everyone thinks the same, that this place is messed up, and nobody wants to go in because it's still standing. I mean, how can something survive all this? Still, I'm too hungry to care anymore."

We went in. The hotel blocked all the noise from outside, muffling the sound of men shouting to each other in the distance until we heard almost nothing except our feet crunching on broken glass and rock. The lobby had been torched, and overhead a hole in the ceiling opened onto a hole in the ceiling above that and so on, until you saw a porthole on the sky, several stories up. A narrow set of stairs led downward.

"Should we go down?" the kid asked.

"After you."

"I don't wanna go down there."

"You hungry?"

"Yeah. I'm hungry."

I grunted again, shouldering my carbine and yanking a pistol free. "So let's go."

The stairs were wood, and I tested them before putting all my weight down, not sure if they'd support a fully loaded soldier or send us crashing to the basement below. They held. We worked our way down until the darkness triggered light amplification, and just to be safe, we switched on chameleon skins, careful to make sure that we had plenty of juice in our fuel cells. Those would go next. We already heard the whispers that fuel cell rationing would start any day, and it had almost gotten to the point where we prayed for Pops just to attack, to get it all over with.

The stairs emptied into a huge cellar, a single room about forty by forty meters filled with shelves and cabinets. Clearly others had already been there. Broken bottles covered the floor, and many of the shelves had been tossed over, shattered in someone's eagerness to get at their contents.

"There's a door," the kid said, pointing. "Over there."

"That's some door."

The back wall was solid concrete, cracked in places where the constant barrage and damage from previous battles had spalled off whole chunks. All the shelves had been pulled away except one. From that distance it was hard to tell, but it looked as though a set of shelving had been bolted to a concrete block, which itself had begun to separate from the rest of the wall to leave a thin crack, perfectly rectangular and barely visible.

We got closer and the kid laughed. "That's a freaking secret door. No shit. I've never seen one."

"Me neither."

The door wouldn't move. It opened outward and we had to move two large blocks of concrete that had fallen from the ceiling before we managed to pry a flat iron bar into the crack. Little by little it scraped open until finally we could see behind it; the kid jumped back.

"They can't hurt you," I said. "They're dead."

A vast storeroom was beyond, stretching out farther than either of us could see, and close to the door lay the bodies of three men in Russian combat armor, their helmets off and skin long since dried out, mummified. The men's cheeks had hollowed, and instead of eyes there were black holes. I inspected the door more closely and saw that it looked like someone had been pounding it from the inside with tools, and maybe bits of fingernails had become lodged in it, as if the men had tried everything they could to get out. We stepped over them to get a better look, and I switched from light amplification to normal before flicking on my helmet lamp.

The shelves in this room hadn't been disturbed, and held stacks of ingots, their metal a bright silver that shone in my lamplight despite a thin layer of dust that had settled. I picked one up. It was heavy, but not silver or platinum heavy, and at the base two Cyrillic letters, *Pe,* had been stamped. I'd seen enough Russian by now to read it.

"Rhenium. Now I know why the hotel is still here.

Pops isn't targeting it because he doesn't want to make it harder than necessary to get this stuff back."

"Screw metals."

"Whatever happened to that speech?" I asked. "You know, how your hometown needs metals to survive, and how we're here to fight Russian aggression?"

"That wasn't me; that was the other guy. And screw you too." The kid moved away from me into the darkness and a minute later yelped. "Who cares about metal? We got *food*."

I ran toward his position indicator, eventually finding him near a wall. Piles of cans rested against it, and I agreed with him that this was the more important find, so we nearly tripped over ourselves and drew knives, not even caring what the cans held. Mine was potatoes. I hesitated before popping the helmet, looking over my shoulder in the direction of the corpses before deciding that I was too hungry to care about the smell, which was true. It wasn't too bad anyway. Once I got my helmet loose, the air seemed stale and gamey, but nothing as bad as I'd experienced in the proximity of the Karazhyngyl corpse trains. It took a few minutes to pound the knife through the can's top and work it around to the point where I could pry the lid off, but soon we got a system down. Half an hour later, the kid and I looked at each other and grinned. His chin was smeared with something, which in the dim lamplight looked red.

"What have you been eating?" I asked. "Blood bags?"

"Cherries in syrup. I think I'm going to be sick."

"We can't tell anyone about this."

"I know. How are we going to hide it, though?"

"Come with me." We filled our pouches with a few

cans and then moved back toward the door, where I lifted my helmet, to aim the light for a better view.

"We can clear the other side of the door and shut it from inside. It looks like the locks are probably still working. We'll just have to hope that we don't get blocked in like they did."

"Won't anyone miss us?" he asked. The nausea must have passed, because the kid was already at work on another can.

"Are you kidding me?"

We were close enough to the surface this time that when the barrage restarted, it was almost deafening, and tiny chunks of concrete rained down from overhead, forcing us to replace our helmets. But it didn't matter. The kid had found water bags, clean, not like the reprocessed stuff we got in the tunnels, and I emptied my water tank to fill it with the good stuff, then sipped slowly from the inside of my suit while we waited. There wasn't anything to worry about. A few rounds came close, but I just knew that as long as we stuck close to Popov's rhenium, we were safe; none of them would hit the hotel. It was as near to happy as I ever came during that time in Almaty.

"How do you think they died?" the kid asked at one point.

"They didn't die of starvation," I said. "This place must seal tight, and I bet they suffocated to death."

The kid kept me sane, for two reasons. The reasons were another epiphany, one that hit me in the darkness of that hotel basement, which we had turned into our personal vomitorium after propping up the three Popov mummies so they stared at us with empty sockets from a few feet away. I lifted my head. The suit sensed my movement and flicked on light amplification, bringing the three corpses into green focus so that as I went through my thoughts slowly, methodically, it was as if the dead men listened with grim approval. First, I hadn't thought about drugs or Ox or my father or Bridgette since I'd met the kid. Not once. Why? Because he soaked up most of my time with his stupidity and didn't know shit about shit, and some unseen force made me feel responsible for teaching him everything—from the best way to strap your waste tubes tight, so they wouldn't dislodge during combat, to the proper way to ram a combat knife through joints in Russian armor. And second, was it selfless of me—was this what being generous meant? I thought about that one for a while, half expecting one of the Russian corpses to start laughing, to get up and puke on my lap, but eventually I came to the realization that it didn't matter. The motivations were meaningless. What mattered was that regardless of whether I wanted to, I was helping someone who had the same goal as me—to stay alive, to make it out—and that act alone had somehow brought with it a measure of grace. If the kid had been hiding drugs, I might have taken them from him. Who knew what I would have done? But he hadn't tried zip, didn't even drink, so it all played out the way it did and subdued the worst part of my mind into some kind of hypnotized state. All the bad crap was still there; being in Almaty wouldn't have helped anyone as far gone as I was to get sane again. But for now it had gone dormant.

The kid stirred and sat up. "What time is it?"

"The barrage is still going, and my chrono is messed. What does yours say?"

The kid pulled his helmet on. "It's midnight."

As soon as he said it, the impacts stopped, sending us back into the tomblike quiet of the basement, and I felt a chill at the realization that the artillery had stopped at such an exact time. I jumped to my feet.

"Let's go."

"What's going on?" he asked. "I thought we were staying here."

"Let's go."

I felt it in my groin first, a kind of fear that forced its way up into my stomach and then my chest, tightening everything so that I fumbled my way through the door, pausing only for as long as it took both of us to make sure the door wouldn't lock once we pushed it shut—in case we wanted back in. The kid scattered rubble to hide the scrape marks, and then we booked up the stairs and back into the hotel.

A loud thump made us duck before I realized what it was.

"That's outgoing."

"Shit."

I glanced out one of the lobby windows and in the distance saw the flash from our guns, the few that had survived the constant threat of artillery and air bombardment, and then watched to the east as plasma flashed; it was too far to see the impact, but I saw the blinking lights against the sky. Then the radio, which had played only static a moment before, cleared, and everything went to hell.

"They're coming," I said.

"Who's coming?"

"Popov." The kid just stood there, his carbine muzzle

scraping the floor as he stared at me. "What?" I asked. "Did you think he was just going to let us sit here all fall, all winter?"

"I don't want this."

I knew where the kid was going, and his hands started trembling so that he could barely grip the Maxwell. I grabbed him by the arm and pulled.

"Don't think about it. Let's get to the command tunnel and find out what's going on."

I kept him moving. Negotiating Almaty's rubble during the day was hard enough, but making it through at night—even with light amplification—was worse, and you always risked falling into some unseen hole or shaft, never to be seen or heard from again. It took forever. By the time we got close to the outer trench line, we heard the shouts of men as they filed out from the tunnels below, taking positions to get ready for whatever came next.

We passed a tank that was still in one piece, and its commander hung from the turret hatch, leaning over to adjust one last bit of rubble. I called up to him.

"What's going on?"

"We got about two hundred thousand inbound infantry, ten thousand vehicle targets, and an unknown number of air contacts. They're all headed this way."

"From the north?"

He sounded astonished, like I could *be* so stupid. "From every direction, dumb-ass." He dropped into his vehicle and shut the hatch.

"I don't want this," the kid repeated.

"Nobody wants it. It just is."

The elevators had already gone down by the time we worked our way through the main entry ramp, weaving through a sea of men whose faces—if we could have seen them—would have been a portrait of everything I felt. How could I have been so crazy, to wish for the attack to happen? Already I missed the hunger and boredom, cursing myself for having been even more stupid than the tanker had thought, for not having enjoyed the past few weeks for what they'd meant: that we were alive. Finally the elevators came and we waited for the soldiers to disembark before pushing our way on.

When we got to the command post, it was almost empty, manned only by a few men in orange coveralls who monitored seismic stations.

"They coming underground?" I asked.

One shook his head. "We're tracking a group of hits that might be borers, but their tunneling ETA is something like two days out. Plenty of time. Topside is another story."

"Where's General Urqhart?"

"Airfield."

The kid and I had popped our lids, and looked at each other before putting them back on, retracing our steps to the elevators. This time, it was going to be nearly impossible to move aboveground.

Topside, the rubble fields lit up with Russian plasma, and it was the closest I had been without being under some kind of cover, without closing my eyes and hiding from the full spectacle of its destructive power. Shells actually came in slowly enough that you could see them. Plasma rounds arced overhead as bright streaks that smeared upon impact before expanding into huge inverted bowls of bright light, like jellyfish that appeared out of nowhere and then vanished almost as quickly as they came. It took me a moment to hear the screams. Then I realized that the kid was screaming and that we had frozen there, like idiots, exposed and protected only by the walls of the entry ramp. I grabbed him and we moved out.

There were no trenches traversing the city, and it would have been smarter to go back down and take the long way, moving from tunnel to tunnel and circumnavigating the city underground, but I couldn't stomach the thought. Anything could happen during the time it would take. By the time we popped up near the airfield, Pops might have already overrun, and we'd be dead the moment we stepped into air.

"Keep moving," I said to the kid, half dragging him from rubble pile to rubble pile. *"Move it!"*

"This is total bullshit."

"Think of it as a party."

I barely heard him when a plasma round impacted nearby, but the kid said something like "You're a nut job," and I laughed.

"Why do we have to find the general?" he asked.

That stopped me. It took me a second to figure it out, and when I did, it wasn't clear if the answer made any sense, but it was the only one I had.

"I don't know. Something tells me we have to find him."

To the kid's credit, it was enough. He followed me now, so I didn't have to pull him along, and we dove under blocks of concrete whenever the scream of shells came too close, waiting for the heat to wash over us and remind us that soon we'd belong to Popov. Without a working chronometer, I had no idea of the time. But eventually we made it to the western perimeter of the airfield, just as the sun had begun to turn the sky pink, and I slid into a trench, grabbing the first guy I saw.

"Where's the general?" I asked.

"Who?"

"General Urqhart, where is he?"

The guy didn't look at me but raised his arm slowly, eventually pointing at an underground entry ramp about a hundred meters east of our position. The ground was completely open. I gave the kid the thumbs-up, and we leapt from the hole at the same instant a plasma round landed in it. My only thoughts were realizations that I had suddenly become airborne and that I had been there before, a long time ago, when I'd first met Bridgette. I landed in the open. It took a moment to get my bearings and regain my wind, but when I finally did, I saw the kid next to me, pulling the remains of his helmet from his head, his hair singed off and eyebrows gone.

"Am I OK?" he asked.

"Yeah. No hair, though."

"What about my face, *is it burned*?"

I heard the panic in his voice and I wanted to joke about it but decided he might lose it completely if I did. "No, kid. You're fine."

We made it to the ramp in less than a minute and dove down, rolling to the bottom before allowing ourselves to breathe.

Russian forces had broken through to the south. The general grinned at me from his chair as he typed commands into a keypad or barked orders into his headset, and he looked like a gnome in green armor, the vision hood lending him a kind of ancient-aviator appearance. The whole scene seemed out of place. I'd never seen him this happy.

Now that there was fighting to do, the old man I remembered was back, and he chewed so hard on his cigar that the end fell from his mouth, severed.

"Oscar, you dirty bastard, got any weed?"

"No, sir. I quit."

He paused to yell into his headset before responding. "Well, ain't that the shit. Good for you. Best thing that could have happened—well, *almost* the best thing; I've got something better."

"What, General?"

"You want to get out of here? Go to Tashkent and link up with the last of our retreating units before they head for Bandar?"

I didn't know what to say. The general's grin went even wider when he saw the look on my face; he snapped his fingers twice, and an Air Force sergeant appeared from nowhere. Neither of them could have known how the question twisted me. I felt my knees begin to tremble, and only then did I realize how much effort it had taken to push the fear down, bottle it up so that I could accomplish the simplest tasks, like walking and breathing. For a moment I felt as though I'd faint.

"Sergeant," the general said, "how long until the autodrone arrives?"

"Five minutes, sir. It's inbound now at Mach three."

I cleared my throat, finally finding my voice. "Sir, what are you talking about?"

"You and your boyfriend." He pointed at the kid. "I'm asking if you want to get out of here. Command wants me to evacuate, leave my boys in Almaty and hightail it out on an evac-drone so Popov will get his hands on one less general. I say to hell with that. I'm staying."

And that was why his men loved the guy. You saw it in the sergeant: a kind of worship as he listened to the general, a look that transcended all the dirt and crap that had affixed to the man's face, turning it from something that resembled a bearded lump of charcoal to the face of a cherub.

"Sergeant, the drone can hold two, right?"

He nodded. "Yes, sir. And if these two won't take it, count me in."

"Ha! My ass. If I stay, you stay." He turned back to me and stopped smiling. "Well? What do you say?"

I looked at the kid. You'd think this would be an easy decision, but it wasn't. The thought of bugging out and leaving everyone behind, especially the general, had instilled a feeling in me that sent tendrils throughout my brain and underscored the sense that deep down I was a coward—that by escaping I'd prove it to everyone. But then the memory of my father came back.

"Thank you, sir," I said. "Yeah. I want to get out of here."

"Don't thank me yet. The drone still has to make it through Pop's defenses—there's a reason we don't use airborne assaults and helicopters anymore—and for all I know, you'll be shot down before you get ten feet off the airstrip. But hell. It's worth a shot."

I shit you not: the kid dropped his carbine and hugged the general, breaking into a tantrum with no sign of stopping.

"Oscar," the general said before extending his hand. "The sergeant will show you guys where to wait."

I took it. There wasn't anything to say, and the only thing to do was stare at the guy and shake his hand, knowing deep down that I'd never see him again.

"Thanks, sir."

"Don't thank me. Just tell your catamite to stop hump-
ing my leg and we'll call it even."

We waited at the entry ramp and crouched against a wall;
the airfield was a mess. It was hard to imagine how a
drone would land on the strip, which had become pockmarked by shallow plasma craters and dotted with the
wreckage of supply drones that had tried to land over the
past few weeks only to get shot down. A stream of tracers
shot past, and I flinched at the snaps. The sergeant gave us
updates every once in a while and he was trying to be cool
about it, like it would help, but the constant reminder
ratcheted up the tension every time. It was almost over.
Not at any other time in Kaz had I been that scared, knowing that whatever happened, it would probably take place
in the next thirty minutes, and either we'd be killed or
we'd make it out. The kid wasn't talking. He just sat there,
staring at the runway and clutching his carbine to his
chest like it was some kind of security blanket. Safety was
in reach, and the fact that it was out there, waving to us,
made it that much harder to accept that irony could rear
its head in a second and swat down the promise of escape
just as quickly as it had materialized. When the drone
screamed overhead, barely clearing the ramp's roof, we
both jumped up and the sergeant had to grab us.

"*Not yet.* The drone will land from the far end and taxi
this way. When I give the word, you break cover and
sprint, but keep your heads down."

"How far?" I asked, but the volume of fire suddenly
increased, drowning my words.

"What?"

"How far will we have to run?"

"About a hundred meters. When the doors pop, you guys will have about thirty seconds to embark; it leaves whether you make it on or not."

My jaw started working, chewing at the insides of my cheeks so that I could keep my teeth from chattering. Our drone had turned into a black dot in the distance and it would have been nearly impossible to see except for the tracers that reached up from Russian positions, pointing to it with lines of red light. When it turned for the approach, it got steadily larger, a gray speck that was slightly darker than the sky and grew with each second until it touched down at the runway's far end in a puff of dust. The aircraft sped down the strip, heading straight for us, and I had the strangest sensation, as though it was a shark with wings. When it got close enough, the sergeant slapped my shoulder.

"That's it. Good luck!" And he left.

The kid and I leapt to our feet at the same time and sprinted. I didn't hear anything, because all my attention was focused on the drone, which had already begun a slow turn, its autonomous computer ticking by the seconds that it had been told were allowed on the ground. It felt as though every Russian gun had been trained on it. Plasma rounds began bursting on the strip, and I noticed the temperature indicator leap all the way from green to red at the same time a shock wave hit, hard enough that I almost fell into the kid and knocked both of us down. And still there wasn't any noise. All I heard was my own breathing and my whispers as I urged myself to run faster.

The kid outpaced me. I watched in horror when a portion of the drone's side cracked open, and thought that

it had begun to break apart, but it was just the door opening, and the kid slid in, turning to beckon as the craft
began rolling. I was still at least twenty meters away. The
next thing I knew, he had grabbed my wrist and pulled me
inside, just before the door sealed shut, locking us into a
narrow space that was barely wide enough for two and
uncomfortably similar to a coffin.

"Are we supposed to buckle in?" he asked.

"I don't know." I found a set of straps and lay flat on
my back, struggling to get my arms through without tan-
gling in the Maxwell. "We should have left our damn carbines on the runway."

"Holy shit. Look out the window."

There was a small porthole-style piece of glass near
my face, and I turned to get a better view as the drone
picked up speed. The ground flashed by. At first I didn't
know what the kid was talking about, but then saw it:
lines of soldiers had made a break for it, hoping to get on
the drone too and sprinting across the runway despite the
exposure. A flash of light made me blink. When I opened
my eyes, I saw the fading gas of a plasma hit and then a
group of blackened bodies where a second earlier there
had been about fifty guys.

"That's really screwed," the kid said.

"It doesn't matter."

"They're all going to die, how can that not matter?"

The plane began to lift off and then pulled up sharply
at the same time its engines roared. It felt as though my
weight had quadrupled.

"It was either you or them, that's why it doesn't matter.
You got parents?"

"Yeah."

"Ask them when you get home; ask them what you should have done. Screw those guys. We're going to be OK."

Don't ask me how I knew, but I did; we'd make it. When the drone banked to the southwest, its maneuver was so gentle that it felt as though I'd made it aboard a passenger plane, and I risked another look out the window. Maybe it was a hallucination—one last flashback to my drugged days or a spurt of insanity that just came with the territory of being a broken toy—but I'd have sworn that someone waved to us from the airfield below, a tiny figure in dark green armor that puffed smoke every once in a while before he disappeared underground. In the distance I saw the line of Russian armor and infantry, crawling slowly over our northern trenches like a wave of ants and beetles. The drone banked violently again. I grunted, trying my best to keep from passing out as it evaded some unseen attack, and without anything to focus on, there was only one thing to do: think.

We'd made it out. The acceptance of that felt as though every muscle in my body relaxed at the same time, and without anything bearing down on me, I started crying. So many men. But I'd meant it when I'd said screw them. It wasn't them I was crying about; it was the general and the fact that he'd made this happen—and that I hadn't really gotten a chance to thank him. A nearby explosion rattled the aircraft and shattered my thoughts just as we went into a steep dive and began rolling. A few seconds later we came out of it. The plane leveled off and its engines settled into a constant whine, each second taking us farther from Almaty and danger.

"You OK, kid?" When he didn't answer, I yelled, *"Hey!"*

"I threw up. I don't want to talk right now."

"That's all right. We're out of that shithole."

The trip to Tashkent took about an hour, and it wasn't long after we'd landed that I heard what had happened. Nobody could have lasted long without a solid defense. Most of the general's men broke and ran, but there was no place to escape, and when they got to city center, they collided with friendlies running in the opposite direction, so the Russians just stopped and pelted the city with more plasma, finishing everyone off piecemeal. Pops didn't take any prisoners. I thought at first that maybe the general had died fighting or committed suicide, but after a while doubted that anything like that had happened, or that it mattered anyway. What mattered was that he was gone and had given us a chance to keep going.

But it wasn't over yet. When the drone landed, a couple of colonels met us, and I could see the shock on their faces when we stepped out to reveal ourselves as a bearded freak and a dirt-faced kid. One of them wanted to shoot us on the spot, because he thought we'd taken the general's place. But I guess the general had uploaded one last message, which the drone transmitted as soon as we got out, and it hit their computers before they could actually do anything to us. I asked one of them to send me a copy and he did.

To the Commanding Officer, Army Group Central:
Decided to stay with my men, so take care of these
two guys for me. Urq.

The colonels left us there and we started walking from the airfield, following them toward a line of sheds.

"Well, kid, we made it."

"I gotta get out of this suit."

"Why?" I asked.

"Because of the puke. Plus my hoses came off when the plane maneuvered. It's a mess in here."

"Hell. *That's* the smell of accomplishment."

SIX

Enter the Cockroach

The main body of Army Group Central had fallen back to Bandar a long time ago, and the forces we linked with in Tashkent formed a rear guard—elements of First Marine combined with the French Foreign Legion's First Cavalry Regiment. The difference between Tashkent's units and the men in Almaty was palpable. There was no sign of hunger in Tashkent, and anywhere you went, you'd hear guys joking, despite the fact that overall nothing had changed; we were still losing. Plasma artillery struck in a constant rhythm on the north side of the city, and to the south our guns answered almost every shot, like a steady and off-beat drum. You didn't need any other reminder that things were still bad. The biggest difference was that we didn't need to watch the air anymore, but old habits were hard to break, and I lost track of the number of times I caught myself staring at the sky or flinching at the sound of overhead drones.

The morning after our arrival, a French lieutenant kicked me and the kid awake as we slept under a concrete slab; I had trouble with the guy's accent.

"Marines?" he asked.

"No. We're not attached to any unit yet."

"Good. The French and stragglers will lead our fall-back on Samarkand, so get up. You'll be with us."

"What?" The lieutenant's voice came through helmet speakers, and while we spoke, our combat suits danced their thing, linked up coms so that in the middle of it I started hearing him over my speakers but with a delay. That, the accent, and my exhaustion made him all but incomprehensible.

"*Samarkand*. We're going to Samarkand. Get up and come with us."

"Why Samarkand?"

"Almaty is finished now, and the Russians move west out of Uzbekistan to flank us. They arrive tomorrow. Get up."

As I understood it, the French had joined us for a percentage of the mining take, and I wondered how much they had gotten out of the deal, how it compared with the men and equipment they'd lost, but when the kid and I fell in, those thoughts evaporated. We loaded into the back of a medical APC and strapped in while Legionnaires pushed on board, searching for a seat. Their armor was basically the same as ours, with slight differences in structure and markings, and while I listened, I noticed the variety of accents; some men were British, and a couple spoke to each other in Chinese. The medic got on last and supervised the loading of a bank of stretchers. It resembled a rolling bunk bed with seven racks stacked on top of each other, and slid into a locking mechanism down the center of our compartment so that we had to pull our legs back and tuck our knees into our chests to make room.

You tried not to look but couldn't *not* look. One of the wounded, a guy in the bottom rack, seemed fine; he didn't have any bandages and rested his head on one arm while he pulled on a cigarette.

The kid elbowed me. "What's wrong with him?"

"How should I know?"

A British Legionnaire next to us chuckled and then kicked the wounded guy's leg, making him jump. "*Cafard*. Nothing but *cafard,* you loafing sack. No wounds, no problems, just a coward."

"Screw you." The one in the bottom rack stubbed out his cigarette and then buried his face in both hands before he started sobbing, mumbling something in French.

"What's '*cafard*'?" the kid asked.

"The cockroach," I said, remembering the word from one of my encounters with the Legion before meeting Ox, and the Brit popped his helmet, nodding after he took it off.

"He knows. Your friend knows. Everyone here should know the cockroach; he's a nasty little thing that slips under your skin while you're not looking and nibbles away until one day you notice that something is missing, but you can't quite figure it out. You know that what you're looking for was there the day before, safe and sound. And so you start looking for it, thinking about it. Then other things go missing. But you can't figure those out either, and it gets worse, because now you're not missing one thing, you're missing several, and it grows on itself, an infection that races out of control, multiplying at a geo-metric rate. Those are the cockroaches, you see, breeding. Infesting. *Le Cafard*."

"Oh." The kid thought about it for a moment, and I saw

his face go red as the guy in the rack kept sobbing. "Can't you shut him up? Why does he have to be with us?"

The entire compartment erupted into laughter at that. Even I laughed, without knowing why. The kid had no idea what he'd said, but whatever it had been was perfect, and the Brit reached into a pouch to hand us cigarettes, patting the kid's cheek with affection.

"Brilliant. You're the smartest American I've met. No, we can't shut him up, for the same reason I can't scratch my head and decide that although this has been fun, I've got a train to catch or a previous engagement that I just can't miss. No, we can't get away from this one. Just ignore him. Don't let *his* cockroaches become *your* cockroaches."

I saw the look on the kid's face, one of total confusion, and paused to light my cigarette before explaining. "He speaks French; he's a native speaker."

"So?"

"So . . ." The Brit grinned at me, and I saw that three of his teeth were absent, the gaps noticeably black, making him look almost as crazed as the one on the bottom bunk. "Go on," the Brit said. "Tell him. This one is young, he needs to *learn*."

"So native Frenchmen can't join the Legion unless they're officers. This guy's an officer. Which makes it worse, because he's cracked up, and since he's an officer, nobody here can get rid of him; they're all enlisted."

"Exactly!"

But before the British guy could say anything more, the APC roared to life, and its rattling shook my teeth, making it hard to concentrate on anything but keeping my head off the bulkhead so I wouldn't shake my way into a concussion. The vehicles ran on alcohol. A plasma-based engine sat dormant as a backup, but only to be used in emergencies, because it robbed the main gun of its ammunition. Comfort was the last thing promised by an APC, and as we began to roll slowly on eight wheels, every bump translated into a jolt that shocked my entire spine, and soon the compartment filled with the smell of fuel alcohol, making it harder to breathe—especially with all the smoke. Someone opened the main vent, which improved the air slightly, and I was about to doze off when the British guy caught my attention again.

"Where are you lads from?"

"The States."

"Not that. I mean have you been in Tashkent the whole time?"

I shook my head. "No. We were in Almaty."

The crazy look left his face then. While before he had worn a constant grin that seemed only to get wider with time, his face now transformed into a network of lines with a look of infinite, somber understanding.

"Bad luck, that."

Retreating forces before us had transformed the northern outskirts of Samarkand into a defensive paradise, and I realized that over time I had become unable to see towns, and might not have recognized one for what it was. It wasn't that I'd studied warfare. Instead it had poured over me for the past years, fully submerged my consciousness into a broth of screaming and blood so that theories had infiltrated through my pores, soaked into my DNA to the point where instead of Uzbek villages I saw fortifications, fields of fire, and cover potential. Uzbekistan even had real people in its towns who occasionally ventured out of their basements to sell or beg. But at the same time, these *weren't* people; they were possible insurgents or, at best, noncombatants, and nothing about them triggered pity, let alone the sensation that they and I belonged to the same species. One child approached the kid and me when we disembarked from the APC, and as I stretched, the kid started gabbing in Russian, holding out his hand so that within a few seconds word must have gotten out to the other Uzbek children that these were new faces, new pockets, a new source of handouts. Instantly a crowd of them surrounded us, and I leveled my carbine at them.

"Get the hell away from me."

"Easy," the kid said. He muttered something in Russian and the children scattered.

"You speak Russian?"

"Kind of. My mom and dad were from Lviv, Ukraine. It's close enough so they get it. I'm surprised after all this time that they still speak Russian here."

A new sensation of respect crept in, and I grinned. "What are you, smart? How do you know about Uzbek history, or what they should or shouldn't be speaking?"

"Just lucky, I guess."

"Come on," I said. "Let's get going."

"Where?"

"We aren't attached to any unit. I wanna see if there's an airfield and check if we can get a flight out to Bandar. I'm done with this crap."

It had only just occurred to me: neither the kid nor I belonged with the Legion, and it might be possible to get out sooner than I had hoped. The dream of escaping seemed so far-fetched that I almost didn't want to think about it, but at the same time, it was irresistible, and as we walked quickly toward the nearest village with a renewed sense of purpose, I thought of little else. The Legion troops, who now headed in the same direction on foot, ignored us.

Units at Tashkent had done their job of holding back Popov so well that they had given retreating engineers more than enough time to build up this, our fallback position, which really encompassed the tiny villages of Bo'ston, Pahtakor, and Jizzakh, with the city of Samarkand at its center. As soon as we passed the outer markers, I felt a sense of calmness that I hadn't felt in a long time. Nothing would get through all this. The outer ring consisted of deep concrete-lined trenches with evenly spaced—and sealed—bunkers, and police units guided everyone through a narrow path marked with tape so that we wouldn't step on any mines. We sensed the tunnels below. And we saw the tops of sentry robots, their emplacements causing them to resemble infinite rows of mushrooms, three deep and widely spaced.

Inside the perimeter there were even more civilians. Lines of them formed at stations where French soldiers handed out food or doctors examined Uzbek children, and as we passed in a group, a long line of Legion troops falling back from Tashkent, the people stared at us. But their looks were not of hatred. The looks were empty, emotionless, as though the Uzbeks were merely curious, the same way you'd be curious about a snake while you tried to figure out whether it was poisonous.

Closer to the center of town, we passed a huge parade field that had been enclosed by dual fences, one inside the other, and each barrier had been topped with multiple rows of razor wire and laced with electrified lines. I stopped. The kid stopped too and we watched as the girls inside knelt and prayed, or exercised, or stood motionless inside the fence, looking back. They all had hair, and unsure of what to do in the face of such beauty, I felt my insides begin to churn.

"What's up?" the kid asked. "They're just genetics."

"Yeah, but the fences."

"Maybe they're under arrest or something."

An engineer heading toward the outer perimeter overheard us and stopped. "They're past their service term. Command told us not to wipe them yet, because we might need them when it comes time to fall back into Iran."

"Which way to the airfield?" asked the kid.

The engineer pointed to the south, shouting over the Legionnaires who kept marching past, all around us now. "Keep on this road and then head south on M-39. You can't miss it, but it's a hike. You'll pass through Pahtakor and it'll be on the right."

The kid and I pressed on south through the town, which, once I saw past the people, struck me as ancient. Our group passed an old stone structure, outside of which sat old men, Uzbeks, dressed in cloth uniforms and holding rifles while they glared. Behind them the building rose from flat ground, and a deep blue dome capped it, so colorful that it made me remember things other than the war, a time when the sky had actually mattered for something besides the threats it sometimes held. This was the east. The men and whatever building they guarded made me feel suddenly out of place and foreign, because it was clearly holy and we trespassed here, unwanted. Our column, us and all the Legion troops, fell silent and we stared back at the men, but I didn't know what the others were thinking, and in an instant a feeling grew that I was a guest who had overstayed his welcome; it became all the more important to get to the airfield as soon as we could, or I might shoot the Uzbeks out of fear.

Outside the village the land was still flat, and I popped my helmet to feel the cold air of late fall, to smell the dusty wind that carried a stink of ore processing. I saw the cloud, not too far away. Even in our retreat, even when we were digging graves or latrines, the rocks and dirt didn't go to waste; they waited in huge piles to be sucked dry of trace metals, anything that might, in turn, be fed into electronics or machines back home. In the quiet I heard it. Somewhere to our west, massive grinders crushed the rock that engineers had removed in digging our tunnels, after which it would be conveyed into the leaching shed and bathed in acid solutions to coax out the important stuff before discarding a poisonous sludge. When we left, what then? I imagined the Uzbek children playing in our abandoned tunnels—some kind of I-dare-you-to-go-as-far-as-you-can game in the darkness—armed with only a candle or a flashlight, going into the deep, where some or all of them might fall into a shaft and never see the light of day again. *Screw them.* I'd paid whatever price was required to walk through this awful country, and if those old men wanted to glare at passing soldiers, they could do it all day, all year, and their children could rot in hell.

When I came back to the present, I realized that we had moved onto the closest thing Uzbekistan had to a highway, and our column of troops stayed on the shoulder, allowing huge APCs to lumber past in either direction; an occasional tank passed, with its commander hanging lazily from the turret and waving. They were all Legion—and happy. How was it they could be happy? I had been in Kaz for longer than I could remember, and surely some of them had been there as long, but few seemed to feel the same weight I did, and most walked easily, actually chatting. Each of the Legion troopers had a white stripe around the top of his helmet, and my brain screamed that it remembered the stripe's significance, but no matter how hard I tried, I couldn't recall the reference. The memory had been trapped, immobilized in the now-crystalline structure that was once my mind. There were no more stories from the past, recollections of my days as a reporter; there was only now.

"Why does the Legion have a white stripe around their helmets?" the kid asked, and I nearly laughed.

"I have no idea."

"How much farther to the airstrip?"

"I have no idea."

But it wasn't much farther. We marched through Pahtakor, where the column thinned considerably as Legion sergeants—with black stripes instead of white—waved many of the men off the road and into positions, while allowing some to continue southward. It got lonely after Pahtakor. Those of us still on the road heard the wind more loudly now, and in such a flat place, without other troops surrounding you, you felt cold and exposed. But eventually we found the airfield and turned onto its access road.

On our way in, a stream of ambulances—commandeered local trucks that held wounded in their beds—roared toward us. The last one stopped and a doctor stepped from the driver's seat.

"You two, you're not Legion?" His accent sounded awful, French, and a cigarette barely clung to his lower lip.

"No."

"Are you assigned to the airstrip?"

"No."

"Come with me; we can use your help at the hospital in the city."

I shook my head, trying to fight off the feeling that we were about to miss our chance to get out. "I'm not going to the city, Doc. The kid and I are out on the next plane."

"No planes are taking out troops, not even wounded; we just came from there. Only airdrops for supplies from now on, and wounded will be evacuated on the ground. Help me."

We flinched at the sounds of detonations from the strip and watched as ten huge gray clouds mushroomed into the air; it was like watching a dream demolished. Engineers, I realized. They had just blown the strip, cratered it so that once we left Uzbekistan, no Popov units would be able to use it—not without major repairs.

I glanced at the kid. "Hop in."

"What? Why?"

"Because." I got in the back and the doctor seemed satisfied, returning to the front seat and waiting for the kid as he climbed aboard. "We're not getting out this way, and at least the hospital is in the right direction. South. The Marines will be here soon, after they disengage at Tashkent, and we'll see what we can do then."

One bit at a time, fragments of my brain put themselves back in place. I didn't notice it at first. It was kind of like returning from a long trip, so long that by the time you got back, you had forgotten that your apartment was *that* small or that in fact the front door wasn't painted dark blue; it was more like an aqua color, with maybe a little purple. It was good news and bad news. The fear of Almaty passed, and I began to see things clearly again and remembered what I had done the day before or even the week before, and every once in a while, I would laugh because the kid said something stupid or funny. On the other hand, the new clarity brought Bridgette. And people reminded me of my father or of Ox, and in those moments all I wanted to do was score, dig in, and cover myself with a pile of sandbags that had been filled with drugs so that I could go back to those days when my mind consisted of little more than goo.

The kid kept me from going back, though. He'd gotten jittery—even more jittery than me—and wouldn't go anywhere unless I went with him, because he was convinced that someone would scope in and notice that he wasn't with his unit and try to attach him to a fighting outfit. They probably would, too. But it wasn't like latching on to me would prevent that from happening, and I explained to the kid that we didn't use tickets anymore, so every time we came within broadcast range of a logistical server, it checked our suit assignments and would figure it out whether I was with him or not. He'd just shake his head. "You don't get it, man" was all he'd say, and he'd shake his head again. "You don't get it. You're my lucky charm."

The doc had put us to work as soon as we got into the city, and gave us a place to sleep in the hospital basement, which was perfect. During the day, we did rounds and emptied bedpans, and one day we even got to shed our filthy

suits for clean, new blue pajamas. The doctor asked me if I
wanted to shave, and I asked if it meant I'd have to use a
mirror, and he looked at me like I was nuts, which I was,
and he said, "Of course. How else would you shave?"
I didn't want a mirror because I was afraid of seeing how
I'd changed, of being reminded that I really existed. In the
end he found a local barber and brought him in to clean me
up. I don't know how it looked, but it felt new. Sparkly.

One day the doc called me into his office. The Marines
had arrived the day before, and so far there had been no
sign of Popov, although everyone knew he'd be on his way
after consolidating in Tashkent. The kid followed me in
and sat on the floor.

"I have a problem," the doc said.

"Maybe we can help."

"A man came to me yesterday and asked for me to
handle what he called a special project. They've already
annexed a building next door, and Marine engineers have
almost finished preparing the operating rooms and labo-
ratory so that they'll all have adequate security."

I took a cigarette he offered, and tried to hide the fact
that as soon as he'd said "special project," my hands had
begun to shake. "Why the security?"

"Look…" He paused to light it for me and then tossed
the lighter to the kid. "That's just it. In America, this
wouldn't be a problem, or in an American unit, but I'm
not American and neither is my staff, half of whom are
Uzbeks. You're used to these things. We are not."

"Maybe you better tell me what's going on."

"I will show you."

The doctor stood and ushered us from his office, leading us down the front steps and into the street, where the

wind bit through our thin clothes and made me shiver. We moved quickly. The next structure over had been an apartment building of some kind, and when we stepped through the door, a pair of Marines stood and asked for identification. I didn't have any, and neither did the kid. Ours was stored in our suit computers, but the doctor held out a card, which the two men scanned, and then he vouched for us. We headed up the stairs nearby, climbed three flights, and then pushed through a pair of double doors into a wide room that looked as though it had once been an entire floor of apartments, whose walls had been completely ripped out.

"This," the doc said, "is my problem."

What got me first wasn't the sight; it was the smell. The room was filled with steel cages about ten feet by ten feet, inside of which had been placed beds, and on most of these lay a genetic. I went numb. The place smelled as though someone had died, and it had been long enough since I'd smelled anything like it that I felt sick.

"What the hell is this?" the kid asked.

The doctor looked angry. "This is what they've given me to handle. Command asked my staff to oversee medical for the rear-guard task force, which I gladly did. But now your Marines want to save these girls and put them on the line again—girls who have gone beyond their shelf life and who are literally rotting alive. Look."

He pointed to the nearest cage, and I didn't want to look but forced myself to, then wished immediately afterward that I hadn't. Bridgette sat on a bed. Her fingers had gone black and she had a vacant look on her face, as though she wasn't seeing anything clearly or maybe wasn't seeing anything at all.

"These are abominations. It's one thing to field combat robots or plasma or any one of the millions of weapons we have, but it's another to play God. I don't want these girls here. My staff doesn't want to come near them."

I cleared my throat. "What do you want us to do?"

"*You* take care of them."

"We're not doctors," the kid said. "There's nothing *we* can do."

"*Oui,* yes. You can do something. You can handle the daily routine, monitor things for me, you can clean their beds, and Marines will help provide security in the event that something goes wrong."

I fought asking the question, but it came out anyway, like someone else had taken over my brain. "Why don't they just shoot them?"

"Samarkand is not just another defense," the doc explained. "Samarkand is where we have to convince the Russians to come no further; it's where we have to bloody them so badly that they won't take another step toward Bandar. What happens if we hold them for a while and then run but don't cripple them?"

"They follow us all the way, and we never make it out," I said.

"Correct. So the Marines have tasked me to find a way to reverse the girls' spoiling, to stop the rot and give them additional life in the field, where they can do the most damage to Russian forces. Every weapon is needed. We have four thousand genetics at the point of discharge, one thousand *beyond* their discharge, and we need them fielded for at least another few months. Perhaps less."

"Can't our scientists just give you some kind of magic formula?" I asked. "To reverse everything?"

"Maybe. Maybe they could." He took a long drag and then flicked his cigarette at the closest cage, where the butt burst into sparks. "But they won't. The Marine general is doing this against orders, so even if he asked for the proper medications, none would be delivered. And one more thing—if you do this for me, and I succeed in reversing their problems, I'll do everything in my power to try and get a plane in here; I'll make sure you two are the first on board, for home."

The room went quiet then, and I noticed some of the girls looking at us, cocking their heads in the same way she always had, and I had to get out. Why me? The new-found clarity that moments before had seemed welcome revealed a major flaw when it unleashed a wave of memories of Bridgette and her hands, which had gone over every inch of me because I was so strange to her. And yet these weren't Bridgette. These were images of her, exact replicas that wouldn't replace anything and only reminded me of what couldn't be had.

I looked at the kid. He grinned, and even though he didn't say a word, I knew what he was thinking: he didn't care about them or Bridgette; he had only heard that we had a chance to get out.

"We'll do it," I said.

"Excellent! We've established a procedure for initial treatment, and some of these girls will have to be put down, because they've lost too much tissue. My staff will handle those."

"Do you have tranq tabs?"

"*Quoi?*" He shook his head. "I don't understand."

My thoughts shifted to Ox and that day we'd gotten high in the observation post. "Tranq tabs are pills, a mixture of haloperidol, fentanyl, and some kind of speed. It helps the girls with their mental crap."

"No. This I do not have, not in large quantities and what we do have is reserved for our human forces. But I might be able to work something with local drug dealers. Do you know how much, the doses?"

I shook my head, wondering if this was a good idea after all, because it would put me in proximity to my favorite drugs again. "I don't know exactly, but I know they take huge doses. Enough to make the sun rise."

We got a short reprieve from duty with the genetics the next day when the British Legionnaire found out where we were; their unit had been assigned an eastern patrol—before Popov arrived—to get a lay of the land and preestablish artillery coordinates on likely spots of cover so we could concentrate fire effectively if the Russians tried an overland assault. He had remembered that the kid spoke Russian, and they needed a translator.

"You're welcome to join us," he said to me, and I hesitated, because it wasn't an easy decision: start the job of watching Bridgette duplicates rot in cages or risk my life on a patrol with the Foreign Legion.

"I'll go." I suited up and sent a quick message to the doctor.

We loaded into a scout car with about ten other men, and they nodded to us, squeezing over to make room. The ride was bumpy. Once we left the area of downtown Samarkand, I saw that we headed north again, back toward Jizzakh, and overhead the clouds looked low and even, the temperature just right for snow. Flakes had started to fall by the time we reached the outer perimeter, and the car slowed to a stop before letting everyone out.

"Where are we?" I asked.

The Brit grinned before buttoning up. "Bo'ston. But not the Boston you're thinking of, mate. We'll head east from here to Ul'yanovo and then do a sweep a few klicks north before heading back overland."

The kid hadn't said a word all day and I clicked my gauntlet against his shoulder. "Everything cool?"

"Yeah. Cool. Fuck it."

I hadn't noticed it until then but should have. When I'd first met the kid, he'd been young still and I'd been foggy with the haze of having just come off drugs, so I'd missed the transition. It was like seeing a butterfly that the day before had been a caterpillar. The short time in Almaty and then here had begun the transformation, and the kid aged without my noticing, but when I looked at him closely, I saw it in the way he carried his carbine—not like a weapon, a separate piece of kit, but like it had grown out of his body. It was meant to be there. On one hand, it was sad to see him warped, but on the other hand, it was a necessary thing, because if we made it out and he wound up back in the world, at least he'd be alive; the warping would keep him safe. And a life twisted was better than no life at all.

"Yeah," I said. "Cool as whatever."

A fight broke out between two of the Legion guys, and one of them fell back against me, knocking me on my ass. The Brit picked me up.

"What's going on?" I asked.

"Okonkwo," he said, "a Nigerian. His term was up last week but the Legion won't let him go, say he's stuck for the duration of the war. It's part of the contract and the boy's an asshole, anyway."

Okonkwo cursed in French, and I hadn't spoken it in years but picked up some of what he said as he faced off against a sergeant.

"I'm not going. Find someone else."

"You're going or I'll shove this grenade launcher up your ass until you shit thermal gel."

Okonkwo threw another punch, which was really pointless in armor, because although he connected, the gauntlet bounced from the sergeant's helmet and left Okonkwo off balance. Within a second the sergeant had thrown him to the ground, sitting on his back before dropping his grenade launcher and pushing a fléchette pistol against Okonkwo's head.

"You're going."

"Shoot me, asshole."

"You're going."

"The Russians are out there; don't you even get it? Why do we have to scout? Can't drones do it for us?"

That got a grunt of agreement from the Brit and a couple of others, and I found myself nodding at the idea—the senselessness of sending twelve men into the unknown. Okonkwo definitely had a point.

"You're going," the sergeant repeated, holstering his sidearm and moving to let the man up.

But Okonkwo didn't move and started crying, pounding his head into a soil that had frozen solid overnight and that now started to look a grayish white from the light dusting of snow. We flinched at the boom of aircraft overhead. But the drones flew northward and were undoubtedly ours, and Okonkwo's tantrum called our attention back when he switched into his native language. Nobody said anything. The Legionnaires slung their weapons and waited, standing in a semicircle around their comrade until he finished whatever it was he was saying and rose slowly to his feet.

"Fuck this," he said.

The sergeant threw him his carbine. "Yeah, fuck it. But you're going."

"I know I'm going!"

"It's all right, mate," the Brit said to me as we started walking. We passed through the outer minefield and then spread out, leaving about ten feet between us as we marched on either side of a dirt road. "He'll be all right."

The road headed east, and with each step I began to shake more, the uneasy sensation that the Uzbek country-side was alive making it hard to concentrate. As we marched, the snow fell more thickly. I still saw the kid on my right and the Brit on my left, but beyond that things got hazy, so I had to trust my suit display, which they had synced to the Legion system before we headed out. On my heads-up, ten blue dots spread out, barely making progress toward the destination marker of Ul'yanovo.

We entered a village. According to my map, it was Zarbdor, population ten thousand, but when we moved into the streets, the narrowness forcing us to bunch a little more, the town looked to me as though it had been aban-doned. My goggles switched to a combination of visible and infrared, and in the distant haze I saw what looked like people, but they were gone before we could get close enough to see clearly, and then, before we knew it, the town ended. At one point the road curved northeast and we continued on a straight course, due east, leaving the asphalt behind.

"Why don't we stay on the road?" I asked the Brit.

"We're heading east, and then we'll hit Ul'yanovo overland from the south. We got some reports yesterday of advance Russian units moving in from Tajikistan and setting up shop."

"I didn't know there were any Russians in Tajikistan."

"Neither did we."

By now the snowstorm had turned into a blizzard. I wouldn't have blamed Okonkwo if he'd just turned and run at that point, because who the hell sent out a patrol when it was clear that the weather didn't have a chance of holding up? What did they expect us to see? The combination of a howling wind and no visibility made everyone jumpy, and just as we prepared to swing northward, I saw a shape charging at us out of the snow, and I fumbled for my carbine, flicking off the safety just in time to open fire at the same instant I yelled like a little girl.

"Contact!"

Whatever it was howled, stumbled a few steps to the side, and then keeled over in the snow. The Brit motioned for us to stay put and crawled forward, seeming to take forever to get there, until he stood and waved us on.

When I arrived, he slapped me on the back. "Goat. Nice shot, Yank."

"What?"

"You shot a goat."

Everyone laughed, even Okonkwo. But then another figure came out of the snow, this time a human, and the man stumbled forward wearing some kind of shawl and carrying an ax, which he waved at us while shouting.

The Brit pointed at the kid. "You catching any of this?"

"He's mad that we killed his goat. He wants money."

"Fuck all. Tell him if he doesn't shut up and get back inside, we'll kill the bastard."

The kid did as he was told but it didn't work and the man kept screaming until he started looking wild-eyed, so we all took a few steps back before turning and jogging northward—hoping to put some distance between us and the crime. I genuinely felt bad. For all I knew, that goat had been like a son to the old man, or his entire winter's food supply, and I'd just shot it without thinking.

Things went smoothly for a while, until I realized that we weren't making much progress, and according to my now-fixed chronometer, it would be dark soon. Then everyone stopped. The snow still fell as hard as it had for the past several hours, and the Legionnaires pulled white sleeping bags from their kits after setting up a wide circle of alarm sentries. The kid and I just stood there.

"What's wrong?" the Brit asked.

"What are you guys doing?"

"Camping. What are *you* doing?"

"I thought we were patrolling Ul'yanovo and then heading back."

The Brit laughed, then pulled the bag over his head before popping his helmet. He shielded a cigarette from the wind; it took a few tries to get it lit, but then he looked up again and smiled. "Mate. It's thirty klicks from Bo'ston to Ul'yanovo. We're good, but not *that* good. Get some rest. We'll finish the patrol tomorrow." Then he raised his voice so everyone could hear. "And, Okonkwo. They sent a patrol because drones have a hard time seeing through snow."

"Fuck you" was the only response he got.

The kid and I collapsed to the ground. Someone eventually produced extra bags for us, and we thanked him, pulling the thin tarps over our suits. The bags weren't really for warmth. But they helped with camouflage and provided at least some insulation from the wind and cold so that the suits didn't expend as much energy keeping us warm.

Before dozing off, the kid asked, "How much more of this shit is there?"

"As much as you want," I said. "Don't worry. Tonight we'll sleep, and tomorrow we'll finish with Ul'yanovo, be back in Samarkand before you know it. Easy as whatever."

I had no idea how wrong that prediction would be.

Someone shook me awake and I tried to jump up, but the bag wrapped around my feet and I fell into a snowdrift before finally coming to my senses. There was at least two feet of new snow. It was still dark but I heard the flakes blow against my helmet as if they were grains of sand, and in the green haze of night vision, I saw it was the Brit who had woken me. The kid stood next to him.

"We're moving out," the Brit said.

"What, no breakfast?"

"Eat while you march."

I didn't taste the food. We resumed our trek northward and the stuff that came out of my pouch felt cold against my cheeks, because the meal pouch had become so frozen overnight that the warming pack barely managed even to

thaw it. Everything had changed. Nobody spoke now and
the Legionnaires moved more cautiously than they had
the previous day, even though the wind and snow kept
most of our footsteps quiet. Once we reached a point
about a kilometer south of Ul'yanovo, the sergeant whispered over the radio.

"Go—" and then a French word I didn't understand.

"Chameleon," the Brit whispered for us. "Go to stealth
mode."

In the snow, the sensation of being invisible made
everything seem like a dream. Now I couldn't see even
the men closest to me, although the kid's footprints
appeared out of nowhere, and a couple of times I felt a
strange vertigo because there was no horizon and the
snow fell so hard that you lost the difference between
ground and sky. Soon the morning came, which made
everything seem more benign, and then, without warning,
we reached the outskirts of Ul'yanovo—a series of low
huts that looked as though they were partly underground.

"Who lives like this these days?" I whispered.

"Silence!" someone hissed back.

A red light popped onto my heads-up, the signal to
stop, and I lowered myself to the snow so I could bring my
carbine to bear on the closest hut. A single blue dot crept
forward. It stopped at a point that looked as though it was
just inside the line of structures, and then my red light
flashed green, so I rose carefully and continued on. When
we passed the first buildings, we heard voices inside—a
woman and some children—which made me breathe with
relief, the realization that a family lived there making
things easier to bear.

Beyond the huts was the town proper, and I climbed

over a low stone wall to slide forward against the side of a
house before peering around a corner at the same instant
the snowfall ebbed. We all froze. In the center of town,
three vehicles idled, one Russian APC and two scout
cars, and what looked like about thirty soldiers were
there. They disappeared a second later when the wind
picked up, hiding them behind a haze of blown snow.

The sergeant's voice clicked in. "Everyone move due
west. Stay clear of the road and make for Bo'ston from the
north. Mission accomplished."

I followed the other dots. Our group moved slowly
along the southern edge of town and at one point we
climbed a low rise onto what might have been a road,
before descending to the other side. As soon as we got
down, Ul'yanovo lit up behind us with plasma.

Someone must have called in the contact, because
without warning, hundreds of rounds fell behind us, turning the snow into colored lights that sparkled with each
impact. I prayed that none would fall short. There was no
need for noise discipline now, and we sprinted, trying to
get out from under the rain of fire that fell on anyone
unlucky enough to have been caught there. You didn't
think about the fact that you'd heard women and children
in town. The knowledge was there, sure, but a wave of
self-preservation instincts kicked in to insist that *yours*
was the important ass to worry about, and that for all you
knew, the rounds would miraculously miss any civilians,
and if they *didn't* miss, screw it.

A loud roar erupted to our front and I dove, shouting to
the kid to get down, but it was almost impossible to see
anything through the curtain of snow. Ahead was a
shadow. Before I could move, the form changed into the

shape of a Popov APC as it bore down on me, bursting through low snowbanks, and there was nothing to do except bury my head in the ground and curl into a ball. The vehicle passed directly over, its belly scraping against the ceramic of my shoulder, and three blue dots blinked out on my heads-up at the same time I heard screams over the radio. When the vehicles had gone, I scrambled to my feet and resumed running, calling out to the kid to stay on my tail, to head west and keep up with everyone else. Maybe someone should have collected our dead. But that wasn't a thought that anyone had at the moment, because it was still unknown what waited to our west, between us and Bo'ston, so whoever had just been crushed would wind up buried in the winter snow to stay there until the following spring.

"Move," the sergeant said over the radio, but it really wasn't necessary.

Throughout the morning we alternated between jogging and walking, eventually shifting into a single-file line to make the deepening snow easier to traverse. Being at the lead was especially awful. Over land this flat, the snow depth varied from a few inches in places, to several feet where it had accumulated in drifts and you had to push through it, lifting your feet high enough to step over or forcing them through—despite the fact that your legs screamed that all they wanted to do was stop. We took turns. After an hour of point, I rotated to the rear and shifted into the role of a walking corpse, a half-human thing whose exhaustion showed and whose mind had conjured up the memories of a similar march, when Pavlodar had first fallen.

Only the sergeant spoke during those long hours, to announce course corrections or to tell the point to move faster. But as soon as we stepped within sight of the Bo'ston perimeter, he stopped us outside the minefield, which was cruel, because all we wanted to do was get inside and go to sleep. I wanted to strangle him.

"Who called in artillery?" he asked.

"You didn't do it, Sergeant?" the Brit asked. I was glad he had survived, and as it turned out, I hadn't known any of the men the APCs had crushed.

"Someone hacked the secure channel, Command, and called in an artillery strike; I checked the records on our way back and it definitely came from our position. Who?"

The wind picked up again, howling over the trenches, which lay a hundred yards to our front, and nobody answered.

"Look, this is simple. I'll find out when we get back to our post, as soon as I have artillery check their records. Who did it?"

Okonkwo chuckled then and raised his hand. "I told you to let me out of the patrol, but no. You had to force it. I called in the artillery."

The sergeant didn't even hesitate; he swung his carbine up and fired a short burst into Okonkwo's chest, and the fléchettes worked their way up as far as his neck. He collapsed into the snow. When it was over, we continued through the minefield and climbed into a waiting scout car, careful to wait for the door to seal before removing our helmets.

"Why'd he call in a strike?" the kid asked.

"I don't know."

"The *cafard*," said the Brit. "Remember the cockroach."

I fell asleep within seconds and don't remember how I made it from the scout car to my rack in the hospital basement; I know only that sleep felt better than I had ever remembered.

We lost girls every day to gangrene. At first it bothered me to see them lying there confused, the dying flesh so black on some that it looked as though they'd dipped their hands in ink, and many of them woke in the middle of the night screaming, so loudly that we heard it in the basement next door. What did these chicks dream of? You couldn't compute the difference in experiences between us and them, because you didn't grow up in a beaker to be shoved onto a battlefield where the only thing promised was the glory of death or this: a lingering decrepitude. But like anything else, you got used to it. Soon I didn't even notice the girls' faces, and every once in a while, I had trouble remembering Bridgette's name. I'd stop and think for a minute, and the kid would have to shout and pull me out of it.

Only one thing animated the girls: pills. *That* computed. The physical deterioration reflected an internal malady that wasted their heads, and sometimes I'd show up to give them the doc's version of tranq tabs—a formula he cooked up using local resources—and would find them standing with their arms poking through the bars, all of them wanting the things. I got that, understood their need, because I had it too, and there were days when I'd stand outside the door with the kid, holding a paper bag full of the tablets. I'd wonder what the drugs were like; a voice from inside woke up when in proximity to the things and whispered that I should just grab a handful and forget everything, that I'd earned it. *Just swallow all of them.* So far I'd resisted. But one morning we pushed through the door with a pair of Marine guards, and I knew that if this went on for much longer, I'd give in.

The whole floor was quiet. Usually they'd be ready for us, standing in their cages, but on that day nobody moved, because the whole group of them, about a hundred, hung limply from nooses they had made out of blankets. The girls could have stood up. Their feet touched the ground, which spoke to a kind of sick dedication on their part, a testament to the fact that the chicks had seen something, a common vision that fed into a calculated ending: *This just isn't worth it anymore.*

Everyone had his breaking point and I'd already reached mine on multiple occasions—in Almaty, Karaz-hyngyl, and places I couldn't remember—but I'd never gone this far beyond it. The sight shattered something in my chest. I ran from cage to cage and tried to force the pills into their mouths, thinking that maybe they'd bring the girls back to life, and as I went, I called over my shoulder at the kid.

"Help me!"

"Oscar, they're dead. Come on."

"No they're not." I was about to ask the Marines to help when I noticed they had vanished. "These chicks don't die, all we need to do is get them wired again, maybe an electrical shock or something. I'll give them their pills, you untie the nooses and get them down, and then we'll rig something up to shock them, Frankenstein-style. Come on. *It'll be fun!*"

"Oscar. *They're dead.*"

When had I told the kid my name? When had he started calling me Oscar? I screamed at him then and threw the bag against the wall to send a hundred tablets rolling across the floor. *"Motherfucker, if you don't help me now, so help me Christ, I will rip you heart out! You don't know me at all!"*

The doc arrived then with the two Marines, and the group started walking toward me. The doc smiled. But I knew, man, I knew that he had something in mind, and all I could think was that the kid had tricked me and I needed to escape or I'd wind up dead like the girls.

"I'm infected, Doc, stay away."

"With what?" He glanced at the kid. "What is his name?"

"Oscar," the kid said.

"What's wrong Oscar? What's infected you?"

The two Marines circled around, trying to get behind me, so I backed against the far wall, looking in either direction as fast as I could. *What was wrong with these people?*

"Okonkwo, the lieutenant in the APC, they gave it to me, man. But if you leave me alone for a minute, I can figure this out. I got this one. Somehow they must have snuck in while I wasn't looking, but I'll get rid of them."

"What, Oscar? What are you talking about?"

One of the Marines slammed into me from the side, and I remember thinking that I had forgotten about them, that it had been stupid of me to forget. The floor came up quickly, slamming into my nose. With the pain came a sudden clarity, as if a spell had been broken, and then I saw the girls differently, their faces calm and pretty, with short black hair that framed those chiseled features. Some of them had died smiling.

"What the fuck is this place?" I asked.

The Marine, a huge guy, bigger than Ox had ever been,

held me down but with a strange kind of gentleness. "It's all shit. Don't think about it, because it's all shit."

"No, seriously, what is this place and how did I get here?" I started crying. The tears came in a constant stream and I screamed into the floor, watching as the doc's feet came closer.

"It's all right," the Marine said. "No shit. It's all right."

"It all got inside me." I tried to think of a way to explain it, but the words wouldn't come and it made me more frustrated, got in the way of my screams. "What's wrong with everyone?"

"You have him?" the doc asked.

The Marine nodded. "Go on, Doc. I got him. He'll be all right; we'll talk him down before we let him go." It seemed to satisfy the doc, because he left without another word, stopping only once to look around at the girls and shake his head.

And that's how I made it through that one—without getting high. The kid sat on the floor next to me and lit a cigarette, the other Marine sat next to him, and the third one stayed on my back, pinning me to the floor as we all smoked in a room full of hanging corpses. The kid put the cigarette in my mouth and lit it for me, holding it there until I calmed down enough to smoke.

"He's right," said the other Marine to his friend. "You know, I get what he's saying."

"Shut the fuck up. Of course he's right, so just shut the fuck up or I'll shoot you both. Right here."

"Why are you still here, Oscar?"

The kid had his helmet off and looked at me with eyes that saw through, and I wondered how long it would be before *he* cracked and a Marine wound up sitting on his back. We sat in an ambulance, in an underground hangar just north of Jizzakh, close to the front line. It had been a week since my breakdown. The doctor had decided that he didn't want us working with the genetics, so he'd assigned us to drive one of the ambulances. We would wait in a frontline APC hangar for the French to on-load their wounded, after which the fun would begin. But first the fighting had to kick off. The truck was solid and had four-wheel drive, so we could make it over some rubble, but our job would be to make our way aboveground as fast as we could to deliver our cargo to the hospital, and then make it back. Most of the time our assignment would be cake; we'd sit underground and smoke. But during that half-hour trip there and back, we'd be exposed, above-ground, a soft target, and I wondered how long it would be before my luck ran out.

I thought about what the kid had asked, and looked at him. "What do you mean why am I here?"

"You're a civilian. You don't have to be here. I mean, you could probably head southwest if you wanted and make for Bandar on your own. Nobody would stop you."

"Because I'd be alone. I don't want to make that trip alone."

"I'd do it. It's worth the risk. Think about it: if you made it back, you'd be home, the States, and every step down the road would be one step away from all this crap."

"I told you. I don't want to be alone." A voice broke in over the general net and said something in French, but I was too tired to translate, and let the words wash over me without really hearing them. The kid hadn't seen Karaz-hyngyl and didn't know what lived out there in the desert

or the steppes—didn't get that I'd rather stay in Samarkand than risk a long trip with only my brain for a companion. "What will you do if someone tries to attach you
to a line unit?" I asked him.

"I'll go. I won't want to, but there isn't much choice, is
there?"

"I guess not."

The kid finished his cigarette and stubbed it on a boot.
"So you're telling me that you'd rather stay here through
an attack and risk getting scorched instead of taking the
road to Bandar on your own?"

I nodded.

"That's whacked-out. You really are way far gone. I
hope I never wind up like you."

It wasn't like I could explain it even if I'd wanted to. I'd
been alone in the tunnels, and in countless hotel rooms
over the years, and the thought of leaving the line without
someone to keep me company was the one that scared me
more than anything. An infinite number of things could
happen when you were alone. But most of all, it was the
fact that my head had become the enemy and when I was
alone, my thinking took over, holding me hostage until
someone happened to pass by and rescue me with a word.
I'd started out thinking that I'd stay with the kid, to take
care of him, but that time had passed and he'd hardened
into something useful, so he didn't really need me
anymore—at least not until he went insane. *I* needed *him*.

There was an old guy, an Uzbek, who manned the hangar doors, which were usually closed, and rested at the
top of a long ramp. We waited at the ramp's bottom. As
we sat in the ambulance, I looked up at the doors, the
tunnel lighting dim and yellow, and I saw the guy check

his watch, carefully get off his stool, and reach for the button to activate the emergency release mechanism, to make sure that it worked. Usually the hangar was controlled inside the tunnel, but the idea was that if the tunnels collapsed, you could still get out using the emergency release. It had become part of our routine. Every hour, on the hour, he performed the check like it was the most important thing in his life, and there was no reason to think that this time would be different. The doors rumbled open and we saw the moon in the distance, full and bright. But then a plasma round detonated, and another, until soon the blasts blotted out the night sky and filled the rectangular opening with a bright glow so that we had to shield our eyes. The next thing I knew, the old Uzbek doorman was at my window, pounding on it with a fist until the skin sloughed off and he slammed his bone against glass, the clicking noise loud and annoying. Then the old man lost it and collapsed next to the truck, dead.

"Holy shit," said the kid.

"Holy shit."

"Did you *see* that?"

I nodded and lit another cigarette.

"No, Oscar, I mean, did you *see* that, the bones and shit? I had no idea plasma could do that. I mean, his eyes were gone, man."

There was a dark smear of blood and burned fat on my window and I did my best not to look at it. "I saw it, kid, I saw it."

The barrage ended a few hours later and we hadn't moved. Another ambulance driver came to my window, so I rolled it down, and he started speaking in French, quickly, and I had to ask him to repeat himself. The guy cursed at me before he switched to English.

"They can't shut the doors from the control station; someone wants us to go do it. Once you use the emergency release, it stays open until someone deactivates it."

"So go shut it," I said.

"You do it."

"I'm not doing it, pal, sorry."

"Why not?"

I pointed to the ground by his feet and flicked my cigarette. "I don't want to step on the dead guy."

Somehow he had missed the fact that the old man had died there, and hadn't seen the corpse. When he saw that it was next to him, the guy shrieked and then sprinted from us, heading up the ramp until we could barely see him, because the moon had moved out of view, plunging the hangar into shadow. The door rumbled until it clanged shut.

"What an idiot," the kid remarked.

"Nah, he's all right. Just an asshole like the rest of us."

"Where do they find these guys?"

"Where did they find us?"

The kid didn't answer, just grunted, and I checked our supply of cigarettes. You kept waiting for someone to tell you to knock it off, because unlike in Almaty, these tunnels had real air handling, but nobody ever did and it had to be because the French held these positions and had some kind of rule that smoking was a God-given right. There were only about three packs left, and I shut my pouch, careful to make sure it sealed so that none would fall out.

"We're running low," I said.

"Whose turn is it to scrounge?"

"Yours."

The kid grimaced and shook his head. "Shit, Oscar, I don't even speak French, man, you go do it. You always get a better deal than me, anyway."

He was right. I grabbed my helmet and buttoned up, handing him the truck keys. The plasma meant only one thing—that Popov had definitely arrived—and at the moment I didn't feel like staying in the truck; a walk might do me good.

"Fine, but move over so I can get out your side."

"What? Why?"

"Because." I climbed over him, barely able to squeeze through the tight compartment. "There's a dead guy outside my door."

SEVEN

Outbound

Doctors and medics treated the wounded underground in aid stations, bringing them to us only when the men needed urgent care at the Samarkand hospital. The rules of war stated that nobody was supposed to fire on ambulances, but that didn't mean anything, and the fact that the red cross emblazoned on our roof had almost completely worn off didn't help. We soon learned that Popov had spotters. For our first trip, medics loaded three guys into the truck bed and I cranked hard on the gas, making sure we had enough alcohol for the trip there and back, before engaging the clutch so that the tires peeled and the truck lurched forward to bring us into the sunlight.

I had made sure beforehand that I knew the quickest ways back to the hospital, but when we came off the ramp, the effects of the barrage made me realize that the preparation had been useless. This wasn't the place I remembered. What had once been Jizzakh now more closely resembled Almaty, or Tashkent, or Shymkent, and the roads disappeared under fallen buildings, and in some places they had become so cratered that you had to go around the road, through what used to be a house. An old woman stumbled in front of me, so I had to swerve. Her clothes had burned off to leave skin covered in layers of gray dust, and for a second she looked like a ghost, the walking dead of Jizzakh. Just as I passed her, the truck bounced over broken concrete and the men in back screamed when the jolting first threw them into the air and then slammed them back onto the bed; their insults forced me to slow down.

Halfway through Jizzakh, the Russians opened fire. Plasma shells fell in single rounds, chasing our progress and occasionally falling well ahead as the gunners tried to bring their rounds on target.

"Go faster," one of the guys in back yelled.

"Last time I went fast, you screamed!"

"I don't care, get us out of here!"

I glanced at the kid. "Why the hell didn't they dig a connector tunnel between the lines and Samarkand?"

"They tried. But the Russians got here sooner than they expected and the engineers had to stop—so it wouldn't mess up our seismic sensors."

"Great."

I gunned it again, switching to four-wheel drive so the truck could climb the piles of debris that blocked our path. Eventually we sped over the low mountains separating Jizzakh and Samarkand, and breathed more easily when the shelling fell behind us.

The rest of the drive was easier. We dropped the wounded off and turned to head back, but as soon as we got to the mountains again, I stopped and looked at the kid.

"You ready for this?"

"No."

"I'm going to go as fast as I can, now that we don't have wounded. Hold on."

"I don't want to go."

The truck whined over the mountain pass and back into the ruins, where Popov had been waiting. We saw the flash of guns in the distance and watched with horror as the shells streaked across the sky, toward us, almost as if they came straight for my face.

"It was better in the other direction," I said.

"Why?"

"You couldn't *see* the firing then."

"Only the ones that hit us are the bad ones."

Despite the plasma, we made it back to the tunnel, and I backed into our slot, shutting down the engine and waiting for someone to fill the tank again. The kid popped his lid and grinned.

"That was really awful driving."

I was happy—a twisted kind of re-verification that sanity had long since left me behind. Maybe the happiness came from a combination of having something useful to do during lulls in the shelling, and being grateful when shells *did* fall, because that meant we'd get to stay safe in the hangar, where every once in a while the Brit would pay us a visit. Sure, we were under attack, but this wasn't Almaty and everyone sensed that the war was almost over. It was as if when we popped our heads from the truck, we could smell the ocean at Bandar. We talked about little else. The main focus was just to stay alive, because as soon as we got the word, everyone would head southwest and back home for good, and nobody wanted to buy it just before shipping out.

And French meal pouches helped. I had forgotten about Ox and his first experience with Legion food until I opened one in the truck, tasting wine-poached salmon as if it was *my* first time, and was barely able to stop grinning. One day the Brit came to deliver a fresh set of meals as the plasma rounds shook the rocks above, and he forced the kid to slide over so that the three of us scrunched together.

"Vodka," he said, and produced a bottle from his pouch.

"For real?" the kid asked. "Where'd you get it?"

"Stole it from one of our supply shites. We better drink it quick before he notices. The sooner we destroy the evidence, the better, because the Legion isn't nice to thieves."

He offered it to me and I waved it away. Something told me it would be a bad idea, not because I was driving but because I'd come to like thinking clearly and wondered if drinking would be another easy escape that would land me in madness. My new mind was better than the old one, cleaner, but I distrusted it and got the sense that it couldn't handle things the way it used to.

"No thanks," I said. "Not a drinker."

"Great! More for us."

I mostly listened, sometimes joining the conversation, but it was more fun to observe, and watching the kid made me glad to see him get wasted. He spoke of Athens, Georgia, in the summertime, and the heat, how it melted the asphalt and made you almost appreciate Uzbekistan, but at the same time his stories made his hometown come to life because of the kudzu and cicadas. I'd never seen a cicada, but I missed the things. And the way he described them would have normally made me sick, but this was different; this was a description of something alive, an insect that despite its ugliness was beautiful compared to the tunnels and ruin, and you knew from listening that the kid had it right, had it all. His sixteenth birthday had gone unnoticed. The kid had kept it quiet and hadn't told even me, but I promised that I'd get him something if we ever made it to Bandar.

"I'm getting laid when we hit Bandar, mate," the Brit said.

The kid nodded. "Me too."

"Have you *ever* been laid, kid?" I asked.

"No. Got a hand job once."

The Brit laughed. "That's nothing. I remember this one brothel when we were stationed in Korea. The Legion actually ran its own houses on base and encouraged us to, uh, stay local, but you'd get bored of the base girls and one day on leave I discovered Don't Tell Mama."

"Don't tell mama?" The kid's speech slurred, and you could tell he wouldn't be with us much longer.

"Don't ask; the name says it all. I spent more money in that place than I want to remember, but when I do remember, I tell myself that every won was worth it."

"What's a won?"

"It's the Korean currency."

"I think I'm going to be sick."

Despite the fact that he was drunk, the Brit jumped from the truck quickly and within a second had pulled the kid out to lay him gently on the ground. He puked. For ten minutes we listened to him before it stopped, and the Brit leaned back out the door to take a look.

"He's out."

We sat for a minute before I realized that the shelling had stopped. A moment later the medics appeared and slid two wounded into the truck bed, and one of the medics climbed aboard, slapping the side when he was set.

"Let's go."

I looked at the Brit, who jumped out of the truck and managed to manhandle the kid back inside, and when he finished, I thought he'd go back to the Legion positions, but he slipped into the passenger seat, forcing the three of us together again.

"Let's go," said the Brit.

"You're not staying on the line?"

"I want to see what this job is like."

"Let's go," the medic shouted.

Nobody had told us about the latest Russian trick. When I gunned the engine and steered the truck from the tunnel, we made it about a hundred meters before the barrage started again—not the single shots they had fired at our ambulance until then, but an incredible volume of fire that made me scream as soon as it came down. It appeared as though the entire earth erupted around us. The Brit gripped the dashboard, his knuckles white, and not knowing what else to do, I slammed the gas down and steered for what I thought was a relatively clear street. We had moved about fifty meters when the truck went airborne.

The landing impact shook my jaw, and an intense heat filled the cab. A thought of burning alive made me feel as though I needed to get out as soon as I could, take a chance on running through the barrage and back to the tunnel, but the truck started to roll over, so there was nothing to do except go with it. And just before I blacked out, someone screamed.

A piercing light made me blink and someone tugged at my leg.

"That hurts," I said.

A voice spoke in French and I didn't catch the words, but then another one spoke, more slowly.

"At least he can feel it."

I lifted my head and saw the French doctor—the one who had enlisted me to assist with taking care of genetics—sawing through my armor, one leg at a time. Sparks flew across the room. The sparks held my attention, because they danced over the floor in multicolored dots that hypnotized me to the point where I realized that I'd been drugged, that no matter how hard I tried, it was impossible to take my eyes off them—until I noticed something else. My armor was all wrong. It had been green before but was now a deep black, and ceramic had melted along the side in gobs of material that froze in the midst of bubbling off. Even with the drugs, it registered just how much heat it took to make the material behave that way, and an image of the corpse trains flashed by. I looked away before they cracked the armor off; you just didn't want to see what waited underneath.

"It will be fine," the doctor said, his voice next to my ear, and then I sensed a distant pinprick. "I'm putting you back under; we'll talk again soon."

I wanted to tell him no and had so many questions about my truck mates, but everything went black again.

The pain flared up, forcing me to scream and arch and clench at the bedsheets with both hands. Then the surroundings came into focus. What looked like a hundred beds filled a long room, and each rack held a bandaged man who stared at me until I got my voice under control. I looked down. Clear bandages encased both legs so that I saw the skin, which had a not-quite-right look to it and seeped blood continuously to be sucked into a machine by the bed. The skin was almost completely white. It draped loosely over my legs in folds, almost making it look like someone had covered them in a white fabric, cut too generously and badly wrinkled.

The doctor appeared out of nowhere. "You had bad burns to both legs."

"What did you do to them?"

"Synthetic skin. Artificial only in the sense that it's manufactured, but the same as human skin. I'll give you a booklet when you leave, and you're going to have to watch out for overheating for a while; it takes some time for the sweat glands to activate."

"It looks dead."

"The skin is bonding to blood cells and nerves, so for now it *is* dead, and the pain very real. Your muscles also sustained damage, and it's normal as we proceed with nerve therapy that you feel the pain as they grow and attach themselves to your new covering."

I remembered the crash and almost lost my voice. "What about the kid and the Brit? My friends."

"I do not understand." I explained it to him, how we got hit in the ambulance, and he nodded. "I am afraid I don't know about the others. You'll have to excuse me. I have other patients to monitor."

"Doc, wait." I grabbed his lab coat to keep him from going. "Who brought me in?"

"I do not know that either. Excuse me."

Once he was gone, I was alone. It didn't matter that a roomful of wounded surrounded me; these were strangers with whom I had no connection, and to be separated from the kid felt as though I'd had an arm amputated. Who would watch out for me? It hadn't been apparent while we'd been together the extent to which I depended on him for a grounding to reality, and as I lay there, it took only a second to convince myself that I'd die at any moment, that something would go wrong. The bandages felt tighter. A fluorescent light overhead swung gently with the vibration of artillery that pounded in the distance, and the moaning of some guy nearby sounded like fingernails on a chalkboard. To make things worse, whatever medication they'd given me after the operation hadn't been enough to help me with the current pain but had been more than enough to make me crave drugs again, drool for them. The old terror took hold, starting in my gut and working its way to my chest so that it became hard to breathe.

Without anything to counter the insanity, I cried. Tears rolled from the corners of my eyes, making it hard to see, and they pattered on the sheets until I reached up and wiped them away. I *should* have been happy. Nobody had told me what had happened out there after I'd blacked out, but the last memories were fresh, of the plasma barrage and the truck; anyone who'd survived the initial strike, the subsequent unconsciousness in the open, under fire, should have been grateful. A normal guy would have thanked some god for another chance. Not me. Everything had gotten so messed that I began wishing I'd died in the ruins of Jizzakh, where plasma could have charred me into a mixed lump of ceramic and flesh. Pain was too much; emptiness was better. Although the artillery was far away, you just knew it was looking for you, aimed at

you, like each round was alive and could sense exactly
where you'd chosen to hide, and the only thing keeping it
from getting into the ward was a little limitation called
effective range. Popov wasn't fighting us; he was fighting
me. In the stillness of the ward, it was easy to do, easy to
convince myself that none of these men mattered, because
hadn't I already proven it? Hadn't my ambulance been
chased by artillery every time it poked its nose out of
the tunnel, until, finally, Pops decided to send everything
he had at once—just to make sure *I* was gone?

I screamed again and a soldier nearby said, "Shut the
fuck up. I'm dying too, you know," which meant he was a
Marine, because he spoke English. And then another
yelled something in French, but I didn't care, because the
screams meant that I was still alive, not that I was in pain.
So I yelled back, "Go to hell," and then a bunch of them
threatened to come over and piss on my legs, so I said, "I
just need something more, something for the pain." Someone put a hand on my shoulder, and it was warm. So warm.

"It's all right," she said.

"Bridgette?"

"No, Sophie."

And it was Bridgette *and* it was Sophie, one of the
genetics we had all seen in the pen outside Jizzakh so
long ago, only she stood right next to me in armor, her
helmet hanging from the belt. She knelt so her face was
next to mine.

"What is wrong?" Sophie asked.

"I am. I'm all wrong; they almost got my legs."

"Jesus Christ," one of the Marines said, "we can't even
get away from genetics while we're dying." And I wanted
to kill him.

"It's going to be just fine," she said, and then smiled.

I grinned back. Sophie glanced at the machine and hit a button, and I watched as a few drops of amber fluid dripped into my IV, disappearing as soon as they mixed with the saline so that in a few seconds the pain vanished altogether.

"That's righter," I said.

"Good."

"I missed you, Sophie."

She cocked her head and then pulled on her hood, shattering the vision by transforming into just another one, another bug-eyed war thing, and I started crying again.

"I do not know you," said Sophie.

"Yes. Yes you do." The drugs carried me away despite the fact that now I didn't want to go, now I wanted to stay with her. The last thing I remember is hearing one of the Marines say "Let's strangle him while he's asleep."

The next time I woke, she had vanished. "Hey," I said, "did anyone see a genetic here earlier, the one who gave me more juice?" But nobody answered. It was the dead of night. I kept waiting for night vision to kick in, until I realized that I'd have to experience the *real* night, without the kid, and with a not-so-complete darkness because a medic sat by the door and stared at a computer screen. My beard itched like mad. I reached up to scratch it and found it gone, the lack of it making me realize what those others had felt so long ago, when I was a green reporter and didn't take, didn't get. Maybe my beard was on the pillow. By the time I'd looked under the bed, the pain from my legs had returned, forcing me to lie back and breathe, trying not to move an inch, to keep the agony in check.

Little by little, the windows got lighter. Popov met the day with a fresh barrage that rattled the frames in place, so I took the pillow and placed it over my face, blotting out the world. I fell asleep. It wasn't clear how much time had elapsed before I woke up again, but light filled the room and some of the men spoke to each other quietly, a few, ones who could sit up, playing cards. That was how my days passed. Without a chronometer, there was no way of telling if a week had elapsed or a year, and then one day the doctor came by and checked my bandages before he smiled.

"Today," he said.

"Today what?"

He pulled a scalpel from a nearby station and returned to the bed, then carefully sliced off the tape that kept the bandages sealed. First one, then the other fell. The air hit the skin on my legs and I winced with the pain, barely able to stand the sudden sensation of cold that ran up them.

"They're cold."

"It's winter. Try pulling your knees up to your chest."

I did my best. Both legs trembled with the strain of flexing muscles, until little by little they bent, but I gave up before my knees made much progress.

"The skin feels tight." They weren't white anymore; they were more like the color of someone who hasn't seen the sun in months, a pale pink, and the doctor seemed pleased.

"Good enough. We'll get you started with therapy tomorrow."

"Therapy?"

"You will find out." He adjusted the machine and sent another bolus of meds into my veins, and I grinned—no complaints—wondering how much longer I'd be there. Before I passed out, I remembered something.

"Doc, where did the genetic go, the one named Sophie?"

"Sophie is a special case. An anomaly. We're studying her because her decay seems much slower than what we've observed in the others. Rest."

I was halfway down a set of parallel bars when they jumped me.

"Get the fuck off!" I screamed.

The kid got up and laughed. "Jesus, you look like you need a tan."

"I think," said the Brit, "that I just broke my arse."

He got up slowly and I stared. The Brit looked the same as ever but the kid's hair had grown longer and his beard fuller, so that he was almost unrecognizable, maybe part man but certainly less boy. I'd never been happier than when it hit me that he was alive. His armor showed the wear of war, and I noticed the tiny patches where someone had quick-pasted a series of tiny holes, which could mean only one thing.

"You get shot, kid?"

He nodded. "Popov hit us with an underground probe. They took me off ambulance duty and attached me to a Marine unit before it happened."

"He's right next to my unit, though." The Brit must have seen the smile fade from my face, and I got angry with myself for having spoiled the reunion by pulling out the topic of war. "So don't worry. I'll keep an eye out for him."

"They have powered armor, Oscar. I've never seen anything like it. They look like monsters, and it must be made of a new composite, because most of our fléchettes don't penetrate. I've never been that close. And they stealth bored, all the way into our tunnel, so we never even knew they were coming, because the guys on watch missed the thermal bloom," the kid explained. "But eventually we pushed Pops back and then sent a team to chase and to blow their tunnels."

"You OK?"

He nodded. "Nothing like what *you* got."

They told me what had happened when the ambulance blew, and I was glad I'd been unconscious. After the truck had stopped flipping, the Brit found me about thirty feet away, where a plasma shell detonated, sending gas to play over my legs. He had pulled me into a hole in the rubble, where the three of us survived the barrage, but the guys in the back of the truck bought it.

"Thanks," I said.

The Brit grinned, and I saw that his teeth had gone a dark shade of gray, with so much dirt and plaque that I couldn't distinguish one tooth from another. "Good drugs?" he asked.

The question sparked the craving, one I'd fought since they'd taken me off painkillers. A couple of times I'd begged the doctor, almost crying, but he was too smart; "I know an addict when I see one," he'd said, and cut me off.

"They're OK, but the doc won't give me anything except aspirin now. How much longer before they let me out so I can come see you guys?"

The two of them looked at each other and started laughing.

"What?"

"They didn't tell you?" the kid asked.

"Jesus, mate," the Brit explained, "you're not coming back to the line. First off, you're a civilian, so they might not have sent you back anyway, but second, you got the magic wound. They're shipping you to Bandar with a convoy as soon as you can walk. We ran into the doctor on the way in and he told us everything; his accent is so bad, though, that I made him give it to me a second time, in French."

My skin went numb, all of it, even the new stuff on my legs, which had hurt just moments before. How did you compute going home? I'd thought the same thing everyone else did, that I'd be stuck in the war until its end, and I'd meant what I'd told the kid, that I didn't want to leave. The road to Bandar should have been an easy prospect: clean living, *I'll-never-complain-about-another-thing-as-long-as-I-live,* and every other thought you should have on hearing that you were going home. Instead the news turned my stomach into a cold knot, and I had trouble looking at them because of a new and mixed bag of feelings that came over me, led by a sense of betrayal— that I'd be leaving them behind, and why did I get to be the lucky one, anyway? Fear soon eclipsed that thought: a fear of getting caught alone on the road by Russians, and surrounded by strangers I couldn't count on in a firefight. *That* was what had happened to me, to my head, a kind of brainwashing. The memories of a normal life were just that—memories—and life on the line was the familiar, what had become so common that everything else shifted into the slot of "unknown quantity," a world in which anything could happen. On the line, it was simple. You stayed suited, buttoned up, and kept underground as much as possible, and everything else was out of your control. I had no idea what the real world, the peace world, held.

"You don't seem all that pscyhed," the kid said.

"I'm not. I don't want to go. I want to stay here, get back on the line. I'll talk to the doc next time I see him and get him to let me stay."

"Like hell you will," said the Brit. "Look, mate. Don't give me any of this. You got a lucky hit, one that means you can go home and grab ass for every day of your life, and that you'll *have* a life, one beyond this craphole."

"Bullshit. I'm staying."

"You're crazy." The Brit looked away before he continued. "I don't know what's wrong with you, but I do know that any other guy in your position would be glad to make it out, to get an early trip southwest to the sea. You'll die here if you stay. Like the rest of us."

"Bullshit on that," said the kid. "I ain't dying; I'm invincible. I'm death in armor and Pops will shit in his pants the next time he sees me. It's a guarantee."

But the mood had broken. What should have been a fun time ended flatly, with the Brit and the kid leaving before they'd meant to, and with me returning to my exercises, trying to retrain my legs to function with only 80 percent of the muscle they'd once had. I hadn't been able to tell them the other reason I wanted to stay, because it wasn't clear how they'd react: I wanted to find Sophie. Something had happened in the short time she'd been at my bed, so I knew staying would be worth it. Through the windows I saw the snow fall, and thought that at least we weren't retreating through *that*.

I should have added "not yet."

At night the city lights went out, and now that my legs had gotten to the point where I could move with a cane, I had taken to standing at the window, staring northward toward Jizzakh. Point defense towers dotted the mountains overlooking the town, and their cannons pulsed when they fired at incoming auto-drones. It was better than fireworks. Rounds burst in the sky, backlighting the mountains so they looked like cutouts, and one night as I pressed my face against the glass, Sophie showed up and leaned her forehead against the window too. It surprised me to the point where no words came, so we stood there for half an hour, watching.

"It's beautiful," she finally said.

"You're beautiful."

"Have we met before?"

"Yes. I know you, but I couldn't convince you to want to live. They discharged you in Shymkent."

She gasped when our artillery opened up and the horizon blossomed with colors reflecting off the snow and ice. We watched quietly some more until she looked at me.

"That was someone else. We are not all the same."

"I know."

Sophie moved so her hip pressed against mine. "They don't want me here, in the recovery rooms with men."

"So why are you here?"

"Because it is a place of honor. The wounded are those who have seen God and returned from His side. And because one day I heard someone screaming and had to know what could be wrong in such a place, and it was you. The doctor found out about my visit, though, and forbade me from returning."

She wore a set of hospital scrubs now, not armor, and the warmth from her leg bled into mine. "Then why did you come back?" I asked.

"I wanted to know you."

Sophie didn't struggle when I pulled her in. I dropped the cane and she wrapped her arms around me, the girl's muscles so hard that they gave me the sensation of having my back wrapped in thin iron bars. She pulled me to my bed. At first it was strange, because you couldn't ignore the fact that guys slept all around, snoring or talking in their sleep, but then it didn't matter, because we wanted it more than anything and my legs didn't hurt anymore. She was mine. We pulled the blanket over our heads and moved quietly but I heard her breathing in my ear and knew that it was impossible to hide all the noise, the clanking of the bed and her soft moans. Until eventually we finished. We kissed and her tongue brushed mine and all I could think was that Sophie's skin felt charged, electrified, dangerous.

"Do you want to die?" I asked.

"I want to go back on the line. And if I die there, then it is good. But if I survive the line, then I will need *more*, and if it is possible to avoid my discharge, I will. Life interests me."

"Why me?"

She touched her lips to my ear, and I wanted her again, moving in and pulling her legs apart while she talked. "Because your face is damaged, your legs were shattered, and part of your ear is missing. You've been where I have. And when I came here for your screaming, you didn't react like the other men. And because I *do* know you. From somewhere."

"You don't even know my name."

"What is it?"

"Oscar."

"That's a silly name."

When she climbed on top of me, I had gone way past caring about whether anyone saw us, and she gripped my shoulders so hard that they bruised. Sophie took her time. Near the end, she leaned over and, in a low voice I barely heard, asked me to need her. I said, "Cool."

Later, before sunrise, she got up to leave and knelt by my head.

"When do you go home, Oscar?"

"I don't. I convinced the doctor to let me go back to my friends in Jizzakh. I tried to get him to let me stay in the hospital, but the last time I was here, it didn't work out so well, so it was a no-go."

She grinned and bit my lip. "This is good. Very good. I will find you there, on the line, if I can. Don't leave without me."

You got the sense that the mining techs could tell the future, because these were guys named Buddy, or Wilson, or Tiny, and they'd immersed themselves in so much rock and sludge that they'd become part of the earth, their orange coveralls long since stained dark gray except at the armpits. These were men of dust and stone. It spoke to them and told them of shifting mantle currents, which brought messages from the earth's core as the men slept with one ear against the rock and as their machinery *ker-chunk*ed and vibrated its song, but never loud enough to drown out the news of what would soon happen. We *all* should have taken notice of them. One day the refineries and leaching pits went cold, the stacks no longer blowing steam and waste into the winter air, and there was the sudden coughing of massive trucks, one after another, as they ground to life. The yellow vehicles lumbered away from the underground concentrator stations carrying metallic cargo and splashing through slush, and one almost ran me down as I moved in the opposite direction, over the mountain pass. A magic must have shielded them, because although ambulances drew fire, the ore trucks didn't, passing through and out of the beaten zone as if nothing could touch them. But I didn't have the sense, or maybe I'd lost the touch—didn't know that I should have jumped on board and gone along for the ride. I didn't know to do anything except head north and link up with the kid's unit, its position a blinking light in the heads-up display of my new armor.

It was risky to walk. But the thought of riding in an ambulance after what had happened last time made me feel sick, and besides, the ore trucks hadn't drawn any fire, right? My legs felt wobbly after the first kilometer and I began to hate both them and the sensation that they'd never be right again, the muscles threatening to quit with every step. Eventually they got used to the exertion, and I climbed over Jizzakh's wet rubble with minor difficulty. They *wouldn't* ever be the same again, and I *wouldn't* ever get the missing piece of my ear back, but none of that mattered, because I'd found Sophie and she wanted to live and soon we'd be out of Uzbekistan forever. The only questions were how I would find her again and then how to get her out.

Halfway to the entrance ramps, an old woman surprised me when she popped from behind the only remaining wall of a half-flattened building, and I wondered if she was the same one I had almost run over earlier in the winter. This one was naked too. As I passed, the woman laughed and said something in Russian, so I moved more quickly, sensing that she knew something I didn't and suddenly aware that I was alone—trying to ignore the chill and the disquieting thought that Sophie's *wanting* to live might not be enough to make it happen. Even if she ran with me, it wouldn't change the simple facts of what she was and what that implied: everyone would want her dead. Eventually I lost sight of the old woman and felt better.

"You lost?" A Marine sergeant sat on a block of concrete next to one of the ramps, its entrance half buried in rubble.

"Looking for a buddy of mine, attached to Two-Five."

"Take this ramp and head down to the main tunnel. When you get off the elevators, hang a left and keep going."

"What happened here?" I asked, pointing at the rubble.

"Freakin' engineers. Probably Army."

The man had popped his helmet and looked southward, pulling on a cigarette and blowing clouds of smoke that wafted back to his face.

"This is no place for human beings," he said, lifting a fléchette pistol that I hadn't noticed. He pushed it into his mouth and fired before collapsing into the dirt.

I ran. The door at the bottom of the ramp was partially open, and after I sprinted through, the Uzbek manning it called out, "Where is Sergeant Tran?" and I called back, "He's dead," but I didn't want to stay and discuss it. The image had burned into my brain. We were so close to getting out, to going home, and the guy must have known it, so it made no sense at all; why would he end it now? But the deeper I went, climbing down a ladder-tube and then stepping into an elevator, the more sense it began to make, because a re-submergence into subterrene brought it all back: the filth and decay. Mold. Past a certain point the walls sweated out their frustrations in rivulets that shimmered green in light amplification, and you heard the low throbbing of the pumping stations, fighting their own little war to keep us all from drowning. In this place, going home meant nothing. In the tunnels, death would come unannounced and instantaneously, so a promise of war's end *next week* would have meant little, because a week might as well have been a year, and we didn't know when the order to pull out would be given—maybe it would be in six months. I wouldn't have pulled the trigger on myself, but it began to get clearer why *he* had. The cockroaches. They'd left me alone for a while, but maybe if they stayed with me as long as they had with the Marine, I'd feel differently; maybe his infestation was more than anyone could take.

It took an hour to find the kid's tunnel and then a minute to find him, slumped against the wall, asleep.

"Hey, asshole. Know where a guy can get laid around here?"

"What?" The kid jerked his hood back so he could look at me in the dim combat lamps. "Holy shit. You can walk?"

"Sure I can walk. The French doctors aren't *that* bad."

"Rumor is they cut your dick off."

"It's true. I didn't need it anymore, thought maybe they could transplant it onto you, since yours never grew in."

He stood up and hugged me. "Listen up, guys, this is Oscar. He's a civilian, so amped up on war and death that he had to come see the sub for himself."

The news drew some stares, and one of the Marines, an old man who looked about eighty but was probably forty said, "Then he must be crazier than any of us, because we *have* to be here," and the others laughed before returning to whatever they'd been doing.

"So what's going on?" I asked.

"We're waiting."

"For what?"

"The Russians are boring this way. Their ETA is in two days, at about fifteen hundred hours, give or take."

It put everything in context. The tunnel was so quiet that you heard the slap of cards and the soft tumble of cigarettes that the Marines threw down to bet, and several others stared into space. My hands started shaking and I wondered: why hadn't I stayed in the hospital?

"Almost makes me miss Almaty," said the kid. "Almost."

"I'm too scared to check my chronometer for some reason. How long have I been away—in the hospital?"

"Three months."

Something felt wrong. It didn't hit me at first, but then everything that had slipped away came crashing back—my father, the urge I'd had in Almaty to get home no matter what, and the faces of the dead. Only one thing made it all bearable—Sophie—but even she was a source of discomfort, because she was somewhere else. Hell. For all I knew, she was dead already.

*   *   *

The use of fusion borers meant that wherever the Russians hit us, they'd own that section of the line, and our guys would have to take it back in a kind of back-and-forth that seemed more like an exercise in ramming one's head against a wall than a coordinated battle plan. Fusion borers did two things: They channeled through rock so you could move troops from point A to point B. They also produced plasma—lots of it. The first thing that happened when a borer broke through to your line was that it sensed the change in forward resistance and opened plasma vents, filling the opposing tunnel with superheated gas. If you were there when it arrived, you cooked. But there was only so much gas to be vented, and the defender usually had more reactors at his disposal, and many of these would be plasma-connected to the defensive tunnels so that as soon as the borer went dormant, Popov would get a dose; we'd dump gas right back at him. Back and forth. Our eggheads had been working on personal anti-plasma shields for decades but so far hadn't produced squat, and even if they did, the power requirements were prohibitive and a magnetic field wouldn't repel heat, so it wasn't clear how much protection a shield would buy you anyway.

The short of it was that if you knew Pops was on his way, you did nothing until he got to a point called the zero-deviation position, the distance from the attack tunnels where we got our best read of his final destination, and the point at which it would be impossible for him to change course. Then you vacated that tunnel and sealed it. Both sides would take turns at squirting plasma into the underground chamber, but at some point neither side would be able to vent anymore, and then everyone charged in to fight for the still-steaming rocks. Fun.

I'd already experienced the attack side of underground engagements, but this would be my first on defense.

"You've defended a tunnel before, right, kid?" I asked.

"Yeah. I wasn't in the first return wave, though. Those guys all bought it almost as soon as they reentered our pos and engaged. Hey, I never asked you. Why are you even here in the first place?"

At first I didn't have to answer. Someone called over the radio, and you wouldn't have heard the message because of all the other traffic, except it was the one message everyone had been waiting for—and dreading at the same time.

"Zero-deev."

The officer in charge of the kid's section, a captain, stood and got everyone moving. Popov was close enough now, about twenty meters away, so we heard the borer chewing through rock and grinding it, a screeching that vibrated the walls and made little ripples in the puddles that had collected on the floor. A section of the wall had begun to glow white on infrared. We filed out the large exit tunnel and waited for an engineering team to maneuver a huge alloy plug into the entrance, sealing it with thin hoses that injected rapid-curing quick paste.

I began to shake.

"So why are you here?" he asked again.

"I used to be a reporter."

"No shit? For real, like with a news station?"

"For real, but not a news station. *Stars and Stripes.*"

He adjusted his hood and tightened its straps. "I thought those guys were all military. But you're not with them anymore?"

We still had time to kill before they broke through, and talking helped keep my mind off what would soon happen, so I told him everything—about Ox and my early days on the line, about Bridgette and the retreat from Pavlodar, and about Karazhyngyl.

"So that's why you're so screwed up," he said.

"What?"

"Drugs. There were a couple of guys in my unit at Almaty who did that shit, zip, and we all stayed away from them. It messes with you."

I said, "Thank Christ."

"What for?"

"I thought you were going to give me a lecture on how messed it was to fall for a genetic."

He thought about that one for a second before snapping his helmet in place. "Nah. They're not bad-looking. I could see that."

Our engineers had just finished placing charges so they would blow the plug at the appropriate moment when it was time to counterattack. We listened. The Russian borer vented into the tunnel we had just vacated, and the noise sounded like the hydraulic brakes letting go on a big rig followed by loud pops as waterlogged rocks exploded, and a few seconds later the plug grew white-hot, groaning as it expanded against the surrounding tunnel. The borer must have moved through the position to hit the other side, because the wall against my back started trembling, making my teeth chatter. I prayed that the plug wouldn't dislodge by accident. Then our vents opened up and we

heard the roar of gas being forced through narrow channels drilled through the rock on either side of us, a noise
that made me grin as I thought that maybe some Russians
had just fried.

Someone issued the general retreat code and we froze.

"Say again?" the captain asked. A few seconds later
he started yelling us. "Back up. *Get to the exits—now!*"

At the time I had no clue what was wrong, but my gut
sensed that things were about to go from kind of crappy to
downright nightmarish, and every nerve told me that I
had to be the first on the elevator. The kid must have
sensed it too. We pushed against the sea of Marines, all of
them fighting to get out, and all of them oblivious to the
captain's pleas to calm down.

Flashbacks of winter in Pavlodar. Once the kid and I navi-
gated the maze of tunnels, the elevators, and then the lad-
ders, we saw what must have been the full mass of our
forces wading through rubble. Words couldn't describe it.
My suit had auto-synced with the kid's unit, and the captain's voice came over, calmly telling us to move in an
orderly fashion toward Samarkand, where our tanks and
APCs had formed up to receive us, but the problem was
that we couldn't *not* bunch up. Units mixed among other
units in a group of men so dense that it pushed me on all
sides and at one point I feared falling down, knowing that
I'd be trampled. Then the Russians opened fire.

As soon as the first rounds fell, all order collapsed.
The kid and I scrambled, at first trying to scuttle from one
rubble pile to the next, but the futility of it soon became
apparent when clouds of men, half molten, flew through

the air, threatening to kill us with their impact. I didn't think about Sophie, or home, or much of anything during moments like those. The entire world collapsed into a bubble that enclosed only me and a single thought—that I needed to be in the mountains, out of range of Russian guns. The kid and I moved through our artillery positions and saw the cylindrical pits, their clamshell ceramic doors wide open to let out the smoke from self-destruct charges that had gone off only a few minutes before, a signal that things were worse than we had hoped; we had blown our guns in place. That meant we weren't coming back.

"What the fuck is that?" the kid asked.

Beyond the gun emplacements lay the ore concentration yards, which should have been empty, since the contractors had left days earlier. But they weren't. Men boiled up from ramps leading to the smelting station, and from that distance it looked as if something was wrong with them; their movements were jerky and their armor so bulky that it made you wonder how they could even walk.

Someone yelled that they were Russians.

"Powered armor?" I asked.

The kid said, "Yeah."

We and several Marines took positions behind rubble piles and opened fire.

At first I thought I was missing, and slowed my trigger finger to take more careful aim. Fléchettes flew from my carbine, their tracers flicking out in groups of a hundred, and when they struck, the projectiles made tiny sparks, so it was clear the rounds were finding their targets but couldn't penetrate. With a sense of horror I realized it: with powered servos you could change the armor completely, make it thicker or of a harder but heavier material so that normal infantry weapons would have little or no effect. It made them more tank than man. Soon *they* opened fire, but instead of using fléchettes, Popov let loose with rockets and grenades, adding to the confusion generated by plasma rounds that still fell, and I ducked when I saw a rocket corkscrew directly at us, blowing the front half of our rubble pile to hell.

"Screw this," I said. "Without grenades we can't touch them."

"I'm with you."

We were just about to make a break for it when a cheer erupted. Ten APCs rumbled out of what remained of south Jizzakh, and had torn through the rim of ruins that separated the ore yards from the rest of the town, opening wide gaps through which poured hundreds of our troops. At first I wondered where the men came from. All of them had been armed with anti-tank rockets, and the first group advanced toward Pops under a cover of plasma fire from the APCs and rockets from troops who had taken positions atop walls. As I watched, it hit me the way they moved without fear or hesitation and coordinated perfectly with hand signals. These were genetics; Sophie was probably with them.

Before I knew what I was doing, my legs, still wobbling with uncertainty, carried me toward them.

"Where are you going?" the kid yelled after me.

"Sophie!"

"Who?" But when I didn't answer, he gave up trying to figure it out and caught up to me. "We're in the open, Oscar."

"I know."

A grenade blew just behind us and droplets of thermal gel hissed on my shoulder.

"We're heading toward the Russians, Oscar, not away."

"I know."

Then another rocket screamed between us, bouncing off a slab of concrete to disappear somewhere to the rear.

"They're shooting at us. You mind telling me what the fuck we're doing here?"

We reached the girls' flank, and I plopped down beside one of them, catching the end of her prayer and ducking when the girl's rocket launcher roared to life, sending out a cone of flame that barely missed my head.

"I know one of them. Sophie. I'm trying to find her." I expected him to be outraged, to scream at me that I'd risked our lives for a genetic and what the hell was wrong with me, was I still crazy? But he didn't.

"Oh," he said, taking cover too.

I slapped the girl's shoulder and shouted, "Where's Sophie?"

"Who?" she asked, not even pausing during her reload.

"Sophie. She's one of you. The doctor in Samarkand said that she was special because she didn't deteriorate as quickly as the rest of you, would live longer."

"Oh." The girl finished loading and popped up immediately, taking only a second to aim before squeezing off another rocket. "That one didn't come with us because she is still with your doctor. And she's not 'special'; she is unworthy."

"Excuse me?" I'd known them long enough to know that to a genetic, it was probably the worst insult imaginable.

"She was not meant to be one with us. You can tell because she doesn't have the mark."

The next time the chick popped up, her head disappeared in a bright flash, probably because a Popov had zeroed on her the last time, had been waiting for her to try it again. Bits of her ceramic slapped my helmet with a snapping sound.

"Come on," I said to the kid.

"Where to now?"

"Samarkand. To the hospital." I jumped up, doing my best to sprint, and he followed me.

"Oh, *now* it's OK to run away?"

By the time we got to the hospital, Samarkand had transformed into something like a riot, with troops pushing through the streets and heading southwest, hoping to climb the next mountain range and make it via miracle over the Turkmenistan plains and onward to Iran. Nobody had been ready for this. The kid and I gave up trying to stay in touch with the Marine unit via coms, and we scrambled through the crowds in front of the hospital. Walking wounded had already assembled and were waiting for ambulances and APCs to arrive to carry them from the city.

There was no guard in the building that used to hold the cages. We vaulted the steps and burst into the room where we had first seen them, where she now waited, standing at the window. She was crying and turned to face us.

"What's wrong?" I asked.

"I wanted to go with them. But the doctor kept me here, said that he wanted to continue testing, but now what?" She had dressed in armor and wore her vision hood, pushed back with one headphone pressed against an ear. "I'm listening to our command net. We will be overrun."

The kid and I looked at each other. "What's going on? Why is everyone retreating?"

"You don't know?"

"We don't have a clue," the kid said.

"Russian genetics are pushing south through western Uzbekistan and will cut off our escape route to Iran within a few days. The others stealth bored into our rear areas here while sending fusion borers to our lines as a ploy. All units have been ordered to fall back immediately to regroup in Türkmenabat, while my sisters hold here."

"Oscar," the kid said, "this isn't good."

"I know."

"Seriously. It sucks. We gotta bail. Now."

"So bail."

I walked over and hugged her, pulling her in close while I tried to do the math, figure out how we'd get her to Iran without being caught by her handlers. "Hey, kid, take off your suit, you're about her size."

"What?"

"*Take it off!*" I turned to Sophie and spoke into her ear. "Your suit is synced to genetic forces. Anywhere we go, they'll know it's you. You have to get dressed in the kid's suit and then we'll move out."

"What about *me*?" the kid asked.

"So *what* if they think you're a genetic? The second you take off your helmet, you explain to them that your suit got fried, so you lifted one off a dead genetic. It's cake."

"Unless they shoot first."

Still, the kid got undressed, and I watched out the window while they traded suits behind me. Below us in the street, the crowd of soldiers parted and a line of APCs, trucks, and tanks pulled up, making me feel safer for a moment. There were so many variables: the Russians and their powered armor; their genetics; and our own Special Forces, who'd be on the lookout for girls like Sophie, ones who tried to escape. But there wasn't another choice.

It was time to go home, as long as we could break through the Russians to our west, and we'd let the cockroaches have Samarkand. Sophie would come with us.

EIGHT

Last Stand

There was an aspect to desperation so positive that it had gone unappreciated in my life, perhaps buried under filth or ignored under a mountain of terror, but when we headed southwest out of the city, my legs felt weightless and there was no hunger. The fear was still there. But it had transformed into something useful, a sense that ahead of us lay unknown forces in ambush but that we'd overcome them no matter what. We *had* to. Popov and our forces raced each other; they tried to cut off escape to our west while we pushed ahead in a mad attempt to get out before the trap closed. And when I say "we," I don't mean just me; the kid and Sophie had the sense too; everyone felt it. Once again our auto-drones and the Russians' weaved and boomed overhead, but nobody looked up and most didn't wear helmets, so as our guys marched or sat on the backs of APCs and tanks, you saw it on their faces, the same look you knew had fixed on yours: grim determination. Desperation was a new friend. There was only one way out, forward, and it felt good to be on the attack, even if it was an attack toward the rear, because of one simple fact: when it was over, if we won, we'd go home.

We had made it out of the city, stopped only once, by a Special Forces patrol that made the kid take off his helmet, but the kid talked his way out of it. Sophie had gone unnoticed. APCs would stop every once in a while and load up with walking troops, so for a time we trudged in a long line at roadside, but eventually the numbers whittled down, until the closest soldiers were a group of five men, about two hundred meters ahead. Just when I was starting to get creeped out, like we had been forgotten in the rear, a passing tank stopped next to us and the commander leaned out.

"Wanna ride?"

"Sure," I said. "Where did you guys come from?"

"We're the last tank out of Samarkand. I'd say the Russians are close behind, but our genetics...you gotta hand it to them."

We climbed onto the back and grabbed hold when the monster lurched forward, kicking up mud and ice as it accelerated.

"How much farther to Türkmenabat?" I asked.

The commander shrugged, answering before he dropped back inside. "A hundred klicks, give or take, but I wouldn't want to walk it. Popov won't be far behind."

I leaned against the turret and looked ahead, listening as windblown snow struck my helmet. The highway went on forever. This section of Uzbekistan had mountains, and the road had been cut in a straight line by our engineers so that it ran through them, pointing directly at a notch in a small distant range. We passed the other group of soldiers and the tank stopped again, but the men waved the commander on after explaining that they were supposed to be there, engineer volunteers left to booby-trap the road and slow the Russian advance. When we started up again, I said a silent prayer, wishing them well, but was secretly grateful that it wasn't me.

Sophie clicked her helmet against mine. "We will not have time to defend in Türkmenabat; the Russians will chase us as soon as they can, but if we stop, we will be trapped."

"I know."

"Do not worry."

"Why not?"

"Because God watches over us, but not them."

I remembered what the other genetic had said to me about her outside the ore concentration yard. "Sophie, what does it mean that you don't 'have the mark'?" She didn't say anything at first, but then wrapped an arm around me.

"I will explain that to you someday. But not today."

As soon as we crossed the Amu Dar'ya River, I flinched and dropped to the tank's deck to make myself small. Engineers blew the bridges. The one we had just crossed dropped in three sections, splashing into the wide river to send up muddy waves, and then a railway bridge next to it leapt upward when a series of detonations swallowed its piers in smoke. It fell slowly. The bridge seemed to sigh with relief as a wide section of it careened over, finally slamming into the river. But I knew it wouldn't stop them. Popov's vehicles were the same as ours, amphibious, but still, just knowing that someone was thinking tactically and that we'd have easier targets once the Russians waded into the river made me feel better; the engineers had just bought us some time.

The sun set, submerging Türkmenabat into the dimness of twilight, and if the last hours of Samarkand had been a riot, *this* place was a scene of total order. We jumped off the tank. A line of infantry had formed on the side of the road and we got in place, waiting our turn for a group of NCOs to tell us where to go.

When I stepped up to the table, they waited for my suit to sync with their terminals. "Who the hell are you?" one asked.

"Wendell."

"I can see that. I mean what the hell are you doing here? You're a civilian."

"I know. I used to be a reporter and then got assigned as a Marine unit historian. DOD."

"Yeah, but you're a *civilian*."

The group of them started talking to each other rapidly, reminding me of a bunch of clucking chickens, and I heard the tired sighs of troops behind us. Eventually the sergeant I'd been speaking with turned back.

"Do you *want* to fight?"

I jabbed a thumb at Sophie and the kid. "I want to stay with them."

"You." The sergeant pointed at the kid, who pulled his helmet off before stepping in range of the computers. "It says here you're a genetic, assigned to Ten Special."

"I'm Army. Private Nelson Jameson, heavy weapons, stole a suit off a dead G when mine hosed up."

"Jesus Christ. Yeah, but the problem I have is that you're *registered as* a G. Look." He spun his computer screen around to show the blinking warning message. "It says here I'm supposed to wipe you because you're past your shelf life. Do you want me to?"

"Do I want you to what?"

"Shoot you."

The kid jabbed his thumb at me and Sophie. "I want to stay with them."

"Of course." He waved Sophie closer and she moved in, not taking off her helmet. "Good. Finally one that makes sense. I suppose you want to stay with them, right?"

She nodded, leaning back and forth.

"Fine. You're all assigned to the northern section, Lieutenant Rivers's area, where he's been tasked to defend the river until the order to pull back comes. Just move to the blinking light. Your orders have been uploaded. *Next*."

"Wait," I said, "defend the river? I thought we had to move out before we get cut off."

The sergeant fixed me with a cold stare and repeated himself. "Next."

We walked along the river road silently. The wind picked up, and although my suit should have kept me warm, I shivered at the temperature and noticed that this far south there was no snow, as if a line had been drawn, beyond which lay a vast desert that we had only begun to see. A group of old men fished by the river, unconcerned with the turn of events, and they didn't look up as we passed. I didn't blame them. We'd just been given what felt like a death sentence, to hold against the Russian attack instead of pushing on to the southwest, and as a result their city would most likely be obliterated. Why should they look at us when we were a premonition of their ruin? Everything in me said that we should take our chances and run. At least then maybe another city would be spared.

"It will be all right," said Sophie.

The kid grunted.

I asked, "How do you know? We should bail now." A scout car turned onto the road at an intersection, and before it passed us in the opposite direction, I flagged it down. The captain driving it had removed his helmet, and looked pissed.

"What?"

"Captain, what's going on? I thought we were supposed to push southwest, that the road to Iran is about to be cut."

"You're wrong," he growled, and just before gunning his engine, he grinned. "It isn't *about* to be cut off, it already *is* cut off. Pops got his shit wired tight."

And he sped off. For the second time the feeling of complete helplessness crept in with shades of Almaty, and once the last bits of sunlight disappeared, the sky went black, sending us into near-total darkness before night vision kicked in. A string of drones flew overhead and we dove to the gutter, waiting for the popping of ordnance drops and the subsequent detonations, but nothing happened, and when I looked up, I saw line upon line of parachutes, below each of which swung a box. It made me feel better. Maybe this wasn't going to be another Almaty, since someone to our south had decided us worthy of a resupply.

The kid led us up the road and I got the sense that nobody had ever considered holding Türkmenabat for any real length of time, because its defenses were thin. A network of trenches lined our side of the river, but we hadn't seen any indication of tunnels. Men had already assembled in their positions. We passed them and overheard bits of conversations about how one guy "was sure that we'd stop them in the river," or another "would bug out as soon as it all started; fuck this shit." But it was *all* bullshit. Without tunnels and proper defenses, it would be only a matter of time before we cooked in place, making me wonder why we should think to defend at all and how it was that I had become so exhausted. I felt about to pass out. But when we made it to our section, an alarm sounded, bringing me back to the present, and once our suits synced to the new unit, a voice came over our speakers—probably the lieutenant the supply sergeant had told us about. He sounded younger than the kid.

"Take cover. I think Russian tanks are now within plasma range."

"He *thinks*?" the kid asked.

"Nelson Jameson? Is that really your name?"

"Nah. It's the name of a guy that we left behind in Almaty. I couldn't use mine, because *she* has my suit now. Do you want to know my name?"

"No," I said. "I like 'kid.' "

Sophie collapsed against the trench wall and slid to the floor. "Oscar. I'm sick." She popped her helmet and for a moment I panicked, because there were guys on either side of us, and if one of them saw her...

But they didn't. All of them were preoccupied with what was about to happen.

"What's wrong?"

"I can't feel my feet anymore. It started in Samarkand, but now I do not know."

The kid and I popped her suit, pulling her halfway out so that she could yank one of her feet from inside the undersuit, and I snapped on my headlamp to get a better look. The ends of her toes were black.

"Jesus," I said.

"It starts now. The spoiling."

"Jesus Christ."

She had been given a bag of pills, the ones the doctor had cooked up to replace the girls' tranq tabs, and Sophie took one before she smiled. "I rot. It is true what the sergeant said. I'm past my shelf life. Did Bridgette teach you nothing?"

"Don't worry," I said. "I'll figure something out. We'll handle this."

"There's nothing to figure out, Oscar. Nothing to handle."

Before we could say anything more, someone slid into our trench and almost knocked me over.

"Did I miss anything?" asked the Brit.

It shocked me how well the Brit took the news that Sophie was a genetic. Someone might as well have told him that the river was made of water for all his reaction, which amounted to his popping his helmet and holding out a hand with a muttered "a pleasure." And as time passed, we talked, the Amu Dar'ya gurgling by while the temperature dropped so low that for a moment I had the terrifying thought that it would freeze overnight, allowing the Russian vehicles safe passage. Around midnight, there was a commotion. We buttoned up, except for Sophie, who kept insisting that she just needed to shut her eyes for a minute and liked the feeling of cold air, and everything went quiet until a group of soldiers in trucks pulled up behind our section. A guy leaned over the trench.

"Fall out for new weapons."

"What?" I asked.

"New weapons. Air-dropped. You'll need them to crack Pops's armor."

The kid, the Brit, and a few others slid from the trench and spent the next ten minutes jogging back and forth from the trucks, ferrying what eventually looked like a hundred grenade launchers and thousands of crates holding clips. We passed them down the line. I had never fired a grenade launcher, and its weight comforted me; you knew something that heavy must be able to penetrate powered armor.

The Brit chuckled.

"What?" I asked.

"Our tanks."

"What about them?"

"I don't see them anywhere. Or our APCs. So where the hell are they? And our artillery is gone, so they must expect us to hold off Popov's tanks with these little things."

Someone next to him, an older guy from the sound of his voice, laughed out loud. "We're done. We may as well break out the white flag, boys, beg for mercy. Maybe they'll take prisoners."

"Shut up," the Brit said.

"What? Why? You said it yourself—we can't hold off Russian tanks with these; so *what* if we can take out their infantry? They won't be *swimming* across the river; they'll come in APCs."

"I said shut the fuck up."

"Really? Shut up? Once the APCs get across, Pops won't even have to debark. He can fry us with plasma and drive back and forth to bury us in this place, save himself time because he won't have to dig new graves for the enemy. This trench will be our tomb. How do we live like this? My ass is infected so badly that the infections have infections, and my crap is black with blood. This trench is where we die."

The Brit slammed the butt of his grenade launcher into the guy's face and then leapt on him, struggling to pop his helmet. The whole time, the guy wouldn't stop talking—didn't even fight back.

"That's right, Legion. Take it all out on me, punish me for telling the truth. You and the rest of us are finished, so take it out on me, and forget about the fact that out there is a beast. If you beat me enough, maybe you can join *their* side."

Finally the Brit got his helmet off and I looked away. I heard the soft thuds of his gauntlet slamming into the guy's face, and little by little the talking stopped, until the Brit had enough and everything went quiet.

I turned back. "Did you kill him?"

"No," the Brit said. "But he'll have to see the medic. Maybe we should call one?"

"Forget it," said the kid. "He can find his own medic."

The Brit took off his helmet and slid to the trench floor, where he lit a cigarette, its tip triggering my infrared sensors so that it looked like a tiny star. "I'm a deserter, lads," he said.

"For real?" I asked. "Fuck it."

"Yeah. That's what I figured. When we got here, the pencil-necks tried sending me to the south side of the city, to the Legion units. I hid out, came back, and bribed them with a bottle of vodka to tell me where you lot wound up. It's not like I ran off to the Riviera."

It was the first thing I'd heard that gave me some hope. "The south side? Could that be where our armor is, like maybe they're going to attack and break out?"

"Maybe. I never got that far, but what's left of our armor has to be somewhere."

There was movement again. I had stood to stretch my legs and to try to acquaint myself with the targeting features of the grenade launcher, which differed from my Maxwell, and peered across the river toward Samarkand. When I zoomed on a boulder, something shimmered next to it, then vanished.

A booming loudspeaker shattered the silence from across the river. "Marines and soldiers of the Foreign Legion. Lay down your arms. You are encircled and there is no place left for you to run. We will be merciful and spare your lives, and you can live out your days at home with your wives and children and girlfriends. Right now in America, in France, everywhere, your countrymen are in bed with your women, and your homes are being robbed because you are here, unable to protect the ones you love. We will spare you. Lay down your arms and for you the war will be over." Then the message repeated itself, over and over.

"Fucking Russians," said the Brit.

"I think I know where the loudspeaker is. Should I pump a few grenades to take it out?"

"No," said the kid, "let it go. At least it gives us something to listen to."

Another set of trucks worked their way up the line and

we listened as they whined, some of the drivers stripping gears as they stopped and started. Another shape appeared at the edge of our trench.

"Anyone here have a heavy weapons MOS?"

The kid and a few others raised their hands. A few seconds later the man returned with help, and they passed rocket launchers and ammunition down to us.

"What are these for?" the kid asked.

"For Popov tanks. All you guys with a heavy weapons will be getting orders soon to form hunter units. It'll be your job to take out any APCs or tanks that try to cross. Good luck."

The kid sat and popped his helmet, then ran his hands through his short beard before he started sobbing. I lifted my grenade launcher, pausing only for a moment to zero on the area where I'd seen the shimmer, then fired a short salvo into the air. It took a few seconds for them to land. There was a quick flash, then two more, and the Russian voice went silent, followed by a subdued cheer from the men in our trench.

"Thanks," the kid said.

Sophie woke the next day and smiled. Her face had gone so pale that as we lay on the trench floor, I didn't notice the mud, only her dimpled cheeks, which trembled in a cold wind that blew across the river and carried away thin clouds of sand to the west. She said something, a muttered thing about her past, but it blew away too. Her voice—and everything about her—stirred memories of Bridgette, and I had to mentally swat them away with near-constant self-reminders that this was Sophie and that she differed from Bridgette in an infinite number of subtleties, despite an identical appearance. Sophie was perfectly dying.

"We cannot linger," she said.

"Why?"

"If we stay here, we are destroyed. Our forces will attack to the south today and then we will immediately move out to follow them. You will see. It is better to stay on the move and risk the offensive. Our leaders *know* this."

I said, "I need to know."

"Know what?"

"The mark. Why you don't have it and what it is."

Her face went blank then, and I wished I could take it back.

"We have a test to pass. Before they release us from the ateliers."

The wind gusted again, howling over the trench so loudly that the kid stirred beside me, but he soon stopped moving. Down the line someone coughed.

"What are they like?" I asked. "The ateliers."

"They are all I ever knew. Once. A long time ago now. It is where they taught us to hunt men and that we served a purpose greater than common soldiers—two purposes, really: to die in war and to spare the lives of human women. Did you have a mother, Oscar?"

"Yeah. Still do."

"These men all have mothers."

I nodded, not sure where she was going.

"Until there are genetics in sufficient numbers to replace *all* men on the battlefield, women are needed for birthing. It is a question of logistics and numbers, of mathematics. I asked our unit mother, Sister Jennifer, why they didn't create us as men—because it was obvious to all of us that men would have greater muscle mass, more aggression, and she told me something that was a secret. She could have been arrested for telling me. Sister Jennifer said that once upon a time, women like your mother would have fought in wars, but that those times had passed, because today it requires so many men to fill the battlefield, millions. Not one woman capable of bearing children can be wasted in war. And when human women wish to serve, and protest not being able to, they might claim that it is unfair not to allow women on the battlefield. But with us, as females, the military can respond that they *allow* women to serve, and that no more are required. She also said that earlier experiments had used male genetics, but that those units had turned on their handlers and were too aggressive. Many humans died."

"But that's all crazy," I said.

"It is a question of numbers and has nothing to do with sanity. I would like to meet your mother."

"Why?"

"Because I don't know what it means to be a girl—not a real girl. In the ateliers, when we complete our training, they line us up for the final test. It is a test of murder, where we kill something... defenseless. The unit mothers monitor the exam, and those who fail are executed later, but most of the girls succeed, joining the sisterhood of warfare—a happy occasion, when the mothers brand them with hot metal. It leaves a scar in the shape of a cross on the back of their head, or the number one; the mark depends on the atelier."

"But you don't have one," I said.

"I failed the test. I carried out the act but my readouts

indicated there was something wrong, and my unit mother led me back to the barracks, where she risked her life to save mine, and when she did it, I asked why, and she said it was because one of us should be closer to human. Sister Jennifer wanted me to learn—to become a woman. She left, and when she came back ten minutes later, she said that she had fixed everything in the computer system so that I would not be executed. They had been planning to kill me that day for my failure, but instead, because of her, I am here with you now. I carry no mark. And I have no idea what any of it means."

I pulled Sophie closer, not caring if anyone saw, and kissed her so that our goggles scraped against each other.

"Why are you sad?" I asked. "Whatever makes you different from the others must be why your spoiling isn't as advanced. It's why you're still with us, at least partially sane. It's a good thing."

"I am old, Oscar. And tired, and dying. The test forced us to kill something very dear, to prove that we didn't care for life, but I did, even back then. I'll never tell you what I killed."

The Brit and the kid leapt to their feet at the same time and peered over the trench lip. At first I didn't know what had woken them. Then I heard it. The wind carried to us a distant and faint sound of tanks and APCs, their high-pitched whines shifting in tone as the vehicles maneuvered somewhere behind a line of hills that rose from the far side of the river.

"They're coming this way, mate."

"Nah," said the kid. "They're leaving."

"Why the hell would they leave? I'm telling you, get that rocket launcher ready. They're coming for us."

Without warning a flash lit the dim morning sky ahead of us, so bright that it frosted my goggles. They cleared a moment later. Then a second flash, a third, and then maybe a thousand more all at once. I smelled ozone inside my suit and glanced at the heads-up to see the readout flicker and jump before finally going dark, and then I heard the deep boom of explosions, so tremendous that they shook the trench and nearly collapsed the wall against which we leaned. A vast curtain of dust and smoke rose in the distance, stretching across the horizon.

"Jesus," said the kid.

The Brit coughed. "They went nuclear. There go all our troubles."

"Nah," I said, "that wasn't nuclear or we'd be getting rad alarms. I think we just used our space-based kinetics, and now there's nothing stopping Pops from using his. We'd better get moving. Soon."

The Brit turned and was about to say something when my backup suit computer kicked in, snapping the heads-up to life; the radio clicked on. Someone announced that all units were to withdraw southward immediately.

"Looks like Command agrees with you, mate," he said.

But we all stopped talking then. The war had just transformed into something more horrible, where you'd be there one minute, gone the next—because an orbital space platform had just accelerated thousands of shielded tungsten spheres to impact on Russian positions, and Pops would be pissed, would want revenge, might even hit us with the same kinds of weapons. Then again, I thought, there were worse ways to go.

*   *   *

We moved through the city and local Turkmen watched at their windows, looking down at us from homes and buildings that had been constructed in concrete. In places it flaked off. The structures were clearly hundreds of years old, but they had painted them in garish colors so that bright yellows and blues contrasted with the filthy gutters, and I suspected the paint hid something rotten, making it even more important to just get the hell out.

Sophie stumbled against me, almost collapsing in the street.

"Are you OK?" I asked.

"I can't feel my feet anymore."

"Did the doctor ever find something that would stop the spoiling—when you were in Samarkand?"

"I don't know. He was getting close, but we left before he said anything final."

"Come with me." I was helping the kid carry a rocket crate and handed my end to the Brit so I could wrap one of Sophie's arms around my shoulder, pulling her forward into the throng of soldiers.

"Where are you going?" the kid called after us.

"To find the doctor. Don't worry, I'll rejoin you later."

We saw a group of military police and steered toward them. "Hey, you guys know where medical is headquartered for now? The French doctors?"

They shrugged and one of them pointed south. "Probably with the Legion, on the south side."

We pushed back into the crowds. The combined weight of the grenade launcher, my kit and armor, and Sophie felt as though it would force my legs to crumble, made them scream a reminder that they would no longer handle this kind of abuse. But we kept going, and at moments Sophie regained some sensation so that she could walk under her own power. It gave me time to recoup. Soldiers around us grumbled, asking what the hurry was. It was a good question, one that made me consider the possibility that I had developed an extra sense, one that felt the light dim—just slightly—at the first sign of trouble, even when it was completely unapparent to those around me. At one point we passed a park and fountain, which had been shut down for the winter, and saw groups of soldiers lounging on bare dirt with their helmets off and cigarettes dangling, or beards stained from the accumulated months of chewing tobacco that inevitably dripped its way down their chins. You saw it in their eyes: these were the ones who would soon die. They knew it and had a kind of stoned look on their faces, so I grabbed Sophie to pull her faster, to get us away from the men and their stares, which told a story of seeing fate and being so resigned to it that no fight remained. It was the same look I'd seen all over Kaz, but it didn't matter; each time was like a revelation.

We broke out of the city and shielded our eyes until the goggles adjusted a moment later. It was still morning, so the sun hung low in the sky, forcing us to stare into it, and at first we couldn't make out our surroundings. But as the vision kits frosted, it was clear that we'd have a hard way ahead. On either side of the highway, tall sand dunes rose, and the wind whipped their crests to send a shifting veil of grit over the concrete, making our boots crunch as we moved on. A long line of APCs and trucks idled by the roadside and we made a beeline for them, their fading red crosses familiar and dreadful at the same time.

A French medic tended to racks of troops in the back of his vehicle and I pounded on the side. "Where is the doctor?" I asked, repeating it in broken French.

"Which one?"

"The one who commanded the hospital in Samarkand."

"First APC, front of the line."

Sophie had begun to lean on me again, and I heard her breathing become shallow and rapid. We made it to the lead APC, and I popped my helmet.

The doctor recognized me almost at once. "It's you! Glad to see you made it." The back of the APC had been cleared of everything except a tall table and operating equipment. He worked on someone who had been stripped of all his clothes, and a long gash ran down his left leg, which twitched while the man screamed. "Get up here," the doctor said. "You can help."

"I'm not a medic," I said.

"So what?"

"But I'm a civilian."

"There are no civilians here, come up."

I motioned for Sophie to sit next to the vehicle and climbed the ramp, ducking at the same time I stowed all my gear in a corner.

"Here," he said. "Hold his leg absolutely still but don't bother taking off your gauntlets; there is no time. I have to reconnect his artery and this asshole keeps jumping."

I did as he instructed and tried not to throw up, but when I looked away, the doctor laughed.

"This is not so bad. You should have seen *your* case when they brought you in. Burns like that are the worst. The outer layers of skin slough off, like when you roast a marshmallow for too long; it becomes crispy on the outside, soft underneath, and everything slides apart."

"What happened to this guy?"

"Tank commander. His vehicle exploded and sent a ceramic plate into his leg, so he will be lucky to keep it; I should probably give up and amputate but he is the son of my cousin."

"I'm sorry, Doc."

"Do not be. He really is an asshole; Phillipe burned down my sister's house when he was sixteen. It was an accident, but the shit didn't have the decency to even apologize, not now, not then. You hear that, Phillipe? *You are a filthy asshole.*"

The man screamed again, and inside the APC his voice was so loud it felt as though my eardrums would burst.

"Can't you give him something for the pain or to knock him out?"

"I did. As much as I could, but he lost too much blood, so there aren't many options. *Just so!*"

The doctor finished whatever he was doing and ordered a medic to complete the sutures. Then he dipped his hands in a tub of alcohol and pulled them out to drip pale red from all the blood that had already collected in the tub, and I ducked from the APC, not wanting to see if any had gotten on my gauntlets. He jumped down after me and laughed.

"You are so broken, American. Why did you come find me?"

"Do you remember you were tasked with finding a way to stop the deterioration in genetic troops so we could use them in the field after their normal service life?"

He nodded. "Not so important now; they all died in Samarkand. Or were captured, which is the same thing."

I gestured at Sophie, who removed her helmet, and the doctor's face went pale. "This is not possible. This is not OK. She should not be alive and you should not have brought her here; I will get the military police."

I drew my fléchette pistol and placed it under his chin before forcing him around one side of the APC so we couldn't be seen from the road. Something had snapped; it was a quick decision, almost reflexive, and although I didn't want to shoot him, I knew I would. "You're not going anywhere."

"What do you want?"

"I want to know if you can fix her. She's deteriorating. How far did you get in your research?"

"I came up with something, a combined treatment using both immunomodulating agents and gene therapy, but the subject became irrelevant when the Russians broke through and killed them all. In any case, I only produced a few vials. What are her symptoms so far?" I told him about her toes and feet and he shook his head. "If you came for my drugs, it will do no good. I could give you the perfect cocktail and it would not reverse effects that have already taken hold. Her toes will have to be removed. And this I will *not* do."

The ground rumbled with the sound of explosions to our south but I didn't take my eyes off him. "Then you die before she does."

"We are at war!" the doctor shouted. "Right now French armor is trying to break through to our south, and have been all morning. I have more wounded than I can

handle, and you want me to stop what I'm doing to take care of *a thing?*"

I pushed the barrel of my pistol against his earlobe, pointing outward toward the dunes, and fired. When the fléchette ripped off a piece of skin, he shrieked.

"*Asshole!* Fine. You," he said, pointing at Sophie. "Get in the APC."

I handed her the pistol and then turned to warn him. "No general anesthetics for her, only locals. When you're finished, give us the immuno-drugs, antibiotics, painkillers, and whatever else she needs to take care of her feet."

"You must be joking. She'll need time to rest. You can't take her from here once I've finished, *she will have no toes.*"

"Do it."

The doctor and Sophie waited for the guy in the APC to finish suturing, after which he wheeled the previous patient out. I pushed a fresh table up the ramp and then shut the two of them in.

We moved as quickly as we could, trying to get away from the line of medical vehicles, when the doctor called after us.

"You are a pair of stupid shits! Stupid! What, do you think that you'll get her all the way to Bandar? I have her toes, *you stupid fucking American*!"

And he was right: it *was* stupid. Almost within the first few steps, I saw that it wouldn't work, because Sophie started sobbing and slumped to the ground, and I had to drop all our weapons. It was the only way I could carry her. Even then my legs wouldn't hold for long, and she almost shouted out loud at every step I took, with her piggybacked and bouncing along to my feeble attempt at running, trying to bury her head in my shoulder. We merged into the crowd of soldiers as it crept southward. For a while I slowed and it became a little easier to hold her, but then the journey degraded into a matter of counting my steps, urging myself to take another ten, just another five, and then promising to nobody in particular that if I could rest—just put her down for a second—I'd get up refreshed and ready to go. But I knew if that happened, I wouldn't be able to pick her up again. Finally I moved to the roadside and into the dunes, where we collapsed in a pile, and she screamed when her foot slammed into the sand at an awkward angle. "I'm sorry," I must have said, but who knew? It wasn't a time for "I'm sorry" or anything close to it, because it had all gotten so clustered, screwed, and ambiguous, and it might have been all my fault.

She popped her helmet and looked at me. "I love you."

"What? Are you crazy?"

"No. I love you."

"I love you too." And then I popped my helmet so we could kiss, and it was the best kiss I'd ever had, one colored by terror and frustration, tinted with the knowledge that I was sub-adequate. It was a *she-was-beyond-beautiful-and-to-hell-with-everything-else* kiss, because I didn't deserve her, didn't know how much longer she had.

"What will we do when we make it to Bandar?" she asked.

"We won't make it to Bandar. Not like this."

"Yes we will."

"You *are* crazy, then, if you really think that." She

laughed and I got angry. "Why are you laughing? There's nothing funny here."

"Oscar, I have never felt pain. Ever. My sisters and I are designed so that we can will our blood to stop flowing from open wounds, to not feel pain and override nerve impulses in order to stay on the field as long as possible. I can't do that anymore. I'm more like you today than I was yesterday, *and my pain proves it.*"

"Sophie, you can't walk. And at any minute Pops could light us up with his overhead kinetics, and even if he doesn't, we need to get to the front and *through* it to see Bandar. How do you expect to fight if we reach the front? This is where we are and where we'll stay. South of Türkmenabat, on a highway full of shit."

"You're wrong." She kissed me again, once. "I know we'll make it; you just have to be enough."

I pulled her close then and wondered if anyone was watching, but the masses of troops moved by in steady thumping, all of them too self-absorbed to notice the pair of discards on the dunes. I popped her armor and slid my hand in, just wanting to feel Sophie, running my finger over her undersuit as she stared into my eyes and smiled again, opening her mouth slightly to moan.

"I wish we could marry," she said.

"Here?"

"Why not here? If there were a priest, I would do it right now."

"They wouldn't let us. There must be some kind of law against me marrying you."

"Why, because I am synthetic?"

"No, because you're crazy."

She laughed and then winced with pain, so I slid my

hand out and resealed her suit. It was late in the afternoon now. The sun hadn't set, but already the moon made its appearance and was full, staring down at us as I rolled over on my back and slid against her side. The section of sky farthest from the sun was an unholy blue, so deep that it was almost black, the kind of color you got only in the desert on a clear day in the winter or early spring, and if you weren't looking directly at it, you saw a single star begin to twinkle, invisible except in peripheral vision.

"Once we rest, we will try again," she said.

"You really believe we'll make it, don't you?"

"I believe in many things. Like you. I knew when I first heard your screams that you were different and that you belonged in war."

"See, there's where you're wrong. I'm a coward. I'm here because I got trapped and because I'm a drug addict whose own parents had disowned him and whose father died thinking that Oscar was a waste. A loser. The worst part about all that?" I remembered that I still had cigarettes and paused to pull one out, lighting it as I spoke. "The worst part is that he was right, and I never got the chance to tell him—even if he *was* an asshole, which he really wasn't. He was just a dad." Even as I finished, I felt my jaw tighten and I fought the urge to cry, turning away so she wouldn't see it if I did.

"I think that's wonderful."

"What?"

"I'd love to be a drug addict—in fact, I think I am— but I don't know enough to know if this is a bad thing or a good thing. It just is. I'd kill to have a father and mother, even bad ones. Even ones who hated me. Because then you know that you belong in this world, and I've listened

to enough men to know that you aren't the only one con-
flicted. I used to sit outside the hospital ward and listen. I
love the way men talk and hate themselves, the way they
are cruel and gentle at the same time, like when one of
them loses a leg and the others make jokes about how
he'll never dance again. It is so human. You have no perspective. You belong, and right now you're alive, yet you
choose instead to focus on death and things that may
never come to pass."

I pulled hard on the cigarette, holding the smoke in as
long as I could, and felt the nicotine work its magic, calm-
ing every nerve. She was deadly. This was the kind of girl
who got it and made me want everything, and for a
moment I *forgot* about everything, including the fact that
she was in such bad shape—that I might still lose her.

"You really think we'll make it to Bandar?" I asked.

"I need you. I want you to make me your wife and
show me a bad life. Or a good one, it doesn't matter. Give
me something to make it so I belong; give me you."

"I will marry you."

"Do you mean this?"

I nodded, then blew smoke in her face and grinned. "I
want you. Yeah."

"Then you *have* to get us to Bandar, because if we
don't get there, you will have shattered me."

I dosed Sophie with meds at 0200 and lifted her onto my
back, then struggled down the dune face until we were
back on the highway, heading southwest. The crowds had
disappeared by then, and men slept on either side. It gave
the night, which was otherwise still, a *Night Before*

Christmas quality, and as I walked, the only things I heard were my footsteps and the occasional rumble of guns ahead of us. Sophie linked to my coms so she could whisper "I love you" or that she had never been happier, so it felt as though something new had been injected into my veins, allowing me to continue when everything else said to stop.

At about three we reached a point where the road transformed from a smooth surface to one heavily cratered, and in my night vision I saw patches where plasma had scorched the concrete, which still smoldered. Empty vehicles lay scattered on every side. Some of them still burned, and the heat made their ceramic plates pop as they expanded. But I recognized where my mind went; this was the retreat from Pavlodar all over again, and the veil of exhaustion was a familiar stew that bubbled around my brain to baste it in taunting thoughts of giving up and going to sleep. Sophie's head lolled when she passed out. Her helmet clicked against mine in a kind of rhythm that I tried to maintain, which kept me going for another kilometer.

Eventually someone hissed at us from the roadside, where three men crouched behind the remains of a burned-out APC. "Where are you going?" one asked.

"We're looking for the front."

"You're there. Find some cover and shut the fuck up."

I moved as fast as I could, heading to the left side and away from them as I looked for cover—a hole, another burned-out vehicle, anything. A shallow depression in the sand opened in front of me and I saw shapes in it: two soldiers on their stomachs, looking forward. I was about to ask if we could join them when I decided to hell with it, I'd ask later, and placed Sophie on the ground before crawling up to one of them and slapping him on the shoulder.

"Who are you guys?" The guy didn't answer, so I shook him. "Hey, buddy, you awake?"

He hadn't answered because he was dead. The entire fronts of his and the other one's helmets were shattered, what was left of their faces spilling onto the sand.

Sophie woke and took my hand. "Where are we?"

"We're at the front. These two are gone."

"Get their weapons."

Once I had gathered their grenade launchers and clips, we settled in to wait for morning.

"I had the strangest dream while you were walking," she said.

"Of what?"

"That I met Bridgette."

The words sent a shiver up my spine, and I flinched when a pair of tanks opened fire to our front, about four hundred meters away. One of them must have hit something, because the rounds burst, then caused multiple explosions in the distance.

"She was beautiful," I said, "but not like you."

"How am I different?"

"Bridgette was curious about men, like you are, but she never really wanted to live."

"Do you still love her?"

I thought for a minute, and we ducked when the entire front lit up with firing from both sides, tiny grenade flashes and plasma bursts mingling in a kind of light show that from farther away would have been interesting, like it had been in Samarkand. As it was, I wanted to bury myself in the sand.

"Yeah," I said. "I still love her."

Someone jumped into our hole and I almost fired on him, which would have been idiotic, because at that range the grenade might have killed us along with him. It was a Legion officer. When he saw our suits, he spoke in almost perfect English instead of French.

"I can't sync with your suits; open a channel." Once we had, he went on. "Good. I've uploaded map data, so take a look at it when you get a chance. Tomorrow we're making the final push. When the time comes, don't stop to gather wounded, just keep going. This will be our only chance at breaking through."

He got up to leave and I stopped him. "Hey, pal, I'm looking for two buddies of mine. They stick together. One is a British guy with your outfit, the Legion; the other is an American kid but he's wearing a genetic combat suit."

"Yes, I saw them. The only reason I remember is that someone tried to shoot the one in genetic armor before he could show that he was human."

"Where? Is he OK?"

He pointed toward the front. "About there, with a tank hunter unit, three hundred meters away and very close to no-man's-land, but he was fine when I last saw him. Good luck finding them, I hope you make it. I hope we all make it."

When he left, Bridgette wrapped my hand with one of hers. "Why don't you know their names?"

"Whose?"

"Your friends'."

"I don't know. I just don't feel the need, maybe because names don't matter that much anymore."

She pulled me in closer and it drove me crazy to be with her and not be able to feel that skin, to instead have to hear ceramic against ceramic.

"I think it's good that you still love Bridgette. She seemed like a very nice person, and I would have liked her immensely. But we shouldn't stay here until morning."

"Why?" I asked.

"Because you should find your friends. Rest. In a while I'll wake you up, and we will move out while it's still dark, because nobody should be separated from their friends unless they want to be."

Sophie didn't need help, because we crept from the hole after switching on our chameleon skins, moving toward the front on our bellies. When we got closer, incoming plasma rounds raised the temperature and I watched the suit indicator climb. Tiny lumps of molten glass spattered the sand around me, hissing when they landed, so that as I pushed forward, the landscape turned into something resembling a moonscape more than anything earthly. Whenever we passed a hole or a group of men, I hissed out, calling for the kid, because I didn't want to risk using the general frequency, which was already busy with traffic. It was excruciatingly slow. Half an hour later we found a strongpoint, which consisted of three tanks that looked as though they'd been toys tossed into the air before landing on their sides, propped against each other; we moved in and deactivated our skins.

A group of men, protected by the walls of destroyed tanks, stood in a circle around something, and I was about to ask one of them about the kid when they all laughed. It was the coldest laugh I'd ever heard. Their conversation played out in helmet speakers, making it impossible to tell who said what.

"You little fuck. Thought you'd get away with it."

"Kill him."

"To hell with that, let's mess him up. Guy wants to play some more, don't you, Popov?"

Then I heard a boy's voice, which sounded even younger than the kid's, and its slightly accented English made him sound innocent, maybe a little slow. "You will all die. Where are your sisters?"

I pushed into the circle to get a better look, leaving Sophie to sit in the sand. In the middle of the circle lay a Russian genetic. His armor had been scorched, and it looked as though it was two inches thick in places, with massive servo boxes at key joints, and tubes that must have held hydraulic systems. The outside was covered by things resembling exposed pipes. But his arms were missing. Both had been blown off and the shoulder pieces dripped what in night vision looked like blood, but I suspected it was more likely hydraulic fluid of some kind. The image of kids pulling the wings off a fly popped into my head. The guy's helmet was off, and he looked like the one I had seen so long ago in Karazhyngyl; he was a boy who should have been in high school and who smiled at all of us, either oblivious to the danger or ignoring it.

I nudged a Marine next to me. "What's going on? How'd he get here?"

"We caught him trying to infiltrate the lines, maybe spotting our pos."

"Shouldn't we hand him over to an officer, let them interrogate him?"

"What officer? You see any around?"

The Russian laughed at that, making me shiver. "Your officers are all gone. Bandar 'Abbas is gone. How long has it been since any of you heard word from Bandar?"

"Shut up!" one of the others yelled. He kicked the boy in the face, and I heard a sickening crunch.

"Is that true?" I asked. "Did something happen in Bandar?"

Nobody answered.

One of the men walked up to the boy and pulled out his combat knife before kneeling by his side. You'd think I would have been horrified at what I knew was about to happen. I wasn't. I *wanted* him to be tortured, and my mind shifted into a gear that had never existed before, one where revenge overrode any scraps of decency that I had managed to maintain, and one where the need to punish this one for everything—for Bridgette, Ox, the general, and even my father—became so intense that I shouted something like "Cut his balls off," and someone shouted back, "He doesn't have any balls." We all started shouting after that so the mob of us became a unified thing, a machine of retribution and God take the Russian. The man used his knife to cut one of the boy's ears off, and the fact that the kid didn't cry out, didn't beg, made me angrier. We wanted him to squirm.

"My brothers will be here soon," he said, shaking the blood off his hair. "And when they come, you will not be welcome in any world."

The man with the knife lost it then and slammed it into the Russian's windpipe, silencing the boy with a thud. The spell broke. My hands shook and it felt as though my suit vents had clogged. A sense of claustrophobia took hold and I grabbed the Marine next to me to keep from falling over.

"You OK, pal?" he asked.

"I'm looking for the kid. He's wearing genetic armor, but he's one of us and is traveling with a Brit from the Legion."

"Mate?" The one with the knife wiped it off in the Russian genetic's hair and then walked over. "You made it!"

The kid, who had been standing in the circle opposite me, joined us and slapped me on the back. "Holy shit. We thought we'd never see you again!"

I should have been happy, but the circumstances of our reunion had changed things, made me wonder how it was that my friends had done this. Then I remembered what *I* had wanted to do to the Russian. It just didn't matter.

"I've been looking all over for you guys. Is it true that we're moving out tomorrow?"

"It's true," said the Brit. "And then on to Bandar."

The kid said, "If Bandar is even still there."

"Why, what have you guys heard?"

The Brit sheathed his knife with a *snick*. "Command lost contact with them two weeks ago, and rumor has it that Pops nuked it, the port and everything. It's why your government OK'd the use of kinetics. Where is Sophie?"

We walked back to where I had left her, and Sophie lay in the sand, curled up with both knees pressed against her chest. She wouldn't respond to me at first. The kid and the Brit dug shallow holes and lay down next to us, arranging their rockets and the launcher so they'd be ready quickly. I rested my hand against Sophie's helmet.

"Are you there?" I asked.

"I'm here."

"What's wrong?"

She said nothing at first but then asked me to take off my helmet and vision hood, which I did. I scrunched down, hoping that no snipers were nearby.

"Would you let them do that to me?" she asked.

"Do what?"

"Torture me like that. Cut my ear off."

My stomach turned and I felt sick again with the thought of what had just happened. "Never. I'd die before I'd let that happen to you."

"But you yelled. With the rest of them. I heard it."

"He was a Russian, Sophie, a genetic."

She slammed her fist into my jaw so hard that my head snapped back into the sand with a thud, and for a moment I thought I'd black out.

"I'm a genetic!"

I waited for someone to say something, to run over and wipe her at that very instant, but nobody moved except for the Brit and the kid, who shifted in their holes.

"You might want to keep that shit down," the kid said. "Just sayin'."

Sophie yanked her helmet off and spat on me before she started sobbing, and I had to pull her close, feeling as though I'd made the biggest mistake of my life and wanting to take it back. But it was too late.

"I'm sorry, Sophie," I whispered. We lay there for an hour, and in the east the sky started to turn a lighter shade, dimly illuminating the sand and wreckage.

"It's not your fault," Sophie finally said. "I would have done the same thing. My sisters would have. It's not your fault."

But something about her voice made me wonder if she meant it. At any moment, the order to move out would come, and I didn't care. In less than a minute I'd managed to fuck up the one thing left that mattered to me, and nothing would change it. As we lay there, my mind raced, trying to figure out a way to make it better, to rationalize what I had shouted at the boy, what I had felt—anything to use to try to explain it all away so we could go back to the way it had been the day before. But nothing came to me.

When the sun rose, orders arrived, flashing on our heads-up displays at the same time someone announced them over coms. An explosion boomed in front of us. I looked up and pulled on my vision hood and helmet, watching as wave after wave of auto-drones swooped down on the Russian positions, and it made me start to feel better, knowing that we'd be getting help from somewhere despite the fact that Bandar might no longer exist. I gave Sophie the next dose of medicine and began to lift her up but she slapped my hands away.

"I can move on my own for now."

The Brit and the kid gathered their things and waited.

"You guys ready?" I asked. They gave the word and we all moved forward. Sophie fell a couple of times and yelled when I tried to help her up, while all around us the shapes of men left their holes in the sand, forming a wave of soldiers that crept toward the line. Our tanks opened fire. Soon they too began to move, inching just in front of the infantry to give us some cover from enemy fire. Sophie was falling behind. I grabbed her then, and she screamed at me to let go, pounded on my shoulders, but I ignored the blows and forced her onto my back.

"You're not going to fuck this up. I don't care if you hate me now, screw it. But I won't let you fuck this up."

Eventually she fell limp and cried. That was how I moved into my final battle of the war: with the Brit and the kid at my side, a broken genetic on my back, and a feeling of dread that I had changed more than I'd realized. I'd become *less* than subhuman and didn't deserve to make it out.

NINE

Second Chances

The war became a blur, my mind a singularity that sucked in on itself so that all I felt was the weight of Sophie and a vague sensation that the kid and the Brit stumbled on in front of me, their shapes sometimes getting lost behind curtains of sand and smoke. There were screaming and forms. Tanks, behind which we marched, rotated their turrets to either side and vomited plasma, but we didn't see if they hit anything, because of the obscurants, dust clouds that defeated our infrared and laser targeting with burning ribbons of magnesium. As I pressed on, it occurred to me that we should have been high, that once upon a time it would have been cool to think that we walked through an infinite sparkler and into some fucked-up land of enchantment. You forgot more than you remembered, but you remembered more than anyone should. There was a group of Popov genetics who had gone unnoticed during the advance and sprang from the sand to ambush a few Legion soldiers to my left, but the Gs didn't fire any weapons. They punched through the men's armor with bare fists and ripped out handfuls of skin, and it was so unreal that I didn't react except to think it was a strange thing to do. Someone fired rockets at the group, killing everyone, and I thought, *Well, yeah, that's OK, because now those guys are gone, out of it all, so it won't hurt anymore.* And then there was a wounded Marine who begged for help because his legs were gone. He said, "Please, don't let me die here," and I said, "It's not such a bad place. I can't carry you anyway." He started crying before I lost sight of him. There were so many scenes that I stopped processing until much later, when they shoved into my thoughts without warning. An hour into the advance, we paused in a Russian trench, popping our helmets and taking the time to recover what strength we could, grinning broadly because whatever else had happened, we hadn't died yet, and from the radio traffic we knew that things were going well. Bandar had never felt closer.

"I love my rockets," the kid said to me.

"They're really good rockets."

"No, you don't understand, old man. Take for once. I really, *really* love them, like I'm the ultimate badass and these are magical things, rounds that never miss. I took off a G's head this morning, hadn't even waited for the tone and just squeezed off, so the warhead never had time to arm, it just took his head, all kinetic. I'm the reaper."

"They're *insanely* good rockets," I said.

"Yeah, man, that's more like it. Insanely good, now I get why you were a reporter, that's a good word for them. Crazy." He paused to take a drag off a cigarette the Brit offered him and ducked when a series of grenades cracked around our position. "Fucking Popovs. I'm ready, Oscar, ready to make it happen, like who cares if we're up against Gs, man? These guys are like little girls, little ape-men."

"You're the rocket man."

"I'm the freakin' rocket man. And a half. Insanely good."

Sophie didn't say anything, and when it came time to leave, I lifted her onto my back again, and we moved out, returning into the haze. The tank commanders waved us on. Something told me that as long I was in a cloud, nothing could touch us, so I positioned myself as close to a tank as I could, walking within the backwash of sand that it kicked up, and catching only glimpses of the battle as it unfolded on either side. I flinched when the vehicle suddenly blew into a cone of plasma because a Russian rocket had streaked out of nowhere and slammed into its reactor section, and I watched as something arched overhead trailing a thin line of white smoke. It thudded to the ground next to me. Once I recognized what the thing was, I pushed on, trying to figure out how the tank commander's head could dislodge from his torso and fly that high, hit the sand, and still have a look of surprise on it as if the guy had been freeze-dried at the moment of death.

We stopped again an hour later and ate lunch underneath the shell of an APC, shoving in as much food and water as we could before our stomachs stopped working out of fear. Exhaustion only masked so much. Once you got used to the walking and dead, fear always found a way back in; adrenaline could keep flowing for only so long and then it hit you again—that you didn't want to die, but that this was the worst possible place for someone with a death phobia.

"I can't taste my food," the Brit said.

I nodded. "I know, this shit is awful."

"No, I mean I can't taste it, can't taste anything, mate."

He ripped off his vision hood and there it was—that look. The Brit was augering in. I just knew that in a few minutes, maybe seconds, he'd lose it, so I glanced at Sophie in the hope that she'd say something to make it stop, but she looked away.

"Bandar," I said.

"What about Bandar?"

"I bet they have good food in Bandar. Better than this crap. I bet by the time we get there, everything nuked will have been fixed, rebuilt, and that we'll get the good stuff as soon as we make it in."

"It's all in Bandar?"

"It's all in Bandar."

The Brit smiled then and shook his head. "Shit."

"You should relax," the kid said. "Just trust in the rocket man and everything will be waxy."

"Hey, kid," I said, and he stopped eating to look at me. "They'll make you give up your rockets in Bandar, you know. You can't take them home."

"That's messed," he said with a genuine look of disappointment. He tossed his pouch to the side and rebuttoned his helmet. "Maybe the war won't end, then. Maybe we'll come back and keep going, push back north."

"Yeah. Maybe."

Our heads-up displays kept us on course, and we had linked with a Legion armored unit, which meant we stopped when they did and pressed on when they said to. So we had a sense of where we were. But the image of a map and the reality of the battlefield were always two different things, and after lunch, when we moved out again, I became lost in a sensation of futility, thinking that maybe in all that time, we'd moved only a few hundred yards and would have to fight like this for months, maybe years. It didn't help that we couldn't see more than ten feet in any direction. Popov armor continuously pelted the battlefield with obscurant shells, adding to a confusion that would have been there anyway and forced you to wonder if at any moment you'd drop off the edge of the earth, step into a chasm that someone had forgotten to map and that you couldn't see because of all the shit in the air. At one point I tripped on something and fell, dropping Sophie so that she rolled a few feet to the side and screamed, and I got up cursing, looking at my feet for what had snagged me. It was a Legion guy. An APC wheel had been blown off one of our vehicles and pinned him to the ground, half buried in sand so that all he could do was wave one arm in the air and ask for water.

"That's messed up," said the kid.

"No shit." I gave the guy some water but he died before drinking it. Sophie waited for me on the ground and I lifted her again, trying to ignore the burning pain in my lower back. "Are you OK, Sophie?"

"I'm fine. I'm sorry for getting mad at you, Oscar."

"It's OK."

"I had forgotten."

"About what?"

"About what it's like. The cumulative effects of watching your family die and what it makes you want. And I was wrong when I said that my sisters would have done the same thing to the Russian genetic. They would have done much worse." She rested her head on my shoulder after that, and everything felt better.

By mid-afternoon, the advance had halted. It wasn't a question of our just giving a little more and continuing the attack, because from the radio traffic, we knew that Popov had pulled off some magic of his own, had set up his defenses so that as soon as we crashed one position, he fell back a kilometer to the next one, wearing us out a little at a time. Our tanks and infantry had become scattered, and whatever remained of Command needed a breather to regroup and get everyone back into order before we made for the next Russian position. We had arranged the bodies of dead Russian genetics, stacked three layers high, so that we could lie behind them and take off our helmets. The firing had died off, and once Pops pulled back, the air cleared; for once we saw sky.

"I like the desert," the kid said.

"It's winter," I pointed out. "Maybe early spring, I don't know. The point is, deserts aren't so bad as long as it's not summer."

"I served in Africa before all this," the Brit said. "God, what a hellhole—at least, that's what I used to say. Now I don't know. The bush wars weren't like this, weren't this bad and didn't make you want to disappear."

"Relax," the kid said. "You're with rocket—"

Before he could finish, the Brit leapt on him, smashing his fist into the kid's face and breaking his nose. The kid scrambled backward in shock. A few seconds later he started crying.

"You're just a fucking kid!" the Brit shouted. "I swear to God, if you say rocket man one more time, I'll cut your fingers off. Don't. Just don't. I'm tired and I just want to smoke cigarettes for a few minutes so I can imagine that I'm back in the bush, maybe back in Korea. What the fuck *do you even know*?"

Once the Brit turned and lit his cigarette, he lay on

his back and stared at the sky, so I moved closer to the kid.

"Don't sweat it."

"I'm cool."

"Well, then stop crying. It'll be cool, just hang."

"I can't stop crying."

"Why not?"

The kid whispered in my ear that back in Türkmenabat he'd stopped off at a brothel with the Brit, after Sophie and I had gone to find the doctor. One of the girls had given him something. "And it hurts, man. I'm way sick."

I laughed then and felt bad for the kid, really, but it was so funny, because he had no idea how cool he was, and it was always cool when someone didn't *know* he was cool.

"That shit?" I asked, waiting for him to look at me again before I finished. "*That* is the least of your problems. Don't even worry about that stuff. I'm just glad you finally got laid."

By three a.m. we were ready to move out, and the tanks coughed to life, although there were clearly fewer of them now and about half as many APCs as we'd started with. The exhaustion had gotten so thick that I couldn't see straight. Someone explained the tactical situation: Popov had raced due south through western Uzbekistan in his bid to cut us off, but to move quickly they could bring only infantry and APCs, which explained why we had made such progress—no Russian tanks. Still, we wore down. Before sunset I had taken off my helmet and vision kit, and saw the dust and sand that had caked to everyone's armor, turning it a matte tan. We had to kick each

other's suit vents every so often to knock the crud loose
and allow fresh air through the filters. And my muscles
hated me. I lifted Sophie in the darkness and she cried
out, but it barely registered, because my arms and back
had fused into a burning mass, threatening to spasm out
at any moment.

Lightly armored Marine units moved to our north and
south, but during the last bits of daylight, most of the
remaining French armor had been transferred to our area,
in the center, so that we massed in a last effort to break
through Popov's line. Beyond him was open desert;
beyond that, about two hundred klicks southwest, was the
city of Mary, and then the Iranian border. I was thinking
about the ocean, how it would feel when we got to Bandar, when we saw the air-attack warning beacon blink on
and dove to the sand, but then a flight of our fighters
swung in to take care of the Russian drones, so we stood
again and moved out, a little more quickly, to mix with
Russian units and hopefully avoid their aircraft in the
process. Still, it made you feel good. Friendly airfields
operated somewhere to the west, close enough to keep up
the support, and it took the edge off an increasing feeling
that we were the only people on the planet.

We had just crested a low dune when multiple rockets
flared up on my infrared, streaking out from the desert.
The APC in front of me opened fire immediately. Its computer tracked the incoming projectiles and spun its turret
wildly in an effort to knock out the inbound, but two made
it through and punched through the vehicle's front armor.
Its reaction seemed delayed. Slow. At first the APC
jumped a little, and then, a second later, every hatch blew
out in jets of flame, and the rear ramp flew past me, less

than a foot by my head, with a *whup-whup* sound, followed by the explosion's shock wave. *We* fired obscurants this time. For a moment, though, before getting lost in the haze again, Popov's APCs saw clearly enough to send a volley of plasma rounds in our general direction, and I fell to the sand again, burying Sophie underneath me and ignoring her pleas to get off. We waited for the smoke to gather and then rose.

The kid screamed in front of me and the haze lit briefly from the backwash of his rocket launcher, and then a few seconds later I dropped into a Russian trench. The kid was on my right, and the Brit on my left. Nobody moved. It was as if the world had gone silent. I heard Sophie's helmet click against mine, but only just barely, because my sixth sense had kicked in to let me know that things weren't normal, that something was off, but I hadn't yet been able to put a finger on it. Then four Russian genetics rose in front of us from the sand, which cascaded off their powered armor, and I don't remember screaming until long after the terror of hearing powered armor for the first time. When I was this close to them, they seemed inhuman—awkward nightmares that clunked and hissed as they moved in our direction at the same time they raised grenade launchers and opened up.

One of the kid's rockets burned a hole through the closest Russian, and then the Brit launched a salvo of grenades, covering another in thermal gel. The thing's hydraulic lines burst, sending the Russian to the sand, where it just lay there. But the other two continued forward.

"I'm jammed," said the Brit, and the kid shouted back, "Reloading."

Sophie yelled for me to get down and I looked at her in

confusion, wondering when I had dropped her, until I saw that she had found a Russian grenade launcher and now pointed it at my head.

"Don't shoot me," I said.

"Get down!"

As soon as I dropped, she opened fire. I couldn't see the impact, but I heard it and then heard the scraping of metal on metal until one of the things finally slid over the trench lip, causing the sand to pour on top of me so that I lay partially buried.

The Brit leaned over. "You alive, mate?"

"Yeah."

"Brilliant! Stay here, we're going hunting." He vanished with the kid and I did my best to brush the mounds of sand away, freeing my legs one at a time.

"You almost shot me," I said to Sophie.

"The only danger was your slow reaction. I would not have shot you."

"What if you had?"

"I would not have. I love you."

One of the Russians, the one the Brit had brought down using thermal gel, popped his armor with a hiss. Sophie targeted him, and just before he slid from the shell, she fired a grenade. He fell, limp, into the sand, where he bled out in front of us.

"I still think you might have hit me by accident," I said.

"Then you don't know me well enough."

At first the sounds of battle were everywhere—men screaming and the noise of rockets and grenades slamming into metal. But slowly it all went away. I knew from my heads-up that we hadn't been left behind, because our main force had gathered only about a hundred meters beyond our trench, but it still felt eerie. The obscurants had drifted off ten minutes earlier, and far overhead the moon was visible, not full anymore. We scrambled from the trench to begin crawling westward toward the bulk of our units, and neither of us had to explain it to the other: being alone was *too* creepy.

There was something about Sophie, and Bridgette had had it too. Even injured and in armor, I could tell who she was and wanted to have her, then and there, in the open desert, because she managed to look sexy just by moving the way she did. Sophie crawled slowly and had to rest every once in a while, and I waited for her. At one point I linked to her personal coms and whispered.

"I want you."

"I want you too."

"No, I'm serious. I think you're beautiful, even in armor, and I know this sounds really stupid but you need to just listen, because I don't know how much longer I'll be willing to say this. I really want to live. With you."

She stopped and didn't speak for a second but then whispered back. "Don't leave me." We kept going then and got to about twenty meters away from the closest friendly when everyone went nuts.

At first I thought they were all screaming in pain, and dropped my head, waiting for rocket or grenade fire, but then it came into focus. They were happy. Something had happened and I stood, helping Sophie to her feet before lifting her onto my back again, and we jogged forward for the last few steps. A second trench line stretched north and south, and scattered around it were the wreckage of about twenty APCs and what looked like hundreds of dead infantry, their armor still steaming. It took a few minutes but I found the kid and the Brit.

"They bugged out," the Brit said.

"Excuse me?"

"No shit," said the kid. "It looks like Popov packed his gear yesterday during the lull and retreated to the north. This was just a token force, left behind to scare the crap out of us."

"Which it did," I said.

The kid snorted. "I'm too sick to feel scared."

Everything refused to register. I knew this was one of those occasions that I'd remember forever, but the significance wouldn't seep in and needed to be absorbed slowly, one bit at a time. The war was over. Nothing stood between us and Bandar now, and for the moment there wasn't any thought of Russian kinetics dropping out of space to end us before we had time to react. After the retreat from Pavlodar, I had been too wasted, too high to grasp the significance of a time like this, but as it began to take hold this time, the enormity made me put Sophie down gently so I could then slide to the trench floor and pop my helmet. It had gotten hard to breathe. Before I knew what was happening, I started sobbing, and there wasn't any thought of embarrassment even though I knew the three of them were just staring at me. Then Sophie lowered herself to my side and wrapped her arms around me. She didn't say anything. Her presence made it better and worse at the same time, so I lost it completely, and when she asked me what was wrong, there wasn't any way to explain—that I was happy and sad and terrified, all at the same time. Happy because I'd never have to look at this place again. Sad because of everyone I'd lost. And terrified because I still had to get her out somehow, and also because it wasn't clear what the real world held for me anymore and I didn't know if I'd hack it. How did you explain that kind of crap? So instead I mumbled that everything was fine and I just needed a minute.

The Brit handed me a cigarette. "It won't be long, mate. You'll be right."

"What the hell am *I* going to do?" the kid said. "I was just really getting good at this stuff."

"There's always the Legion, mate."

"I can enlist?"

"Sure," the Brit said. "Especially if you're an idiot. But let's not get too happy yet, because there's over a thousand klicks of desert between us and Bandar. We have a long trip ahead of us."

We spent the rest of the night in the trench, and at some point I fell asleep on Sophie. It was the best sleep I'd had in ages. It worried me at first that it wasn't clear where we'd go or how she'd get out, but exhaustion swept over those thoughts and everything went dark.

Just before dawn, we piled our wounded into APCs. Collecting them took all morning and I had to hide with Sophie in the trenches, because I couldn't risk leaving her alone, in case someone tried to talk to her. It's not like it disappointed me. The last thing I wanted was to carry guys with no legs or spend the day wading through wreckage and the bloating dead. On the other hand, by the time they gave the signal to saddle up, I was close to mad with the desire to just move. Sophie had gone unconscious from the drugs again, and as I was left to my own thoughts, they quickly turned to whether the Russians would hit us with kinetics, until finally the orders to move out arrived.

There was no room inside any vehicle, so we climbed atop an APC and watched as others did the same to form a long column of vehicles bristling with men, some of whom had to ride on the sides, grasping anything just to hold on. The Legion had commandeered a couple of Pops's APCs, but as soon as they turned the engines over, the vehicles exploded. I watched as men flew through the air. Their landings sent up clouds of sand, and a few of them got up or crawled back to the road for help, but the ones who struck the highway made a crunching sound and never moved again. Once they got things sorted out, the column started southward.

All afternoon we traveled. I popped my helmet and felt the breeze move through my beard and wondered how long it had been since the last time I'd showered, which led me to think of other things I hadn't considered: how long it had been since I'd slept in a bed or had a real meal, and what it would be like to have a real job that didn't involve death. Sophie slept next to me, and I was glad for the quiet. It gave me time to sort through the flood of images that our victory had unleashed, things cloistered in a dark part of my mind because for so long I never *really* thought I'd make it out. All the dead visited me in what must have been less than a minute but felt like a year, because their pictures crystallized in my head, exactly how they had looked in the last moments I'd seen them. Nobody said anything. I guessed that the Brit and the kid both were thinking the same things, because they stared into the distance but their eyes never moved. They were seeing something that wasn't visible to anyone except them. If the Russians had hit us with an air attack then, it would have succeeded; the will to fight had been sucked out, leaving each man in a state that resembled a human husk, barely there and dazed from having gone so long without peace. I *tried* to sleep. But there wasn't enough room on the APC's roof, and every time it hit a pothole or braked to avoid slamming into the vehicles in front, my eyes blinked open to make sure that we weren't under attack. Sleep would have to come later—in Bandar or wherever else we wound up. By the time we reached the next city, Mary, we were in such a bad state that Command decided to hell with security and let everyone drop where they stood, which resulted in a highway littered with snoring men.

When I snapped awake, the suit chronometer read 0500, and the Brit sat next to me, watching whatever it was that had woken me in the first place. A group of trucks pulled alongside our APCs.

"Who are they?" I asked.

"Air Force. They were the only ones left in Mary—volunteered to stay behind when everyone else bugged out so they could give us air support."

"I heard an explosion."

"They're blowing all their aircraft and ordnance in place, and for about an hour they've been transferring all their fuel alcohol to us, enough to get us into Iran, so we won't have to run on plasma. Someone oughta buy these guys a drink, mate. Or something."

"Or something."

Another boom broke the morning silence, and to our north I saw a cloud of smoke rise, billowing flame as it shifted in color from black to gray and then white. Everyone woke up with the noise. We took an hour to eat and gather gear before crawling back onto the APCs, where we elbowed each other for room to lie down, or to get as far from the engine vents as possible because of their heat.

Sophie rested her head in my lap. "How far to Bandar?" she asked.

"I don't know. Your helmet is scratched. Dented. Are you OK?"

"Fine. Just tired."

"It's gotta be a couple of days away; we haven't even crossed into Iran yet."

I'd been thinking about her all morning—the problem that would soon face us—and thought that maybe talking about it would help. "I don't know how we'll get you out yet, Sophie. Or where we'll go."

"It will be fine, just trust."

"I wish I had your faith."

"It's not faith." She raised herself on both elbows and leaned her head back to look at me. "It's something else. We're not in Bandar yet, and you said it yourself: we have days on the road. Anything could happen in that time. We'll think of something."

When she lowered herself to my lap again, I laughed, and Sophie punched me. "What's so funny?"

"I was just thinking what my mom would say—if I brought you home."

"What *would* she say?"

"Not much. I think she'd have a heart attack. Hell, she'll probably have one when I step through the door. I haven't seen her in years."

"You think too much, Oscar."

The APC lurched forward and we held on again, doing our best not to think about whether we'd make it. It was too sudden. The transition from a war in which millions had been wiped—so many men that they'd had to be replaced with boys and the elderly—to the prospect of peace was almost more than you could bear. You couldn't think about it too much. I glanced around and saw many of the guys on our APC, including the kid and the Brit, break out bottles of vodka and tilt them upward so that the morning sun glinted off glass. That was when another thought struck me. Back in Türkmenabat I'd seen those guys in the park, the ones who looked as though they were dead already. *These* guys, though, the survivors, had a different look, one that spoke of comfort in battle, or at least a pseudo understanding of its concepts and reality. But now that we were at peace, now what? If the guys in Türkmenabat had the look of death, we had a look of discomfort and malnourishment. We were so sculpted by war that imminent peace didn't auto-register as a good thing, because it was the unknown, a change that might be for the better, but what if it was for the worse? If you hadn't been there, that thought would sound crazy, but it was true; these were men who weren't sure if they'd fit in anywhere *except* war, not anytime soon—maybe never.

I saw myself in them and realized something: none of them were kids anymore, and everyone looked the same. You knew that some of them *had* to be kids, because the facial features were there, but a lot of them were ancient, arching their backs in pain because someone had handed them a carbine, given them five weeks of training on how to use a suit, and ignored their protests about how the family doctor had assured them they were too old for combat. Didn't glaucoma make you ineligible for the draft? All of them shared a common feature that you wouldn't recognize if you hadn't eaten sand with them. If you hadn't felt the mold grow against your back in those wet tunnels or nearly gone crazy whenever someone's suit valve opened to drop turds by your feet, you couldn't take, and unless you'd done the time, you'd be shit for recognizing that the true horror of it all wasn't the combat—those brief moments of adrenaline and letdown, adrenaline and letdown, *there's a dead guy,* and *wow, does it hurt to lose three fingers?* Combat, in some ways, *was a relief.* Take this: the real horror of it all was time, and how slowly it passed, giving you ticktocks to think about the millions of ways you'd buy it—slow or fast, dirty or clean—and then when the action ended, you had more time, slow days to remember everything you saw, and if you couldn't remember it at that moment, it didn't matter; those things popped up in nightmares so that someone had to shake you awake because in the tunnels screams are about a thousand times louder. Time had changed every one of these guys, blurring the line between sixteen and sixty, and what really started to make me want to drill into my head, to silence the part of my brain that made me think about all of it, was the memory of that corpsman from so long ago, when I made my first trip into subterrene, when I hadn't been able to compute how a young guy talked like he was an old man. Now I knew. Now I was surrounded by those young guys, and the old men, and grasped that the corpsman hadn't been speaking in terms of age; he had been speaking in terms of a parallel existence that nobody could explain, only experience. He had been talking about a different world, and to experience it meant you no longer belonged in real time. And now that I had finally figured it out, I wished I hadn't. Experience and time: both were cancers.

They were all crapholes, the cities and the towns. Mashhad. Moghaan. And then little villages not even on the map, where the local Iranians poked their heads out of mud-bricked huts to see what all the commotion was about, not sure if they should cheer that we were finally leaving or cry because maybe it meant the Russians would be coming next, and would they be any better? Some of the guys threw their empty vodka bottles at them, the glass shattering against their homes, and I understood the gesture, cheered with the others whenever someone came close to hitting a goatherd. We wanted to be left alone. It felt as though they knew everything and when the locals stared, they didn't just look at us with passing interest; there was a sense that all your secrets had just been exposed and that if you could get them to look away, you'd be whole again and the illusion of humanity would drape itself around your shoulders once more until someone else peeked out.

Iran passed in a blur of tan and brown, and the nights were cold enough that we slept with our helmets on, even Sophie, who had started to get better. Her feet still hurt. Every once in a while, we'd pop them out of her suit to take a look or change bandages, and it struck me how clinical these things had become. Once upon a time I would have been horrified by someone who had lost so much flesh, but not anymore. Now it was normal. It was a question of ranking your wounds to decide just how bad they were, with the loss of both legs or both arms being at the tops of everyone's list, just below having your face melted enough to disfigure but not enough to ki!l. Toes were nothing. You didn't need them to hold anything, and from the looks of things, they were healing, so in all, Sophie's progress made me happy. She tried walking once or twice when we stopped, and I knew it would be some time before she got used to the new sense of balance, but for now she was still in one piece, and that was what mattered.

One day out from Bandar we had a close call, making me think about how far we were from getting her to safety. The column had stopped for the night, and Sophie and I retreated into the desert to be alone so I could inspect her for signs of rot. She was still suiting up when a Marine wandered over and saw everything.

"Is that a G?" he asked. When we didn't answer, he stumbled down a dune face and came closer. "Are you a G? For real?"

Sophie nodded. "Yes."

"What's it like?"

"I do not understand. What is *what* like?"

"Afterward. They teach you about death so you whack jobs want it. What's death like?"

"It's about glory. Acceptance. Death is a passage from this world to a seat at His right hand and a life eternal."

"Do you have to die in combat to get it?"

She cocked her head. "No. One can be discharged."

"Executed, you mean."

"Or self-discharge."

"Thanks," the guy said, and he shook her hand. "That's what I wanted to know."

The Marine dropped his grenade launcher and in the fading light of dusk climbed the next dune face, using his hands to help him up the slope. I handed Sophie her helmet. Just before he made it to the top, the facts that his conversation had been so odd and that he had seemed so unconcerned by her identity finally got to me.

"Hey, pal," I yelled. "You're going the wrong way. The column is in the other direction."

"I know. I'm not going back."

"What?"

"I'm tired of all this. I want to live for a while without a suit on, take a shit in the open for once—a real shit, not one that I have to squeeze through a tube—and besides, the desert seems like a nice place to die. Watch out on the road. There's a rumor going around that Special Forces set up inspection points outside Bandar to find and kill genetics; some of the Gs are trying to get out."

When he disappeared over the dune, Sophie and I looked at each other. "That's not good," I said.

She didn't say anything.

We hit our first checkpoint at Lar, and everyone jumped off the APCs to wait for the Special Forces units to check suit computers and identification. The line barely moved. Days had turned hot now that we had moved so far south, and as our forces milled on the highway, the APCs rolled through the inspection post first, then stopped on the other side to wait for us. I heard the grumbling. Nobody was happy with waiting, having just come through the worst fighting that many of us had seen, and there was a sense of indignity about having to submit to another delay when Bandar was so close now—close enough that those who had removed their helmets could smell the ocean. By the time the last APC passed the checkpoint and the infantry began to move up, some of the men were cursing as one by one the soldiers in front removed their helmets and submitted to questioning.

I had no idea what we'd do.

"She can head for open desert, mate," the Brit suggested. "Just loop around and meet us on the other side somewhere."

Sophie said, "No. There are auto-drones overhead looking for that. They'd spot me in a moment."

It was maddening to have gotten this far only to think that I'd lose her. "This is such bullshit."

"You're damn right it is," someone else said. Then another Marine started shouting toward the head of the line until everyone had begun screaming. A war cry erupted from the Legion troops, and almost the entire mass of them began pushing forward, all order disintegrating. The Special Forces units began backing away from their wire fence, leveling carbines at us. One of them opened fire. Without hesitation, the rest of us—those who still had weapons—lit up the highway with grenade and rocket fire, some of the men throwing themselves on the fence until it buckled under our onslaught, crushed underfoot as our unit moved forward. These weren't new troops. Our guys were salted and hard, rotten on the inside from having lived through the trial of combat, and I marveled at the stupidity of the Special Forces guy who had opened fire. Four Legion troops fell on him, wrenching his helmet free and then pounding him to the ground with the butts of grenade launchers.

I grabbed Sophie and pulled her so that she stumbled. "Come on. *Now*."

The kid and the Brit kept up as we hurried with the others, pushing through the mangled fence line and ducking at the occasional explosion, and we laughed at the calmness of it all—compared to what we had just experienced. It almost seemed fun. There was no plasma or obscurant, no Russian genetics, just a few Special Forces with carbines who only now realized their mistake and disappeared into the dunes, a few of them pausing to turn and fire a quick burst, making sure that we didn't chase them. Who wanted to chase them? We just wanted to go home, and the mob had spoken so that nobody could stop it now as it swept upon the APCs and loaded up. The officers I saw did nothing. One of them, a French colonel, his armor torn off at the shoulder and head bare except for a bloody bandage, smiled warmly at his men while a single tear rolled off his cheek.

"I told you, Oscar," Sophie said after our APC started moving.

"Told me what?"

"To trust."

"We still haven't made it to Bandar, and what then?"

"We will find a way."

Three hours later, the convoy wound through a mountain pass, and we stopped talking to stare at the wreckage that had once been a thriving port city. I'd been to Bandar on my way in, years prior; this wasn't it. For as far as we could see, the buildings had been leveled so that a flat plain, with spires of concrete wreckage and steel that occasionally poked up from rubble, now rested where a city had once stood. The ground had been scorched. In the middle of it all was a huge crater, at least a hundred meters across, from which radiated black char marks, and when we got closer, our rad meters kicked in, warning us of the danger and reminding us to keep helmets on. Signs had been posted by the roadside, alerting everyone to the fact that the doses were acceptable but instructing people to keep moving toward Qeshm. A few women and children walked through the remains of the city, and they all looked for something, but then we got closer and I saw that they were blind, trying to feel their way through bricks and dust, maybe looking for something to eat, so I threw a ration pack as far as I could.

"That's cold, dude," someone said.

"Why?"

"They can't see. You think one of them will ever find it, or even know that it's food?"

"Fuck you," I said. "This is Bandar, and it's over."

A few others started throwing ration packs, then more, and within a moment the air filled with them, tiny black packages that curved space and raised clouds of radioactive dust wherever they landed. I laughed. Sophie looked at me, and what could I tell her? That for me Bandar had turned into some maniacal Easter egg hunt where only the blind kids could play, and then only if they were willing to soak in radiation? If I was braver, I'd take off my armor too, and undersuit, throw it all away, because the gear felt like a toxin now, soaking into my skin so that no amount of scrubbing would take it off or make anything safe again.

"Screw it," the guy said, dumping his rations too. "It's still cruel, but I'm not hungry anymore."

The column made its way as quickly as it could toward

a new bridge, one that had been recently erected so that we could access the military's sceondary port on Qeshm Island. We rolled across and I glanced back. It was the last time I'd see Bandar, and I already missed it, knowing that this was another one of those special moments, a transition from one major set of events to another—like saying goodbye to your first girlfriend after high school and promising to call every day but deep down knowing that you wouldn't. Bandar was where we had made our first deal, without even knowing it. We'd all stepped off a boat, civilian and military, and walked up the hill to whatever waited for us and subconsciously signed off on an agreement to leave the world behind and go down the rabbit hole.

A sign announced that winds were blowing to the north, and I took my helmet off, letting the breeze dry my tears. Sophie touched my face with a warm gauntlet.

"They are still here," she said, and then touched my chest. "In here. All of them."

"I know. It's not why I'm sad."

"Then why?"

"Because I don't know where *I* am. And you're right, I think too much."

When we saw the port, I started feeling better. The APCs wound through a mountain road, and at one point it looked over the piers, new ones that had been erected to handle transports and warships, huge things that resembled footballs half submerged, with openings to let their weaponry breathe. The docks swarmed with Navy personnel, and as I watched, they pushed APCs and tanks off the end of a pier, into deep water. The sight made some guys laugh. Soon we'd be down there, waiting again for however long it took for a clerk to enter our names into the system, assign us a berth for one last trip. I didn't laugh. Sophie wouldn't get a berth unless we figured something out quickly, but then I had no way of knowing that someone who I hadn't seen in a long time waited down there, someone forgotten, someone who always had all the answers.

Dan Wodzinski's voice rang out, cutting through all the noise of Marines and Legionnaires as they jostled for position in the crowds, waiting to board one of the ships.

"Oscar Wendell!"

I saw him and grabbed Sophie's hand, dragging her with me and telling the Brit and the kid I'd catch up with them later. When I got close enough, Dan hugged me.

"Jesus. When I saw you, I almost didn't recognize you; you look half dead."

"What are you doing here?" I asked.

"Came back. I had to see the final days, you know? I left after the last time I saw you, and thought I'd never come back, but something about this. Just had to be *here,* you know? Report it all. Funny, but nobody else is around. The story's dead and everyone thought I was crazy to want to cover it."

There wasn't a lot of time. We had spotted Special Forces patrolling the docks, and every once in a while, they'd zero on someone who still had his lid on, asking him to remove it. I grabbed Dan by the collar.

"I need your help."

"Sure. With what?"

"This is Sophie. She can't take her helmet off because

she's a genetic and if Special Forces spot her, they'll kill her. We need to get her out of here." When I finished, I assumed that he'd tell me to get lost, or give us up on the spot, but to my amazement he just nodded and turned to walk in the opposite direction, away from the military section of Qeshm port. When he saw that we hadn't followed, he stopped.

"Are you coming or what?"

"Where are we going?" I asked.

"There's a way to get her out; she's not the first, you know. Hundreds of them escaped, and most are heading for Thailand. The Thais have some enlightened position on genetics and offered them amnesty as long as they're willing to serve in the army as instructors, to help them in bush wars with the Burmese. I think I know a way to get her there."

"See?" Sophie whispered as we jogged to catch up with him. "All you had to do was trust."

"It won't be easy," Dan continued, "but a bunch of Korean ships just docked here a day ago, hoping to get some salvage deal for the vehicles and equipment we're discarding. Find the right one, a captain willing to take a chance, and she's in. I hope you have money, though."

I thought for a second. "You have a satellite phone?" He tossed me one and I struggled to remember a phone number I hadn't called in years, trying three times before getting it right as we moved into the civilian port area. Ten minutes later I hung up. "I have money. Haven't had anything to spend it on since I got here, so it should be enough. In fact, I'm loaded."

"Good. You'll need it. Thank God these guys all speak English."

I wouldn't have known where to start. Sophie moved close to me and it wasn't clear if she was afraid, but I figured she had to be, because this was it, and either it would work and she'd disappear and I wouldn't know when I'd see her again, or it wouldn't and she'd die. There was a lead weight in my gut and I wanted to run back into the desert with her, just bug and figure out a way to live in Iran with the blind kids. Instead we walked the quay and looked at the ships. Dan pointed to one that was dirtier than the rest, an old fishing vessel that had so many APCs stacked on its deck that it seemed about to founder, and the vehicles hung over the edge so that their front wheels spun slowly. The captain stood at the gangplank and pulled on a cigarette while his men prepared to cast off; he smiled as we approached, showing teeth that were somewhere between yellow and brown.

"You headed to Korea?" Dan asked.

He nodded. "Pusan. Long trip."

"Any chance you'd take a passenger?"

"All of you?"

Dan shook his head. "Just one. A girl." He gestured for Sophie to take her helmet off, and when she did, the captain's smile disappeared.

"No way. Too risky. Bad luck."

"We'll pay. A lot."

The captain thought for a moment and then glanced over our shoulders, back at the warships. "Anyone see you come here?"

"No."

"Pusan is a hundred thousand. More for me to take her all the way to Bangkok."

And then she was in. As Dan haggled for us, I pulled

Sophie to the side, between a pair of huge crates, and kissed her when she started crying. We stood there for a minute before she looked at me and smiled.

"Will I get to Thailand?"

"We'll get you to Pusan," I said. "And we'll have to figure they'll do what they promise and take you to Thailand from there."

"You'll come for me. Soon."

"As soon as I can. I'll head for Bangkok and the first of us to make it will find the other. I've been there once before and stayed at the Mandarin Oriental. Just go there every Sunday at noon and we'll meet in the lobby."

Dan walked over and put his hand on her shoulder. "It's time. Two hundred thousand, Oscar." He handed me a slip of paper with the name of a bank and an account number, and as I phoned in the transfer, my voice trembled, because I couldn't shake the feeling that I might never see her again. Everything happened quickly from there. Once the captain confirmed the transfer, he ushered Sophie onto the deck, and before she disappeared below, she glanced at me one last time, just for a second, with a look of terror that burned into my brain.

"It'll be OK, Oscar," said Dan. "She'll make it. There wasn't any choice, anyway." A horn sounded from the military docks and Dan pushed me toward them, breaking into a jog at the same time. "That's for us."

You would have thought that Marines and Legion troops were all muscle, like heavyweight boxers with no necks, but they weren't. Before they loaded us onto the ship, we lined up for delousing and a trim, and everyone, including me, the Brit, and the kid, had to dump his suit and under-suit into a mountainous pile at the quay's edge and stand naked in line. Dan laughed as he watched. The Navy turned hoses on us one by one and sprayed a mixture of cold water and chemicals so that we all bellowed with pain, the water pressure great enough to make it feel like a stream of needles. From there we moved to barbers, who shaved us all down with electric razors until our skin had been exposed from scalp to cheek. There wasn't a big guy in the whole group. All of them looked like scare-crows, with thin wiry builds and the kind of body that comes only from months on the march and a constant worry of death, the skin pale from an internal disease of the mind and near-total lack of sunlight. After the haircut, they issued us khaki uniforms, and I slid my only remaining possession, my wallet, into the front pocket. A line of clerks waved us onto a ship and we stepped aboard with uncertainty, unsure of what waited for us belowdecks.

On our way down I passed a stainless steel cabinet, its face so shiny that it acted like a mirror, and I froze. Who-ever looked back wasn't me. Thermal gel had pockmarked his face, the right ear looked ragged where the bottom half had been removed by fléchettes, and his cheeks had become so sunken that his head looked more like a skull than anything of flesh—something resembling an old Abraham Lincoln. Dan pushed me forward so the line would keep moving, and I stumbled on, dazed.

"That doesn't look like me," I said.

"It's you. When's the last time you used a mirror?"

"Months. Maybe years."

"Well, take it from me, Oscar—it's you and you've changed."

We got to our berthing area, which happened to be in one of the cargo holds that had been packed with crates, each of them marked with the symbol for the metal it held. In a way, we were all rich. The kid and the Brit found flat spots to lie down, and Dan and I sat next to them, waiting for the ship to begin moving. It was my last moment of fear that we'd be attacked without any way to defend ourselves, and the thought that we couldn't see outside made me sweat. I looked around for Sophie, panicking when I couldn't find her.

Dan handed me a cigarette. "She'll be all right."

"Sophie make it out?" the Brit asked. I told him what had happened and he smiled. "You did well, mate. Not bad. Hell, we all did. I didn't expect any of us to make it out, but here we are."

I introduced them finally to Dan, and we all talked for a while, until the ship got under way. The engines thrummed throughout the hold, shaking the crates underneath us, and we felt the gentle bump as the vessel pulled away from the quay. After an hour we must have made it to deeper water, where the swells rocked us back and forth, and every once in a while, a Navy guy would shout from overhead to stop smoking, and someone would shout back to go to hell. I was about to fall asleep when Dan tugged on my shirt.

"It's over. You'll be home soon."

"I know."

"You haven't been back in a while, have you? How long?"

"A year or two."

Dan sighed. "It's different, Oscar. Not bad, just... weird. Nobody even remembers that this war happened, and there's a backlash against genetics, to the point where within a couple of years the major powers will probably sign a treaty—banning their production."

"That's OK with me. I won't be staying long. Just long enough to tie up loose ends at home, then head for Thailand."

"Just don't forget that it'll be cool no matter what."

"No it won't. Nothing's cool anymore. Never was."

Dan nodded, pulling on his cigarette before blowing a series of smoke rings. "I'm not going back to the States."

"Where, then?"

"I met a girl in London. I think I'll leave the ship in England."

"How long?" I asked. "Before we get there?"

"I don't know."

Our return trip took over a month. The truth is that I don't remember much of that trip, because the accumulated exhaustion hit me all at once, and my body released all its tension at the same time, so I slept for most of the voyage, threw up a lot when I was awake, and smoked with the kid and the Brit for the rest of the time. Dan and the Brit left us in England. The kid and I said goodbye to them and we promised we'd keep in touch, but it wasn't true, because the fact was that I didn't want to keep in touch with them—maybe someday but not soon. Already my mind had convinced itself that none of the war had happened and that it would be safer to stay away from the things that reminded me that it *had*, and that I was its product. A stillborn son of conflict. When we crossed the Atlantic, there was the added bonus of watching the kid unravel and having to hold him in the middle of the night while he screamed that he didn't want to go home and could someone give him some armor because he didn't want to die when we got to port. I promised him that there would be armor waiting when we got there, but eventually enough guys in the hold complained about his shouting that a pair of corpsman showed up one morning to take him to sick bay, where I suppose he passed the rest of the trip on psychotropics. It was the last time I saw him.

About a week out of Norfolk it hit me that I'd be heading home. Until then it still hadn't felt real, and for the first time in months, I needed to get high, so I spent my days scrounging in the hold, asking everyone if they had any drugs—but they didn't—and then working the rest of the ship with no success. My father was dead. Sophie was too, for all I knew, and although part of me missed her to the point where it felt like an ulcer eating its way slowly through my soul, another part felt terrified by the prospect of finding her. What if it had been all about the war and had nothing to do with love? What if we met in Bangkok and it hit me that she was a genetic, a thing, not real and just as disgusting as I had once thought they were, as everyone thought they were? Ox and Bridgette laughed at me in my dreams until one day a chaplain showed up, making the rounds and talking to everyone before we docked the next day. He stopped and glanced up at me as I looked down from my crate.

"Hell of a thing, isn't it?" he said.

"What is, Father?"

"The truth."

"I don't know what the truth is anymore."

"The truth is that everything they told you, about how you were doing your country a service by going off to fight the Russians so they couldn't steal our resources, it was all bullshit."

It was strange to hear a priest curse, but in a good way—a way that made you trust him. "I'm not military, Father. I'm a civilian. They didn't tell me anything."

"Oh." He paused to drink from a flask and then winked at me. "Then you don't have anything to complain about. You should have known it all along, that the truth was nothing but a fucking joke."

As soon as he walked out of sight, I turned a corner. I didn't know what the world held, but I knew that the guy had been right and that if a priest could have it wired that tight and swear like a Marine, maybe things would be OK. Not great, but not all bad either. There was still one more day before we docked, and I spent it sleeping.

This time there weren't any nightmares.

TEN

Accommodations

The maglev from Norfolk made a hissing sound that I had forgotten about, the first reminder of a world buried for years, a time capsule that seemed bigger and shinier than I had remembered. At first guys like me—men in khaki uniforms and flip-flops heading for northern destinations—filled the car, but the train stopped every once in a while to let them off and to allow civilians on board, forcing us to mix with regular people. They seemed like children. Civilians smiled at everything and had a way of laughing that made us marvel, astonished us with their ability to convince us that *here* were people who really *didn't* have a care in the world, who felt no weight other than that of the decision of what to eat for lunch. They complained about the car's temperature, about the food, or whined about how it was behind schedule, and more than once I looked down at the floor, ashamed because I didn't know that you *could* complain about such things, because after where we had just been, the temperature seemed a silly thing to worry about, the food tasted real, and who cared if we were off schedule? At least nobody was shooting at us.

At one stop, a girl sat in the aisle seat next to me. Her blonde hair was perfectly straight, and I smelled it from that close, barely able to keep myself from burying my nose in her neck after having been immersed for so long in only the stale air from my suit. She began putting on lipstick and I stared at her reflection in the window, terrified, because what if she talked to me? What the hell did I have to say to anyone not from the tunnels? When she finished and looked around the car, my hands started shaking again, and I pushed them under my legs, praying for them to stop.

"Are you a soldier?" the girl finally asked. Our train had reached its next stop and she wasn't really focused on me, but instead watched to see who got on.

"Pretty much."

"Are *all* you guys soldiers?"

"Yeah."

"Where did you come from?"

"We just got off the boat from Iran."

She looked at me then and I imagined that she saw through, and could she have sensed the rot in my head, smelled it faintly, even over all her perfume? I wished that I could crawl under the seat in front of me to hide. "What happened to your face?" she asked.

"I was wounded, in battle. Well, a few battles, actually."

"Really? Was it scary?"

I just stared at her. My mouth had stopped working, like somewhere between my brain and lips the nerve impulses jumped the tracks, synapses mutinying to sabotage my voice. But that couldn't have been the case, because my jaw worked up and down, trying to talk, but the only things I could think to say were too horrible for her, because what did *she* know? I'd infect her. This girl was something unique, because I hadn't seen anyone untainted by Kaz in so long that it was like looking at a snowflake, which, if I breathed on it, would melt into nothing. After a minute of silence, she rolled her eyes and looked away, and I turned back to the window to watch the cities flash by. Ten minutes later the train slowed and she got up to leave.

"Your stop?" I asked.

"No. I'm moving to another car."

Once she had left, I whispered, "Yes. It was scary."

Union Station in D.C. was like a mental collision, a light show that slammed into my retinas, making me blink as I stepped from the platform into the main station, where news and ad-screens, plastered to every flat surface, blinked images as quickly as you absorbed them. It was raining. I stood at the front door, staring into the street as people pushed by in a rush, and felt the panic begin in my feet, locking them in place with the thought that to move outside would mean being seen by everyone who looked at me. Instead I turned and headed for a men's store. It had become clear that the khaki uniform—or maybe something about my face—made people stare. Maybe if I looked more like them, they wouldn't notice the scars, wouldn't put two and two together to realize that a ripped ear and a uniform totaled to the horrors in which I had participated, ones that I didn't want anyone to ask me about again since my experience with the girl on the train.

An elderly man stood behind the counter and sized me up. "Just come back from overseas?" he asked.

"Yeah."

"And you want clothes. Want to get out of your uniform."

"Yeah."

"You have any money?"

"I don't know." Somewhere in all the mess of getting Sophie out and fighting to retain my sanity on the ship, I had forgotten my bank balance, but had a vague sense that there should be plenty of money as I handed him my card. It took him a moment to run it through his computer.

He handed it back. "You're rich."

"I inherited some, earned the rest. And there's not much to spend money on in Kazakhstan."

"Well, what are you in the mood for? Suit? Business casual?" He listed a bunch of other stuff and my eyes fixed on the floor; then I closed them, trying to focus on the words but failing. Finally he sighed before holding up a scanner to pulse me for measurements. "I've got some ideas. Come this way."

We got to the casual section and he started handing me shirts and pants. "Try these. And we've been getting a lot of rain lately; you might think about a coat. Or at least an umbrella."

He showed me a dressing room and, before shutting the door, patted me on the shoulder. "I was in the service too. A long time ago. How long have you been back?"

"A day."

"It's not like home anymore, is it?"

"No. It's not."

Before closing the door, he sighed. "It will be, but it'll take time."

"Maybe the clothes," I said, "normal clothes, I mean.

Maybe having these will make it a cakewalk." But the man just shook his head.

Styles had changed. Not in a major way, but enough that I felt odd in a shirt that seemed two sizes too large until the old man assured me that everyone wore them that way. And pants were shorter than I remembered. He handed shoes over the door, and they looked like blocks of plastic, thick-soled. How long had it been? A couple of years at the most, but it dawned on me that in all that time, I'd been cut off from the real world—no news feeds in the past year, nothing except a few emails from home, dispatches from a world for which nothing could have prepared me. The changes were subtle—so subtle that if you'd been in the peace world the whole time, there wouldn't have *been* any noticeable changes—but to me it was obvious. I was a foreigner.

When I stepped from the dressing room, he handed me a bag with the rest of the clothes and then held out an umbrella. "I've already charged you, gave you the employee discount."

"What war were you in?" I asked.

"The last three. And you might not believe it, but I miss them."

"What?"

He looked over my shoulder, not focusing on anything, and then I knew that this guy understood and wasn't full of it, that whatever he said came from experience, because he had the look. It was faint, faded, but there. The guy's face made me want to stay and never leave. "You'll take, eventually. It's not going to settle in for a while. But one day you'll forget about everything except the good stuff, and believe me, there *was* good stuff, and even the ones you lost won't be so scary to think about anymore, and then every once in a while you'll start smiling again. I did, anyway." He looked back at me and clasped his hands together, his face turning red as if he'd said something that embarrassed him. "Well, on your way, I guess. Good luck."

When I stepped into the street, the rain hit me in a cold wash, underscoring the fact that I hadn't felt it in so long because the helmet and suit had always kept me insulated from the world. It took a second to pop the umbrella. The rain pelted it, increasing in volume until the handle vibrated with the impacts, sheets of water falling off the edges on all sides. Cars crept by, three-wheelers whose plastic bodies looked insubstantial compared to the monsters of Kaz—the APCs and tanks, and even the scout cars—and mentally I estimated how easy it would be to take them out with just a carbine. Yet the drivers seemed unconcerned by the lack of protection. Some of them talked on phones or laughed, while a few looked about to kill, maybe angry because of all the traffic, but none of them seemed to realize that a single plasma round would burn them all in an instant, and I wanted to shout it at them, shake them by their collars. They all looked crazy.

A group of men loading a truck nearby hadn't registered until one of them dropped a box so that it slammed to the concrete sidewalk with a bang, and I dove into the street, rolling as close as I could to the gutter, where a small river of water soaked me. One of them saw it and helped me up, handing me my umbrella.

"You OK?" he asked.

"Yeah."

"Why'd you do that?"

What I couldn't tell him was that for a few seconds the scene had transformed from D.C. to Almaty, the cars into lines of Marines on the retreat, and the bang into a bloom of plasma that charred everything in a ten-meter radius. Instead I said, "I don't know," and wandered off, looking for a cab.

But the cab was dirty, its driver an immigrant whose accent sounded Russian when he asked, "Where to?" and it made me close my eyes to keep reminding myself that this wasn't war, this wasn't Kaz, and he wasn't a Russian genetic. Where *did* I want to go? I didn't want to see my mother, not yet, but there was someone else.

"Five hundred block, Fourteenth Street, northwest."

He gunned the engine, its whine filling the tiny passenger space so that closing my eyes didn't help, and when I opened them, I would have sworn for a second that it had turned into an APC, with rock walls on every side as we descended into the tunnels. When he spoke again, it all melted away.

"You heard about the Chinese?"

"What about them?" I asked.

"They're at the Urals now. Not long to Moscow, and it went nuclear a few days ago."

It took a second for the words to make sense, but the thought of Chinese in Russia seemed so bizarre that I shook my head, trying to make it stick. "What are you talking about? The Chinese invaded Russia?"

"Yeah, where have you been? It's all over the news."

"Did this happen just over a month ago?" It had all begun to click—why the Russians had pulled out of Uzbekistan, why they hadn't kept chasing us to Bandar.

He nodded. "Yeah, that's about right."

"God bless the Chinese."

"Bullshit."

The rest of the ride was quiet. I must have offended him, because the guy lit a cigarette and blew the smoke back on me, every once in a while glaring into the rearview mirror, but I didn't care. It felt good to know that Pops was getting it, the Chinese pushing through his territory, taking it all, and it didn't matter who was invading, because it could have been aliens for all I cared; what mattered was that they were losing. It made me smile. I imagined their boy-thing genetics being washed in thermal gel, or having tanks drive over their smiling faces, and it felt like finally everything was being put in its proper place, like maybe there was a reason to hope after all, because the Russians had made a critical error. They'd pushed too far, too hard, overextended. But the joy the news had brought was short-lived, and before I knew it, my thoughts turned back to uncertainty—of what I'd say when I got to my destination.

Half an hour later the cab stopped, pulling over to the curb, and I paid the guy before climbing out onto the sidewalk, where I stared up at the building that had once been like a second home. The lobby was black marble, and a receptionist glanced up before returning to her computer, leaving me to head for the bank of elevators on my own. A crowd of people waited there. I recognized some of them but couldn't remember their names, and they had no idea who I was, other than a man who was soaked by the rain and whose face showed the scars of something awful.

I got off at the third floor and entered the suite. The words "Stars and Stripes" were printed on the glass door in large black letters. The place hummed. People laughed from behind cubicles and I smelled a whiff of coffee, which made my mouth water a little because I hadn't had any in so long. Finally someone saw me standing there and came over.

"Can I help you?"

"Phil Erikson. Is he back from Iran?"

She nodded. "Is he expecting you?"

"Tell him Oscar Wendell is here to see him. He'll be surprised."

The secretary shut the door behind me. Phil sat at his desk, a huge oak thing buried in paper and junk, from which a single computer poked out and cast a pale green glow on his face. Somehow he had managed to find a clear spot in the mess where he could prop his feet up. I didn't know what to expect. The unknown grabbed hold of my chest and squeezed, making it hard to breathe, because I'd half convinced myself that he'd jump over and punch my lights out—and I thought it might be a little deserved.

"Oscar Wendell. No shit. When Sheila told me you were here, I nearly freaked."

"I nearly freaked coming over."

"What do you want? We don't have any jobs for you."

I shrugged; it was a gesture I'd have to get used to again after not having done it in years, and I felt my neck muscles cramp. "Not here for a job."

"For what, then?"

"I was an asshole."

Phil grinned. It was all toothy, and I recognized it

immediately as one we all had used—to put our sources at ease, get them talking. He stood and walked around the desk, grabbing my hand and shaking it.

"Shit. It's forgotten. We heard you got trapped in the Pavlodar encirclement and then we lost track of you. Didn't know you'd made it out until Wodzinski called a few weeks ago."

"Dan's a good guy."

"He's an asshole, like the rest of us. Just hides it better. It must have been rough over there. Tell me what happened."

And before I even knew what I was saying, the story spilled out. Everything except Bridgette and Sophie. When it came to Almaty, his eyes went wide, and Phil jumped back into his chair to start typing.

"They said nobody made it out of Almaty; you've gotta be kidding me. You were *there*?"

I nodded. "And then we retreated to Bandar. I saw the kinetic strike we used, the whole thing."

"We heard about that. What did Bandar look like after the nuke?"

The memory of the women and children was so intense that the office disappeared, then returned a few seconds later, when I found him staring at me, waiting for an answer. "You OK?" he asked.

"Fine. Bandar was wasted, gone. I don't want to talk about it anymore."

Phil stopped typing and leaned back in his chair. He lit a cigarette and handed it to me, saying something about how "no smoking" didn't apply to him, and what were they going to do, anyway, arrest us? There were other words, a whole discussion about the new business of journalism, the importance of neo-holo, and who had died in

Kaz, but it was too late to pay attention, as my thoughts had drifted far away from it all, to Sophie and the kid, to Dan and the Brit. I wondered if everything was OK. Phil stubbed out his cigarette and coughed.

"You know, that last email from you pissed me off."

I nodded. "I'm really sorry about that, wasn't myself."

"You still get high?"

"No. Not anymore."

"Good. You and drugs were never a good mix. So what does an Oscar Wendell do now? What are your plans?"

I thought for a moment. It was a good question, and although I knew I'd head for Thailand, it wasn't going to happen immediately, because there were still loose ends to tie. But what *would* I do once I got there?

"I don't know. My father died and left me a bunch of cash, so I might do nothing for a while and just live. You know?"

"No. No I don't, but it sounds good. Listen, you've been gone a while, and just be careful around the city. There's that whole uproar about you guys and genetic troops."

"What uproar?"

"Protestors. People afraid that they'll grow genetics to do all our jobs, and somehow it got linked to anyone who was in the war. No offense, but you don't look like a regular guy anymore. You look military."

I started to feel sick, then angry at the thought of people so stupid that they'd think genetics would take over, or that it was somehow my fault. "That's a load of crap."

"I'm not saying I'm one of them; I'm just saying to avoid groups of people carrying picket signs, and to stay away from the Pentagon—or any place near it. Just be careful."

I finished my cigarette, sucking it down to the filter, and rested it on Phil's ashtray before standing to leave. He showed me to the door. Outside, the cubes went quiet as we walked through, and it gave me a queasy feeling, like I had done something wrong, my mind spiraling as it tried to figure out what.

"They know who you are," said Phil.

"What?"

"You're famous around here. I think you may have even surpassed the great Dan Wodzinski."

"But I didn't even write any stories for you after Pavlodar."

"Oscar." Phil opened the front door for me and then stood in it, watching as I walked to the elevator and hit the button. "I'm not talking about writing stories. I'm talking about something else entirely. Why do you think I typed the whole time we talked? You *are* a story."

By nightfall the rain had stopped, and I stood outside my apartment door, hesitating to put my hand in the bio scanner, for fear of what waited inside. I knew there wasn't anything in there. But I hadn't been back in years, and wondered if ghosts would rise from behind the couch to ambush me with reminders of what I'd left behind, and besides, once I closed the door behind me, I'd be alone. It wasn't like I hadn't been alone the whole time I'd been back. But until then, there had always been people around, in the train station, in Phil's office, and during the hours after I'd visited him, when I'd wandered up and down

Wisconsin, trying to absorb the way everything had changed since I'd left, wondering if D.C. would ever "fit" again. Inside the apartment, my thoughts would be my only company, and there wasn't any way to know where they'd take me left unchecked. Then again, I couldn't stand in the hallway forever, because sooner or later someone would notice and maybe call the cops; I opened the door and went in.

A layer of dust covered everything and my shoes left dark marks on the wood floors, raising clouds wherever I stepped. Nothing had changed. Except for an enormous stack of letters, which slumped on my coffee table and spilled to the floor when I collapsed onto the couch, everything was where I'd left it—including the syringe. It rolled out from under the couch and tapped against my shoe, so I reached down and picked it up, pinching it between two fingers and unprepared for what came next. Cockroaches. They'd followed me all the way from Kaz, waiting for a moment just like this, and when I put the syringe on the table, trying to push it away, it didn't help. No matter what I did now, the sight of the thing and the memories of its last use had opened the door to them, forcing me to cover both eyes with my hands and let out a moan. *Alone.* One by one the things crawled through my thoughts, dropping crumbs of remorse as they went, making me cry because my refrigerator was probably empty and there wasn't anyone I could call to come over and talk me down from the ledge onto which the cockroaches had pushed me. I ran, out the apartment door and back into the street, so quickly that I stumbled over a homeless guy and didn't even mutter an apology, the thought that I'd find a dealer and be done with it making me run harder;

only one thing was guaranteed to keep them out: getting lit. There were too many of the things, and if you couldn't kill them, at least drugs would silence the part of your mind that screamed along, egging the things on and agreeing with every thought they evoked. I passed a hotel taxi stand and hopped into the first one.

"Take me to the Navy Yard—waterfront. Somewhere around there."

"Wanna be more specific?"

"I'll know when we get there." I glanced at him and saw he had a tattoo, one I'd seen before, of a scorpion with its tail piercing the side of a tank.

"You were in Kaz?" I asked.

"Yeah. You?"

"Yeah. How long you been back?"

"Six months. I got out just before they hit Bandar."

"Lucky for you."

He laughed, but it was halfhearted, a kind of *whatever-you-say* laugh. "Yeah. Right. Sometimes I think it would have been better to just go out that way—quick, in a flash."

The world evaporated, and all that existed then were the cab and its driver, grabbing my attention so that nothing else mattered, because he spoke my language. I *knew* what he meant. That was the instant when I thought maybe the Gs had something with this God stuff, because what were the odds that on my way to find a dealer, I'd jump a cab with a veteran, who took, who listened, and who summed things that shouldn't add and made them fuse?

"Man," I said, "me too. It's a hell of a thing to say, but there it is."

He laughed again, and when he looked back, I saw that his left eye was gone, covered by a patch. "That's because it's the only way to make it all go away. Sometimes. Other times you just have to cut slack and let it all roll over until those voices are too tired to keep telling you that it's all a waste of time, like you wear them down with infinite patience until finally they just decide 'fuck it.'"

The cab wove through Georgetown, angling down a slope and under the elevated highway so that as I looked out, I saw the scum settle off the Potomac in waves of foam, black from the glow of streetlights. And the bums. I'd never remembered seeing so many, and they stood at the water's edge, looking toward the opposite banks as if maybe something more promising waited over there. It reminded me of the time on Lake Balkhash, men trying desperately to shed their suits and jump in before the plasma engulfed them, but these guys just stood there, resigned to whatever arced over to land in their midst.

"Those are us."

"What?" I asked.

"Us. Ninety percent of those guys are veterans, just back from the East. The dirty East. And if you don't get it wired, you'll hang just like them, with no focus except on what can't be anymore."

"I don't get it," I said.

"They all want things to be the same way they were *before* they left, before the war. You know. *Normal.*"

I was getting angry. I wanted it to be normal again too, wanted to get rid of the roaches forever and heal the rot that had grown in my gut, working its way upward into my chest. It wouldn't be long before it took over everything.

"There's nothing wrong with normal. Everyone wants normal."

"That's just it, man." He pulled over and flipped the meter off, sending the cab into darkness. "Normal is how we are now. You can't go inside with a scalpel the way a surgeon goes in for an appendix, snip-snip, and then—voilà—everything is back to normal. To do that they'd have to wipe everything from your brain, rehab your soul. Normal for us now means getting by with the new guy, getting used to garbage that's sloshing around inside us until it's just another thing. Adapt to it. Because it's never going away."

We talked for another hour, and a couple of times the bums came up to the cab and he'd give them cigarettes, and both of us smoked everything we had. It felt right. The smoke filled the car so that it gave me the impression of being hidden in obscurants, safe from targeting systems as long as I stayed inside and didn't move. I used to read a lot, and while sitting in the cab, I recalled an old article from the twenty-first century, some psycho-horseshit about how people with depression tended to smoke more, have a higher chance of nicotine addiction, and when I told the cabbie, he laughed; we both did. I mean, how could it have taken so long for someone to figure *that* one out? For the crazy and depressed, something had to have gotten them there in the first place, and the thing about nicotine was that while you smoked or chewed, it gave you something else besides the drug, something to do to *forget* what it was that had got you there. It gave you a thing to focus on, to pass the time with minimal thought, because for those brief minutes you had to concentrate on lighting or pinching, inhaling or spitting and just let it all sweep in to repair the walls between you and whatever thoughts were trying to kill you that day. *Hell yeah* it made sense. And when you finished one cigarette or dip, you had to decide if you could hack things for a while, or if you needed another that very second, that instant. Sure, nicotine killed people. But for some, risking *that* was preferable to taking life completely straight.

By the time one a.m. rolled around, we were both tired, and he asked if I still wanted to go to the Navy Yard.

"Nah. Take me back to the stand where you picked me up. What do I owe you?"

"No money. Most of us are on our own, except for when we're not."

I nodded but didn't say anything. When he dropped me off, I shook his hand and then walked the few blocks to my apartment, not hesitating this time to stick my hand in the reader. The place was still dark. But this time the syringe didn't grab hold and I walked into my room, where the bed lay bare, because I had left it like that, with no sheets or blankets. Only instead of lying down, I moved it, just far enough that I could squeeze between the bed and the wall and lie on the floor. There wasn't any way I'd be able to sleep on a bed. A floor was better, like the tunnels, and when I started sobbing, the only thing that made me feel better was the thought that in a few minutes I'd fall asleep, which was almost as good as nicotine or drugs—for making everything go away. The only problem with sleep was that most of the time you woke up, but that was hours away, and for now the promise of unconsciousness was good enough.

Tomorrow, I told myself. Tomorrow I'd find the courage to go see her.

*   *   *

The opulence of my upbringing came back in a flash. My mother's home was more a compound than a dwelling, with tall brick walls that faced Nebraska Avenue and had been topped with broken glass. A wrought-iron gate swung slowly while I waited, and before I had even mounted the front steps to the door, her butler had opened it, stepping outside to keep me from getting too close.

"I'm sorry, sir, but I couldn't hear you clearly through the intercom. What did you say your name was, and what business do you have with Mrs. Wendell?"

"Just tell her I knew her son. I go by my nickname, Scout."

"*Scout.*" He said it the same way you'd look at a bug, unsure if you should just let it crawl away or stomp on it. "One moment."

A few minutes later someone came to the door. She was older than I remembered, and her hair had gone completely white so that as she stared from behind thick glasses, it gave me the odd sensation that a stranger had taken over my mother's body. Still, something in me shifted. I didn't know why, because I hadn't spoken with her in years, but I felt my insides begin to slide, like they had all softened and melted at the edges, and for the first time since my return, it felt like everything would be OK.

"Can I help you?" she said. "I'm told that you knew my son. Is he dead?" She said it with such detachment that it surprised me.

"No. He's not dead. He's me, Mother. Oscar."

A look came over her face. You'd think it wouldn't

be possible for someone so pale to turn white, but she managed, and with one hand she grabbed the doorframe while clutching at her chest with the other.

"Oscar?"

"Yeah. I..."

She grabbed me. It was the second surprise of the morning, because for the life of me I didn't recall ever having been hugged by my mother, and yet there it was, her holding on with such force that for a moment I thought she'd knock the wind out of me.

"They all said you'd died. You didn't keep in touch and so I thought you were dead, because we heard so many stories about what happened over there."

"I made it. I'm home."

She hugged me some more and then cried for about five minutes, and then we walked into the sitting room, where she stopped to wipe her tears away, which was when the woman I remembered came back. Her voice went cold. She sat on a chair across from me and straightened her skirt before replacing the glasses and fixing me with a stare that I'd never forget.

"Your father died without knowing where you were; he died assuming that you were gone."

"I'm sorry, Mom."

"Did you come here for money? He left you a lot of money, but I'm guessing that you've already spent most of it on drugs."

"I didn't come here for money, and most of what he gave me is still there. I just came to let you know that I was OK, and to say that I was sorry."

"Sorry for what?"

I thought about how to answer her. What *was* I sorry

for? For wasting the time I'd had with my father, for spending most of it stealing from both of them or fighting, or for being, in general, such a selfish prick that it had taken a war to make me figure it out? It finally registered that it was a question that had no answer, so I shrugged and looked at the floor.

"I guess I'm sorry for everything. I should have stayed in touch, and it was wrong for me to not let you know I was alive."

Her face softened some, but I could tell she'd regained control. There wouldn't be another hug. That had been a lapse in sanity as far as she was concerned, but although she didn't know it, that hug would be the last good thing I remembered about her, the one moment that stayed with me, even after she died a year later.

That was the thing. I'd been scared to see her because up until then, I'd assumed that it had been up to me to make everything better, to make up for everything I had done. But that thinking had been all wrong. Nobody could make up anything to her; it was the way she'd been wired—to think that in D.C. society you just didn't do certain things, and once you had, forget it. You'd never be let back inside. And I held a special place among the fallen, because I had invented *new* ways to offend her, ones that involved so many drugs and so many girls— some the daughters of her closest friends—that there had never been any hope for atonement. So if the goal had been to change her opinion of me, then I *should* have been scared and dreaded the meeting, because no words in the universe could have been assembled in the right order to make her change her opinion of me—to get her to forget what I had done, or let bygones be bygones. It was only much later, maybe after she had gone, that it became clear: I'd done exactly what needed to be done. It made me feel better to know that by the time she died, I'd taken care of my problems and gone to see her, to try and make it up, even though I knew there *was* no making up for things; I'd made the effort, and that was what counted.

For what seemed like hours she went on about my father, and it got to me. Nobody needed to point out that I hadn't been there when it happened, or that the last conversation we'd had was for shit; I knew that. And she *knew* that I knew that, which made it a thousand times worse, because I had to just sit there and take it, knowing that she was right. It occurred to me to run, but I couldn't do that, since this was a sort of penance, my sitting there and giving her the chance to describe what a shithead I was, a punishment that I'd evaded for as long as I could but that, in the end, found me anyway. There was nothing else I could do. He was gone, and for the rest of my life I'd regret the way we'd left things, but I had to figure that if my dad ever spoke to my friends in the afterlife, he'd understand why I'd done the things I had. At the very least he'd know I'd finally straightened up.

When the topic finally shifted to my facial scars, I explained what had happened, and she sunk into a horrified silence. I almost thought she'd hug me again, but the moment passed. I stood, taking advantage of the respite, and she walked me to the door.

"Where are you off to now? Hookers? Go and get drunk?"

"Actually, I'm heading to Thailand. I met a girl and she's waiting for me there."

"How nice."

"No, really, I think you'd like her. I met her in the war."

"Give me a break, Oscar. There aren't any women in wars these days; the only ones they have are leftovers, high-ranking officers or those ... *Oh dear God.*"

I turned and walked down the stairs, smiling as I left, and called over my shoulder, "I'm serious. You'd like her. When I get there, I'll send you my contact info so you can fly out and stay with us for a while. You always said that Thailand—"

But the door slammed before I could finish. It was true: she'd always liked Thailand. That was where she and Dad had gone for their honeymoon.

Now that I'd done what I'd come to do, there was nothing in D.C. to keep me there. As it turned out, she never made it to Thailand again, and later I got a letter from one of her friends that she'd died angry. Alone.

I hopped into a cab and had the driver stop at my apartment so I could grab a few things and then hit the airport. It took a while to find my passport. By the time I got back, he'd downloaded the day's news, and he handed me the reader so I could see my picture on the leading story, "One Last Dispatch," by Phil Erikson.

"You're famous," the driver said.

"Great."

When I handed it back to him, he gave me a look as though I was crazy. "You're not going to read it?"

"I don't need to read it. I lived it."

"Where to?"

"National Airport."

Driving down George Washington Parkway was one

of the best moments of my life. Not because something happened or occurred to me, but because *nothing* happened or occurred to me, only a general sense that the war was really over and that as soon as I stepped on the plane, I'd be shutting the door on a part of my life that I didn't care to see again. It was sunny. Joggers moved along the bike trail near the river, and alcohol-burner motorcycles flashed by every few seconds or so, making me feel as though everyone else was in a hurry, concerned about getting somewhere on time, while for me time had become something meaningless, a thing usually to be endured or feared, except that for the moment it was enjoyable. Sophie might not be in Thailand yet, and it would take a while for my flight to connect and land in Bangkok, but who cared? There was a sense of *everything-will-be-all-right* in the air, and I breathed it in.

By the time I bought my ticket, checked my bag, and boarded the plane, six hours had elapsed. It was nearly dinnertime, and if I managed it, I'd sleep through the first leg of the flight. It couldn't have been more perfect. But then a pair of flight attendants saw me from the other end of the cabin and whispered something to each other. After I had seated myself, one of them came over.

"Are you the guy from the news story today?"

"Yeah."

"Oh my God, you're like a celebrity. What was it like?"

"What was what like?"

"The war. We heard a lot about it for a while, but then other things started happening, and now the Chinese and Russians are at it. So *what was it like*?"

I wanted to scream at her. For a second my hand

clenched into a fist, preparing itself to slam into her windpipe and knock her back into the seats, wipe that smile
away, because she had just proven herself an idiot. It
might have been honest curiosity, and it probably was, but
that didn't matter, because she had just erased the entire
day, robbed me of the warm feeling, one that I hadn't had
in years and that now was sure never to come back, so the
only thing to do was to ruin her day with violence.

"It was awful," I said instead. "You couldn't shower
for months on end, and you had to take dumps in your suit
so that by the end of a rotation on the line, your ass had
developed all sorts of skin infections that no amount of
medication helps."

"Ew," she said.

"Exactly. And that's not even the worst part. Do you
even know how hard it is to shoot children when they're
running away? I mean, they're such small targets. and I'll
be damned if they can't run just as fast as an adult. I swear
it took twice as many rounds to take down your average
kid as it did a woman, but that's if you include pregnant
women, who were really easy to hit."

Her smile faded and she stepped away, glancing back
at her friend, who was still smiling from the front. "That's
really sick. You killed pregnant women?"

"Lots of them. You killed anything that moved."

I got the best service during that flight. The attendants
left me alone unless I wanted something, and always
made sure that I got a soda as soon as I asked for it, and I
never regretted anything I'd said to the one girl—because
to hell with her. To hell with all of them.

A day later we circled over Bangkok and I nearly lost
it. Out the window I saw the city, its towering buildings

visible from some miles out, bordered on every side by lush green fields, so green that they reminded me of something. Then I felt it all shift: it wasn't a passenger plane; it was a drone, and the kid was strapped in next to me as we circled around the Almaty airfield, turning west for Tashkent. General Urqhart waved at me from the ground, and for some reason I could see him clearly, saw his mouth move as he tried to tell me something, and then his face melted to be replaced by a Russian genetic's, and he slowly raised a carbine to point it at my face.

When I came back, the plane had landed and emptied, and my hand gripped the flight attendant's wrist, twisting her arm to the point where she cried out.

I let go before it snapped. "I'm so sorry. What happened?"

"Get off the plane before we call the cops." She screamed at me: *"Get off, you freak!"*

I've avoided air travel ever since; you never knew what would set you off.

It was the fourth week, and still no Sophie. A typhoon warning had been issued and I watched while the locals scurried along, tying their boats to docks on the Chao Phraya as its muddy water turned white in gusts of wind. The lights flickered off, but from my balcony I could still see, because the sun hadn't set, although thick clouds made it gloomy enough that I couldn't see far. Tomorrow would be another Sunday. Maybe she'd be there, but it was getting harder to hope every week, and each trek to the lobby to wait for her seemed to make the hole in my gut grow larger. I'd seen a genetic or two already and called out to them, but each time they'd scurried away in fear, running for the nearest alley. The concierge explained it all when I asked. He said that Americans disguised as tourists had been showing up, and that the Thai government thought they were hit squads sent to eliminate as many of the girls as they could find before the assassins disappeared over the border into Burma.

In the dusk and without any lights, the city became like a ghost town, and I imagined that every building was empty, the spires of high-rises vacated to create a theme park of desolation. I couldn't see the port from the hotel, but I'd gone there every day to check for the Korean ship, cursing myself for not having made sure to remember its name. But it had happened so quickly in Bandar. There hadn't been time even to say goodbye before she left, and then I'd had to board my ship, so it had never occurred to me to take note of the name. The dockhands had gotten so used to my asking every time I showed up that they greeted me with either "no, no Koreans today" or "yeah, yeah, over there, go check," which would send me running. Two weeks before, I'd found a ship that might have been the one, rusted so badly that its name flaked off in chunks, but its crew had disappeared, and the next time I returned, it was gone, so there hadn't been a chance to know for sure.

Lightning flashed in the distance, toward the ocean, and a few seconds later came the crack, making me flinch involuntarily. Suddenly the lights flickered back on. Almost at the same time, my phone went off, and I ducked through the curtains, back into my room, where I grabbed it before the third beep.

"Hello?"

The voice on the other end spoke perfect English, and I recognized it as the concierge's. "Mr. Wendell, there's a young lady here to see you. Shall I send her up?"

My throat went dry. I wanted to say yes, and tried, but I couldn't figure out the word until finally it came out in such a hoarse whisper that I would have sworn that someone else had said it.

"Fine," he said, "she'll be there momentarily."

Time went into slow motion, and as soon as I hung up, my feet shuffled across the floor, bringing me slowly toward the door until I stopped ten feet away, pausing to catch my breath and figure out what to say. I'd just decided on saying "hi" when someone knocked.

She stood in the doorway, smiling, and wore a minidress and some kind of combat boots, making me realize I'd underestimated how amazing she looked. "Hello, Oscar."

"It's not Sunday."

"I couldn't wait until Sunday."

"Good for you."

It took me less than a second to carry her to the bed and toss her there before climbing on top, and we kissed for a long time, until she stopped me.

"I've been here two weeks."

"What?" I asked. "Why didn't you come find me?"

"My sisters took me in, made me see a special Thai doctor—one who reverses our spoiling and fixes everything, things the French medication didn't. It was...painful. But everything is OK now; they have wonderful doctors here."

I pushed her dress up, barely able to control myself, but she stopped me again.

"Wait. There's something you have to know."

"What?"

"I can have children now."

And that was when I decided to have my first kid. Having Sophie was like sinking into a dream that I never thought would become real, but did, and then once I got it, I realized that the real thing was even *better* than the dream. She moaned and I went faster. She grabbed my arms in that grip of hers and I bit her neck until she cried out, and when it was all over, we just stared at each other for about an hour.

"Let's keep doing that until I'm pregnant," she said.

"Yeah. Let's."

"And don't leave me. Ever."

Epilogue

It's been ten years and the cockroaches still visit me. You never get rid of the things entirely, and that's another shitty thing about war: it leaves a mark like a scar, which fades over time but never really goes away, except that *this* scar is on your soul. Sophie knows enough about the roaches to leave me alone when they come, and usually I crawl into bed or curl up in a corner of our house to cry it off, but the really bad ones come at night to force me awake with the sudden realization that nothing will ever be OK again. But it doesn't happen as often as it used to.

I got a call from Dan once, a few months back, and he said that he'd gotten married and they'd like to come to Bangkok for their honeymoon. "Sure," I said. It was a decent time, but we left them alone for the most part, because neither of them was totally cool with Sophie, and it pissed me off, but Sophie didn't mind, because to her Dan didn't matter. And he told us about the Brit. The guy had stayed in the Legion and got his wish—a return to Africa, where an APC ran over him in the darkness of some mosquito-infested shithole. Dan didn't know what had happened to the kid, and I never found out—probably never will.

The simplest way to explain all this—what I learned and what it all meant to me—came from a drunken Australian I met in a local bar one night, when he asked me about my scars. I told him how they happened and he laughed.

"Why'd you go to war if you didn't have to, mate?" he asked.

"I wanted to see it," I said, "to experience it, like maybe it would make me a better person, like maybe I'd grow up."

"And did you?"

"Yeah. In a way."

"To hell with that, mate. You're just crazy. You know how I know?"

I shook my head. "How?"

"Because there are heaps better ways to grow up, mate. *Heaps.*"

There wasn't anything to say, because he was right. Sophie and I have two kids already, and if there's any way to do it, my plan is to have them grow up the easy way. If I can do *that,* maybe they'll never meet any cockroaches.

ACKNOWLEDGMENTS

This book wouldn't have been possible without the support of my wife, Carolyn, and the understanding of my children, Liam, Lily, and Reece. Thanks also to my mom and my sister. Special appreciation goes to Alberto Patiño Douce (who taught me to think), Gena Harper (who taught me to believe), and John Swegle (who taught me the value of money). Others were equally instrumental in getting *Germline* out: Nick Mamatas, for critiquing the original novelette; Lou Anders, for introducing me to so many in the genre; DongWon Song, my editor, for working with an unknown; and my agent, Alex Field, for believing in *Germline* from the start. Last I'd like to thank Edmond Chang, who deserves special recognition because he taught me how to write; for that there are no adequate words of thanks.

For George Plimpton, and Kevin, and Scott.

extras

orbit

meet the author

T. C. McCarthy earned a BA from the University of Virginia and a PhD from the University of Georgia before embarking on a career that gave him a unique perspective as a science fiction author. From his time as a patent examiner in complex biotechnology, to his tenure with the Central Intelligence Agency, T.C. has studied and analyzed foreign militaries and weapons systems. T.C. was at the CIA during the September 11 terrorist attacks and was still there when US forces invaded Afghanistan and Iraq, allowing him to experience warfare from the perspective of an analyst. Find out more about the author at www.tcmccarthy.com.

interview

If you could go back and give advice to the sixteen-year-old T. C. McCarthy, what would it be?

You'll be bald by thirty-six, so enjoy having hair now.

Give a brief arc of your writing career; how'd you get started?

Look, I'm no different than any other writer; I've always written. But what's more important is that I've always read. Magazines, comic books, graffiti, and books—you name it and I've read it. Childhood meant California— Bay Area—and our mom had this thing about no television, so she threw it away, which meant we could either go home with a latchkey or trip it to the library (riding a bike), where we'd read for a while, then throw water balloons at cars. There was a lot of running from neighborhood bullies too, and, after that, more reading. So by the time I picked up a pen (we didn't have computers in the '70s and early '80s, and forget about having access to a typewriter), I'd already gotten that sense of story. Constant reading branded it into my brain. And story-sense provided enough juice to keep me going through the early stages, when writing was about fumbling with words more than working with them, but to be honest, the story-sense was a curse at first. I knew the kinds of stories I wanted to write. But that's not the same thing as being able to put the words on paper, and it took twenty-five years of practice before I wrote anything worth reading, let alone anything someone would buy.

What's the best advice you've been given when it comes to writing?

To not become a writer. George Plimpton gave the commencement address at my high school, so what did I do? I walked right up to the guy and said, *Mr.-Plimpton-I'd-really-like-to-be-a-writer-can-you-give-me-any-advice?* Like he'd never been asked *that* before. Well, George gets this look on his face, like he needs to find the can, and then takes a deep breath before shaking his head. And that voice; you know the one: pompous and arrogant but with the chops to back it up, so you just let it steamroll. "Don't do it," said George. "There are far too many of us in the world already and you'd be better off going into banking, or being a doctor or lawyer." What in hell did you say to something like that?

Except…

Plimpton was right. UVA's creative writing program denied me entry (I submitted science fiction as a writing sample, which apparently was a big no-no), so the dean gave me permission to drop out and surf Australia; I gave up on the whole English major/MFA thing. Still, here's the thing: I wrote. Never stopped. By then someone had invented a thing called a PC, then the laptop, which made writing easy, and my eventual path as a PhD student and scientist primed me with all kinds of material that I never would have gotten had I concentrated on being "a writer" from the first day of college. Here's to you, Plimpton.

You've written short stories for literary, horror, and science fiction venues. What gives? Can't you just pick one? Which do you like best when it comes to short stories?

First let me caveat my answer: I have a lot to learn. There are plenty of writers out there who can define what literary fiction is, and I've read the blog wars over the Academy snubbing genre writers, etc., but these discussions are beyond me. So right now, none of that stuff matters; I write and read. Sometimes I feel a mainstream/literary story in my gut, and it just comes out, and I've had success with those, having published in *Per Contra* and *Story Quarterly*. I've only written two literary shorts, so that's a one thousand batting average! In fact, I wrote my first literary story because my SF had been rejected so often from pro venues that I was furious and decided screw it—time to write something else. In contrast to the SF venues, a professional-rate online magazine bought that short story within a month of my submitting it. What the hell does that mean?

And no, I can't just pick one genre and don't have a favorite—anything goes.

Who is your favorite author?

Here are my favorites by country:

USA: Ray Bradbury, Michael Herr, Joe Haldeman
UK: Hector H. Munro, George Orwell, John Christopher
France: Guy Sajer
Russia: Artyom Borovik
Kazakhstan: Kanatzhan Alibekov
Israel: Ron Lesham

You have a day job and a family; when do you write?

On my days off, but usually between eight and eleven p.m. and four and seven a.m. I get very little sleep. Maybe that's why so many of my stories and books tend to be dark.

The protagonist in Germline *is an interesting character with some major flaws; how did you choose* that guy, *and what went into fleshing out Oscar Wendell?*

I'll never reveal everything about that process; it was personal. But Oscar is like a lot of people I've known growing up, especially in a world where children are exposed to drugs at an early age. For guys like Oscar it's too great a temptation. I mean, of course people will take or drink "stuff" that makes them forget that they're embarrassed to dance in public, makes them uninhibited when it comes to talking to the opposite sex, and makes them, essentially, fearless. These, however, are lies. In the case of Oscar, addiction prevents him from learning fundamental principles "normal" people take for granted, like the fact that using war as a springboard to fame is insane. Oscar, however, is lucky. I've known plenty of people who go down a similar path and don't make it back alive or, if they do, are just damaged goods. I wanted a character that overcomes all that; in a way, *Germline* is a coming-of-age story (albeit an unusual one).

What book is in front of you right now?

Counterinsurgency Warfare: Theory and Practice, by David Galula. I have to stay sharp, you know?

introducing

If you enjoyed GERMLINE,
look out for

EXOGENE

The Subterrene War: Book 2

by T. C. McCARTHY

ONE

Spoiling

*And you will come upon a city cursed, and
everything that festers in its midst will be as
a disease; nothing will be worthy of pity, not
insects, animals, or even men.*

MODERN COMBAT MANUAL
JOSHUA 6:17

Live forever. The thought lingered like an annoying dog
to which I had handed a few scraps.

I felt Megan's fingers against my skin and smelled the paste—breathed the fumes gratefully, for it reminded me that I wouldn't have to wear my helmet. Soon, but not now. The lessons taught this, described the first symptom of spoiling: when the helmet no longer felt safe, a sign of claustrophobia. As my troop train rumbled northward, I couldn't tell if I shook from eagerness or from the railcar's jolting, and gave up trying to distinguish between the two possibilities. It was not an *either-or* day; it was a day of simultaneity.

Deliver me from myself, I prayed, *and help me to accept tomorrow's end.*

Almost a hundred of my sisters filled the railcar, in a train consisting of three hundred carriages, each one packed with the same cargo. My newer sisters—replacements with childlike faces—were of lesser importance. Megan counted for everything. She smiled as she stroked my forehead, which made me so drowsy that my eyes flickered shut with a memory, the image of an atelier, of a technician brushing fingers across my cheek as he cooed from outside the tank. I liked those memories. They weren't like the ones acquired more recently, and once upon a time everything had been that way. Sterile. Days in the atelier had been clean and warm—not like this.

"Everything was so white then," I said, "like a lily."

Megan nodded and kissed me. "It was closer to perfect, not a hint of filth. Do not be angry today, Catherine. It's counterproductive. Kill with detachment, with the greater plan."

I closed my eyes and leaned forward so Megan could work more easily, and so she wouldn't see my smile while smearing paste on my scalp, the thin layer of green thermal block that would dry into a latex-like coating, blocking my heat. The replacements all stared at us.

"Can you tell us what to expect in Uchkuduk?" one of them asked. "It's my first time—the first time for most of us. They mustered us a month ago from the Winchester atelier, near West Virginia. How should we prepare?"

"It's simple," I said. "There's one thing they don't teach in the atelier: Bleeznyetzi."

Several of them leaned closer.

"Bleeznyetzi?"

I nodded. "It's Russian for 'twins.' "

"You are an older version," one said. "We speak multiple languages, including Russian and Kazakh, and we know the word."

"Then you know what our forces call us—the humans."

"No. What?"

The train squealed around a sudden bend, pushing me further against the wall. I braced a boot against Megan, who had just fallen asleep, to keep her from slumping over.

"Bitches and sluts. The tanks taught English too, right?"

They left me alone after that. It was no surprise—we all learned the same lesson: *"Watch out for defeatists, the ones near the end of their terms. Defeatism festers in those who approach the age. Ignore their voices. Learn from their actions but do not listen to their words. When you and your sisters reach eighteen, a spoiling sets in, so pray for deliverance from defeatism and you will be discharged. Honorably. Only then will you ascend to be seated at His right hand."* The replacements wouldn't associate themselves with me for fear that I would rub off on them, the spoiling a contagion, and for some reason it made me feel warm to think I had that kind of power.

"You're incorrigible," I whispered to Megan. "It is *not* your turn for rest." But she didn't hear, and exhaustion showed on her face, in thin lines that I hadn't noticed before, while she slept. "I'll tell you a secret: hatred is the only thing keeping me from spoiling, the only thing I have left, the only thing I do well."

The armored personnel carrier's compartment felt like a steam bath. Heat acted as a catalyst, lowering the amount of energy it took for the phantom dead to invade my mind, and I focused on my hands, thinking that concentration would keep the hallucination at bay. It was no use. The APC engine roared like a call from the past, and Megan melted away to be replaced by the dusty outskirts of Pavlodar, a bird jabbering overhead as we jumped off from the river. Five Kazakhs stood in an alley. They looked at me as if I was an anomaly, a dripping fish that had just stood up on two legs to walk from the Irtysh, and they failed to recognize the danger. Our girl named Majda moved first. She sprayed the women—who began to scream—with fléchettes, her stream of needles cutting some of them in half as she laughed. Majda wouldn't laugh for much longer. A rocket went through her, leaving only a pair of twitching legs...

Megan was shouting at me when the vision evaporated.

"Catherine!"

The APC compartment reappeared. We sat encased in a tiny ceramic cubicle, strapped into our seats and struggling to breathe alcohol-contaminated air as the vehicle idled.

"You're spoiling," she said. "You were laughing."

I nodded and tongued another tranq tab—my third in the last hour.

"It's an insanity," Megan continued. "I worry. The spoiling seems to be worse in you than in any other, and someone will report it. One of the new girls."

"It doesn't matter. Soon we will kill again and then it will be as if nothing was ever wrong, as if destruction was a meal, maybe toast and honey."

The turbine for the plasma cannon buzzed throughout the vehicle, vibrating the twenty cubicles like ours along each side and the three large ones down the vehicle's spine. We had two ways out: the normal way, a tiny hatch in the floor, where we would come out underneath and roll from between the APC's huge wheels; and an escape hatch in the roof, where we could pop out in an emergency. It wouldn't be long before everything stopped and time would dilate with excitement, with the freedom of movement and a sudden breakout into the open, where one could find targets among men.

The turbines went quiet and I saw a tear on Megan's cheek.

"It doesn't matter," I explained, "not because I don't care about you. I do. It doesn't matter because we're dead anyway tomorrow. And I don't *want* to die."

"Don't."

"I don't want to be discharged."

"You speak like them, like the non-bred."

I shook my head, ignoring the insult, and placed a hand on her shoulder. "Haven't you ever wondered what it would be like to live past the age? Maybe the spoiling goes away. *Fades.* I have more killing to do, and they will rob me of it at eighteen."

Megan shook her head. She turned and I saw from the movement of her neck that she had begun sobbing, which made me feel even worse, because my actions ruined the moment. This was to have been a sacred time. It was said that in quiet seconds during battle, when the firing paused, as it sometimes did without explanation, one heard His voice in the wind or in the silence of the suit, His hand on your heart to let you know that you were a sacred thing among the corrupt. So the time before an engagement was to be used for reflection, to prepare for glory in an hour of meditation that climaxed with a flash of anticipation, of wanting to prove one's worthiness. But words ruined everything.

There were plans and strategies, mapped out in advance by human generals and run through computers, semi-aware, able to calculate just how far we could go before our systems reached their limit. It was a ritual beyond us—the way our leaders communicated with God and channeled His will. Nobody gave us the details. For the past two years, neither Megan nor I had known why the war existed, except what we had caught in passing during interactions with men, with human forces, the non-bred. But those were glimpses. They weren't enough to answer all the questions, and soon we stopped asking, because it was enough to know that we fought Russian men, and we prayed that God would make the war last forever. A feeling of satisfaction filled me as I thought about it, as if knowing that God was a part of the plan was enough, something that made us invincible because He trusted us to cleanse this part of the world, to allow a lily like Megan to exercise her will.

We would move out soon. Far below us, the advance shock wave of our sisters was already attacking, underground, pushing into Russian tunnel positions and killing as many as possible before we followed with the main force—a mixed army of humans and my sisters, exposed aboveground for the greater glory. Our attack would make Megan feel better, I was certain. Waiting never helped, but war?

War made us feel fifteen again.

They played it over the speakers when we were born at fifteen-equivalent—the hymn, a prayer known only by us, our first lesson, a call to the faithful:

*This is my Maxwell. It was invented over a
century before I was born but this one is new, this
one is mine. The barrel of my Maxwell consists
of an alloy tube, encased by band after band of
superconducting magnets. I am shielded from the
flux by ceramic and alloy barrel wraps, which
join to the fuel cell, the fuel cell to the stock. My
Maxwell carbine has no kick; my carbine has
a flinch. It is my friend, my mother. My carbine
propels its children, the fléchettes, down its length,
rapidly accelerating them to speeds ranging from
subsonic to hypersonic. It depends on what I
choose.*

*My carbine is an instrument of God. I am an
instrument of God. Unlike ancient firearms, the*

*fléchettes have no integral chemical propellant
and are therefore tiny, allowing me to fill a
shoulder hopper with almost ten thousand at a
time. Ten thousand chances to kill. My fléchettes
are messengers of God. My fléchettes are killers.
The material and shape of my killers make them
superior armor penetrators. But my killers are
not perfect. I am not perfect. My killers are too
small to work alone and must function as a family.
But I shall not worry. My Maxwell will fire fifty
fléchettes per second, and fifty is a family. With my
Maxwell I can liberate a man of his head or limbs.
With my Maxwell I will kill until there is nothing
left alive.*

    With my Maxwell, I am perfect.

It was then, at fifteen, that Megan and I met our first humans. Until that point, the technicians kept us in atelier tanks; we were alive and conscious, fed information and nutrients through a series of cables and tubes. The tanks gave us freedom of motion so we could put movement to combat scenarios played out in our heads, lending our muscles the same memories fed to our brains. Fifteen-equivalent was our birthday, when we became the biological equal to a fifteen-year-old human and slid from the growth tanks to feel cold air bring goose bumps and, along with them, a sense that the world was a both hostile and promising place, full of danger but also the opportunity for redemption.

First steps were awkward. Megan had stumbled when trying to stand and crashed into me, sending us both to the cold floor in a heap. We giggled. *I'm Megan,* she had said, and I told her my name, after which we looked into a mirror, and I thought, *She looks just like me.* We were skinny girls, with leg and arm muscles that flexed like pistons under gravity, and that I knew could be used to kill the human technicians around us in hundreds of different ways. They had hair. Our heads had been shaved perfectly smooth and Megan and I sat there, on the floor, rubbing the tops of them and tracing our fingers over the scabs where only a few days before, cables had penetrated, and the thought occurred to me that if I killed one of the humans, we could take his hair, to glue it onto our heads just to feel what it was like. But the technicians were kind. They helped us both up, guiding us to the dressing area, where they gave us our first uniforms, orange, and bright enough that their color glowed under fluorescent lights. The sounds—not muffled by the gallons of thick fluid that normally surrounded us in the tanks—were enough to make me dizzy. I vomited on the floor.

A new voice spoke through the speakers while we organized. "Glory unto the faithful. On this, the day of your birth, a choir of angels sings your praise in heaven, telling God that He should watch for the time when you join him, to sit at His side after serving mankind. This you *shall* do, in honor of your creators.

"It is said that 'all the earth shall be devoured in fire. For then I will restore to the peoples a pure language, that they serve my Masters with one accord. From beyond the rivers the daughters of His dispersed ones shall bring offering. On that day I will not be ashamed for any of my deeds in which I transgressed against God; for then he will take away from our midst those who spoiled, and they shall no longer be haughty in His holy mountain. He will leave in our midst a meek and humble people, and we shall trust in the word of our Creators.'

"Rejoice, for *you* are His daughters and ours, a holy Germline, Germline 1A, and you will bring to Him eternal glory through death and with sacrifice. So sayeth the *Modern Combat Manual*."

While the voice read passage after passage, Megan helped me into my orange jumpsuit, and when we looked at each other, I knew she was the one.

It didn't matter now, in Kazakhstan, that those memories were old; it was the same look I gave her on that afternoon, when we slid from the bottom hatch of our compartment and stretched outside the APC under a dim sun. We smiled. I didn't need to say it to her: it was an amazing day, cold and bright like on the day we were born, and we would be together when the enemy turned to face us. My hatred burned with an intensity it hadn't mustered since the day before, and both legs trembled, wanting to move out regardless of whether the others were ready.

Our APCs had stopped across the border, west of Keriz and inside Kazakhstan where vehicles spread across the countryside. To our north, contrails marked the passage of autonomous fighters, semi-aware drones that fought on instinct, twisting through the sky in patterns like braided white ropes. Russian ground attack craft tried to cross south, the APCs making an attractive target as they stopped in the open to assemble, but so far our fighters had kept the aircraft away. Every once in a while you saw a black streamer fall, followed by a cloud of fire and then a distant thud.

"It is here," said Megan, "in the air."

I nodded. "Death and faith."

"I will kill all I see."

"And we will bathe in the blood of mankind, washing ourselves of their sins."

She said, "Let it go. Detach."

But I didn't answer.

You could tell a battlefield from its smell. Burned metal tinged with rot, acrid enough that it felt like it would singe the tissue in your nose, foreign enough that it made you clench fists with the impatience to wade in. Only about half of us remained. Many of my sisters—the ones who had led the shock assault earlier that day, underground—had partially melted armor, bubbled from plasma attacks. Several were absent an arm or a hand. Despite the wounds, they would feel nothing, because the nerves had shut down, and blood vessels had sealed themselves to prevent further fluid loss. A plug of ceramic—locked in place with quick paste—would seal the suit breach and maintain thermal integrity. I felt proud. This was *my* unit, and none of us had spoiled to the point of being combat ineffective, so our dead now looked down from Heaven with the same sense of pride. Our wounded were the new girls, the replacements, and before they helmeted, you saw that their faces still glowed, but now it wasn't the glow of nervous expectation; it was the glow of having killed, of *knowing*.

We began our advance, following on foot behind APCs, which moved at jogging pace, sending sheets of mud and snow into the air and coating our suits in a dripping mess. Our feet made sucking sounds as we plodded. On either side of us, a full division of Foreign Legion and Marines advanced at our flanks. *Human*.

There were no words to describe it, no way to understand except through experience. Trudging. Fighting against
the mud with every step so that within five minutes your
muscles screamed, and then having to continue like that
for thirty minutes, an hour, two. I was near the edge of our
formation, close to a group of Marines. You could see
some of them, their armor almost new, as they twitched
with every explosion or dropped to the mud at the first
hint of tracer fléchettes. Many of them began stumbling
and barely lifted themselves, falling behind as we continued. Nobody cared. The exhaustion got so thick, so fast
that it was all anyone could do to keep her eyes open, let
alone pull a straggler from the mud. I could have blocked
the pain, willed it away the same way I twitched a finger,
but the sensations reminded me that I hadn't been discharged yet, so they became comforting things, reminders that there was more killing. Pain was familiar now.
Welcome.

At times a walking plasma barrage moved ahead of us
so that we moved faster, jogging over a crust of hard
glass. It was a godsend, and I heard Megan whisper her
thanks. We spent the whole first day of the advance like
that, walking, then jogging, and soon I remembered that
distances in Kazakhstan killed resolve almost as easily as
the spoil. A tree on the horizon might look close. But as
you walked through the day, it barely changed position
and was enough to drive you mad with the feeling that
you would never reach it.

Then, at last, contact. Close to sundown, Megan and I
found ourselves in a hole with three Marines. One of them
screamed as Russian grenades cracked on every side,
sending sprays of thermal gel over our position to hiss

and smoke as the droplets melted whatever they touched. The other two men were hardly better. Both huddled at the bottom of the crater, screaming to us that we had encountered the outermost positions of a Russian defensive line.

I kicked one. "How can you aim from there?"

"Get up and fight," said Megan, but the men cursed at her.

She grabbed the grenade launcher from one and peered over the lip of the hole. I fell beside her. A hundred yards away, behind a small rise, tiny flashes marked the position of a Russian grenadier whose helmet and shoulders the low sun outlined, and we had to duck when a spray of white tracer fléchettes kicked up the dirt around us. Megan dialed in the range. At the same moment she popped back up and fired, I sprinted from the hole, doing my best to zigzag through the mud toward the Russian position, not able to think through the haze of fatigue.

We continued like that for a few minutes. I would drop to the ground when she stopped firing, until her grenades started detonating ahead of me again—my sign to get up, keep going. Finally I got close. I waited for her to stop and almost immediately saw the shape of a Russian behind the edge of a fighting position. His helmet was black, with paired round blue vision ports instead of a single slit like ours, and a series of cables connected the outside of the helmet to a power pack so that they draped over the man's shoulders like thick strands of hair. You almost forgot why you were there, transfixed by the realization that he was so close, his proximity releasing an influx of hatred that made you want to scream. The man shimmered in the light. I saw all of them then, the ones who jeered at us as we waited for the cars in the rail yard, who pelted us with empty food packs, but especially the ones in white lab coats, always there when we returned from the front, eager to punch data into their tablets as they forced us to answer questions. This was a man. It was rare to get this close, and it made you want to savor the moment, to get even closer and rip his helmet off so you could watch his expression change with death.

I slipped a grenade from my harness, hit the button, and waited for its detonation before rolling into the hole to push the dead Russians aside. "Check fire, Megan. Clear."

A set of three shafts led straight down in the center of the hole, the only way the Russians could have survived our plasma barrages. I tossed in grenades to make sure the shafts were empty, and then let the exhaustion wash over in a warm tide, numbing my muscles and nearly sending me to sleep. The sun set at that very moment, and according to our locators, we had made it to a point west of Karatobe. *They* were in Karatobe. The Russians had retreated there to establish a major defensive line on either side of the Syr Dar'ya River, with Shymkent well to the south.

Tomorrow, I thought with a shiver. *Tomorrow is our day.*

Megan flopped down next to me and yanked off her helmet. She laughed. I removed mine before kissing her, after which we lay against the dirt wall of the hole and stared up—the sky turning an unbelievable reddish orange as the sun's light faded—waiting for the stars, something we never got tired of seeing. Megan especially loved stars, and they always brought wonder to her face. Soon I would dream. Sleep was a thing feared, something that resurrected buried memories and then twisted them into nightmares, a time to avoid. But you couldn't evade sleep any more than you could avoid the men in white coats.